THE
DYSON
FILE

BAEN BOOKS by JACOB HOLO

The Gordian Protocol (with David Weber)
The Valkyrie Protocol (with David Weber)
The Janus File (with David Weber)
The Weltall File (with David Weber)
The Dyson File

THE DYSON FILE

A GORDIAN DIVISION NOVEL

JACOB HOLO

THE DYSON FILE

A Baen Books Original

Baen Publishing Enterprises
P.O. Box 1403
Riverdale, NY 10471
www.baen.com

ISBN: 978-1-9821-9301-0

Cover art by Kurt Miller

First printing, November 2023

Distributed by Simon & Schuster
1230 Avenue of the Americas
New York, NY 10020

Library of Congress Cataloging-in-Publication Data

Names: Holo, Jacob, author.
Title: The Dyson file / Jacob Holo.
Description: Riverdale, NY : Baen Publishing Enterprises, 2023. | Series: The Gordian division ; 5
Identifiers: LCCN 2023029026 (print) | LCCN 2023029027 (ebook) | ISBN 9781982193010 (trade paperback) | ISBN 9781625799388 (ebook)
Subjects: LCGFT: Science fiction. | Detective and mystery fiction. | Novels.
Classification: LCC PS3608.O49435648 D97 2023 (print) | LCC PS3608.O49435648 (ebook) | DDC 813/.6—dc23/eng/20230626
LC record available at https://lccn.loc.gov/2023029026
LC ebook record available at https://lccn.loc.gov/2023029027

Printed in the United States of America
10 9 8 7 6 5 4 3 2 1

To David.
For taking this shy engineer under his wing.

PROLOGUE

"A DARK AND STORMY NIGHT," THE MAN UTTERED WITH A DEEP frown. "How appropriate."

He gazed through outward-slanted windows to the black, roiling thunderheads. Ferocious streaks of lightning revealed the caramel hues of ammonia ice clouds, and a dusting of ammonia snow melted off the window's vacuum-insulated outer layer.

Technically, it wasn't night at all. Not according to his wetware's internal clock, but that was because Saturn's ten-hour-and-forty-two-minute days were ill-suited to the biorhythms of organic citizens, leading most places in and around the gas giant to follow an Earth-centric calendar.

The man harrumphed, took a sip from his wine glass, and continued to gaze out the window with heavily lidded eyes. The skin of his round face was pale and slightly moist, his salt-and-pepper hair oily and uncombed. He wore a dark green suit—mostly because he had to for the party—though the garment's precise tailoring seemed to hang off his slouched shoulders in a slovenly manner, as if both he *and* the suit didn't want to be there.

His dynamic scarf hung around his neck like a thick piece of limp linguini, its surface animated with a looping pattern of abstract shapes in muted colors.

He raised the wine glass to his lips once more.

His name was Esteban Velasco, Senior Macrotech Engineer

for the Atlas Corporation, and though he stood on the cusp of his greatest achievement, his brooding demeanor and unkempt appearance hinted at the dark thoughts within his mind.

A distant bluish light drew his eyes, partially obscured by the ammonia clouds. The source of the light was a tall floating megastructure called Janus-Epimetheus, named in honor of the two moons demolished during its construction. The locals called it the "Shark Fin," for it did indeed resemble a brilliantly white downturned fin, though one that measured over one hundred kilometers tall and flared at the top into an expansive oval plateau two hundred kilometers across and fifty wide.

Velasco couldn't make out much beyond a distant silhouette haloed by a faint aura created by the lights from external buildings and short-ranged craft, all obscured behind the churning storm clouds. The powerful glow from its banks of nine massive engines—aligned in compact triplets vertically along the megastructure's trailing edge—grew brighter as it made what was probably a minor course correction through the *comparatively* gentle winds of Saturn's fortieth northern parallel.

The senior engineer stood on the bottom floor of the Atlas mobile headquarters as it floated through the storm, trailing Janus-Epimetheus on its endless journey around Saturn. The building resembled a miniscule silver top drifting behind the giant, downturned fin.

Velasco raised the wine glass to his lips once more, but then paused and stared into the golden, bubbly fluid. His wetware interfaced with the glass, and an infographic for the beverage appeared in his virtual vision beside it. He skimmed over the summary.

It was an expensive wine. Not synthesized within the miniaturized chemical factory of a food printer, but produced the old-fashioned way, starting with grapes grown in a vineyard. A *Saturnite* vineyard, in this case. The infographic said the drink had been imported from Old Frontier, a large agricultural city located about two-thirds of the way down the Shark Fin.

"Boaz broke out the good stuff tonight," Velasco muttered to himself. "A shame."

He relaxed his hand, and the glass slipped from his fingers. At this altitude, Saturn's mass produced a natural 1.065 gravities, and the glass fell to the floor much as it would have if he'd let go on Earth. It bounced once and rolled until it stopped against the outward slant of the window, leaving an expensive streak on the self-cleaning carpet.

"What the hell, butterfingers?" sniggered a man behind Velasco. "Can't handle a few drinks?"

Velasco let out a weary sigh.

"This is all I need right now," he grumbled under his breath.

"You say something? I'm sorry, but I'm having trouble understanding you over your booze slur."

Velasco turned around—slowly and with great lack of enthusiasm—to face Leon Traczyk, another macrotech engineer, though not as senior as himself.

The two formed a stark contrast. Traczyk stood half a head taller than Velasco, with impeccable posture, chin held high as he looked down his nose at the other man. His tawny mane was slicked back, without a hair out of place, and his beard was neatly trimmed and combed. He wore a crimson business suit with a diamond pattern alternating between lighter and darker shades, accentuated by a large ruby at his throat.

The suit didn't look very fashionable to Velasco, but knowing Traczyk, the pattern was probably based on some new Lunarian or Jovian fashion trend. Behind him, the party was in full swing. Around seventy people from Atlas' senior staff mingled in the wide half-moon space at the bottom of the mobile headquarters. Catering drones weaved through the crowd, offering drinks and hors d'oeuvres, while their boss, Julian Boaz, climbed up onto a raised dais at the back, perhaps in preparation for a speech.

"Leon," Velasco grunted to his coworker.

"Esteban," Traczyk replied with a smirk.

"Don't you have anyone else to pester?"

"'Pester'? Don't be absurd. Can't I stop by simply to say hello?" He raised his wine with a twinkle in his eyes. "I'd offer you another glass, but it seems you've already had enough."

Velasco didn't say anything. He simply stared at the other man, his face sullen and his eyes dark with secret intent. Traczyk, while annoying and overly ambitious in a boardroom-backstabbing sort of way, had been reduced to the equivalent of white noise in his frayed mind.

Traczyk snapped his fingers in front of Velasco's face. The senior engineer wasn't sure how much time had passed.

"Something wrong with you?" Traczyk asked, then smiled.

"Perhaps you should seriously consider retirement. Or at least a sabbatical."

Velasco locked eyes with the younger man. "Why don't you say what's really on your mind?"

"Where's this coming from?" Traczyk shifted uneasily from one foot to the other, perhaps taken aback by his colleague's sudden directness.

"Go on and say it," Velasco taunted. "Unless you're afraid to."

"Afraid?" Traczyk's face reddened and his voice grew softer, yet more forceful at the same time. "Listen here." He jabbed Velasco's chest with a finger. "Everyone here might think we won the contract because of you, but I know the truth. I was in the trenches each night trying to hold your sorry excuse for a design together. The boss is about to get up on that stage, and I'm sure he's going to shower you with praise. Praise everyone else thinks you've earned, but the truth is you didn't earn shit. You know it, and I know it. I carried your worthless, deadbeat carcass across the finish line. *I* did! That should be *me* he's about to recognize. Not a has-been like you!"

Velasco let Traczyk's scorn pour off him like the pointless bleating it was.

"Well, I wouldn't worry too much," he replied evenly. "I have a feeling you're about to get exactly what you've wanted all this time."

"What the hell is that supposed to mean?"

"You'll see."

Traczyk frowned as Velasco slid past him. He weaved through the crowd, heading in the general direction of the room's center.

Julian Boaz, Atlas CEO, stood on the dais and surveyed the crowd. He was a big, bald, broad-shouldered man that exuded an air of approachability despite his physical stature and position within the company. He surveyed the crowd with warm eyes and an affable smile, though Velasco knew those features masked his real personality. Boaz could put on whatever friendly airs he wanted, but he knew—and had been on the receiving end—of the man's ruthless nature. All Boaz wanted was to see Atlas on top, and he didn't care who got caught in the grinding treads of their progress, be it their competitors or the company's own engineers, programmers, and physicists.

"Ladies and gentlemen!" Boaz began. "Your attention please!"

The room grew quiet, and all eyes focused on the CEO.

Boaz held out a cupped hand, and an abstract document materialized over it.

"I have here the letter from the Senate's Megastructure Subcommittee. I won't bore you by reading through all the legalese, but suffice it to say, Atlas has been awarded the Dyson Realization Project. We did it, people! We're the ones who'll go down in history as the builders of the very first Dyson swarm!"

A cheer rose from the crowd.

"I know this project has had its ups and downs. I was so proud of all of you when our bid was selected as one of the two finalists"—he paused for dramatic effect—"alongside SourceCode."

Someone in the crowd booed, and Boaz chuckled on stage.

"Now, now. Let's all keep it classy. Our competitors have had a *very* bad day."

The crowd laughed in agreement.

"And, in a way, what they're going through now isn't all that different from what we faced earlier this year. I know I shared everyone's shock and disappointment when our first major replication trial was sabotaged."

Sure, you did, Velasco thought. *Which was why you called me to your office afterward and screamed in my face for an hour straight. I still remember the flecks of spittle hitting my eyes.*

"But all of that is behind us now," Boaz continued. "Our design—and design *team*—came out on top. In fact"—he wore a sly grin and held up a finger—"I've got something of a treat for everyone. A...friend, shall we say, on the subcommittee passed us a video from SourceCode's botched trial. Who'd like to see it?"

The crowd cheered and laughed.

Velasco felt a hand on his shoulder.

"Hey, Esteban?" asked a soft, concerned voice, the sound cutting through the cheers by using his virtual hearing.

Velasco turned to find Horace Pangu, a senior consultant on the project, standing next to him. The slender man possessed a narrow face with sunken cheeks and sharp, dark eyes that nonetheless exuded a sense of warmth and genuine concern. He wore a subdued dark blue suit with a slowly changing starscape on his scarf.

"You okay?" Pangu asked, giving Velasco's shoulder a friendly squeeze.

"I'm fine," Velasco lied.

"You sure? You look like you've seen a ghost."

Velasco winced at the word "ghost" before he could catch himself. He tried to pass the gesture off as a shrug.

"Something wrong?" Pangu asked.

"It's nothing. Just a lot on my mind."

"Want to talk about it? We can slip away while Boaz isn't looking."

"No, thanks. Maybe later."

"Okay, but you know my door is always open."

"Thanks, Wiz." Velasco gave the man a thin smile. "I know it is."

"Get a load of what happens next!" Boaz crowed as the video played at high speed in a virtual window behind the dais.

Velasco had missed the start of the video, but he knew how the trial would play out. SourceCode's design utilized microbot swarms to reassemble raw material into components for the Dyson project. One of their swarm seeds had been fired at a test asteroid from a SourceCode construction cruiser, which also played host to the megastructure subcommittee and members of the press.

The initial deconstruction and replication phase had gone well enough, with the swarm reaching ten times its initial size before the first errors occurred. It *should* have stopped at that population level and switched from replication to construction, but instead the swarm continued to self-replicate. SourceCode engineers had attempted to halt the rampant replication, but unidentified errors prevented the shutdown command from being accepted, and the swarm continued expanding at an exponential rate until the entire asteroid had been converted into self-replicating microbots.

And then the situation grew worse. The swarm began ejecting spores at nearby objects, which included the SourceCode cruiser and the government guests inside. Microbots began to eat through the ship's outer hull, forcing the subcommittee to call for aid. It had taken a concerted effort from six Consolidated System Police cruisers to rescue the crew and contain the outbreak.

No one had been hurt in the accident, but in the following days the subcommittee passed a motion to disqualify SourceCode, resulting in the contract being awarded to Atlas by default, despite their own mishap earlier that year.

Velasco watched the video play out almost absently, as if he were experiencing events from outside his own body. It didn't seem real to him, and yet paradoxically it felt more real than his own flesh and blood. His mind didn't second-guess what the video showed, didn't question how SourceCode had failed so spectacularly.

Instead, it accepted the images as the pure, unfiltered truth they were.

Because he knew the swarm had done *exactly* what it had been configured to do.

"Wow!" Boaz put a splayed hand to his chest. "What a disaster! I thought *replication* was in SourceCode's wheelhouse, but this makes it look like they're experts at replicating *failure*!"

The CEO's captive audience laughed at his lame joke with the enthusiasm of people who looked forward to continued employment and who enjoyed receiving large Esteem bonuses.

"Good one, sir!" Traczyk shouted above the crowd.

Velasco would have rolled his eyes if he'd cared enough.

But he didn't.

None of this mattered anymore. Not the project. And certainly not the inane office politics.

He turned away from the dais and weaved through the crowd until he found himself on the edge of the room near the windows. He followed a path along the windows, which took him out of the half-moon hall and down a curved corridor with windows on one side. The executive floor of the mobile headquarters was split into two sections: the open half-moon hall and an equally large area split into about a dozen executive offices, including his own.

He palmed the door lock. Programmable-steel split open and he stepped inside.

His desk was a mess. Plates, eating utensils, and empty food wrappers littered the surface, stacked precariously high and shoved to either side in a vain attempt to form enough empty space in the center to work.

Abstract technical sheets were pinned in the air over his desk, and more hovered against the back wall, covering it from end to end in macrotech diagrams, programming language, simulations, and other documents of his trade. It must have looked like a chaotic mess to any outsider, but he knew where to find every file, even with his eyes closed.

A potted plant sat next to his desk as a reminder of one of the company's "Personal Wellness Measures." It was brown and dead. A few dry leaves lay on the floor, though most had been removed by the self-cleaning carpet.

He rounded his desk and collapsed into the programmable-foam of his chair. The foam morphed to support his body for maximum comfort, but it brought him no relief today.

He dismissed the abstract diagrams and stared blankly across his desk at the door he'd walked through. The door and the wall appeared as a thin crosshatch over an abstract view of the windows. The virtual imagery let everyone know that, yes, there was indeed a wall there, but here, have a nice view of the outside.

The storm had picked up, whipping flakes of snow against the pane while distant lightning forked from cloud to cloud. The blinking lights of a quadcopter flew past on its way to Janus.

"Enough," he said after a long pause.

He set his jaw and unlocked the bottom drawer of his desk. He pulled it back and gazed down at the pistol. It was a Popular Arsenals PA7 "Judicator" heavy pistol, loaded with explosive-tipped rounds. There weren't many civilian threats the weapon couldn't handle.

He took it out and placed it in the center of his desk, adjusted it so the barrel aimed to the side. He wasn't supposed to keep a weapon like this in the office. But then, there were a lot of *other* things he shouldn't have done.

He'd spoken to no one about what he planned to do next. That, in a way, had been the easiest part. He'd become skilled at keeping secrets, given the company he'd kept recently and the truths they'd shared. This was but one last omission, one he felt no urge to share, lest people try to persuade him otherwise, to urge him back from the precipice.

Deep down, he knew he was running away. Someone stronger would face this problem head on, but not him. There was no fight left in him. Only weary resignation.

The only way through . . . he thought to himself, *is out.*

He picked up the gun and sent the keycode that unlocked its safeties.

The weapon was armed now.

His heartbeat quickened.

He licked his suddenly dry lips, turned the gun inward, and opened his mouth. He stuck the barrel down his throat, gagged a little, tried to take a calming breath through his nose, but gagged again and withdrew the weapon.

He stared at the gun once more, heart pounding in his chest.

"I just want out," he said mournfully.

He placed the barrel back into his mouth, closed his eyes, took one last deep breath—

—then pulled the trigger.

CHAPTER ONE

SUSAN CANTRELL LOGGED INTO THE *SOLAR DESCENT* GAMING SES-
sion and let the environment unfold around her. The physical sensa-
tions of her real body back in her apartment faded away, replaced
with the game's virtual world. She found herself standing in the
middle of a wide pedestrian boulevard suspended within the can-
yons of a vast, inverted city of glass and metal. Inverted because the
buildings seemed to have been built *down* from a mechanical sky.

Her avatar came into focus next, clad in a set of blue armor
that hugged her body's athletic curves. Her deployable helmet
was retracted into her collar, revealing an approachable face that
seemed ready to face the challenges of the day without letting
them fluster her. Her bright red hair was groomed into a neat
pixie cut, and her hazel eyes were open and alert.

The face matched her real one perfectly. Mostly because creating an avatar from scratch in the game was a *lot* of work and
she didn't want to hold up the other players.

Her drone floated by her side, shaped like a kite shield, and
a spell-sword hung in the scabbard at her hip.

Susan had chosen the stellar vanguard class for its combination of durability and flexibility. She often found it a good idea
to lean toward more defensive strategies when trying out a new
game's mechanics, and the stellar vanguard's starting gear and
stats certainly fit her preferred playstyle.

She checked her character status in a discreet pop-up window on the inside of her wrist. Both her Health Regen and Impact Reduction auras were active, and her spell-sword came primed with an Immolation charge.

"Good to go," she declared with a nod. "Now, what next?"

According to the session primer, the city was called ClearView, and when she looked down, she understood why. The transparent walkway afforded her a view of the Everdark Eye, a black hole that played a key role in *Solar Descent* lore, being the source of many of the setting's science fantasy antagonists.

Which means ClearView must be built along the bottom of the Loop, she thought.

She turned in a circle, taking in the full panorama around her. Sure enough, she could make out the thinning silvery line of the Loop shrinking into invisibility ahead and behind her. If she recalled correctly, the Loop was an orbital ring constructed around the Eye, and it seemed ClearView had been built along the ring's underside.

"Okay, so now I know where I am." She looked around again. "But how do we get this scenario rolling?"

A steady stream of pedestrian traffic flowed around her in both directions. Most of them possessed a certain genericness that informed Susan's highly experienced gamer senses that they were unimportant. However, two individuals stood out with their characterful flamboyance.

One was a smallish, mousy woman, hunched forward by her heavy backpack. Her helmet and torso plating looked a size too large for her and were covered in gray-and-black digital camo.

The second woman's platinum skin gleamed under the street-lights, and her fiberoptic dreadlocks pulsed with a kaleidoscope of technomagical energies. She wore a flowing robe that glittered so brilliantly it gave the impression of having been spun from gold.

The two women stood at the darkened mouth of an eatery that—judging by all the dynamic graffiti and the trash on the ground—might as well have put "Shady Bar" over the door in bold letters. Susan assumed the two vibrant characters must be her fellow players, Grace Damphart and Nina Cho, though she wasn't sure which was which.

The more colorful of the two women waved at Susan, and she walked over.

"Greetings fellow adventurer!" the metallic woman began in a boisterous version of Nina Cho's normal voice. Her luminous eyes were white from end to end. "My name is Radiant Blaze, laser mage extraordinaire. And this here is Medic-One-Forty-Four, the latest in a long line of mass-produced combat medics who have served as my faithful companions on many adventures."

"Medic-One-Forty-*Five*," Grace corrected. "One-Forty-Four was my last character."

"Really?" Nina asked, the bombast vanishing from her voice entirely. "I thought your last character was One-Forty-Three."

"With you and Isaac, sure. But I was running a separate campaign with the kids."

"Ah. Okay, got it."

"Also, how would Radiant know any of my other characters? I'm not clear on that."

"You don't like my little improv backstory?" Nina crossed her arms, and her eyes changed from white to dark blue.

"It's not that I don't *like* it. I just don't see how it would work. This should be the first time you've met any of us."

"But can't I have met some of your past clones?"

"I guess, but we're all starting fresh characters for the new season. What adventures are you referring to?"

"Okay, yeah, good point."

"I suppose we *could* have a shared adventure in our backstories if you want me to add one?" Grace offered.

"No, no. I can work with this." Nina cleared her throat and returned her attention to Susan. Her eyes brightened. "Sorry about the confusion, fellow adventurer. It seems I was mistakenly thinking of someone else. Clones, you know? Who can keep all of them straight?"

"Understandable," Susan said.

"And what might your name be?"

"Susan Cantrell. Stellar vanguard."

"Susan?" Nina said, her voice becoming quiet once more.

"Yes?"

"I'm asking for your character's name. Not your real name."

"This *is* my character's name."

"You're using your real name for your first *Solar Descent* character?"

"By mistake," Susan admitted. "I got confused during character creation. When it asked me for a name, I wasn't sure if I was supposed to give mine or make up one, and by the time I realized the error, I was already fifteen screens deep in the creation process and didn't feel like backtracking."

"She does have a point there." Grace gave them a knowing nod. "The whole character creation interface really needs an overhaul. It's the worst part of this game, if you ask me."

"Okay, fine. Let's just move on." Nina cleared her throat once more. "Welcome to ClearView, Vanguard Cantrell! I assume you're here like us to investigate the disappearance of renowned star seer Natli Klynn on behalf of the Solar Guild?"

"Umm." Susan smiled bashfully. "Am I?"

Both Nina and Grace nodded.

"Then yes, I am."

"Wonderful!" Nina beamed a bright smile. Literally. Her teeth were translucent, and light leaked through them from the back of her mouth. "That makes three of us. However, the Guild believes abyssal cultists may be involved in Star Seer Klynn's disappearance, and they've arranged for us to be joined by an expert." She bobbed her head toward the bar door. "He's inside."

"Go inside, meet expert," Susan summarized. "Got it."

Susan stepped toward the door, but Nina placed a hand on her shoulder to stop her.

"I must warn you, though. This expert is a harbinger, a master of abyssal energies and a worshipper of Singularity, one of the dark gods of the Abyss. We have no way of knowing how far the rot of his twisted faith has spread."

"Be on guard. Got it."

Susan started for the door once more, but the laser mage held her hand firm.

"Also," Nina added in her normal voice, "we may have trouble recruiting him."

"Why's that?"

"He prepared a backstory for his character," Grace said with the slightest hint of a frown.

"Is that bad?"

"Could be." Nina faced the door and tugged her robes taut. "We'll just have to see for ourselves. Let's go." She led the way inside.

The dim, smoke-filled interior fit Susan's expectations of a shady space bar. A few of ClearView's denizens sat at round tables, eating, drinking, or smoking, while a robotic bartender served drinks from behind protective iron bars. Most of the patrons were of the same generic nature as the people outside, all except for a lone hooded figure seated in the corner.

They approached the dark figure. Purple runes glowed along the hem of his black cloak, and a pair of purplish, luminous eyes shone from beneath his cowl. He picked up a fistful of small cubes covered in runes and cast them across the table. His glowing eyes surveyed the results.

"The gravity waves have ... spoken of your arrival," Isaac Cho said, giving his voice a throaty, ethereal quality.

"They say anything about the job the Guild's offering?" Nina asked, crossing her arms.

"My divinations have not been ... that specific."

"Well, the Solar Guild asked us to hire you. We're searching for Natli Klynn."

"Ah, the renowned star seer. I too found her disappearance ... curious."

"This is official Guild work, so the job pays well. Interested in helping out?"

"Money is not a ... concern of mine." He cast his divination cubes again and inspected the results.

"Okay, well"—Nina shrugged—"how about you join us for the hell of it then? We could use a party member who's familiar with the abyssal arts."

"I'm afraid I ... cannot."

"Here we go," Grace whispered, drawing Susan's eye.

"And why the hell not?" Nina placed a hand on the table, looming over Isaac.

"There is a ... personal matter that requires my attention."

"A personal matter?" Nina asked. "Do you have to take care of it *now*?"

"I do. A regret from my past has ... revealed itself. The window of opportunity to resolve my mistake is ... closing."

"So, basically, you want us to ignore the main story in order to waste time on some side quest you threw together. Does that about sum things up?"

"I'm afraid I don't ... understand your question."

"Uhh!" Nina groaned. "Enough, Isaac!"

"What? Is something wrong?" Isaac replied in his normal voice. He pulled back his hood, revealing sharp eyes framed by short, black hair. The face closely resembled his real one, with the exception of the glowing eyes.

"Yes, something's wrong," Nina said. "Don't you want to get the main quest rolling?"

"Well, yes. Of course, I do."

"Then why are you being such a pain about it? Let's party up and move the story along!"

"I'd love to, but you have to convince my character first."

"Convince him? But you *control* him!"

"True, but it's called roleplay for a reason, and he's not a trusting individual. You see, at a young age, Dominus Souleater encountered a traveling—"

"'Dominus *Souleater*'?" Nina snorted out a laugh. "What? Was Evil McEvil too on the nose for you?"

"The name follows the lore guidelines for the harbinger class. Besides, I thought it'd be nice for us to gain a level or two before we hit the main story. I finished laying out the scenario last night, and Cephalie agreed to run the NPCs for us."

"Can't we do this after the main quest?"

"No. Dominus has a very tragic backstory. You need to earn his trust."

"But we don't have the time!" Nina complained. "It's been a total pain trying to schedule sessions that accommodate all of us. We all woke up early this morning so we could fit in a few hours before work, and *you* want us to waste it on some home-brewed quest instead of the main storyline!"

"Then why didn't we play last night? We would have had plenty of time that way."

"Sorry, but I couldn't." Grace raised a hand. "Niece's birthday party took priority."

"Also," Nina continued, "does your character have to talk like that *all* the time?"

"Talk like what?" Isaac asked.

"With stupid...overdramatic...pauses...sprinkled in your sentences."

"It's a verbal tic. Dominus picked it up during his—"

"Tragic backstory," Nina finished with a roll of her eyes. "Yeah, I get it. I'm sure your *Solar Descent* fanfiction is thrilling, but I want to find out what happens to Klynn! This season is kicking off a new story arc, and I want to experience it for myself before someone spoils the ending for me."

"Eh." Isaac shrugged. "I found the ending rather lackluster. You see—"

"Don't you *dare!*" Nina pointed a stern finger at him.

"Wait. Hold up," Susan interrupted. "Isaac, how do you know the ending already?"

"He watched spoilers," Grace explained.

"He *always* does that," Nina added.

"Of course, I do," Isaac said. "That way I can relax and enjoy the ride rather than stressing about how it'll end."

"You dare come *close* to spoiling the ending, and I'll use Irradiate on Mister Souleater! See how his tragic backstory likes being flooded with gamma rays!"

"Then the joke's on you, because I know how touchy you can be sometimes, so I planned ahead. I already have a Nullify counterspell queued up. Go on and waste your Irradiate cast on me. It'll fizzle into nothing."

"I just might! You got two Nullify charges on you? Because after I Irradiate your ass, Susan can Immolate it!"

"Umm, just to be clear," Susan said, "I'm not immolating anyone's ass. Least of all someone I work for."

"Work *with*," Isaac corrected. "We're partners."

The comment put a smile on her face, though it quickly vanished as the twin siblings dove headfirst into a long, protracted "disagreement" over spoilers, schedules, and gaming etiquette.

Grace walked over to the bar and sat down on a stool. The twins didn't seem to notice.

Susan sighed and joined her. "Are they always like this when they play *Solar Descent*?"

"Not always," Grace said.

"Sometimes, though?"

She nodded.

"Often?"

"Well . . ." Grace shrugged without answering.

"By the way, it's nice to finally meet you, Detective Damphart," Susan said, careful to pronounce the last name as "Damp-Heart" rather than her first guess, which had been the equivalent of "Damn-Fart." She extended a hand to the other woman.

"Likewise." She twisted around on her barstool and gave Susan's hand a firm shake. "And please, call me Grace."

"Sure thing, Grace."

"Thanks for pronouncing my last name correctly, by the way. Not everyone does that."

"You have Isaac to thank there. He was quite insistent on how I should pronounce it, for some reason. I'll admit, my first instinct was to say—"

"Please don't."

"Right. Sorry."

The two of them glanced in unison back at Isaac and Nina. The twins were still going at it.

"I heard about your work on the Gordian murders," Grace said. "Nasty business there, especially at the end. Glad to see both you and Isaac made it through alive. It would have been terrible for us to lose one or both of you on your first case together."

"Yeah, it was a close thing," Susan said, recalling the torrential storm on Saturn's moon of Titan, the frigid sheets of liquid methane lashing their crashed aircraft with Isaac unconscious in the cockpit while she ventured outside to face the horde of weaponized drones encroaching on their position. "A *very* close thing."

"I bet," Grace agreed.

"Okay, you've made your point!" Isaac exclaimed.

"Then can we skip your stupid side quest?" Nina asked.

"If you *insist.*"

"We ready to move on?" Grace asked, stepping off the stool.

"I *guess,*" Isaac said. "I'd still like to do the side quest at some point. I spent a lot of time on it."

"*After* the main story," Nina said.

"All right. After," he agreed with a sigh. "Back in character?"

"Yeah. Let's get this session moving already."

"Okay. Here goes."

Isaac pulled his hood up then cast his divination cubes onto the table. He ran his hand over the cubes, then used a finger to flip most of them to a different side. When he was done, all the cubes showed the same starburst symbol.

"The gravity waves have deigned to whisper to me once more. I have received a...revelation. It seems I am fated to join you on your quest to find the missing star seer."

CHAPTER TWO

DETECTIVE ISAAC CHO SAT AT HIS DESK ON KRONOS STATION, IN orbit around Saturn.

Or, more accurately, he slumped in the chair with his neck arched back across the headrest. His arms dangled over the sides, and his legs were extended under the desk.

He stared up at the ceiling, mouth open as his eyes flitted from one light fixture to another.

He wore the dark blue of the Consolidated System Police over his slender frame, and the golden eye and magnifying glass of Themis Division glinted on his shoulder. He wasn't short or scrawny, but he doubted there was a single soul in the whole wide solar system who'd call him physically imposing.

He used his foot to kick off the floor, sending his chair spinning in a circle. The lights blurred overhead, forming luminous arches across his vision. The only person who saw him do this was Susan, who sat in the desk opposite his, and she was otherwise engrossed in abstract documentation she'd been reading for the past hour. The spacious office contained more than enough desks for the department's hundred or so detectives and specialists, but most of them were empty, their occupants out in the field.

Which is where we belong, Isaac thought morosely.

He felt an urge to check the time once more but resisted. Checking it over and over again wouldn't make the day go by any faster. In fact, it seemed to have had the opposite effect so far.

"Hey, Isaac?" Susan asked.

"Hmm?" He stopped his spin and sat up.

Susan shifted her virtual document aside. She wore the slightly lighter blue of a Peacekeeper special agent, with a silver shield over her left breast and a peaked cap on her head. She was the only person on Kronos—indeed, the only person anywhere near Saturn—clad in such a uniform, because *this* uniform didn't belong to SysPol or any of its divisions.

That was because Susan was the first member of the officer exchange program between the System Cooperative Administration (more commonly referred to as the Admin) and Isaac's own Consolidated System Government (or SysGov for short).

The two governments shared at least a *few* things in common. If you squinted hard enough. Both were based on Earth, for example. But even that similarity came with an asterisk because they were centered around different versions of Earth. The Admin came to be in a timeline split off from SysGov history circa 1940 with the assassination of Adolph Hitler, and the differences compounded from there all the way up to modern day 2980.

And that, by extension, meant Susan came from another universe, as strange as the concept was for Isaac to wrap his head around.

He still had no idea why she'd been assigned to *him*—a thirty-year-old detective who'd only just finished his five-year probationary period—to serve as his deputy. The Admin had a reputation for militarism, xenophobia, and oppressive laws against anything that sniffed of artificial intelligence, so it would have made sense for his superiors to assign her to someone with more experience or, at the very least, someone who knew the first thing about transdimensional politics.

But they'd selected Isaac Cho. For reasons that continued to elude him.

"Got a question for you," Susan said.

"Shoot."

"I've been pondering my vanguard build. You know, plotting out perks and spells I want for each level, and I was wondering if I could pick your brain a bit."

"Sure. What do you want to know?"

"Well, I can pick out a second spell at level two, and I've

narrowed it down to two candidates. Which do you think would be better: Gravity Spike or Solar Flare?"

"Gravity Spike," he answered without hesitation.

"You sure? Solar Flare does more damage."

"True. But Gravity Spike can debuff or even disable enemies outright, giving you a crowd control option. It's more versatile and synergizes well with your character's role as the party tank."

"Good point!" Susan pulled her screen back over and underlined one of the entries.

"Shouldn't you two be working?" Grace asked from the next row over. The senior detective didn't bother to look up from her own virtual screens.

"Yes, absolutely," Isaac replied. "*If* Raviv would give us another case." He craned his neck back over the headrest. It made it seem like Grace's desk was stuck to the ceiling. "Got anything we could help you with?"

"Nope." Grace blew a breath out the side of her mouth. "Just slogging through these missing persons reports before I head down to Janus. The case has been stalled for over a week, and Raviv is sending me in to take charge."

"Anything interesting?"

"Not so much interesting as weird. The first few disappearances were all kids from the Second Engine Block, so my gut reaction would normally be human trafficking. But the most recent reports are adults with *very* different backgrounds, and I cannot for the life of me find the pattern." She scratched her head. "I don't know. Maybe it'll come to me on the flight down."

"Want help sifting through those reports?"

Grace glanced up from her screens. "Are you really that bored?"

"What's it look like?"

"Like Raviv needs to assign you your own case."

"Couldn't have said it better myself."

It wasn't that Isaac disagreed with the decision to put him and Susan on desk duty after their first case together. Not on principle, anyway. Both of them had almost *died*, and it made sense to give personnel who'd been through that sort of trauma some downtime.

But Isaac had been unconscious for the worst of the episode. All he remembered was alarms going off in their aircraft, and then his head cracking against the wall. After that, he woke up in a ship's medical bay with the worst sore throat of his life, courtesy of a short whiff of Titan's freezing atmosphere.

Susan had gone through far worse than him, but she seemed utterly unfazed by the ordeal, taking the damage to her synthetic body in stride. She still held that she got "shot at less over here," even though their aircraft had been downed by a missile and she'd received what Nina had charitably referred to as a "bullet massage" while defending the crash site.

That was one of the things he'd learned early on about Susan. There wasn't much that could faze her. Granted, she'd transitioned from organic to synthetic at the tender age of twenty-three. That was nine years ago, so pain was a distant memory to her. Her current body wasn't just any old synthoid either, but a top-of-the-line military-grade model from the Admin's Department of Temporal Investigation.

And if *that* wasn't enough, she could transfer her connectome—the neural map of her mind—into an even deadlier combat frame. Isaac had been horrified when she'd first shown him the humanoid war machine bristling with weapons, but he had to—*begrudgingly*—admit it had come in handy on the Gordian murder case.

"So how about it?" Isaac asked Grace.

"How about what?"

"You let me look over those missing persons reports?"

"No thanks, Isaac. I've got this."

"What if I say, 'Pretty please'?"

"What if *I* say, 'Get your own case. Raviv will give you one when he's good and ready'?"

"Fair enough." He sighed and sat up in his chair.

"This isn't so bad," Susan said. "Look on the bright side. We've gone a whole week without being shot at."

"I don't want you to take this the wrong way," Isaac replied carefully, "but your perception of a typical workweek might be a little skewed."

"You could be right." She gave him an indifferent shrug and returned to her character planning.

"Any other questions?" Isaac rocked back in his chair. "Gaming or otherwise?"

"Actually—"

The avatar of a miniature woman appeared on Isaac's shoulder, roughly as tall as his head. For today, she'd chosen a long indigo coat and matching hat with a lavender flower stuck in the side. Her eyes were obscured by a pair of opaque circular glasses, and she flourished a wooden cane in one hand before smacking it against his earlobe.

Her name was Cephalie—short for Encephalon—and she'd been Isaac's integrated companion for the last five years. The blow to his ear was as virtual as her avatar, but Isaac's wetware conveyed the strike's physical sensation to his brain. He turned his head to the side with a mildly annoyed expression.

"What did I do this time?" he asked dully.

"Nothing." Cephalie pushed her glasses up the bridge of her nose. "*This* time."

"Then why hit me?"

"Because I thought you should know."

"Know what?"

"That Raviv is on his way," she said, then vanished.

Isaac bolted upright and scooched his chair up to his desk. He sat up with ramrod posture, set his forearms on the desk, and knitted his fingers. Susan closed her gaming literature and assumed a similar—if slightly less rigid—pose.

Chief Inspector Omar Raviv paced into the Themis Division office less than a minute later. He held a SysPol blue mug in one hand with the words CRIMINAL TEARS written on the side in golden letters and held an abstract document above his free palm. He seemed engrossed in the document as his legs guided him forward at a brisk clip, navigating the rest of his body through the wide grid of desks as if on a form of autopilot.

The legs brought him to a halt next to Grace's desk.

"Chief?" she asked, gazing up at him over her missing persons reports.

"Typical," he grunted, closed whatever document he'd been reading, then took a sip from his mug. "What do you think?"

"About the Second Engine Block disappearances?"

"You have a chance to look over the case log?"

"Most of it. It's a weird one."

"Facemire keeps saying the same thing."

"Given what I've seen so far, I have to agree with his assessment. There's no discernable pattern. Not when we include the most recent incidents."

"Maybe, but he's in over his head. He's floundering, and we need to get this case back on track." Raviv raised an eyebrow. "Unless you feel I'm being too harsh on him."

"Well..."

"Be honest with me, Grace."

"No, I think you've made a fair assessment. I've already got a list of three leads Facemire hasn't checked into that seem obvious to me, and I'm not even through all the reports."

"You ready to go down there and bail him out?"

"I am, but are you sure this is wise? You can still leave him in charge."

"Officially, it'll remain his case. Whatever his shortcomings may be, I'm not going to throw him to the wolves just because he missed a few leads. But on the other hand, we have a responsibility to find those people and find them soon. So, the story is I'm sending you down as support only. But make no mistake, you're the lead on this one. Clear?"

"Clear, Chief."

"If Facemire gives you any bruised ego bullshit, you send him straight to me. Got it?"

"I'm sure that won't be necessary."

"I wish we didn't have to play these games, but this case has dragged on too long. I can already see the political shitstorm on the horizon. The state police have been making noise about our 'incompetence,' so we might as well be ready for it to get worse."

"At least this one isn't all over the news like the Apple Cypher."

"*Yet*," he pointed out. "How soon do you head down to Janus?"

"Within the hour."

"What about forensics backup?"

"I've already lined up a dedicated team and briefed them. They'll meet me in the hangar."

"That's what I like to hear." He gave her a thin but genuine smile. "Good luck down there."

"Thanks, Chief."

Raviv stepped over to Isaac's and Susan's face-to-face desks. Isaac somehow found a way to sit up even straighter.

"Sir?" he asked in a tone he hoped didn't sound too eager.

"Hey, you two," Raviv said with a sad, almost pitying expression, his voice quieter than before. "How've you been? You both feeling all right?"

"Never better," Isaac said.

"Same here, sir," Susan added. "Ready to get back to it."

"Isaac, how's the throat?"

"Just fine. I can't even tell the medibots operated on it."

"Good." Raviv nodded, though he didn't seem convinced. "Good. And you, Susan? Are you happy with the repairs to your synthoid? Any problems with the Admin parts we had to print out?"

"No issues to report." She flashed a quick smile. "Both my general-purpose body and combat frame are ready for action."

"Good, but let's not be too hasty. You both have been through a lot."

"I've had worse," Susan said.

"Still, I insist. And since I'm the boss, I can insist pretty hard."

"Then why not send us out there as support for another detective?" Isaac suggested. "Something like a . . . Oh, I don't know, a missing persons case?"

"You mean the Second Engine Block disappearances?"

Isaac nodded, perhaps too eagerly.

"No. Trust me, you don't want that one."

"Sounds like Grace could use the extra pairs of eyes down there."

"Maybe, but that one's a hair's breadth from going political in a nasty way. I give it fifty-fifty odds I'll be heading down after Grace sometime tomorrow to run interference for her. It's best if *both* of you"—he gave Susan a meaningful glance—"stay clear of this one. Don't want either of you getting tarnished by association."

"He does have a point there," Susan said to Isaac. "Especially with me."

"Yeah," Isaac sighed, sitting back.

"You two sure you're up for another case so soon?" Raviv asked.

"Absolutely," Isaac said.

"Ready and willing, sir," Susan added.

"Okay then. I'll see what comes up. I don't have any easy ones right now, but I'll get with you if any come in from the super. How's that sound?"

"That—" Isaac was going to complain about being given "easy" leftovers, but he thought better of it. An easy case was better than the nothing he had right now. "That'd be great."

"All right. We'll see what comes in. Take care of yourselves."

"Will do," Isaac replied.

"Thank you for your concern, sir," Susan said.

Raviv nodded to both of them, clearly satisfied he'd done his bossly duty, then headed out of the office.

As soon as he left, Isaac blew out a breath and slouched in his chair. Susan let out a little sigh and opened her character sheet once more.

"Hey, Isaac." Grace walked up beside him. "Since I'm going to be neck-deep in a case, you two can go ahead and schedule the next session with Nina. I'll catch up later."

"You sure? I thought you were really invested in this season."

"Yeah, but don't worry about me." She patted Isaac on the shoulder. "Might as well enjoy the short hours while they last."

"Thanks," Isaac groused.

Later that day, Isaac took the station's network of counter-grav tubes out from the Themis offices, located near the middle of the station's upper half, and down to Becky's Quiet Corner, which earned its name from both its atmosphere and location.

Kronos Station may have been dwarfed by megastructures such as Janus-Epimetheus, but the space station still housed and supported a standing force of over one million federal police officers, with a slight majority of those being physical citizens. Its dark blue hull took the form of an octahedron, as if two unusually tall pyramids had been sandwiched together base to base, and Themis Division took up dozens of levels around the middle of the upper pyramid.

The station was a city in its own right, and while its core activities revolved around law enforcement, the station was also home to a plethora of civilian businesses, with the most common taking the form of food and entertainment venues.

Becky's Quiet Corner was one such establishment, a modest café nestled in the hard edge of one of the station's corners, one level above the central hangars. The square "equator" where the two pyramids met formed a solid wall over ten levels tall and housed the majority of the station's hangars for corvettes and other craft of similar sizes, while larger vessels docked externally. Patrons at Becky's watched the comings and goings through two of the cafe's inward-slanted walls.

Isaac stood at the threshold for a moment, his eyes taking in the room. The café was packed for the midday rush, but the seating was arranged so that it didn't feel crowded. Its hardwood floors and cloth drapes pulled back from the windows gave the establishment an old-fashioned, earthy ambiance. He spotted Nina at a small table by the window, walked over, and sat down across from her.

"Any luck?" Nina asked, her cheek resting on a fist as she stared out the window, her tall, perspiring glass of cherry cola fizzing beside her. Outside, the massive sphere of a *Sentinel*-class cruiser slid past on its way to a nearby docking arm.

"I don't know. Raviv still hasn't assigned us a new case."

"Give it time. It's only been two weeks."

"Two weeks I could have been doing some good out there rather than warming my office chair."

"Yeah, but look at it from his perspective. He almost lost two people under his command."

"It's not the first close call—or worse—the department has had. Not by a long shot."

"No, but it *is* the first one since he took over."

"I suppose you have a point there," he conceded.

A waitress in a brown summer dress served him his iced mocha before he ordered it. He and Nina followed a predictable routine when they met at the café, and the employees at Becky's knew their patterns well. He picked up the drink, nodded to the waitress, and transferred a generous Esteem tip to her account. She gave him a quick smile in recognition of the gratuity, then headed to her next table.

"Plus," Nina said, "I bet he has a soft spot for you."

"I don't know about *that*."

"Why not? You mentored under him for how many years?"

"Three."

"And you think that isn't a factor?" She leaned toward him and spoke softer for emphasis. "Come on. Raviv may have taken lessons from porcupines on how to make friends, but we both know he's got a good heart. He'd stick his neck out there for any one of us, and I bet that goes double for you."

"You think he's coddling me, then?"

"No, I wouldn't call it that. But maybe—just maybe—*he* needs to get over your near death, too."

"I almost wish *I* needed to get over it. I was unconscious for the whole thing! Cephalie had to show me videos of what Susan went through."

"What about her? Is she really okay with what happened?"

"Honestly, I think so. I know I found some of her DTI stories a little hard to accept when she first shared them, but looking at her now, it's clear that wasn't the first time she's had limbs shot off."

"Good thing you had someone like her watching your back."

"Yeah. No kidding." Isaac took a sip. "How about you? How's your day been?"

"Richeny keeps trying to drop spoilers from the new season. It's getting annoying."

"Richeny..." Isaac thought for a moment. "Isn't he the one who's been hitting on you?"

"Yeah." Nina paused, then frowned. "Well, one of them. *Anyway*, the sooner I get off this station the better. And I was *this close*, too!" She held up her thumb and forefinger.

"What's keeping you here?"

"Lack of seniority. You hear about all those people disappearing in the Second Engine Block?"

"I've heard."

"I wanted to be on Grace's forensics support. Was even on the list to fly down before I got booted off. I'm not sure who it was, but someone decided to restrict the job to senior specialists only."

"That might have been Raviv. He made it sound like SSP was about to stir up trouble over our lack of progress."

"Well, of course they are. It's their favorite pastime. Next you'll tell me space is black and Saturn is tan."

"Point taken," he agreed, shaking his head. "By the way, Grace said we can go ahead without her."

"Really? She sure about that?"

"I asked, and she said she'd catch up later."

"Well then." Nina shrugged. "In that case, what about a session right after work?"

"Hold on." He opened an abstract window. "Let me check my calendar. I *may* have an opening."

"Yeah, yeah," Nina laughed, knuckling him in the arm.

CHAPTER THREE

TROOPER RANDAL PARKS OF THE SATURN STATE POLICE COULDN'T shake the feeling that something was wrong. This wasn't his first corpse while working for the SSP. He wasn't *that* green, but it was the first corpse that made him go "hmm" in a meaningful way.

He focused in on the corpse of Esteban Velasco once more, and his avatar bent down as if taking a closer look.

He wasn't physically in the room. More to the point, he didn't have a physical body to begin with, being a purely abstract entity. He'd transferred his connectome from the police quadcopter to the Atlas HQ's infostructure shortly after he and Sergeant Boris Chatelain had arrived, and that was the first time he'd gone "hmm" to himself during this call.

That first "hmm" wasn't related to the crime. At least he didn't *think* it could be, but it didn't change the fact that the abstract environment within Atlas was one of the most barren, depressing virtual realms he'd ever visited. No style. No personality. No *flair*. Just an endless black plain with a dark gray grid stretching out to infinity beneath a black sky. Why would *anyone* want to work in such an environment?

The few ACs he encountered inside didn't bother to acknowledge his presence, and their simplistic avatars—mere glowing points moving from node to node along the grid—made him feel unwelcomed and out of place, since his avatar was the only object with any sense of realism in the stark expanse. He wore the dark green of the SSP with a cap over his dark green eyes. He'd once considered changing his sandy brown hair to green as well, but that might have been pushing it.

Back in the victim's office, he scrutinized the corpse through a combination of the local infostructure, the feed from a disk-shaped SSP conveyor drone, and the senses of any physical citizens who'd set their wetware to PUBLIC, which was exactly zero since only the sarge was present. Parks could see the room through his eyes, too, but that was over a secure link shared between them and the drone.

The corpse reclined unnaturally in the chair, jerked back and somewhat to the side by the weapon's discharge and the secondary detonation of the shell. A fist-sized hole had been blown out the back of the man's head, splattering bits of brain, bone, and hair in a conical pattern behind the desk and up the back wall. The gun sat on the desk, the end of the barrel slick with saliva.

"Welp." Chatelain stuck his thumbs behind his belt. "I think we have the cause of death figured out."

"No note," Parks said.

"Excuse me?"

"He didn't leave a note."

Chatelain ran a finger along the edge of the desk. He came across a sticky sauce spill underneath a plate and wiped the goo off on his pants.

"Anything local?" he asked Parks.

"I checked the desk infosystem and ran a search through the unrestricted parts of the company's infostructure. No note."

"Not every guy who kills himself leaves a note."

"He was legally obligated to write one."

"Somehow"—Chatelain gazed down at the corpse's open mouth and vacant, rolled-back eyes—"I'm guessing that wasn't a priority for him."

Suicide was technically legal within SysGov, though it was by no means encouraged from both a legal standpoint and a societal one. SysGov was a culture where synthetic bodies and abstracted minds left people virtually immortal after they transitioned into a post-organic state, and it was inevitable that some citizens would yearn for the exit door as the centuries rolled by.

Saturn State law required any citizen planning an act of self-termination to submit their plan for government approval before carrying out the act. Parks had some serious doubts about the wisdom behind said law, but he supposed it had been put in place as one more measure to discourage citizens from taking their own lives.

As for how such a law could be effectively *enforced*, the politicians had left it up to SSP's "discretion," for what little sense *that* made.

"No note means we should investigate further," Parks stated.

"What? Are you kidding?"

"No," Parks replied, somewhat defensively.

"He *clearly* blew his own brains out."

"The victim did not declare his intent to die."

"He did that when he stuck the barrel in his mouth!"

"Which happened under suspicious circumstances."

"Suspicious!"

"The company had just landed the biggest contract in its history, and he's the lead engineer on the project. Why would he kill himself after receiving news like that?"

"Who knows what was going through his head?" Chatelain let out a quick snort. "Besides the bullet, I mean."

"This doesn't make sense."

"So what? One piece of good news doesn't mean jack in the long run. Everyone's got problems, and who knows how deep his ran? The motive could be anything. For one, his wife could have been sleeping around."

"Ah!" Parks perked up. "Good thinking! Should we interview her?"

"Uhh, how about this? How about *I* file the report with the station, which will declare this an open-and-shut suicide, and you"—Chatelain knocked on the conveyor drone's hull—"can collect the body for processing. All hundred or so pieces of it."

"I—"

"Don't worry. If something weird happened here, the autopsy will spot it."

"But—"

"Hop to it, Rainy. That body won't bag itself."

Chatelain stepped through the virtual police cordon over the door and headed down the corridor.

Parks returned his focus to the body. He switched his avatar off since there was no one physically left in the room. Alive, anyway.

"Hmm," he murmured, unsatisfied with where his disagreement with the sarge had ended.

But he had his orders, so he interfaced with the drone, set its operational mode to evidence collection and corpse removal, then specified the work area. The drone floated over to the rear wall, and its two flexible limbs began the tedious process of collecting the victim's brain spackle.

Parks watched the drone's progress through its own sensors as it placed each piece of flesh or cut-away blood splat into separate sealed containers, which it then stored in an internal rack. It would take some time for the drone to complete the evidence extraction, and Parks used the delay to mull over what he knew about the suicide.

He understood why Chatelain had been so dismissive. The *what* of the death seemed painfully clear, barring an unforeseen piece of evidence turned up by the forensics review.

But that wasn't what bothered him; it was the *why* that continued to stick in his mind like a splinter. Why would Velasco kill himself? And not just kill himself, but do so after receiving news of the winning bid?

Death didn't have to come invited or need some special meaning. Lives began and ended all the time, but Parks couldn't shake how something felt off about this one. A suicide following bad news made logical—if morbid—sense to him. A suicide following good news? Not so much.

But Chatelain would be the one to file the report, and so that would be the end of it.

Unless... Parks thought as a second possibility came to mind. Chatelain would be the one to file the *state police* report, but there was the possibility of a *federal* look at the death.

He opened a personal folder with all the presentations and manuals he'd received during basic training and ran a search for "SysPol." The search flagged a single document, and he opened it and skimmed through it until he found the entry he was looking for.

I was right, he thought. *Any member of the state police can request assistance from SysPol, regardless of rank.*

The connection string for the support line stood out in vibrant text.

He considered his next actions carefully.

This might tick the sarge off, he thought. *But will it be worth it?*

"Hmm."

He didn't know the answer to that question.

He placed the call anyway.

"SysPol Support," the dispatcher said warmly. "Good day to you, Trooper Parks. How may I be of service?"

"Umm, hello."

"Hello."

"Yes, umm." Parks cleared his nonexistent throat, which was purely a delaying tactic as he composed his thoughts. "I'd like to put in a support request."

"I can certainly assist you there. First, are we dealing with an active emergency?"

"No, nothing like that."

"Always good to hear. What sort of issue are we looking at, then?"

"We were called out to Atlas HQ for a death by gunshot. Initial impressions are it's a suicide, but I'm not so sure. I'd feel better if someone from SysPol could take a deeper look at this."

"Sounds like a job for Themis Division. One moment while I open a new case. Can you send me the call record and any other pertinent files? I'll attach them to the case log."

"Sure thing." Parks grouped all the files he had together and transmitted. "Sending them your way."

"And...received. Thank you. Are you making this request yourself or on behalf of a superior?"

"Myself. Why? Is that a problem?"

"It's not so much a problem as a matter of priority. SysPol resources are limited, and we do take the requestor's seniority into consideration when allocating resources. Since there is no active emergency, you may experience some delay before Themis Division can dispatch a detective or specialist to your location."

"Oh, I see."

"Though, there are a few measures you can take to reduce the delay. Is there a sergeant nearby or—even better—a lieutenant who can endorse your request?"

"Umm, no," Park replied, choosing his words carefully. "No one I can get to endorse it."

"Then, do you have anything you'd like to add to the case file before I forward it on to Themis?"

"No, that's all I've got so far."

"Understood. Your case is now in the queue. You can expect follow-up instructions from Themis once the case has been assigned."

"Got it. And thank you. You've been very helpful."

"My pleasure, Trooper Parks. Have a pleasant day."

✧   ✧   ✧

Parks waited for the drone to finish, ordered it back to the quadcopter, then transferred his connectome. His perception of the physical world blinked from Velasco's office to the copter's tandem-seat cockpit.

Chatelain sat in one of the chairs, which he'd spun around to face the cramped cabin, a deep scowl on his face as he rapped his fingers on the top of a knee. Parks appeared in Chatelain's virtual vision as his usual avatar seated across from him.

"Hey, Sarge."

"Hey yourself, Rainy."

"Drone's finished. Should be back here with the body in a few minutes."

"Is that so?"

"What do you mean?"

"Oh, nothing." Chatelain shrugged his shoulders. "Nothing at all."

"Is something wrong?"

"What makes you think something's wrong?"

"You seem a little off. That's all."

"Well then." Chatelain leaned forward until his face almost touched Park's. "Maybe it's because my partner called SysPol behind my back!"

Oh dear, Parks thought. *He knows. How could he—*

"I'm guessing by your dumbfounded face you don't know how this works."

"Uhh."

"You see," he began in a conversational tone, even though his eyes were pits of fury. "If you'd ever put in a support request before, you'd know one of the first things the call center does is set up these annoying automatic updates for everyone. And that includes all the troopers on the original call."

"Oh dear."

"Which means I received one of their little messages right after you finished." Chatelain drummed his fingers on the dashboard. "Care to explain yourself?"

"I thought they might be able to help."

"That wasn't your call to make. It's *mine!*"

"I'm sorry, Sarge, but I don't see the harm in being thorough. This suicide doesn't sit right with me, and I'd feel a lot better if someone were to take a closer look."

"You only think that way because you haven't had to deal with SysPol before."

"That doesn't mean I'm wrong."

"Doesn't mean you're right either." Chatelain let out a heavy sigh. "Look, you're new, I get that. I remember how I was when I started out, just a regular bundle of optimism and energy, ready and willing to help everyone. Before I came to grips with reality. Before it sank in that not everyone can be helped, and not every story receives a happy ending."

Chatelain opened an abstract window and pulled up the alert from SysPol. He scrolled to the bottom and tapped the highlighted connection string.

"What are you doing?" Parks asked.

"Fixing your mistake."

"SysPol Support," a woman said over voice chat. "Good day to you, Sergeant Chatelain. I see an existing case number referenced in the call. Give me a moment to pull up its status. Ah, here we are. Looks like the case hasn't been reviewed for assignment yet. How can I help you?"

"I need to cancel the support request." He shot Parks a fierce eye. "My partner placed it by mistake."

"Sarge—"

Chatelain made a sharp slashing motion across his throat.

"Of course, Sergeant," the dispatcher said. "I can take care of that for you. Can you please give me the reason for the cancellation?"

"Lack of communication between me and my partner. We weren't on the same page when he called earlier."

"I'll put that down as 'incomplete information.' Since you're Trooper Parks' superior, you have the authority to close his support request yourself. Please confirm you wish to close it."

"Yes. I want it closed."

"Very good. I have appended the case with your cancellation request. Is there anything else I can help you with today?"

"Nope. That'll do it."

"Then have a good day, Sergeant. SysPol Support out."

The comm window vanished, and Chatelain turned back to Parks.

"I'm going to let this one slide just because you're new at this, but if you *ever* pull shit like that on me again, I'll make sure it ends up on your permanent record. You can argue with me all you want. I'm a big boy. I can take it. But once your superior makes the call, that's that. Get in line or get out of the force. Have I made this clear enough for you?"

"Yeah, it's clear."

"Good." Chatelain switched on the quadcopter's rotors. "Now let's get this corpse back to the station."

Mitch hated meetings.

Which wasn't surprising, since there were a lot of things he hated, and he wasn't shy about sharing his ever-growing list of disdain with those around him. For one, he hated when people asked him "Mitch what?" as if they found the simplicity of his name offensive.

Which, he considered, was perhaps a form of symmetry since *he* found most names from his fellow abstract citizens to be pretentious drivel. What was wrong with "Mitch?" He saw no reason for anything fancier. It was the name he'd chosen to identify his artificial connectome. What more did he need? Certainly not an example of audible diarrhea like "Quantum Luminary" or "NeoHawking."

He let his actions speak for themselves, without the baggage of frivolous word association. It was one of the reasons why he preferred to keep to his own quiet corner of the Kronos infostructure. The solitude allowed him to focus on what was important, which was overseeing the many Themis departments under his command so that they continued to shove their boots up crime's figurative ass.

He loved that part about his job the most, especially the look on a criminal's face/avatar when he/she/it was brought to justice. It represented the moment when a measure of beautiful order was restored where only chaos had once reigned, and it was as sweet to him as a tall glass of ice water at the end of a long day working in the sun.

He didn't drink, of course. Didn't eat either, virtual or otherwise. He'd never seen the point in integrating with some walking meat terminal so he could experience the physical world through shared organic senses. Why were so many of his fellow ACs obsessed with "eating food" through the senses of an integrated companion? What was the point? The solar system would be a better place if everyone would hurry up and abstract already, but he'd accepted long ago that for all the advancements in medical science, there still wasn't a cure for dumb.

He'd been rereading one of Horace Pangu's books recently. His most famous one, in fact. It was titled *A Tale of Stars and Meat*, and it advocated for the complete virtualization of the human race. The book was one of his favorites, and he tried to find time to reread it once a year.

Mitch's austere views extended to his choice of avatar for this meeting. As a being of pure data, he could manifest in the meeting with any shape he wished. His fellow superintendents often criticized him for his rudimentary approach to avatar selection, but what they didn't realize was he took extra care in selecting the most annoyingly simplistic designs he could find.

Today he'd chosen a large circle suspended over his seat at the conference table like a yellow full moon, complete with exaggerated eyes and mouth. The face wasn't smiling or frowning. Rather, it was locked in a dull expression, neutral and unimpressed.

His fellow superintendents all sat at the table physically, most of them old enough to have transitioned into synthoids, along with a virtual representation of Colonel Raj Heppleman from the SSP, who'd joined their meeting remotely from the Second Engine Block. He'd spent the entire meeting complaining.

"Well, Mitch?" Ishii Takuya asked pointedly, arms crossed as he glared at Mitch's expressionless hover-face. "Got anything to add for the colonel?"

Ishii was head of the Kronos' Arete Division, in command of SysPol First Responders in the Saturn State. He was a bicentennial in what Mitch assumed was meant to be a "ruggedly handsome" synthoid body clad in the red of Arete Division. He was also no fan of Mitch's methods or personality, and the feeling was very, *very* mutual.

Mitch had a lot of opinions about Ishii, most of them negative. For one, the Arete superintendent had a truly obnoxious habit of scheduling meetings for pretty much everything, as if talking about a problem was somehow the equivalent of *solving* the problem.

"No," Mitch replied. "Not especially."

His avatar's mouth didn't move with the words.

"If the Themis superintendent doesn't," Heppleman said, "then I do. This lack of results is intolerable. We informed SysPol of these disappearances nearly two weeks ago, and what do we have to show for it? A big, fat zero. That's what. The city council is breathing down my neck on this one. They've been doing their best to keep public perception of the case under control, but sooner or later we"—he made a sharp, all-inclusive gesture around the table—"need to show them and the public we're not sitting around picking our noses!"

"Colonel, please." Ishii put on a forced smile. "We've demonstrated for you how seriously we take this problem. Arete has dedicated a full department to supplement the city's own police force."

"Throwing more people and equipment at a problem is a start, but where's the progress? Where are the results? Where are our missing people?!"

"I'm sure it's only a matter of time, Colonel."

"And what about Themis?" Heppleman demanded, eyeballing the floating yellow face. "What about the investigation itself?"

"Mitch?" Ishii asked with a raised eyebrow. "Care to field this one?"

"Appropriate resources have been allocated to the case," he answered simply.

"Yes," Heppleman scoffed. "One additional detective!"

"And support staff," Ishii said.

"Hardly a meaningful addition!"

"I disagree," Mitch said.

"And why's that?"

"Because you, like everyone else at this table, seem to be in a state of perpetual confusion." The table sucked in a collective breath, but Mitch continued before any of the others could cut him off. "And that's because you fail to grasp the difference between quantity and quality. Tell me, Colonel, what matters more? That we throw large numbers of aimless head count at a problem, or that we put the right people with the right experience and support in the right place? Which do you believe will produce the best results?"

"This case has been poorly staffed from the start."

"You raise a point I've already conceded," Mitch said. "Yes, we underestimated the extent of the problem, and the initial resources we allocated were insufficient for the task at hand. However, that issue has been rectified to my satisfaction."

"*Your* satisfaction?" Heppleman sneered.

"Indeed. The Themis department now has the right people on the case. What more could you possibly want?"

"How about some damned progress? What are *you* doing to solve the case?"

"Nothing at all."

"And why is that? Your colleague from Arete is practically tripping over himself to help us out, and yet you insist on sitting this one out?"

"That's because I'm not a micromanaging jerk." Mitch didn't say the words "like the rest of you here." He thought he showed considerable restraint with that omission.

"Ex-*cuse* me?" Heppleman said.

"Listen, Colonel. Management, at its core, is a simple vocation. Either you have the right people working for you, in which case you should trust them to do their jobs, or you don't, in which case you should replace them. Or at the very least give them tasks that better match their lackluster skills."

"Then you don't believe this case warrants your personal attention?"

"No. It doesn't."

"I think what my colleague is trying to say," Ishii said, "is all of us here have to be attentive to *all* the issues in the Saturn State, not just your own case, and that we must apply our time accordingly." He shot Mitch a stern eye. "Isn't that right?"

"Sure," Mitch said. "You can think of it that way if it makes you feel better."

His avatar changed for the first time since the meeting started, snapping from its bored expression to a toothy grin with wide, exaggerated eyes. A detached thumbs-up appeared beside the face.

Heppleman snorted.

"Perhaps there's more we could be doing," Superintendent Fergus Kayson offered, speaking up for the first time in the meeting.

He wore the black of Argo Division's patrol fleet. "I could move one of our larger cruisers down to Janus and position it near the Second Engine Block. From there, it could provide logistical support for the other divisions. Its presence would also serve as a clear visual reminder of how seriously we're taking the problem."

"An excellent idea," Ishii said. "Colonel?"

"At this point, I'll take whatever I can get."

Mitch didn't pay much attention to the rest of the meeting, mostly because the presence of the Argo cruiser would serve no practical purpose other than to "show people how much we care," and that sort of style-over-substance decision-making held its own slot on his list of disdain.

He transferred back to his work area once the meeting wrapped up and began processing his mail, starting with a review of any unassigned cases. He worked through the newest messages, rejected a couple nuisance calls that Dispatch let slip through and forwarded the rest on to different departments depending on location, capacity, and the nature of the case.

He was near the end of the list when he stopped, his work-flow halted by an unusual support request. Not because of the nature of the suicide case—the fundamentals seemed straight-forward enough, at least on the surface—but because of the call record. A Trooper Randal Parks had placed the initial call, which was unusual in its own right. Troopers rarely placed such calls themselves unless it was an emergency, and a room temperature self-termination didn't qualify. Even stranger, his sergeant had canceled the request almost immediately.

These two facts sparked Mitch's curiosity. SSP troopers tended to reach for the simplest conclusion, and this suicide might be an example where the new guy saw something his more seasoned partner didn't. Or didn't *want* to see because of the extra work it entailed. Not all SSP troopers shared this lack of attention to detail, whether deliberate or otherwise, but it was a common enough trait to be a problem for Themis detectives.

The two troopers were flying to Janus, so Mitch sent them new orders, routing them back to Atlas mobile headquarters where they would await the arrival of a Themis detective. He checked the caseload of the departments working on or near Janus and forwarded the case number to Omar Raviv for assignment.

CHAPTER FOUR

"HERE WE ARE AT LAST!" NINA DECLARED, HER OVERACTING A
sure sign she'd returned to her Radiant Blaze character. She
brushed back one of her fiberoptic dreadlocks and smiled at Isaac
and Susan. A nearby atmospheric unit switched on, and garbage
fluttered across the street outside the dilapidated warehouse.

"Doesn't look like much," Susan said, surveying the building.
She'd been looking forward to the *Solar Descent* session since
Isaac had mentioned it after lunch. The day, like the ones before
it, had dragged on with very little to occupy her time, and she
welcomed the after-work diversion.

"Looks can be deceiving, though," Isaac said, his purple eyes
glowing from beneath his hood. "If our information is correct,
the cultists behind Klynn's disappearance will be inside."

"Vanguard Cantrell!" Nina swung around to face her. "Since
you're the most heavily armored of us, would you be so kind as
to check the door?"

"Sure."

Nina and Isaac took a few steps back, almost as if they
expected something bad to happen. It was a simple sliding door,
rusted and unlocked. She grabbed the handle—

—and the door exploded outward into flame and scything
shrapnel, throwing her back across the street until she skidded
to a halt in a mound of trash.

"An exploding door?" Nina waved her hand back and forth to clear the smoke. "Really? What is with these developers and trapped doors?"

"Maybe they think it's funny," Isaac said. "You okay, Susan?"

"Umm." She checked her health on her wrist display. "Mostly. Regen's kicking in." She rose to her feet, brushed herself off, and drew her sword. "I take it the bad guys know we're coming."

She paced toward the door with long, meaningful strides.

"Hold up," Nina said. "Maybe there's another entrance we can— And she's gone inside."

There was a spaceship in the warehouse. Not a nice, new, sleek spaceship, but one that looked like it had been cobbled together from junk and held in place with welded metal and prayers. It sat in the warehouse like a misshapen, metal egg on four squat legs. An elevator platform dropped down from the belly on four extendable poles.

Several figures stood on the platform, jammed so close together they resembled a singular, horribly mutated blob of flesh and machinery. They were humanoid rats about half Susan's height armed with short swords, maces, and scimitars, their bodies augmented with all manner of cybernetics in place of their limbs and eyes.

"Rats," Nina grumbled from the blasted doorway. "Always with the rats."

"For the dark gods!" shouted one of the cyborgs, and the cultists charged off the platform.

A message alert from outside the game beeped next to Isaac.

"Hold on. It's work." The cyborg ratmen froze mid-charge, and he opened the comm window. "Hello, sir."

"Isaac," Raviv said. "Sorry to disturb you after hours."

"It's no trouble. What can I do for you?"

"The super sent in a new case, but it's an odd one. On the surface, it looks like a straightforward suicide, but the deceased is a major player in the Dyson Project, and that makes me nervous. The case *shouldn't* take more than a quick trip down to Janus, but we need to be certain this really is a suicide before we close it. Would you and Susan mind taking this one off the pile?"

Isaac made eye contact with Susan, who gave him an emphatic nod.

"Not at all, sir," he replied. "We'd be more than happy to take care of it for you."

"Wonderful. I'm sending you the details now."

"We'll get right on it." Isaac closed the comm window.

"Does that man ever go home?" Nina asked.

"It's not *that* late," Isaac said, opening the case summary. "Deceased is named Esteban Velasco, one of the senior engineers for Atlas. Discharged a pistol into his own mouth."

"Ouch." Susan winced.

"We should go over the rest before we leave. Meet you back at the office?"

"Sure. I'll head right over as soon as we disconnect."

"Wait up." Nina pointed to the cyborgs. "Can't we at least reach a good stopping point? We've got space rats to kill."

"Sorry, Nina." Isaac gave her a sad smile. "Duty calls."

"I can see why Raviv is torn on this case," Isaac said once he and Susan were back in the office. He stood next to his desk, an array of abstract screens hovering before them. "Nothing stands out as unusual besides the SSP call record, and even that appears to be little more than a disagreement between two troopers. On the other hand, Velasco was a huge player in the Dyson Project, which has been notorious for the ugly politics and sabotage attempts that have dogged it since day one. That, plus the obscene amounts of money at play mean the project's rife with temptation for bad actors. It's no wonder he wants us to be extra certain on this one."

"What kind of company is Atlas?" Susan asked.

"Large-scale construction with a heavy focus on megastructures and, to a lesser extent, terraforming. Atlas is best known for their macrotech constructors. They eschew the use of self-replicating swarms whenever possible."

"Why's that?"

"Mutations mostly. Any self-replication system, no matter how well designed, runs the risk of unexpected mutations as it expands. There are always countermeasures in place, but the risk of a dangerous change is never zero. By approaching their design problems on a macro-scale rather than a micro-scale, Atlas has earned a reputation for robust, reliable solutions, even if they give up some flexibility in the process."

"Now that's a philosophy I can get behind," Susan said.

Isaac thought he understood her sentiment. Self-replicators were a Restricted technology in the Admin, and that was "Restricted" with a capital R. One of the Admin's purposes was to enforce the Yanluo Restrictions on forbidden or limited technologies, and Susan—as a Peacekeeper—was sworn to uphold them.

Self-replicators were also one of the few things Isaac knew Susan feared, so much so that she'd almost ripped her own uniform off when its smart fabric became contaminated. She'd mistaken a harmless gangster virus for something far more sinister, but fortunately, he'd been able to talk her down before she stripped in front of the SSP squad.

"Technically, Atlas does use self-replicators," Isaac said, "but those machines—their constructors—are significantly larger than your average microbot."

"How much larger?"

"It varies. Sometimes they're hundreds of meters across."

"Good enough for me. It's when they're microscopic that those things give me the creeps."

"Atlas was actually in the news today," Isaac said. "They won the Dyson contract, which was a heavily contested competition between them and rival company SourceCode. That's a *massive* coup for Atlas, since the Dyson Project stands to be the largest macrotech endeavor in SysGov history."

"What's Atlas been up to recently? Besides shooting for the Dyson contract?"

"Not sure. Cephalie?"

His IC popped into existence, seated precariously atop one of the virtual screens.

"The Atlas mobile headquarters is currently down near Janus." Cephalie stood up and paced across the top of the screen. "They're busy executing a contract for an expansion to Janus' power and propulsion systems, as well as building up the basic framework for what will become the Fourth Engine Block city, situated around the reactors and thrusters. The main engine assemblies are going in along the trailing edge of the Shark Fin, beneath the Third Engine Block, which is itself situated below the Second Engine Block." She shrugged. "I think you get the idea.

"Setting the Dyson contract aside, Atlas used to be a much bigger deal than they are now. They're Saturn-based, which by itself is unusual for a major player in the megastructure scene; most of those companies are headquartered around Earth or

Jupiter. Atlas dates back to the founding of Janus-Epimetheus. That's where they made a name for themselves and built their initial fortune. The company expanded from there, though they've hit something of a slump recently, focusing on smaller projects while losing numerous bids to their competitors."

"Which would make the Dyson contract even more important for them," Susan said.

"It goes a bit beyond that." Cephalie floated down to Isaac's shoulder. "The scale of the Dyson swarm's construction will keep them busy—and guarantee their income—for *centuries*. They've just become the envy of the entire macrotech industry."

"And Velasco was one of their top engineers," Susan said. "Who, all of a sudden, decides to ventilate his own head. How should we approach this?"

"Simple," Isaac said. "All suicides are treated as homicides until either we or the state police declare otherwise. And even if the SSP do declare it a suicide, we have the authority to over-rule them."

"Do you think there's a chance this could be a homicide?"

"Not at the moment, but there are the occasional outliers that surprise us. If so, the autopsy will tell us more."

"Would that be enough reason for SSP to call us? Wanting us to perform the autopsy?"

"Not usually. Our forensic equipment is better than theirs, but they'd typically handle a body like this on their own."

"Which makes me wonder why we were called down there in the first place."

"We'll have to talk to Trooper Parks once we're on site," Isaac said. "And that brings up the question of transportation. There aren't any regular flights that connect to the mobile headquarters, so I say we take a V-wing down."

"Armed?"

"Uhh." Isaac frowned at her.

"It *did* come in handy last time."

"Susan, all we're looking at is a trip down to Saturn and back. We're not going to be shot at." He paused, then added, "Again."

"You never know."

"But I'd say probability is in our favor."

"You thought taking weapons last time was a bad idea, too."

"I— Yes, you've got me there."

"Those weapons saved our lives."

"Technically, *you* saved our lives."

"Right. Because I was armed to the teeth."

"Susan—" He stopped and let out a resigned sigh. "Fine. I'll ask for some guns on it."

"Thank you."

He opened a comm window. "Dispatch."

"Dispatch here. What can I help you with, Detective?"

"I need to requisition a V-wing to take down to Janus, preferably one that's ready to go. The case number is attached." He glanced over at Susan. "Also, I'd like the V-wing to be armed, if possible."

"Expecting some action, Detective?"

"I hope not."

"Let me see what's ready to deploy. Yes, here we are. One V-wing powered and loaded with a standard defensive package. It's ready to go in Hangar Three-Twenty-Two. Shall I reserve it for you?"

"Yes, please."

"Very good. There. The V-wing is yours. I've added the keycodes to your case log. Anything else I can do for you? Will you need any accommodations while on Janus?"

"I don't think so. We hope to be back on Kronos tonight. Thanks, Dispatch."

"My pleasure."

The comm window closed.

"Head out next?" Susan asked.

"Almost. I'm going to grab my overnight bag just in case this takes longer than we expect. Also, it wouldn't hurt for us to head down with a forensics specialist. That way we can knock out any weird possibilities with the body or crime scene while we're at it."

"Don't you normally request that through Dispatch?"

"True, but I have an alternative in mind." He opened another comm window and waited for the response.

"Radiant Blaze Adventuring Services," Nina answered. "You pay, we slay. Now accepting murder hobo applicants. Please click the link to apply for membership."

"We are *not* murder hobos," Isaac protested.

"Don't judge. Radiant's desperate now that all her partners have abandoned her."

"You sound bored."

"Wow! How astute! Are you a detective?"

"This is a serious call."

"Sorry. Couldn't help myself. What do you need?"

"How would you like a date with a corpse?"

"Depends. Work related?"

"Yes."

"Will it get me off this station?"

"At least for a little bit."

"Good enough for me."

The variable-wing aircraft descended through the Saturn atmosphere as light from the distant sun caressed the cloud tops. Thunderheads of ammonia ice glowed almost golden in the new light, casting long, dark shadows behind them.

The V-wing braked through the atmosphere, its hull passing through wispy vapors above the storm clouds. The craft's delta wing morphed outward, reforming into a narrow straight wing more appropriate for low speeds and higher maneuverability.

Isaac pressed his forehead against the canopy and glanced down at Janus-Epimetheus. He could see the megastructure's upper crown, an oval expanse over two hundred kilometers long and covered from end to end in teardrop-shaped towers, one side of their glass and metal structures shining in the new day. The triangular body of the Shark Fin dipped down from that upper megacity, cutting through the Saturn clouds like the bow of a great white ship.

The fortieth northern parallel was a zone of relative calm on Saturn. Travel too far north or south, and it wasn't uncommon to experience regular windspeeds above four hundred kilometers per hour. But along Janus' path, nestled between two great storm bands, the weather was far more manageable. Air pressure was one atmosphere at the top of Janus, though the megastructure was so tall the pressure climbed to ten atmospheres near the bottom, where reddish clouds of ammonium hydrosulfide replaced the surface weather of ammonia ice.

Lightning flashed from cloud to cloud and the V-wing lurched upward. Restraints bit into Isaac's shoulders, and he grunted out a short exhale.

The V-wing flew across Janus's long axis, just above the local traffic patterns. Aircraft and spaceships took off and landed in a constant ballet along the crown's rim.

The V-wing glided past it all, then began a descending corkscrew behind the megastructure's trailing edge. A trio of Janus' huge thruster ports glowed blue, casting cool light over dark clouds too deep for the rising sun to have reached them at this hour.

A silvery object glinted below them, like a metal top following Janus through the clouds.

"Is that Atlas?" Susan asked.

"That's it," Isaac said. "The Atlas mobile headquarters. Cephalie?"

His IC appeared on the dash.

"Have you spoken with Atlas traffic control?"

"I have. We're cleared for landing."

"Thank you. Take us in."

The V-wing dipped down, closing with the mobile headquarters. The structure's upper surface was segmented into large hexagonal plates. Some of the hexagons were missing, revealing recessed machinery pits. One hexagon detached from headquarters and lifted upward on graviton thrusters. Two of its sides were open, exposing a cavern of intricate mechanisms. The hexagonal plate leaned in the direction of Janus and accelerated toward a gaping hole in the trailing edge, situated below the Third Engine Block's massive thruster nozzles.

"Macrotech constructors?" Susan asked.

"That's right," Nina said. "Working on the Fourth Engine Block."

"Pretty big for something that can self-replicate."

"And they can get bigger," Isaac said. "As I understand it, they can merge when they need to work on larger projects."

The V-wing banked inward. A hangar near the facility's midsection yawned open, and the V-wing glided inside. The outer door sealed shut behind them, and the air cycled.

Isaac checked in with an Atlas representative, transmitted his badge to verify his identity, and then followed her directions to the hangar with the SSP quadcopter. Susan, Nina, and one drone trailed him.

The drone was his LENS, which stood for Lawful Enforcement and Neutralization System. It was a standard-issue Themis device that Cephalie controlled for him when in the field. The spherical drone resembled a floating metallic eye slightly larger than his head and could perform a wide variety of functions by manipulating its fast-reacting prog-steel exterior. It also contained a number of internal systems in addition to its small graviton thruster, allowing it to perform support tasks such as light forensics work or infostructure hacking.

The hangar was the next one over, so they didn't have far to walk.

The SSP quadcopter was a low, roughly oval vehicle surrounded by four outboard propellers encased in cylindrical shields. The front and back were dark green around a black-and-white checkered midsection with the copter and precinct numbers on the hood, sides, and, Isaac assumed, the belly. This was quadcopter thirty-seven from the Third Engine Block's 103rd Precinct.

Two members of the state police waited for them, a physical sergeant and an abstract trooper. Sergeant Chatelain leaned with his back against the copter side door, arms crossed. He did *not* look happy to be there.

In contrast, Isaac thought he saw a hint of shy eagerness in Trooper Parks' dark green eyes. A shade of green, he noted, that matched the individual's uniform. He doubted that was a coincidence.

The AC's avatar began to approach them but stopped when Susan entered the hangar. His expression soured, eagerness coming into conflict with trepidation. Isaac and the others stopped next to the copter.

"Sergeant. Trooper." Isaac greeted them each with a curt nod. "I'm Detective Cho. This is my deputy, Agent Cantrell, and behind us is Specialist Cho, who'll handle any forensics work while we're here."

"Cho and Cho?" Chatelain's mouth twisted as if he were chewing on the inside of his cheek. "You two related?"

"That's right."

"How quaint."

"Sergeant, we're here in response to an SSP support request. Shall we get down to business?"

"Look, I know why you're here. However, there's a slight problem."

"Which is?"

"I seem to recall canceling the request. Were you aware of that?"

"Yes. I read the call transcript."

"Then you should know I don't believe there's any point in you being here."

"Your opinion seems clear in the matter."

"So why *are* you here?"

"Sergeant, you're free to complain about the situation all you want. Our work will proceed with or without your help, but that work will go more smoothly—*and* you'll be free to leave sooner—if you stow that attitude of yours for the time being."

"Yeah, yeah. No need to get pushy about it. I know how you Themis types enjoy throwing your weight around."

"Then shall we get on with it?"

"Sure." He put on a smile devoid of warmth. "Whatever you want, name it. It's not like we have any other places we need to be."

"Let's start with the initial call. Trooper Parks?"

The abstract trooper didn't respond immediately, his eyes fixed on Susan and a worried grimace on his face.

"Trooper?" Isaac prompted once more.

"Yeah?" He continued to watch Susan.

"I'd like to discuss your call to SysPol, if that's all right."

"Okay . . ."

"Is there a problem, Trooper?"

He finally tore his gaze away from Susan. "I guess not."

"Then, if you don't mind, let's start with the reasoning behind your call."

"The suicide felt wrong to me."

"Can you be more specific?"

"It doesn't make sense. Velasco killed himself right after news came in that Atlas had won the Dyson contract. Why would he do that?"

"A good question. Which means part of our task will be to establish a plausible motive for the suicide. What else?"

"I . . ." Parks seemed to struggle with his own thoughts for a moment, then shrugged. "No, that was it."

"I see. We'll need access to the body and the crime scene."

Chatelain slapped the copter door, and it slid open. He made an exaggerated welcoming gesture toward the interior.

"The body's all yours."

"I'll call one of my drones over and get to work." Nina opened an abstract interface and began inputting commands.

"Thank you." Isaac turned to the troopers. "Would one of you care to show us to the crime scene?"

"Parks will." Chatelain slapped the AC on the back. His hand may have moved through empty air, but his wetware interfaced with Parks' AC to create the illusion of a connection, and the trooper's avatar stumbled forward.

He turned back to the sergeant with a worried expression.

"Go on." Chatelain shooed him away. "This is what you wanted."

"I guess you're right." He gave Susan one more wary glance, then shook his head and made a beckoning gesture at the copter. A conveyor drone detached from the copter's roof and hovered down to him. "Come on. It's this way."

Isaac passed through the police cordon and rounded the desk in Velasco's office. The chair was the first object to draw his eye with a chunk missing from the headrest, followed by the shallow divots in the floor and back wall where evidence samples had been collected by SSP. Susan and two drones followed him in, and Parks materialized beside the desk.

"Let's see it, Trooper," Isaac said, watching the empty chair.

Velasco's body and the scattered contents of his head took form in their shared virtual vision, superimposed upon the reality of the room. Isaac drew in a breath, then let out a slow exhale as he gazed down at the dead man's face, its mouth agape, eyes open and rolled back into the skull.

He was no stranger when it came to death; his time with Raviv as a deputy detective had exposed him to a wide variety of dead bodies, and that experience had imparted a certain degree of callousness when it came to working around corpses.

But that exposure didn't make him ignorant to reality. He was staring at the end of a life, the end of someone's story, and he could almost feel death's cold fingers glide along his spine. Hours ago, this shape had been a living, breathing human being, but violence had robbed it of vitality, reducing it to an inert sack of water, proteins, fats, and minerals.

He found organic bodies the worst. In contrast, there was something sterile about a synthoic body. No blood. No flesh. No bones. Just broken machinery, sometimes wrapped in a facsimile of organic life. Abstract deaths were even more intangible. Not even a body to recover for those, just the absence of data in an infostructure.

He supposed the permanence of organic death contributed to his feelings as well. Synthoid and AC deaths weren't always permanent. Some citizens elected to save copies of their connectomes in mindbanks as protection against unexpected death, but modern science provided no such options to organic citizens because the transition from organic to synthetic was a one-way trip.

Organic bodies still bothered him, still elicited a primal, emotional response in him, a sense of sadness and loss and regret, even if his experience and professionalism provided a buffer against those feelings.

Desensitized but not immune, he concluded for himself.

He glanced over at Susan. She'd elected to transition at the tender age of twenty-three when most people took the leap sometime after their first *century.* She hadn't even been an adult by SysGov reckoning when her connectome had been read by the Admin. She'd willingly thrown away decades of her natural life to be transformed into a living weapon, a decision she could never reverse.

He wondered if she ever regretted the choice.

She crouched next to the blood splatter, a forearm on her knee as she took the pattern in.

"That's a significant amount of spray," she said. "What'd he hit himself with?"

Parks didn't immediately respond.

"Trooper?" Isaac prompted.

"What?" Parks gave the impression of being both surprised and distracted.

"Agent Cantrell asked you about the weapon."

"Oh." He grimaced, and his eyes flicked to Susan and back. "Velasco shot himself with a PA7 loaded with explosive tips, hence the mess." He tapped the abstract version of the weapon on the desk. The real one would be in the copter.

"PA7?" Susan asked.

"A heavy pistol design by Popular Arsenals," Isaac said. "Any clues as to how he came by the weapon?"

"Looks like he printed it out himself using company runtime.

I turned up the production log when I searched for public files in Velasco's infosystem." Parks pointed at the desk. "It's from three days ago, so he may have been contemplating the suicide for at least that long. He used a valid multiuse permit to replicate the weapon, and I found the same permit stored in his wetware."

"Then the weapon was legally his."

"Yes, sir."

"However, I don't recall seeing the permit or production log in the case folder."

"Sorry. I probably should have sent those when I opened the case."

"That's all right. Just transfer the files to my LENS, please."

"Right away. Sorry again."

"Would any old printer crank out a weapon like this?" Susan asked.

"No," Isaac said. "Parks? Any thoughts?"

"The production log came from one of the Atlas prototyping printers. There's not much a machine like that won't replicate with the right authorization."

"And as one of Atlas's senior engineers, Velasco had all the access he needed. A valid permit and an unrestricted printer he could use whenever he wanted. Doesn't seem like there's much mystery to how he produced the pistol and killed himself."

"Which still leaves the question of why." Susan stood up and joined him at the desk.

"We can start by talking to his boss and coworkers. Maybe they can shed some light on the matter."

"His boss is Julian Boaz," Parks said. "The CEO took personal charge of the Dyson bid, so Velasco was reporting directly to him. There's also Leon Traczyk, another engineer and one of two people who said they spoke to Velasco right before he killed himself. The second one is a contracted employee, not a direct hire. He's acting as a consultant on the project. Name's Horace Pangu."

"I'm sorry." Isaac's eyes widened. "Did you say Horace Pangu?"

"That's right," Parks replied, clearly not seeing the significance.

"Horace Pangu," Isaac repeated. "Are you telling me Atlas hired the *Pinball Wizard*?"

CHAPTER FIVE

"WHO'S THIS 'PINBALL WIZARD'?" SUSAN ASKED ONCE THEY WERE alone in Velasco's office.

Parks had transferred back to the quadcopter, clearly relieved to get away from Susan.

"That's not easy to explain," Isaac replied. "How familiar are you with the Near Miss?"

"Not terribly. I think I came across it in my cultural notes. It's a formative event in SysGov's past, right?"

"More like *the* formative event. The Near Miss was a massive industrial accident that turned a lot of China into pinballs."

"I'm sorry." Her eyebrows rose in surprise. "Pinballs?"

"Yeah. Pinballs. The Chinese were experimenting with self-replicating systems and one of their tests got a little out of hand. And by a little, I mean a lot. The swarm could have killed off everyone and everything on the planet if no one had intervened."

"But why pinballs?"

"I'm not sure, actually."

Cephalie poofed into existence on Isaac's shoulder. "Here, I'll field this one."

"Be my guest," Isaac said.

"Okay, pay attention, everyone. Class is in session." A small chalkboard with a map of Earth appeared next to Cephalie, and she tapped the center of Asia with her cane. "The outbreak started

53

as a manufacturing test in One Asia, the unified Asian government of the time which later became one of the founding states in SysGov. Industrial firms wanted to see if they could produce simple objects quickly and cheaply using a self-replicating system with very loose requirements for base materials. They chose a pinball as the target output for the test and then let the system rip!"

"After which, the swarm grew out of control," Susan concluded, a dark edge to her voice.

"Right you are. Back then, there were almost no protections in place against microtech mutations. In fact, we now know the design team was actively *encouraging* adaptive mutations in an effort to improve the system. Unfortunately for them, one of the mutations rendered all their shutdown commands useless.

"So, after the swarm ate the design team and turned all their bones into pinballs, it then chewed its way out of the test compound and expanded from there across mainland China. *Millions* died as the swarm carved its way across the continent, creating a trail of carnage a thousand kilometers long and seventy-five kilometers across at its widest."

"Did the swarm continue to mutate?" Susan asked.

"You better believe it did, growing nastier and more resilient with every iteration. One Asia's military threw everything they had at it, but it proved too tenacious for anything short of nuclear bombardment to even slow it down.

"*Fortunately*, the United Territories of America and the European Cooperative sprang into action around that time, and together with the brightest minds from One Asia, were able to formulate and deploy a nonnuclear solution to the swarm. Basically, a counter-swarm that modified and turned the original swarm against itself. The team that developed the counter-swarm was led by two leading pioneers of AI integration: Doctor Horace Jeong and his personal AI assistant, who chose the name Pangu after achieving self-awareness."

"The Pinball Wiz-*ards*?" Susan asked.

"More or less," Cephalie said. "Back then, those two were pushing the boundaries of integration between the physical and abstract, charting new territory for connectomes, both organic and artificial. They became the first instance of full integration between two connectomes, and most histories reference *him* in the singular, either as Horace Pangu or the Wizard."

"The Near Miss," Isaac said, "led directly to the formation of SysGov in..." He paused in thought.

"2455," Cephalie stepped in, "with the signing of the Articles of Consolidation by the five founding states: the United Territories of America, the European Cooperative, One Asia, the Federated States of Africa, and the Lunar State."

"So then," Susan said, "there might not even *be* a SysGov if Horace Pangu hadn't stopped the swarm?"

"Pretty much," Isaac said.

"And the Horace Pangu from the Near Miss is the same one here at Atlas?"

"That's what Parks said."

"Wow." Susan shook her head, her eyes growing distant. "That's so different from how events played out back home, though there are some interesting parallels."

"How so?" Isaac asked.

"Where you had the Near Miss, *we* had the Yanluo Massacre."

"Sounds ominous."

"As it should. Yanluo was a weaponized AI that went rogue, took over a microtech swarm, and slaughtered its way across China, Mongolia, and parts of Russia. It was eventually put down by a ruthless campaign of nuclear bombardment."

Isaac opened his mouth to say something like "Why am I not surprised?" or "Of course the Admin was formed in response to an evil, genocidal AI. Makes perfect sense!" but then he thought better of it and stopped himself before the first sound escaped his lips.

"You looked like you had something to say there," Susan observed.

"It's nothing."

"You sure? I've seen you make that face before."

"I'm not making a face," he replied, more out of reflex than anything else, but then he asked, "What face?"

"It's the one you make right before you poke fun at me." She shrugged. "Or the Admin."

"Okay, granted," he said with a frown, "I may have had a thought along those lines. But, I'll have you note, I didn't say anything."

"This time," Cephalie chimed in, and Susan chuckled.

"You are *not* helping." Isaac glared at his IC. "Look, how

about we get back to work? Cephalie, would you mind setting up the first round of interviews for us?"

"Boaz, Traczyk, and the Wizard?"

"That should do it for now."

"Anything else?"

"I'd like you and Nina to go through Velasco's infosystem. There might be more to find than what Parks turned up."

"You've got it, sir!" Cephalie snapped off a salute with fake enthusiasm and vanished.

Isaac shook his head and sighed. Susan stepped up beside him.

"So," she began with a crafty smile on her lips, "what *were* you about to say?"

"I'm keeping that to myself!"

The first thing Isaac noticed about Julian Boaz was the smile, sad and "sincere" and just a little too perfect for the moment, as if Boaz wanted everyone to know he was there for them, his shoulder ready to accept anyone who needed to let it all out after Velasco's suicide. He might even pat them on the back and say "There, there."

It was such a sincere smile.

Or rather, a "sincere" smile.

Isaac placed deliberate mental quotes around the descriptor because he knew a social mask when he saw one. Whatever was going on inside Boaz's head, none of the thoughts or emotions reached his face muscles without his permission. He might be grieving or laughing or raging on the inside, but that sad, "sincere" smile would stay fixed to his face until he decided to change it.

The forced expression didn't tell Isaac much on its own. People hid their true feelings for any number of reasons, plenty of which were perfectly legal. But even so, that smile set Isaac to wondering what was *really* rattling around inside the bald, broad-shouldered CEO's brain.

"Mister Boaz, thank you for agreeing to speak with us," Isaac said, taking his seat in front of the oval, smoked-glass desk. A second chair formed out of the programable-steel floor, and Susan sat down next to him. The LENS settled into a holding position behind their backs.

Boaz's office was roughly the same size and shape as Velasco's except for the natural view of the Saturn sky through the side wall. The storm thundered outside, and wind whistled past the window, shrouding the view with a thick haze like tan soup. The window's vacuum insulation prevented most sounds from penetrating, but the window seemed to be configured to pass through a muted version of the outside soundscape. Three diffuse lights from Janus' Third Engine Block thrusters glowed in the distance above their position, serving as the only indication of the immense bulk of the megastructure's trailing edge.

Physical awards and virtual pictures covered the wall across from the window, showcasing Atlas' project history and accolades, with the early periods in Janus' construction displayed prominently along the top.

Boaz smoothed out the front of his black business suit with a large hand.

"It's no trouble, Detective. I'm just a little shaken up, that's all." The smile grew sadder and more pronounced for a moment. "Didn't think the day would take such a terrible turn."

"Of course," Isaac replied neutrally.

"Also"—that smile grew warmer—"I'm sure you're aware of this, but I've already been interviewed."

"Yes, by the state troopers." Isaac opened the case log and pulled up the relevant file. He adjusted the position of his interface, which only he and Susan could read due to the privacy filter.

"I answered all their questions," Boaz assured him.

"I'm aware of that."

"Which makes me wonder why the three of us are sitting down for this chat." He held up a hand. "Not that I'm complaining or trying to be critical of how you do your job. Investigating suicides isn't my wheelhouse, after all."

"The reason is simple enough, Mister Boaz. SSP has asked us to review Velasco's death, and so that's what we're here to do."

"But why? I mean, the man shot himself, right? At least that's what it looked like to me."

"All suicides are treated as homicides initially. Beyond that, it would be inappropriate for me to comment on an ongoing investigation. Now, if you don't mind, shall we proceed?"

"Certainly, Detective. Please." Boaz spread his open palms. "Ask away. I've got nothing to hide."

"Let's start with your relationship with the deceased."

"Easy enough. I'm his boss." He paused, and the sad smile grew sadder. "*Was* his boss, I should say."

"Could you be more specific?"

"I'm the Atlas CEO, so my responsibilities generally involve high-level management. I set our goals, determine our overall corporate strategy, deal with how our company is organized. Those sorts of things. I keep an eye on our relationships with our most important customers, often state or federal government entities. I also take a leadership role in key projects, such as the expansion into the Fourth Engine Block and the bidding war for the Dyson Realization Project. Bear in mind, that's not always the case, because I delegate the management of most projects to our senior engineers."

"What determines whether or not you take an active role in a project?"

"Mostly it's a judgment call as to how important the job is. I also take into account our overall capacity. The macrotech industry has a history of going through a sine wave of feast-or-famine periods. Sometimes we're scraping the bottom for whatever work we can find, while others we're so swamped we're rejecting jobs we know our competitors will pick up and earn a ton of Esteem on.

"We're currently going through what you might call a 'minor famine' period, so I'm directly involved in the Fourth Engine Block. On top of that, I want this install to go in extra smooth because some of our recent projects for the Saturn State have experienced a few bumps. Nothing too serious, but not up to our standards either. This company made its first big break with Janus, and that's a legacy I don't want to see tarnished. For the Dyson Project, well, I think the scope and historical significance of that one speaks for itself!"

"Which projects was Velasco working on?"

"He was dedicated full time to the Dyson Project. Essentially, he was the number two on Dyson right under me, though I should specify that hierarchy is from a management perspective. For engineering decisions, he was the lead. On Dyson, I took care of the budget, scheduling, head count, customer negotiations, and so on, while Velasco took the lead on the design work and prototyping."

"Why was Velasco assigned to the Dyson Project?"

"Seniority and talent. His designs have helped shape us as a company. Have you heard our motto?"

"I have not."

"Premium macrotech solutions!" Boaz spread his arms grandly. "With an emphasis on the macrotech part. Most of our competitors utilize microtech and nanotech swarms for large-scale construction projects, but we take a different approach. We use macrotech to build even bigger macrotech. In fact, we're one of a handful of companies who take this approach. Velasco may not have invented our macrotech constructors, but he most certainly contributed to their refinement over the years. Sure, self-replicating swarms are an easy to use, versatile, and scalable solution." He smiled slyly. "When they work without defects. But all that generalization comes at a price."

"Jack of all trades?" Susan suggested. "Master of none?"

"Precisely!" Boaz beamed at her. "I couldn't have said it better myself. Yes, most self-replicators suffer from a bad case of overgeneralization while also running the risk of mutation, which SourceCode demonstrated quite spectacularly during their last test. If you want to build big, you need to *think* big. And self-replicators, with all their advantages, aren't always the right tool for the job. Far from it, in fact."

"Then why do most macrotech companies use them?" Isaac asked.

"Because it's easy, not because it's *better*. It also doesn't help that a lot of our competitors—SourceCode included—have large numbers of ACs working for them."

"What's wrong with that?"

"Nothing on its own," Boaz added quickly. "I don't have any problems with us hiring ACs. We have a few among our ranks, after all. But we've had our share of ACs not work out over the years, and that makes us leery of hiring more."

"Why didn't they work out?"

"It's hard to pinpoint one consistent reason, but I think it's part of their nature. An abstract citizen is, by definition, separated from the physical. And the physical realm is where we at Atlas do our business. The physical *is* our wheelhouse, you could say. Not only that, but we conduct that business on a grand scale. ACs are often . . ." He smiled without warmth. "A lot of them are too detached from reality to fit into this line of work. If you don't interact with what's real, what business do you have demolishing planets and terraforming atmospheres? That's one of the reasons why almost all Atlas employees have a physical body, and integrated companions are a rarity among us. I know Velasco didn't have one, for instance."

"Getting back to Velasco, did you notice anything unusual concerning either him or his work on the Dyson Project?"

"Unusual." Boaz leaned back and took on a thoughtful expression. "Not really. I mean, the man was strung out. That much was clear, but we have phases like that in this industry. Feast or famine, remember? We all can get stretched thin from time to time, but I don't recall anything alarming about his behavior."

"Do you believe Velasco was overworking?"

"Perhaps."

"And yet you said Atlas was in the middle of a workload famine."

"I did, yes. A mild one, though."

"Then why was Velasco overtaxed? Why not divert more resources to the Dyson Project?"

"Because my options were limited without additional income streams," Boaz said. "The Fourth Engine Block was our only large-scale project until we won the Dyson bid, so it's not like I was in a position to hire tons of contractors to supplement our workforce. Not if I wanted to keep the books balanced. We had to make do with the people we had until we secured more work. Which we *did*, I might add, so Velasco's workload would have tapered off if he'd..." Boaz trailed off. His demeanor calmed somewhat, and that sad smile came back. "I'm sorry. I think you know the rest."

"Did Velasco say or do anything that led you to believe he might commit suicide?"

"No, nothing that told me he was stressed out any more than the rest of us."

"What about the quality of Velasco's work near the end?"

"I didn't notice any problems there, though again, the technical side of the business isn't where I spend most of my time. I don't recall any complaints, either from the project team or the customer, so let's go with no news is good news on that front."

"Fair enough." Isaac jotted down a few notes. "What will become of the project's leadership moving forward?"

"We'll move on as we always do. This isn't the first vacancy I've had to fill on short notice, though the *cause* is a bit more dramatic than I'm used to." He let out a somber sigh. "Anyway,

Horace Pangu will take over as engineering lead, though in truth that's a bit of publicity sleight of hand."

"How do you mean?"

"Unofficially, I'm going to have Leon Traczyk take over Velasco's responsibilities. Traczyk will head the day-to-day project work while Pangu will continue to act as a figurehead for the project. I hired Pangu as more of a PR stunt than anything else. The Pinball Wizard himself, working for Atlas! Even managed to poach him from SourceCode two months back. I needed to do something to turn around our public image after the Society sabotaged one of our trials, and Pangu had reached out to me, expressing an interest in our company. So I took him up on it."

"Why is Traczyk taking over?"

"Two reasons. He's already on the project—he was part of Velasco's team—and he's a hell of an engineer. I almost chose him over Velasco when I was putting together the team to handle Dyson."

"One more question, and then I believe we can move on for now. Do you know or have any reason to suspect why Velasco committed suicide?"

"I'm sorry, Detective, but the answer's no. We've already touched on the stress he was under, but his demeanor didn't seem unusual to me. Tired, yes. Stressed, absolutely. To the point of suicide? No. Every project has its rough patches, and we've all had to push ourselves to clear them, Velasco included. On top of that, we'd just been awarded the project! Velasco would have received some well-earned downtime while I worked to bulk up the project team. Thinking of it that way, his death doesn't make *any* sense."

"Understood. Thank you for the information, Mister Boaz. That'll be all for now. Would you be so kind as to send for Mister Traczyk next?"

CHAPTER SIX

THE FIRST THING ISAAC NOTICED ABOUT LEON TRACZYK WAS HOW he picked at his beard, sometimes plucking pale brown hairs free and flicking them away, only for them to flutter down onto his flashy red business suit. The senior engineer didn't seem cognizant of the tic as he waited for Isaac to prepare his virtual screens.

Isaac tried not to rely on his "gut" when he could help it. He preferred the steely comfort of facts over the ephemeral strengths of intuition, but sometimes his intuition tickled the inside of his mind and he listened.

Because more often than not, it was right.

He closed all his screens then began opening the same ones all over again, one by one, at a painfully slow pace, then proceeded to fine-tune their positioning to form an orthogonal grid.

"This is my first time being interviewed by SysPol," Traczyk offered, perhaps to fill the silence as he shifted in his seat uncomfortably.

"Is it now?" Isaac asked without looking up. He shifted one screen a millimeter to the right, then nodded. Everything lined up perfectly now.

"Yeah." Traczyk flashed a friendly smile. "You'll go easy on me, won't you?"

"Is there a particular reason we should go easy on you?"

"I don't know. Maybe because I'm nervous?"

"And why might you be nervous?"

"Uhh..." Traczyk grimaced, then turned to Susan. "Hey there. You with SysPol, too? Which division are you from?"

Susan must have detected Traczyk's unease on her own, because she stared back at him with cold, unblinking stiffness. If her eyes had been drills, they would have bored into his skull.

"Sorry I asked. Sheesh!" Traczyk looked away and adjusted his collar. "Did you turn the heat up in here or something?"

"Mister Traczyk," Isaac began, "I'd like to start by discussing your relationship with the deceased. Could you describe it for us?"

"We were working on the Dyson Project together, but I'm sure you already know that. He was the engineering lead, and I was his second. We formed a pretty good team."

"How was he to work for?"

"Fine, though it was more about working *with* him than *for* him. We were a team. In the trenches of the project together, figuring our way through one headache at a time. The primary technical specs were very much a collaboration between the two of us."

"Did you see any indications Velasco was overworked?"

"Of course, I did, but that's nothing new. We all pushed ourselves hard, especially near the end, and Velasco pulled his weight with the rest of us." Traczyk let out a long sigh. "He'll be missed."

"Did you speak with Velasco shortly before he committed suicide?"

"Yes."

"Did he give you any indication he was about to commit suicide?"

"No. Nothing like that."

"Did he say anything that might explain why he killed himself?"

"Can't think of anything, sorry."

"What did you talk about?"

"The project." Traczyk shrugged. "And whose efforts Boaz would acknowledge during the party."

"Would you say you knew Velasco well?"

"Oh yeah. Definitely. You don't spend as much time as we did on the same project and not get to know the other guy."

"Did you consider yourself friends with him?"

"Friends?" Traczyk sat back. "Yeah, I guess you could say that."

"How close were the two of you?"

"Umm, I don't know. Hard to say. Not super close or anything."

"Did you sometimes hang out after work?"

"Sometimes. When we could. We were both so busy."

"Did the two of you play any games together?"

"I don't know. Sometimes? Who doesn't unwind with a little VR?"

"Which games did you play?"

"I don't remember off the top of my head."

"You don't remember?" Isaac asked doubtfully.

"Oh, wait!" Traczyk snapped his fingers. "Yeah, of course. It wasn't often, but we played *Solar Descent* a few times together."

"What type of character do you play in that game?"

"I have a few accounts, but my favorite is an abyssal shadow. I've always enjoyed stealth mechanics in games, so shadows are right up my alley. He's a Nadirian named Swift Blade-in-the-Dark. Most people I play with call him 'Swifty.'"

"Is that the character you used while playing with Velasco?"

"Umm. Yeah, probably."

"Are you sure or not?"

"Yeah, I'm sure. I was using Swifty."

"Which class did Velasco play?"

"I'm sorry?"

"Which class did Velasco use while you and he played *Solar Descent* together?"

"Uhh...why do you want to know?"

"Please answer the question."

"Well, I'm not sure..."

"Why not? You had no trouble describing your character. You're clearly familiar with the game and enjoy it to some degree. Plus, you said the two of you had played together."

"A few times. I don't remember his class."

"Then what archetype did he use? Melee or ranged? Solar or Abyssal? Attacker, defender, or support?"

"A ranged combatant of some sort."

"What kind?"

"I'm not sure. There are a *lot* of classes in *Solar Descent*. You can't expect me to remember all of them."

"A fair enough point," Isaac conceded. "Did his character wear any armor?"

"Uhh..."

"Surely you have some recollection of what his character looked like."

"Of course."

"Did his character have armor?"

"Nothing that stood out to me."

"Then his character's face wasn't concealed by armor?"

"Not that I recall."

"What race was he playing?"

"Uhh..."

"Let me guess." Isaac let out a resigned sigh. "You don't remember that either?"

"We didn't play that often!"

"Or perhaps there's another possibility. Perhaps you and Velasco weren't friends. Perhaps you never gamed together, and you've been lying to us this whole time."

"About a game!" Traczyk blurted.

"And how much else, I wonder?"

"Well, I thought..." His eyes flicked over to Susan.

"Don't look at me," she said in a cool, stern tone. "Between the detective and me, he's the nice one. If you're forced to deal with me, then you're already in deep trouble. Do you know what I did to criminals in my last job?"

"What?" Traczyk asked, his voice cracking.

"Shoot them dead."

He shrank back from Susan's intense stare, a horrified expression on his face.

"She's being honest, too." Isaac knitted his fingers on the table. "Now then, why don't you start telling us the truth? *Before* I decide to charge you with lying to a police officer." He glanced over at Susan. "Or perhaps I'll let my partner interview you alone."

"Okay." Traczyk held up his hands. "Okay! I'm sorry! No need to get all dramatic on me. Look, I just...this is really awkward for me."

"What's awkward?"

"Talking about Velasco."

"Why?"

"Because I hated his guts, all right?" Traczyk's face twisted up with a combination of shame and snarling anger. "He's dead, and I'm just so angry!"

"Why?"

"Because now that lazy bum has saddled me with even more of the workload!"

"Then the part about you and him working well together?"

"A lie, yes. I don't know what happened, but Velasco's work has been absolute garbage for months, leaving me to pick up the slack."

"Any idea why?"

"Not a clue, and that's the truth. If I'd known what was wrong, I would have tried to fix it. If for no other reason than to make my life less of a living hell!"

"Did you mention any of this to your superiors?"

"No." He snorted. "What? You think Boaz cares? He'd just tell me to stop being such a whiner. 'Being crybabies isn't in our wheelhouse,' he'd say. 'Suck it up and get the job done.' I've been down that road before. I know where it leads."

"Why lie to us about this?" Susan asked.

"Because, like I said, I felt awkward. I know I was angry at Velasco, but I didn't want to speak ill of the dead. Is that really a crime?"

"It is if you lie to us," Isaac pointed out. "Do you know why Velasco committed suicide?"

"No."

"What was your working relationship with Velasco really like?"

"We butted heads, but most of the time we kept it professional. It wasn't until the last few months that things grew worse. That's all I know, okay?" He sighed. "Anything else you need from me?"

Isaac gave Susan a quick look. She replied with a shake of her head.

"That'll be all," Isaac said, "for now."

The first thing Isaac noticed about Horace Pangu was how normal the man looked. He wasn't sure what he'd expected after learning he'd be interviewing the Pinball Wizard, but a baseline humanoid synthoid hadn't been one of his guesses. Pangu had renounced his SysGov citizenship centuries ago, choosing instead to live in the Oort Cloud Citizenry where restrictions on self-modifications—be they physical or mental—were almost unheard of.

And yet there he is, Isaac thought, *in a synthoid that matches the appearance of his original body. I wonder why.*

Horace Pangu settled into a comfortable slant on the chair, one elbow on an armrest and a leg up across his knee. He wore the slightest hint of a smile on his thin lips. It was a polite and pleasant expression, though not a happy one, and his dark eyes acknowledged the grave event that had drawn SysPol here.

"Good day to you, Detective." Pangu nodded to Isaac, then to Susan. "And to you... Agent, I believe?"

"That's correct," Susan answered. "Agent Cantrell."

"From the Admin's Department of Temporal Investigation," he mused with a subtle shake of his head. "How quickly the landscape can change. Makes me curious to see what the *next* six centuries might hold for us."

"Thank you for agreeing to speak with us, Mister Pangu," Isaac said.

"It's quite all right. I was one of the last people to speak with Esteban, so it's only natural. And please, feel free to call me Wiz. Most everyone here does."

"I'm surprised to see you looking..."

"Like a humanoid meat sack?" His eyes twinkled with genuine mirth.

"I would have worded it differently, but yes."

"You're not the only one." He gestured down his body with one hand. "Most people are surprised to see me like this. I commissioned this body after Atlas hired me. I don't know if you noticed yet, but Atlas—in terms of their company culture—likes to keep things natural. They employ few ACs, and most of the synthoids who work here can pass for baseline humans. Cosmetically, at least. Using my original body as a template seemed like a good fit for the job. The path of least resistance, as it were."

"That said, you've never been shy about your views on the future of the human body."

"Or rather, its *lack* of a future," Pangu corrected. "The human form, while tremendously successful on Earth, is a horrible way to expand out into the stars, but people still cling to it for irrational reasons. The only place it can survive without artificial aid or terraforming is the thin film around one rocky planet. Space is vast and inhospitable. It doesn't care how well evolved we are for one gravity or one pressure or how much we crave oxygen.

"Human flesh is a prison. Modern technology may have breached its walls, but the inmates are so accustomed to their cells that most remain inside, out of fear of change or nostalgia or any number of poor reasons."

"'Flesh shackles the mind,'" Isaac quoted.

"It would be more accurate to say the human body is a liability we should all leave behind, though I still hold my original quote is catchier. I take it you've read *A Tale of Stars and Meat*?"

"A while ago. It was required reading in high school."

"What did you think of the points I raised?"

"Hard to say. I remember struggling to meet the minimum word count on my report. Beyond that..." Isaac flashed a bashful smile. "Philosophy's not really my thing."

"You might want to give it another look," Pangu suggested. "If I'm not mistaken, you're alive right now because of the advantages I preach."

"How so?"

"I merely refer to your encounter down on Titan. I don't pretend to know more than what's been made public, but can all three of us agree you'd both be dead if Agent Cantrell didn't have a synthetic body?"

Isaac glanced over at Susan, who nodded with a frown.

"He's got a point," she said.

"Both of you are alive in part because she chose to abandon her flawed original body." He leaned toward Susan. "You did transition willingly, yes?"

"I did."

"Good." He grinned at her. "I didn't want to assume. I don't know much about the Admin, and some of the rumors are a bit on the ugly side, I'm afraid."

"It's all right. I'm used to it by now."

"Why switch to a company whose culture is at odds with your own beliefs?" Isaac asked.

"I know it must seem like that, but the truth is I wrote *A Tale of Stars and Meat* four centuries ago, and it was even more controversial back then. The backlash is one of the reasons I became a citizen of the OCC. But time is a funny thing. People over here have become more open to my ideas, and I guess you could say I've mellowed a bit with old age."

"But why Atlas?"

"Because I wanted to be a part of the Dyson Project, and I believed at the time—and still do—that Atlas put forth the better design. That's the main reason I reached out to Julian about switching companies. It's quite an honor to be a part of this project."

"Why did you conclude Atlas has the superior design?"

"I'm sorry, but I can't answer that. Not without a court order, I'm afraid. SourceCode has me under a nondisclosure agreement, so I'm not at liberty to discuss my time working with them."

"Of course. I understand," Isaac replied. "Moving on, did you work closely with Velasco during the last two months?"

"Yes, though a lot of my time here has been spent bringing myself up to speed on the details of Atlas' approach."

"What was your opinion of him?"

"He was a very skilled engineer, and a good man to work with, but he was also under tremendous pressure, and it showed at times."

"How so?"

"He seemed...unfocused near the end."

"Do you know why?"

"No, sorry."

"Did you speak to him right before the suicide?"

"I did, though briefly. We didn't have much of a conversation. All he really said was he had a lot on his mind and then left." He pursed his lips. "I thought he was talking about the project, though perhaps not. Perhaps he was referring to something else."

"Such as?"

"It's a matter he complained about from time to time regarding the local chapter of the Society."

"You're referring to the Mercury Historical Preservation Society?" Isaac asked.

"The same."

Isaac frowned at the mention, then turned to Susan.

"The Historical Preservation Society is a loosely organized movement known for their anti-macrotech and anti-terraforming politics. The Mercury arm of that organization is focused on preserving the planet as it is today."

"Which would place the planet's resources off-limits for the Dyson Project," Pangu added, "if the Society had its way."

"Which they haven't," Isaac said. "All of their legal challenges have been shot down in court, but that doesn't mean they're not ready to 'fight the good fight.' I've never dealt with them personally, but I'm familiar with their reputation in SysPol.

They're known to play fast and loose with the law, blurring the line between peaceful protest and illegal action. They're also the group behind the sabotage of an Atlas constructor during one of their Dyson trials earlier this year."

"Their stance on Mercury always struck me as immature," Pangu said. "The planet represents a wealth of resources well positioned for conversion into a Dyson swarm, but the Society would see it twirl around the sun uselessly rather than be reshaped into a megastructure that'll benefit the entire solar system."

"How was Velasco involved in the Society?" Susan asked.

"From what I gathered, they were harassing him, though how and to what extent, I can't say."

"You okay?" Susan asked as they walked back to the counter-grav tubes, the LENS floating behind them. She spoke to him in SysPol security chat, which would come across as gibberish to anyone without the translation key.

"I am. Why do you ask?"

"It's just I've never seen you interview someone that way before."

"What do you mean?" Isaac asked, genuinely curious.

"You were being awfully nice to him."

"Well, that's because I didn't see any reason to bring extra pressure to bear." He turned to her as they walked. "Did you?"

"No."

"But?"

"Nothing," Susan said. "Other than, at times, it felt more like you two were having a conversation, rather than us conducting an interview."

"You really think so?"

"I do."

"She's right, you know." Cephalie appeared on his shoulder.

"You too?" Isaac replied with a grimace. "Look, maybe I was a *little* softer than usual, but the man's a legend. How many people can say they've actually spoken to the Wizard? We might not even have a SysGov if it weren't for him."

"I suppose we can't blame Isaac too much," Cephalie quipped to Susan. "He was blinded by all the stars in his eyes."

"Was not," Isaac protested.

"He caught you off guard with the book question," Cephalie continued.

"I *know*! That was so embarrassing. I had no idea he was going to quiz me on his writings."

"Did you even read it back in high school?"

"I ... skimmed most of it, I think. At least enough to put a report together."

"That would be a 'no,' then."

"I was in my teens. What did I care about the future trajectory of the human form?"

They stepped into the grav tube and took it up to the hangar bays. The graviton current dropped them off near the headquarters midsection, and virtual arrows guided them down a long corridor. They followed the arrows until they arrived at the hangar with the SSP quadcopter.

Chatelain slouched in the cockpit with a sports article suspended over his chest. He didn't look up. They passed the cockpit window, then entered through the side door to join Nina in the back.

"Hey," Isaac greeted.

"Hey yourself." She sat on a stool next to a retractable shelf with Velasco's corpse and a rack of evidence canisters. Two of her drones hovered over the bagged corpse, each with a dozen metallic tendrils penetrating the surface. She leaned over the shelf, a hand smooshed into her cheek as she studied the readouts from her drones.

"How's it going?" Isaac asked.

"Fine. Just wondering why we're even out here."

"You mean besides the superintendent wanting this death looked at?"

"Yeah. Besides that. You find anything yet?"

"Not really. Sounds like Velasco was under a considerable amount of job-related stress. The quality of his work had fallen off—enough to rile up one of his coworkers—and it's possible the Society was making matters worse for him in their own special way."

"Those jokers?" Nina rolled her eyes. "Some people can't take a hint."

"How about you and the body?"

"A whole lot of nothing." She sat up and copied her screen over to Isaac and Susan. "No injuries or signs of trauma beyond the obvious. No recent injection sites. No software anomalies in his wetware. Tissue samples came back negative for residual micro- or nanotech. Neural pathways and musculature from the head down to the right hand all look normal."

"Why check those?" Susan asked.

"In case an external factor forced the arm to shoot himself against his will," Isaac explained. "Such as with an invasive microbot injection."

"Ah. Got it."

"Toxicology test shows he had *a drink*, so unless this guy *really* can't hold his booze, he was in complete control when he blew his brains out. His last drink was a glass of Old Frontier Sparkling Hixon 2965, in case you were wondering. It's the same wine everyone else at the party was having. I could tell you what he had for breakfast if you like."

"That won't be necessary. Anything else?"

"Trauma to the head is consistent with a PA7 loaded with high-explosive rounds. The barrel was in his mouth when he pulled the trigger. Both the pistol and ammo were printed about three days ago."

"Conclusions?"

"The poor guy cracked and blew himself away." She threw up her arms. "Besides that, I've got nothing."

"Any sensory records in his wetware?" Susan asked.

"Nope, sorry. His privacy settings were maxed out, so his implants won't have a digital trail."

"But there might be something in his desk," Isaac said.

"Could be," Nina agreed. "I saw Cephalie add the job to my queue. I'll head down to his office as soon as the drones finish up." She leaned back on the stool, her head resting against the back wall. "How about you two? About ready to call this one a suicide and move on?"

"Not quite. I'd feel better if we had a clear motive."

"Maybe there isn't. At least not a rational one. Maybe he's just a poor soul who cracked under the pressure. Not every tragedy hides something sinister behind it."

"I know, and so far I agree with you, but let's be as sure as we can about it before we close the case. Cephalie?"

"You rang?" She appeared on the shelf next to the corpse, then poked the bag with her virtual cane.

"What do we have for Velasco's next of kin?"

"Public records show he's married with no kids. Wife's name is Cynthia Velasco. I have the address and her connection string, courtesy of Atlas. Most of their employees have been staying in a Third Engine Block apartment complex nestled in Exchanger Row. SSP flew out there and let her know about her husband while you two were conducting the interviews. Want me to set up a meeting?"

"Please."

"Okay. On it." She vanished from the shelf.

Nina's drones retracted their tendrils and bobbed out of the copter. She stood up and tugged her uniform straight.

"Want us to wait for you to finish?" Isaac asked.

"Nah. I'll hitch a ride with the troopers and catch up later." She followed her drones toward the hangar exit.

"Aren't you going to tell them?" Isaac called out after his sister.

"Why? It's *your* case." She grinned at him before she and her drones disappeared around the bend.

Isaac grimaced and let out a short exhale, then walked out of the quadcopter and knocked on the cockpit window.

Chatelain bolted upright with a start. He looked around until he spotted Isaac waving through the window.

"Sergeant."

Chatelain opened the window. "Done already?"

"More or less."

"Then we're free to go?"

"Not exactly."

CHAPTER SEVEN

THE V-WING GLIDED THROUGH DARK CLOUDS KISSED BY SUNLIGHT across their billowing thunderheads. The view cleared, and the trailing edge of Janus came into focus. The three massive thrusters of the Third Engine Block formed a triangular formation of gaping nozzles slightly below and to the side of their approach. Six more thrusters stood out high above, shadowed by the oval megacity crown atop Janus. A rectangular hole gaped below where Atlas constructors broke down and reformed raw material for the Fourth Engine Block.

The V-wing slipped into formation behind a row of inbound aircraft. Their wings straightened and elongated, and they slowed as they passed under the shadow of Janus' crown.

"The Third Engine Block is a city built around one of Janus' propulsion units, right?" Susan asked.

"More or less," Isaac said.

"How large a city are we talking here?"

"Very. Not as big as the capital, Ballast Heights, but close. About sixteen million people live here, and the other two Engine Blocks are both older and more populous. Residents are predominantly Saturnite with a smattering of people from other states.

"The largest industries revolve around harvesting and utilizing Saturn's natural resources, which is why atmospheric processors and refineries take up a considerable portion of the Central

District, and many of those focus on separating deuterium and tritium from the air, which they feed to the fusion reactors and the propulsion units in the Edge District.

"There are also pumping stations that supply excess or unwanted material to other cities. Plenty of industrial printers, too, what with all that cheap power, which helped the Engine Blocks become a major manufacturing hub. One of the larger in the Saturn State, in fact, though the cities remain best known for their power generation. Together, they supply about ninety percent of the megastructure's energy needs."

"*Fusion* power?" Susan asked, her tone somewhat incredulous.

"You sound surprised."

"I don't know. I'd assumed Janus' power came from hot singularity reactors. Aren't those the SysGov standard?"

"Depends on who you ask. While it's true fusion reactors have fallen out of favor in many parts of the solar system, you have to remember where we are."

Susan glanced out the window to the shadowed cloud tops.

"A gas giant?"

"Which is ninety-six percent hydrogen."

"Ah. Right."

"We couldn't run out of fuel if we tried. Both types of power plants have their pros and cons. For example, hot singularities are very mass and space efficient for the amount of power they put out, which makes them the go-to choice for SysPol cruisers. Meanwhile, Janus sits in a vast reservoir of free fuel, which makes fusion the more economical choice. It also helps that fusion reactors are easier to produce; no exotic matter required."

"Makes sense to me."

The V-wing followed the line of aircraft toward a honeycomb of openings in Janus' outer wall. The elliptical bulk of a passenger liner obstructed their view in the final moments of their approach, and then they dipped beneath it and landed in one of the open bins.

The outer door closed, the air cycled, and unseen robotic arms moved their bin to another area within the Janus wall. They shuddered to a halt, and virtual indicators along the front wall lit up green.

"This is our stop." Isaac opened the cockpit and climbed out, and the LENS bobbed after him. Susan joined him by a rectangular depression in the prog-steel wall. A door formed, and they passed through it to a wide pedestrian corridor with a clear view of the city.

"Oh, nice," Susan breathed, a grin on her lips. She walked up to the wall-height window and rested her elbows on the railing.

"Welcome to the Third Engine Block." Isaac joined her, always pleased to see someone impressed with Janus.

The central corridor of the Third Engine Block gaped before them with gargantuan structures extending back from the three thruster nozzles to form a mass of machinery that continued down the center, meshing with other edifices farther down that populated the industrial sectors of the city. Their side of the corridor went on for over eighty kilometers before it veered off to the right.

Residential housing took up most of the outer walls, built on stacks of open shelves that extended toward the center to varying degrees, filled with everything from tightly packed amalgamations that must have been separate buildings at one point to quaint separate structures and even vibrant parklands. Numerous bridges spanned the residential and industrial sectors, and some of those were large enough and wide enough to feature their own buildings.

The height of buildings along the wall shelves was regulated in most cases by the position of the shelf above, but sometime in the past the residential zone had spilled out over the corridor's floor and ceiling, which featured the city's tallest and most opulent towers.

A luminous beam—one of the city's two "sun rods"—ran along the side of the industrial sector for its entire length. The rod provided most of the illumination on this side of the city's central industries and helped its citizens keep to their Earth-centric circadian rhythms.

"Have you been here before?" Susan asked.

"Only once, I believe. It was during a school field trip." He pointed to the structure behind the closest thruster. "We got to tour part of the thruster assemblies *while* they were firing. Quite the sight. The whole place was shaking. *I* loved it, but I think it gave my teacher motion sickness."

Susan chuckled, staring out the window at the "skyline," her eyes drawn to the many towers extending down from the ceiling.

"Where are we headed?" she asked.

"An apartment complex in Exchanger Row. It's where most of the Atlas families are staying. It's on the ceiling pretty close to the airport. Sounds like a nice part of town."

She nodded, still gazing out the window.

"Come on," he urged with a hand on her shoulder. "Let's pick up our rental."

"Right."

✧   ✧   ✧

The Hanging Gardens apartment complex featured two blocky towers situated on either side of a street-level parkland. The towers extended far below the park, and while most of the apartments must have required elevator or counter-grav access, Velasco's was situated conveniently at street level.

"That's a lot of cars and copters," Susan commented as the rental came to a halt in a parking space within sight of the Velasco home.

"Friends and family, most likely." Isaac climbed out of the vehicle, and the door slid shut. "It's been several hours since she found out."

"You want to handle this yourself? Or should we both go in?"

"We'll go in together, but I'm leaving the LENS behind. You might want to take your hat off as well."

"Sure thing." She took off her peaked cap, then combed her hair with her fingers and stuck the cap under an armpit.

A group of kids played hide-and-seek amongst all the vehicles. A young boy of six or seven years wearing gray-and-black-striped coveralls crouched with his head down behind a cherry red luxury quadcopter, counting down from twenty. A girl about the same age ran past Isaac, giggling as she took up her position behind their rental. Other children hid themselves behind vehicles or nearby trees. Some still wore their abstract goggles, which allowed them to experience the local infostructure, though most had hung their goggles from bands at their necks.

It had only been five years since Isaac had received his wetware. Five years since he legally became an adult at the age of twenty-five, the age where the human brain typically stopped growing. He grimaced as an unbidden picture of a teenage Isaac Cho shot through his mind, the lanky kid running around with a ridiculous pair of purple sunglasses. The thought sent a shiver of embarrassment through his being.

"This must seem an unexpected treat to them," Susan said. "All of a sudden they're hustled into cars for a surprise visit with the relatives."

"Mmhmm." Isaac stepped up to the door and palmed the buzzer.

The door split open a minute later to reveal a short but compact man with a blotchy complexion wearing part of a black business suit. He'd taken off his jacket and undone the collar around the thick reddish trunk of his neck.

"Can I help you...officer?" he asked in a weary tone.

"Detective Isaac Cho, SysPol Themis." He transmitted his badge. "And this is my deputy, Agent Susan Cantrell."

"Hello, sir." Susan dipped her head toward the man.

"We're here to speak with Cynthia Velasco concerning the death of her husband. My IC called ahead to let her know."

"Right. Yeah. I took the call for her." The man sighed and backed up, gesturing for them to join him in the apartment. "Cynthia's in the back. I'm Jeremy, by the way. Cynthia's older brother."

Jeremy led them through the apartment to an oval dining room with a view of the park's rolling hills. A dozen people crowded around the table, about half seated in chairs that matched the faux-wood patterning of the table while others used simple plastic seating that might have been freshly printed.

Gift baskets of food and vases of white flowers covered the table to the point of overflowing. A bottle of red wine stood open and nearly empty, while wine glasses ringed the table, some drained and others untouched.

Everyone's eyes fell on the two detectives as they entered. Everyone except for the woman at the head of the table who continued to stare into her empty glass of wine, spinning it slowly with two fingers.

"Cynthia," Jeremy said quietly.

The woman looked up at him, and Isaac could see the family resemblance in her round, blotchy face, thick neck, and husky build. Her eyes were dry but reddish from recent tears.

"The SysPol detectives I mentioned? They're here to see you."

"The detectives," she repeated with a frown. "Yes, I remember. What do they need?"

"We have a few routine questions to go over with you," Isaac said. "But before we begin, let me apologize for our intrusion during what must be a difficult time, and to also pass on my condolences for your recent loss."

"Thanks." She took a deep, shuddering breath, which seemed to help her composure. "Might as well get this over with. Where do you want to do this?"

"Anywhere in your home is fine. Right here if you prefer, though I'll have to ask the others to leave the room."

"Here then." Cynthia glanced around the table. "Everyone, if you don't mind?"

The occupants began to disperse. Three of them took turns giving her brief hugs or pecks on the cheek before departing. Isaac and Susan sat down next to Cynthia after everyone else had left the room. Jeremy sealed the door on his way out.

"Is SysPol normally called in for suicides?" Cynthia asked, refilling her wine glass with the dregs of the bottle.

"Sometimes. It depends on the circumstances of each case."

"And what circumstances brought you down here this time?"

"We've been asked to help ascertain your husband's motive for the suicide. We were hoping you could shed some light on the situation."

"I've been asking myself that same question." She took a shallow sip then set the glass down. "The last few days have been playing out in my head on an endless loop, as if my brain were trying to slot the puzzle pieces together."

"Any thoughts on why he did it?"

"No." She shook her head. "He was stressed and on edge, but it's nothing I hadn't seen before, to one degree or another. Maybe this had been an unusually tough project for him, but it's hard for me to say, because he always managed to push through the grind in the past."

"Did he talk about the Dyson Project with you?"

"A little. To tell you the truth, we'd been going through a rough patch ourselves, talking less, hanging out after work in different rooms."

"Was this a recent change in your marriage?"

"No. This has been going on for a few years now." She let out a long sigh. "And steadily growing worse. I tried to convince him to see a marriage counselor with me. Made the case to him a few times, but he never listened. Those talks always ended badly, so it's been months since I tried."

"How did they end badly?"

"Fights, mostly. And not just about our marriage. Any number of things could set him off. Sometimes it felt like navigating a minefield blindfolded would be easier than talking to him."

"Did your fights ever become physical?"

"No. Nothing like that. Just lots of angry shouting." She took another sip of wine. "We may have had our disagreements, but he never laid an improper finger on me. Still, I'd be lying if I said all those fights didn't wear on me. I'd even contemplated filing for divorce at one point."

"Did he know about this?"

"No. You're the first people I've ever shared that with."

"Did the two of you have any recent fights?"

"Yes, we did."

"How recent?"

"We had a big one within the past week."

"Can you be more specific as to when it happened?"

"Oh, about three or four days ago. He'd just come home from work. We were about to sit down for dinner when I asked him how his day had gone and he just...blew up at me. Started raging at me about every little thing wrong with our marriage."

"Such as?"

"He yelled at me for cleaning his office. He was a bit messy, and he had a bad habit of stacking dirty plates on his desk. So, sometimes I cleaned his desk for him."

"Anything else? Anything stand out as unusual about the fight?"

"No. Nothing I'd call unusual." She let out a slow breath. "Unfortunately, a fight like that was pretty typical for us, though I have no idea what set him off that time."

"Did your husband talk much about his boss, Julian Boaz?"

"On occasion."

"How would you characterize their relationship?"

"As good as can be expected, I suppose."

"What do you mean by that?"

"I don't think he had a very high opinion of Boaz, but I sort of took it as the typical noise people make about their bosses. He never brought up leaving the company, so I suppose you could say he tolerated Boaz as a boss, and not much else."

"How about Horace Pangu? Did your husband talk about him at all?"

"Now *that* was a rare bright spot in his life. He was delighted to have met the Wizard, and even happier to be working with him."

"What about Leon Traczyk?"

"That *snake.*"

"Am I correct in assuming they weren't friends?" Isaac asked, surprised by the amount of venom in her voice.

"Oh, heavens no! Quite the opposite."

"How so?"

"If you look up 'duplicitous coworker' in a dictionary, you'll see Leon's picture there. He's been after Esteban's job for at least two years. Always looking for a place to stick the knife." She paused and then frowned. "Figuratively, I mean. I suppose I should choose my words carefully, given who I'm talking to."

"That's quite all right," Isaac assured her. "Can you give us an example of the friction between Traczyk and your husband?"

"There weren't any big incidents I can recall. It was more of a constant drip of antagonism. Like how Traczyk would turn into this petty little suck-up whenever Boaz was around."

"Moving on, did your husband have any interactions with the Mercury Historical Preservation Society?"

"Yes."

"Can you tell me about them?"

"Those idiots would sometimes harass him on the way to work. They had a protest zone outside the airport, so they'd shout at him as he entered the terminal, calling him names like 'planet killer' or some other nonsense. As if a dumb lump of rock has a life."

"Anything else?"

"They got a hold of his connection string and would call or send him messages, but Atlas set up software to block them out. They did show up at the apartment a few times. Made quite a ruckus. I had to overlay my sense of hearing just to get a good night's sleep. Fortunately, Atlas hit them with a restraining order. Even so, SSP had to arrest a few of them later for violating the order, but that seemed to do the trick. Their stupidity calmed down after the arrests, thankfully."

"Did they ever threaten him with violence?"

"Oh, yes. He didn't show me all—or even most—of the Society messages, but I know some of them were death threats."

"Were any of these threats reported to the police?"

"I don't think so, sorry."

"That's all right. Mrs. Velasco, thank you for answering our questions. As one final order of business, would you mind giving us access to your husband's home office?"

"Sure. Right now?"

"In a little bit. The forensics specialist working this case will be joining us once she's finished at Atlas headquarters. I'd like her to take a look your husband's home workstation. I'm especially curious to see these messages the Society sent him."

The SSP quadcopter landed next to their rental. Isaac leaned against the car's hood, and Susan stood nearby, arms crossed while they waited. The copter settled to the ground, its engines switched off, and Chatelain and Nina stepped out. Parks materialized next to the sergeant.

"Anyone *else* you want ferried around?" Chatelain asked.

"Not at the moment," Isaac replied evenly. "Specialist Cho?"

"I grabbed an image off Velasco's desk, but it'll take a while to sort through it all. I'm sure his filing system made sense to him, but hell if I know how he could keep that mess straight."

"Velasco also had a workstation in the apartment," Isaac said. "I'll need you to pull that as well."

"Great," she sighed. "Looks like it's an all-nighter for me. After I grab the image, I'll head over to the nearest station and settle in."

"That would be ours," Parks offered. "The 103."

"Works for me."

"You can off-load the analysis to Kronos if you think that'll help," Isaac suggested.

"Nah, I can handle it," Nina assured him. "Just got to slog through."

Cephalie appeared, seated atop the LENS. "I'll pitch in as well. All-nighters don't bother me."

"Thanks," Nina said. "That should make the work go faster."

"Anything of note in the desk image?" Isaac asked.

"Other than it's a godawful mess?" Nina shook her head. "No. Ask me again in the morning."

"Fair enough."

"Now, if you'll excuse me, duty calls." Nina whistled, and

one of her drones floated out of the copter and followed her to the apartment.

"So, where does that leave us?" Susan asked.

"Spending the night in the Third Engine Block," Isaac said. "No point heading back until we can make a clear determination."

"Have you lot found *anything* to show it's not a suicide?" Chatelain griped.

"Not yet," Isaac admitted. "So far, we've come across three possible contributors: workplace stress, martial issues, and harassment from the Society. Of all those, the Society's involvement is the one I'm most interested in."

"Were they threatening him?" Parks asked.

"That's what his wife said. We should know more once we look over any messages left in his office."

"You know, it's funny that there's a connection to the Society," Parks said. "I've been thinking about Atlas' sudden swing in fortune. How SourceCode's last trial failed so catastrophically. They were the clear favorite beforehand."

"Government officials tend to frown upon self-replicators that almost eat them," Isaac said.

"Yes, I get that. But *why* did the trial fail? Was it a case of bad engineering? Or maybe something else? What if the Society was involved?"

"That's . . . tenuous at best," Isaac said. "There's no evidence of their involvement."

"That we know of," Cephalie countered. "Remember, the Society sabotaged an Atlas trial earlier this year. It's not unreasonable to think they'd give it another go."

"Granted," Isaac said, "but any sabotage by the Society should have been revealed by our own division's review of the incident. But either way, it might help for us to take a look at the official report."

"I'll send a request to Argus Station for a copy," Cephalie said.

"Thanks." Isaac glanced over to Parks, then back to Cephalie. "And even though I doubt there's a connection, request the Atlas sabotage report as well."

Parks gave him a nod, looking pleased with himself.

"If for no other reason than to have it in case we need it," Isaac stressed.

"Consider it done," Cephalie said.

"What's got you so happy?" Chatelain nudged Parks in the arm.

"Just that I was right." He smiled at the sergeant. "There's more going on here than just a suicide."

"*Maybe*," Isaac said. "Though, it's true the lack of a clear suicide motive has begun to bother me as well."

"Not you too!" Chatelain rolled his eyes.

"Yes, me too," Isaac replied. "Anyway, all speculation aside, we'll need to wait for the forensics report."

"Does that mean we're free to go?" Chatelain asked.

Isaac paused for a deliberate moment before saying, "Yes, Sergeant. You may return to your regular duties."

"Woohoo!" Chatelain threw up his arms. "Sweet, sweet freedom!"

"And us?" Susan asked.

"We'll give Dispatch a call and have them reserve hotel rooms for us."

"If you're looking for a place to stay," Parks began, "there's a hotel not far from our station."

"That should work," Isaac said. "What's the hotel's name?"

"Plume Tower. It's part of the Ring Suites hotel chain. You can even see it from here." Parks pointed toward where the ceiling cityscape met the wall shelves. Sure enough, Isaac could make out a fiery abstract banner for the Plume Tower along with the dark green of an SSP precinct building a few shelves below. A large, virtual "103" rotated beside the police building.

"Ring Suites?" Susan asked Isaac. "Isn't that the chain you really like? The one where they print out your preferred room furnishings before you arrive?"

"The same. You set up your profile?"

"Yes." She gave him a slightly embarrassed smile. "I'm not making *that* mistake again."

"Good to hear." The image of an uncharacteristically worried Susan Cantrell came to mind, standing outside his hotel room, soaking wet with nothing but a bath towel for modesty. It wasn't an . . . unpleasant thought.

But it was an unprofessional one, and he shook it away.

"We'll give Dispatch a call then check in for the night," he said at last.

"Works for me," Susan said.

CHAPTER EIGHT

THE 103ʀᴅ PRECINCT BUILDING WAS A WIDE TEN-STORY BUILDING that took up the entire span between shelves twenty-eight and twenty-nine, its "roof" melding with the upper shelf. Its broad, flattened front contrasted with local architecture that featured sinuous curves and colorful translucent exteriors, as if the buildings had been formed from sculpted fluids frozen in place.

A pair of quadcopters flew out from the upper hangars as Isaac and Susan stepped through the open doors at the ground floor. Three desk sergeants sat or hovered behind a row of desks with civilians awaiting their turn in a crowded, snaking queue.

An abstract sergeant saw them enter and waved them forward ahead of the queue. At least, that's what Isaac thought it was trying to do. The sergeant's avatar was composed of barely enough polygons to provide a basic humanoid shape, each surface covered with pixels so chunky he couldn't read the AC's expression. Even its SSP uniform was rendered in the same low-fidelity style.

Groans of disapproval spread through the queue as he and Susan skipped it.

"Oh, come on!" griped a lanky man with a shock of purple and yellow hair split down the middle. His jacket and pants matched his hair.

"Police business!" snapped the polygonal sergeant in an unnatural, synthetic voice. "Wait your turn!"

"I'm waiting! I'm waiting! That's *all* I've been doing all morning!"

Isaac stepped up to the sergeant. "Good morning. We're here to see—"

"Specialist Cho?" the sergeant asked abruptly.

"Yes," Isaac replied with a slight frown. "Could you—"

"Conference room seven." A navigation arrow blinked into existence and traced a path to the left and down a corridor. "Next!"

"Thank you." Isaac's frown deepened as he and Susan followed the arrow into the station.

"*Friendly,*" Susan sighed with a shake of her head.

"It's fine. As long as they don't interfere with our work."

They found conference room seven. Isaac palmed the door open and walked in to find Nina asleep at a rectangular table with what might have been a coffee thermos cradled in her arms. A thin brown film remained at the bottom of a nearby mug.

"Sure, I don't mind..." she mumbled, a line of drool leaking from the edge of her mouth.

"Nina?" Isaac said softly.

"Just let me slip into something more comfor-bab-bull, yeah..."

She snuggled up to the thermos and rubbed her cheek against it.

"Nina?" Isaac repeated, then gave her a soft poke in the shoulder.

"Ah!" She bolted upright in her seat so fast Isaac flinched. Her eyes flitted about the room.

"Good morning," Isaac said, recovering.

"Mornin'." Her gaze darted to one side, then the other. "Third Engine Block?"

"That's right."

"103rd Precinct?"

"Right again."

Her eyes scanned the room once more. "Where'd Jefe go?"

"Who's Jefe?"

She looked around one last time, then down at her own attire, then finally let out a groaning sigh. Whatever energy had propped her up oozed out of her body, and she slumped onto the desk, hugging the thermos close.

"Damn it!" she moaned. "That was a *dream*?!"

Isaac cleared his throat noisily.

"I know!" She rested her forehead on the desk. "Give me a minute."

"How late did you stay up?"

"Too late! If Velasco were still alive, I'd kill him myself!"

"Please don't say things like that."

"But he was such a *slob*!"

"I'm getting that impression."

"And on top of that, the worst kind of slob!" She thumped her forehead against the desk twice. "I've never seen an infosystem so poorly organized. It's almost like he went out of his way to make it counterintuitive. Every time Cephalie and I thought we were almost done, we'd turn up some new anomaly. It was horrible! I should have dumped this on a Kronos team and called it a night!"

"Why didn't you?"

"Because I thought it'd only take us a few hours tops!"

"Find anything?"

"Maybe." Nina waved her hand, and her report materialized over the table. "It's all there."

"Thanks." Isaac copied the file. "Anything you'd like to cover in person?"

"Nah. Everything should be clear in the report."

Cephalie popped into existence, seated atop the thermos. "I can give you the deep dive, if needed."

"Sounds good. Then Nina, why don't you head to the hotel and catch some winks? We had Dispatch reserve a room for you. You've got your own rental, too. It's waiting in the parking garage next to the station."

He sent her the rental's keycode.

"Aww," she cooed. "My little brother's the best."

"I try," he replied dryly. He helped her up out the seat, then gave her a pat on the back. "Go on. Get some z's. You've earned it."

"Damn right I have."

She shuffled out of the conference room, the thermos tucked in her arms.

"Shall we get to work?" Susan asked.

"Let's." Isaac pulled up a chair and expanded the report into separate screens.

✧   ✧   ✧

"Someone tampered with his desk at Atlas?" Isaac's eyes narrowed as he reviewed Nina's report.

"That's our conclusion." Cephalie twirled her cane as she

paced across the table. "Carefully targeted, too, though not exactly subtle. My guess is whoever did this was in a hurry."

"Any chance it was Velasco?" Susan asked. "Perhaps he wanted to clear out some embarrassing files before he...you know." She mimed firing a finger-gun into the side of her head.

"Not unless he set it on a delay timer," Isaac said. "Look at the timestamps on these deletion jobs. They're eight minutes *after* Velasco shot himself."

"On top of that, the program seems to have been inserted remotely," Cephalie added.

"Right. Never mind." Susan opened a new tab in the report. "Do we know what was deleted?"

"We have a good idea." Cephalie shifted both of their reports to the correct tab. "Nothing remains of the missing files, I'm afraid. The deletion program did a thorough job of that, and it also tried to clean itself out after it finished executing, but we got lucky. The program *didn't* have administrator rights to Velasco's infosystem, so it couldn't clean up *everything*. Some evidence remained, such as in temporary system memory or nodal communication buffers. This allowed us to extract fragments of the search queries."

"What were the queries looking for?" Isaac asked.

"Keyword 'ghost.'"

"Ghost?" Isaac asked. "Anything else?"

"Not that we know of, though it's possible other search parameters were used. We know the recovered queries are incomplete."

"Hmm. Ghost."

"Perhaps a project name?" Susan suggested. "Maybe a secret project?"

"But why delete it before SSP arrived?"

"An illegal secret project?" Susan added with a shrug, though she sounded doubtful.

"At a company vying for the largest macrotech contract in history? I don't buy it."

"Actually..." Cephalie pushed her glasses up the bridge of her nose, and they glinted dramatically. "We have reason to believe 'ghost' refers to a person."

"Why's that?" Isaac asked.

"Because whoever wiped these 'ghost' files from Velasco's office at Atlas *didn't* have access to his home."

Cephalie cycled their reports to a new tab, and Isaac began to skim through the entries.

"'Reminder: Schedule a meeting with the Ghost,'" Isaac read. "'Reminder: Call the Ghost tomorrow.' 'What to do about the Ghost's proposal?'"

"These notes go back two whole months," Susan said.

Isaac scrolled down the list. "Find anything juicy?"

"Unfortunately not," Cephalie said. "They're all just as generic as the ones you read. Velasco must have kept the details in his head."

"What about these mentions of meetings and calls?" Susan said. "Any records of those?"

"None we could find," Cephalie said.

"Hmm." Isaac leaned back and crossed his arms, staring at the list of unusual—if generic—reminders.

"Thoughts?" Susan asked.

"I was somewhat hesitant to declare this a suicide before, but this clinches it. A man mysteriously kills himself, and then someone comes in *immediately* after he's dead and wipes specific files from his desk? That reeks of something rotten, which means it's our job to keep digging until we can untangle this mess. Not every tragedy hides something sinister," Isaac added, echoing some of Nina's words from the day before. "But perhaps this one does."

❖   ❖   ❖

"Ghost?" Julian Boaz asked, his image visible through the comm window.

"That's right, Mister Boaz," Isaac said. "Does the reference mean anything to you?"

"Ghost...ghost...hmm." He worked a screen off to the side. "No, nothing's coming up. Besides, I don't recall—" His eyes widened with sudden recollection. "Wait a second. Maybe there's something. Give me a moment to check elsewhere."

He leaned to the side, leaving only the back of his head and a shoulder visible on the screen.

"Yes, here it is." Boaz settled back into his chair. "Mattison's Retreat. Otherwise known as the Ghost Town. It's an old project of ours—from about nine years ago—and not a very successful one. I just checked our records, and Velasco was a part of that team, though not in a leadership role. Is that what you're looking for, Detective? I can send you the project brief."

"I'm afraid that doesn't sound like a match. Our evidence suggests the Ghost is a person, not a place."

"A person, you say?" Boaz frowned and turned back to the side screen. "No, I don't think so. If there was a customer with that name, we'd have a record for it. Or an employee or subcontractor. I ran a search through all of those. No matches. Nothing even close." He leaned forward. "Are you sure this Ghost is a person and not a place?"

"I suppose we could be mistaken."

"Because Mattison's Retreat would be a good match. It really is a ghost town nowadays, nestled between the Second and Third Engine Blocks. Like a band of diseased frosting between two layers of delicious cake. How did you say you came across this information?"

"We have evidence related files were deleted from Velasco's desk."

"Huh. Well, that could be Mattison's Retreat. That project was a complete disaster! The first—and *last*—time we ever partnered with SourceCode! In fact, I think it's safe to say Mattison's Retreat is the source of the bad blood between our two companies. Bunch of backstabbers hiding in their abstract realms."

"Mister Boaz?"

"The retreat was supposed to be an easy score for both our companies. Atlas started by hollowing out a section of the barrier between the Second and Third blocks—which was unnecessarily thick from day one—and then both our companies began processing the excavated material into an idyllic resort town." He chuckled and flashed a smirk. "Only it didn't go well."

"Mister Boaz?"

"SourceCode's self-replicators started chewing up our mini-constructors, and they even ate through some of the buildings we made!" He stopped with his mouth open, then shut it and paused in thought. "Or was it the other way around?" He tapped his chin with a finger before giving them an indifferent shrug. "Anyway, the whole project went to hell. Both of our replicator systems started fighting each other, tearing down buildings faster than they could be erected, which is when the Saturn State stepped in. They paid us for the work we'd performed up to that date, closed the remaining project scope, and then kindly told us both to fuck off."

"Mister Boaz?"

"Such an embarrassment." He shook his head with a bemused smile. "You know, I think those machines are *still* fighting it out to this day. Kind of like our two companies are. I wonder who's winning?"

"Mister *Boaz*," Isaac said, this time with added force.

"Hmm? Yes? Sorry, I seem to have gotten sidetracked. The Ghost, right?"

"Are you certain Atlas hasn't had any dealings with anyone using that name or alias?"

"Yes, quite certain. Otherwise, there'd be a record."

"Then I thank you for your time."

✧   ✧   ✧

"Someone called the Ghost?" Horace Pangu replied. His image in the comm window sat back.

"That's right."

"I've run into a few individuals over the years who went by that moniker. You'd be surprised how many times I encounter repeat names, especially when it comes to ACs. A lot of them seem to gravitate to the same tired references. That, and I suppose my age plays a factor, too."

"Would any of these 'Ghosts' happen to have a connection to Velasco?"

"None that are obvious to me. It's been..." He stared off in thought and let out a slow sigh. "Oh, about twenty years since I worked with someone named Ghost, though to be precise her full name was Ghost *Seeker*. She was a lovely Oortan engineer with some innovative takes on synthoid design. We got along quite well."

"Nothing more recent?"

"Perhaps. Not a *person*, but... well, it's something. Though now that I consider it, I doubt this'll help you."

"Any piece of the puzzle could prove useful, even if the use isn't immediately obvious."

"Of course, Detective. It's actually something I said to Esteban before he... went back to his office and ended it."

"Something *you* said?"

"Yes. Strange, I know, but there it is. He seemed a bit pale to me, a bit out of sorts, so I went up to him and asked if he was okay. Then I said, 'You look like you've seen a ghost.' I'd intended it as a simple jest, but his reaction surprised me."

"How so?"

"He flinched. As if I'd inadvertently hit on a sensitive subject."

"Hmm."

"That's all, I'm afraid."

"Did Velasco say anything else? Perhaps something right after he flinched? Anything that might provide some clue as to who or what this Ghost is?"

"Only that he had a lot on his mind, which seemed true enough, given what followed."

"A colleague named 'Ghost'?" Cynthia Velasco said.

"Or some other acquaintance, Mrs. Velasco," Isaac said.

"Now that you mention it, I do recall him talking about someone with that name."

"Can you be more specific as to when you heard it?"

"Maybe a few times in the past month or so. I assumed it concerned his job in some manner. I never really paid much attention to what he did for a living. He seemed incapable of simplifying things down to a level digestible for people not in the industry, and our conversations would devolve into a flood of technical jargon and meaningless acronyms."

"Then you don't know whom he was referring to?"

"No, Detective. Sorry."

"That's all right, Mrs. Velasco. What about his tone when he spoke of the Ghost? Or perhaps his mood at the time?"

"Frustrated and annoyed. Sometimes excited. Usually a mix of those."

Frustrated? Annoyed? Isaac thought. *But also excited? How do those fit together with someone who ends up committing suicide?*

"Anything else?"

"No, sorry."

"Then I thank you for your time, Mrs. Velasco. And for your understanding. Again, I'm sorry for interrupting your day once more."

A pair of SSP troopers escorted an agitated Leon Traczyk to the conference room.

"Have a seat, Mister Traczyk," Isaac said from behind the table, alongside Susan.

"What the hell!" Traczyk gave the troopers a foul look before walking in. "You picked a swell time to drag me out here! You could have called, you know!"

"Under normal circumstances I would. But your previous lack of truthfulness has left me…disappointed, shall we say? And so, I thought a change of venue might be beneficial for us to conduct our business more smoothly."

"You trying to be an ass?"

"Nothing of the sort, I assure you." Isaac indicated the seat opposite him. "Now please, if you don't mind?"

Traczyk sank into the chair with a huff.

Technically speaking, Isaac didn't have the authority to *force* Traczyk to show up at the station for the interview, but he *had* insisted, and the insistence of a SysPol detective carried a certain degree of weight, even absent the strict letter of the law. He'd even dispatched a pair of troopers to Atlas to keep an eye on the man, just in case he tried to flee Janus or take some other unusual action.

So far, Traczyk had given no indication he might try something stupid, which boded well for the man in Isaac's mind but still left the matter of his earlier dishonesty to consider. That was another reason Isaac had insisted on the second interview taking place at the station; he preferred to interview victims, witnesses, and the like in locations they found comfortable, but recalcitrant or dishonest individuals earned a different approach. The mere fact they were in a police station could sometimes provide the necessary pressure for him to tease out the truth, whatever it might be.

"Well, I'm here." Traczyk gave them an exaggerated shrug. "Can we get on with it?"

"In a moment." Isaac finished arranging his virtual notes, then faced Traczyk, studying his demeanor. He sat in the chair at an angle, head tilted to the side with the beginnings of a snarl on his lips.

"Take an abstraction, Detective. It'll last longer."

"Tell me, Mister Traczyk. Does the name 'Ghost' mean anything to you?" He watched the man for any sign of unease or recognition.

But saw none.

"Ghost?" Traczyk echoed. "What's this about?"

"Please answer the question."

"I have no idea what you're talking about. Ghost?" He let out a loud harrumph. "This isn't about *Solar Descent*, is it? I already fessed up that we didn't hang out together."

"No. This isn't about games."

"Well then, I haven't got a clue." He leaned his head back and stared up at the ceiling. "Ghost. Ghost?" He sat up again, a perplexed expression on his face. "There's that ghost *town* between the Second and Third Engine Blocks. Is that what you're interested in?"

"No."

"Can you at least give me a hint, then? I have no idea what you're after."

"We believe the Ghost to be a person Velasco was in contact with before he killed himself."

"A person?" Traczyk's brow wrinkled in deepening confusion. "Someone Velasco was talking to?"

"Yes."

"Recently?"

"We believe so."

"Hell if I know." Traczyk snorted. "Why you asking me? We hated each other's guts!"

"You were colleagues on the same project."

"Yeah? So? Doesn't mean I spent my time around him. Quite the opposite, in fact. There were times when we'd go *days* without saying a word to each other in person. Just messaging back and forth."

"About what?" Susan asked.

"Dry technical stuff. You want to hear the epic saga of how we handled the DAC-90 pattern prepper revisions? Hmm?" He indicated both detectives with a cupped hand. "Either of you? No? It's a *thrilling* story of iterative design." He smirked at them. "I have a patent pending for my work on it."

"Then you have no idea who the Ghost might be?" Isaac asked.

"Not a clue. And that's the truth."

Isaac frowned and made a note on his screen.

The rest of the interview proved equally fruitless.

✧   ✧   ✧

"Death threats, huh?" Susan remarked doubtfully after she and Isaac began to wrap up their review of the Society messages from Velasco's two desks.

"That's what the wife said," Isaac replied dully, resting his cheek on a fist.

"I don't see how *any* of these qualify. Do you?"

"Not really."

"Take this one for instance." She opened the message and guided it into the space between them. "All they're doing is hurling insults at him."

"And juvenile insults at that," Isaac added. "How exactly is the entire planet of Mercury supposed to fit up a person's behind anyway?"

"Well, it does make for an interesting graphic."

"Hmm," he murmured, inspecting the image between them. The cartoonish version of Velasco appeared to be in a great deal of pain, which was understandable, given the anatomical impossibilities on display. The tears pouring out of his straining eyes were a nice touch. "I suppose this could—under certain perspectives—be considered a loose threat of bodily harm."

"Loose?" She flashed a half-smile. "You mean like his asshole?"

"Susan, please. Let's keep it professional."

"Sorry."

"The bottom line is the Society was actively hostile toward him, which makes this an angle worth following up. Especially given their previous illegal actions against Atlas."

"What happened with that trial, anyway?"

"Give me a moment." Isaac opened one of the case files Cephalie had requested for them. "I remember catching it briefly in the news but never really paid much attention to it. Ah. Here we are. Atlas was showcasing one of their constructors for the government near L4. Looks like Boaz, Velasco, and several other high-ranking company officials were present in person. So were members of President Byakko's cabinet and a handful of senators, including representatives from Saturn, Venus, and Jupiter."

"Then this was *very* high profile."

"Indeed. Atlas had maneuvered a small asteroid into position, but instead of processing the material into the framework for a Dyson collector, the constructor instead produced a significant number of smaller panels shaped like extended middle fingers."

Susan snorted and leaned forward with a hand over her mouth.

Isaac raised an eyebrow at her.

"Sorry, sorry." She straightened and waved him on. "Please continue."

"It turned out one of Atlas' own engineers—a woman named Lisa Schmidt—had altered the constructor's core programming. Arete Division First Responders promptly arrived on the scene, both from the nearby Arestor Station and transmitting in via connectome laser. They quickly diagnosed the source of the problem and arrested Schmidt.

"Shortly after that, Schmidt loudly and proudly declared herself as a new member of the Society, after which she started spouting their usual propaganda. The Society never took credit for the incident, but neither did they disavow it."

"Interesting," Susan said, "but doesn't strike me as relevant to our case."

"I'm leaning toward the same conclusion." Isaac opened a separate case file. "The *SourceCode* trial, however, is a little more relevant. The trial began much the same way Atlas' did, starting with the SourceCode self-replicating swarm being seeded on a test asteroid, and ending with the swarm replicating out of control.

"According to the report, this was a case of poor engineering and insufficient protections against replicator mutation. No charges have been filed, though it seems fines against SourceCode are still on the table. SourceCode management pinned the blame on an engineer named Antoni Ruckman, who they then fired."

"Okay, but why did you consider SourceCode's blunder relevant to the case?"

"Because"—Isaac's eyes glinted—"Cephalie found correspondence between Ruckman and Velasco on the home infosystem."

"Ah! Velasco and this SourceCode engineer were in touch with each other? Even though the two companies were in fierce competition for the same contract? Now, *that's* intriguing!"

"Quite. Cephalie, can you summarize for us?"

"Sure thing, kiddos." The AC appeared on the table and clicked her cane against the surface. "From what I can gather, Ruckman and Velasco go way back. I can't be sure from the correspondence alone, but it looks like they met at Amalthea University while Ruckman was a microtech professor there and Velasco an engineering student. Seems like they've kept in touch ever since."

"The SourceCode engineer Velasco kept in contact with is the same guy blamed for the mishaps at their trial?" Susan narrowed her eyes. "Suspicious."

"Agreed." Isaac shifted the two files aside. "It seems to me we have three potential leads: a deeper forensic look at Atlas, a talk with the local Society chapter, and the same with the SourceCode executives."

"Nina's going to be *thrilled*."

"We'll let her know once she wakes up. As for us...Cephalie, where's the SourceCode headquarters right now?"

"Checking." A blackboard appeared next to her, and white chalky text scrolled across it at unnatural speed. The text stopped and she looked up. "Near the Atlas Shoal."

"The *Atlas* Shoal?" Susan asked.

"It's part debris field, part macrotech construction zone," Isaac explained. "It's where the moons Janus and Epimetheus were broken down to construct the Shark Fin. Atlas played a huge role in that project, hence the name." He leaned back and grimaced down at Cephalie. "How long would a trip out there take?"

"Depends on when we leave. The Shoal has a pretty fast orbit. Call it a rough two and a half hours if we leave soon."

"I suppose we could ask a representative to transmit to us, but they *are* local, so the proper way to handle this is face-to-face." Isaac shrugged. "At least we already have the V-wing."

Susan sat up. "Cephalie, what if it were just me flying to the Shoal?"

"At max acceleration? Less than an hour."

"An hour there. An hour back." She nodded with a faint smile and looked over to Isaac. "What do you think? I can take care of SourceCode while you follow up with the Society. We'll cover more ground this way, *and* it'll cut down on travel time."

"I..."

His first inclination was to object. Susan only had one SysPol case under her belt, and her lack of experience presented any number of pitfalls, especially when it came to SysGov laws. That, plus negative reactions she sometimes garnered made Isaac hesitant to cut her loose. He preferred to be nearby in case someone gave her a hard time.

But, on the other hand, she'd served as an Admin Peacekeeper for twelve years, and as a STAND for nine, serving under their Special Training And Nonorganic Deployment command. She knew how to handle herself, and she'd demonstrated excellent professional restraint during their last case whenever people slung insults at her.

And look at her, Isaac thought. *She's actively seeking out ways to contribute. She wants a larger role in our investigations. Besides acting as the occasional death machine, no matter how helpful—or* indeed, critical—*those moments have proven.*

"I like your initiative," he answered at last, and her smile grew. "Good thinking, partner. We'll do it your way."

CHAPTER NINE

ISAAC DROPPED SUSAN OFF AT THE AIRPORT THEN SET THE LOCAL Society chapterhouse as his destination.

The drab building possessed a faint church-like quality with an exterior styled into gray stone blocks broken up by tall stained-glass windows depicting the natural bodies of the solar system. The rental had to stop some distance from the chapterhouse due to the congestion of other vehicles parked in front.

Isaac climbed out of the vehicle and walked over, the LENS floating a few paces behind him. He stopped in front of the tall wooden double doors, palmed the buzzer, and waited.

The doors split open to reveal a young, rail-thin woman with a long face that narrowed to a prominent chin. Tears streaked down from blue, reddened eyes, and her wiry hair was pulled back into a heavy clip, almost as if it were held under tremendous tension and would snap out into an afro if released.

"Oh, thank you for coming!" she sobbed with outstretched arms and advanced on Isaac. He fought a compulsion to dodge out of the way before she embraced him and buried her face in his shoulder.

"Uh, ma'am?" he asked, his arms out to the side, stuck between the instinct to return the hug and the urge to push her off.

"Thank you! Thank you!" She rubbed her dripping face across his shoulder, then blew her nose onto his collar.

"Excuse me, ma'am." Isaac placed his hands on her shoulders and eased her back. "There appears to be some mistake."

"There's no need to hide it," she blubbered, then rubbed a puffy sleeve under her runny nose. "You're among friends now."

"Ma'am, if you would just listen—"

"Please, come in." She sniffled, but then seemed to compose herself. "We have cupcakes."

She turned and disappeared inside without another word, leaving a mildly frustrated Isaac behind her. He glanced over at the LENS, where Cephalie appeared and shrugged at him.

"You do like cupcakes," she tittered, then vanished again.

"Not the point," he breathed, then walked in.

He followed the woman through a small foyer to a round, central chamber with a heavy, faux-wood table which was, as promised, laden with cupcakes from edge to edge. The cupcakes formed a sea of gray frosting and black candles with the occasional glimpses of reddish cake underneath. Most of the two dozen or so Society members in attendance held cupcakes in varying states of consumption. The physical ones, at least; there were a few AC avatars floating about. Drink bottles stacked the side tables, chairs were scattered around in haphazard clusters, and an off-scale and time-accelerated representation of the solar system rotated overhead.

"Here you go, dear." The woman handed him a cupcake. "Help yourself. There's plenty more where that came from."

"Thank you," Isaac replied blandly before handing the cupcake off to the LENS. The drone extended a prog-steel pseudopod, doused the candle, and drew it into an internal storage compartment.

The woman looked him up and down. "I'm sorry. Have we met before?"

"Doubtful."

"Well, we can fix that." She put a hand to her chest. "My name's Bonnie Rosenstein, though Bonnie is fine. I'm the assistant chair of this chapter, so if you need anything, you only need to ask. Now dear, what should we call you?"

"Detective Isaac Cho."

"Oh my! A *detective*!" She flashed a smile at him. "We don't get many people from the police over here."

"I can't imagine why."

"I know! Right?" She sniffled again, pulled out a soggy handkerchief, and blew her nose into it.

"I'm sorry," Isaac began, politely but firmly. "I hope you'll excuse my ignorance, but what exactly is going on here?"

"It's my husband, you see." Rosenstein dabbed under her leaking eyes. "He's going to die."

"Oh, I'm terribly sorry. I didn't know. Please accept my condolences."

"It's all right. We only found out yesterday."

"I hope you don't think I'm intruding, but what's wrong with him?"

"Nothing." She shook her head defiantly. "Which is the worst part of it. He has such a *long* life ahead of him, but the *imbeciles* in charge of our government are going to execute him!"

"He's to be executed? What was his crime?"

"Being in the wrong place at the w-w-wrong time." Rosenstein began to cry again. "You see, SysGov is going to take him apart, piece by piece!"

"Take him…" Isaac creased his brow. His eyes swept over the cupcakes once more. Gray frosting with red cake. "Mrs. Rosenstein? What's your husband's name?"

"He goes by many names, some more famous than others. I'm sure you've heard of at least one or two of them. Many have gone out of fashion. Utaridi. Suisei. Soosung. Otaared. Hermes. He even went by Udu-Idim-Gu once, if you can believe it." She shook her head. "There's no accounting for my husband's tastes, I'm afraid."

"Yes, I believe I see where this is going."

"But nowadays, he goes by the name he's most famous for." She stretched an open hand toward the ceiling, and one of the planets above glowed brighter.

"Mercury," Isaac filled in with a pronounced frown. "You think you're married to the planet Mercury."

"And not just me!" she declared, her eyes brightening. "Many of us aspire to become Spouses of Mercury. I finally became one last year. Oh, it was a lovely ceremony! We held it right here in the chapterhouse. You should have seen it!"

"I'm sure it was quite the spectacle," Isaac replied, believing every word.

"What a magical year it's been!" She placed a hand over her chest and gazed off in a dreamy manner. "I wouldn't give it up for anything."

"I'm almost afraid to ask, but doesn't the long-distance nature of your . . . marriage . . ."

"Make intimate matters difficult?" She batted her eyes at him.

"That wasn't what I was going to ask, but okay. We'll go with that."

"It's easy." She opened the collar of her blouse and pulled out a long chain necklace with a glass bulb on the end about the size of her fist. There was a rock inside the bulb.

A gray, uninteresting rock.

"A piece of your 'husband'?" Isaac surmised.

"So that he's close to my heart at all times." She flattened the necklace against her chest. "At *all* times," she emphasized.

"I believe you."

"Even after he passes, I'll still have this to remember him by." She gestured around the room. "We've all received one. Even those of us not ready for marriage yet. Have you received yours?"

"No, and no thank you. I don't need any rocks."

"But it's no trouble." She turned away. "Here. Let me get one for you."

"Mrs. Rosenstein—"

"Please, there's no need to be shy about it." She stepped over to one of the drink tables, shifted bottles aside, and opened a black bag made of heavy fabric. "We have plenty to go around." She reached into the bag and drew out a hefty stone.

"Mrs. Rosenstein, this really isn't necess—"

"Here you go." She took his hand into hers and planted a rock in it.

Isaac stared down at the stone. It covered the palm of his hand.

"Treat him with respect, and he'll do the same to you."

"Thank you." Isaac wasn't sure what else to say. He handed the rock over to his LENS, which stored it with the cupcake from earlier. "Mrs. Rosenstein, you said you were the assistant chair of this chapter?"

"That's right."

"Is there someplace we can speak in private?"

"What for?"

"I have a few questions to ask you."

"Questions?" She seemed to regard him and the LENS more fully. "Oh. Oh my. Why didn't you say so earlier?"

"I tried."

"Right. Sorry, I've just been so flustered since the news hit us." She composed herself, straightening her posture and smoothing out her clothes. "Yes, of course I can answer your questions. Here, we can use this."

She led him back into the foyer and closed the door to the main chamber.

"All right. How can I help you?"

"Do you know Esteban Velasco?"

"The Atlas engineer?" Her lower lip quivered. "Yes."

"Have you been in contact with him?"

"Me personally?"

"Or the chapter as a whole?"

"Well, yes, but it's nothing unusual. We've been sending him a steady stream of educational material in the hopes he might mend his ways."

A cartoonish example of the "educational material" flashed through Isaac's mind, but he said nothing.

"We also tried a few times to appeal to him directly, but then Atlas hit us with a restraining order"—she held up a finger—"which we have abided by, I assure you!"

Except for the members SSP arrested, Isaac added silently.

"Detective, may I ask what this is about?"

"Velasco committed suicide yesterday."

"Oh." She placed shaky fingers across her lips. "Oh my. Dead?"

"Very."

"*Permanently?*"

"He was organic, so yes. There's no backup connectome."

"Oh dear." Her shoulders slumped. "Detective, please understand, we only wanted him to see reason. Not *kill* himself! We never wanted *that*! Why, what even would be the point? Atlas is still moving forward with their plans, right?"

"They are."

"Then what would we have gained by driving a man to suicide, even if we *could*?"

"A fair enough question," Isaac admitted. "What about the chair of the chapter? What's his name?"

"That would be Desmond. Desmond Fike."

"And is Mister Fike here today?"

"No. He's working remotely again."

"Again?"

"He hasn't been to the chapterhouse in weeks. Been working on a big publicity project this whole time. Not sure what it is, but it's shaping up to be quite spectacular, from what he's told us. We've emptied almost all of the chapter's Esteem funds into it."

"You don't know the nature of this project?"

"Not really, no."

"But you're the assistant chair."

"I leave the money and big-picture stuff to Desmond. It works out better that way." Her eyes gleamed. "He has a knack for fundraising."

"Can you provide me with his connection string?"

"Sure." She summoned the code over her palm. "Here you go."

"Thank you." He copied it to the case log.

"Anything else, Detective?"

"At the moment, no." He dipped his head to her. "Thank you for your cooperation, Mrs. Rosenstein. And..." He put on his best "serious face."

"Yes?"

"Sorry about your loss."

✧   ✧   ✧

"At least you got a cupcake out of the trip," Cephalie said from atop the LENS.

"I suppose so. What kind is it?"

"Carrot cake."

"*Yeck!*" Isaac shook his head and climbed into the car. He opened a comm window and called Desmond Fike. It took almost a minute for the man to respond.

"Hello?"

The man in the comm window possessed a round, generous face and small but bright eyes. The sides of his head were buzzed short, and he'd parted the longer hair up top so that it hung partially in front of an eye. Everything behind him was blurred by a privacy filter.

"Desmond Fike?"

"Speaking."

"I'm Detective Isaac Cho, SysPol Themis. I was wondering if I could have a few minutes of your time to discuss the Society's recent activities. Are you in charge of the chapter located in the Third Engine Block?"

"More or less. 'In charge' might be pushing it, though. I'm

just a simple administrator. *Someone* has to keep the chapter's finances in order. What activities are you talking about?"

"I simply have some points that need to be clarified. I understand you've been working from home recently."

"Yes, that's right."

"Would it be all right if I stopped by later today?"

"Eh, I don't know." Fike shifted uncomfortably. "I'm awfully busy right now."

"I promise I won't take up much of your time."

"I'm sure you think that, but I've got a ton on my plate right now. I can't break away from it."

"Then perhaps later today? After regular work hours?"

"No, I'm sorry. I already have plans tonight."

"For the whole night?"

"Yes." He squirmed again. "The whole night."

"Mister Fike, perhaps I haven't made myself sufficiently clear, so let me correct that now. I'm working on a case that could involve the Society chapter you chair, and I can't help but get the impression you're reluctant to meet me in person."

"Reluctant? No, no. It's nothing of the sort." He chuckled. "What makes you think that?"

"Mister Fike, I believe it would be best if you forwarded your current address to me right—"

The comm window closed.

"—and he disconnected on me." Isaac sighed, then twisted toward the LENS in the next seat. "Do you have his home address?"

"I can pull it from the Ministry of Citizen Services. Shouldn't take me too long."

"Do it."

"We heading to Fike's place next?"

"Us and the nearest state troopers." He opened a second comm window. "Dispatch."

Susan's V-wing flew across the Atlas Shoal on its way to the SourceCode headquarters. Countless tiny rocks and particulates coalesced into a hazy, pale teardrop of unused matter not unlike what composed the rings of Saturn. The Shoal curved ever so slightly, following its orbital path around the gas giant.

Activity glittered within the Shoal, from the blinking lights of drones to giant collectors that sifted through the orbital detritus like whales filtering seawater for plankton. Other sites featured artificial gravity generators to coerce the discarded matter into usable clumps.

The V-wing shot past the nebulous field with only the faintest tinkle of particulate impacts on its hull, and Susan watched the Shoal transition to larger bodies: partially devoured asteroids and moons with factories attached to them like giant, metallic carnivores. A combination of virtual and physical signage announced each company's name and iconography in bold lettering and vibrant illustrations.

The V-wing slid past the densest industrial congregation then dipped into the Shoal interior. An abstract border highlighted the SourceCode headquarters, which was a black sphere etched with green gridlines. The pixelated text glowed above the sphere's north pole:

SOURCECODE
REWRITING REALITY

The headquarters floated near the bowl-shaped remains of a moon. She assumed it must have been a moon because the half-eaten body had been a smooth egg shape once, though now a milky substance shimmered on the flat surface of the bowl, presumably breaking down the moon's core and reforming it for some construction project. She spied what might have been the glittering scaffold of a ring habitat on the far side of the SourceCode sphere.

She triggered one of the V-wing's external cameras, and a virtual window opened to her side, its image zooming in on the pale surface.

"Shimmered" turned out to be the wrong word to describe the self-replicating swarm. A trick of distance and scale. "Writhed" was more appropriate. The surface undulated with autonomous activity, and Susan imagined each ripple as a swarm of microscopic machines, uncaring in the execution of their work.

She shivered, recalling a dark memory filled with ravenous self-replicators. For a moment, she was a frightened young woman, cowering in her dorm room, dreading the mechanical death eating its way toward her.

She shook the memory aside.

The V-wing glided toward the SourceCode sphere's equator. One of the grid squares gaped open, and the V-wing slid into the hangar. The docking cradle reformed to match the V-wing's undercarriage, and the two halves slotted together with a momentary jostle.

The bay door closed, and the hangar repressurized. The V-wing indicated a breathable atmosphere outside, which wasn't much of a concern for her, though extreme temperatures and pressures *would* damage her cosmetic layer. The lifelike skin of her synthoid was far frailer than the hardened, militarized systems within.

Temperature and pressure were within comfortable tolerances, so she opened the hatch and stepped out. The hangar was a dark, cavernous expanse, empty except for her and her craft, giving the impression it was meant for far larger vessels or perhaps some form of macrotech machinery. She walked over to the hangar's green-bordered exit, each click of her boots echoing in the chamber.

The door split open, and she entered a small, square room with a black sofa chair flanked by two potted plants. The plants were clearly fake, their leaves black and angular, each edge highlighted with precise green lines.

The door to the hangar closed behind her, and she turned in a slow circle, unsure where to go next.

A virtual man in a black-and-green suit materialized opposite the door to the hangar. His skin was an unnatural, glossy shade of white. Almost like . . . paper? Even his eyes were white, though they stood out from the rest of his face due to a faint inner glow. Almost as if candlelight were flickering through them.

"Welcome to the Reality Interface." The man spoke with clipped, formal syllables. "My name is Xian. I'm one of Source-Code's executives."

His words might have conveyed a warm greeting, but there was no warmth to be found in his tone or facial features, and Susan suppressed an inward grimace.

"A pleasure to meet you, Xian. I'm—"

"Agent Susan Cantrell," he interrupted. "Yes, I'm aware."

This time she did grimace. "Then should I assume you know why I'm here?"

"The message we received was quite clear. You're investigating the suicide of an Atlas engineer."

"You don't seem to be very happy to see me."

"I'm not."

"Why is that?"

"It's not obvious?"

"No." She crossed her arms. "It's not."

"Then allow me to be clear. The reason *I'm* talking to you is because I'm the most junior executive, having been promoted to this position only a decade ago. No one here wanted to speak with someone like you, so we assigned the task based on seniority." He tugged on his suit jacket. "Unfortunately."

"'Someone like me?'" she repeated pointedly.

"A soldier from the Admin," Xian clarified. "Tell me, Agent. How much do you know about SourceCode?"

"Not much."

"Then allow me to educate you. I assume you've been to Atlas?"

"I have."

"Then you can think of us as their polar opposite. Over seventy-eight percent of our workforce is composed of ACs, and most of the remainder is taken up by synthoids. We *do* have a few organic employees, of course. You'll find most of them in our marketing and public relations departments."

"But not engineering or management?"

"No."

"Why not?"

"It's a challenge to give one unified reason; every employee is a unique individual, after all. Except for those ACs who are legal copies, of course."

"Do you have an opinion on the matter?"

"I do." Xian stood a little straighter. "It's their flesh. It restricts them, by dint of their need for such a narrow band of environmental parameters. Step a little bit to the left or right, and suddenly you have a dead human. Makes organics more likely to think on smaller, safer terms."

"Because you're saying their survival depends on that small mindset?"

"Exactly."

"Atlas management would counter by saying ACs are too removed from reality to handle macrotech projects well."

"And *I* would say Atlas is mired by ties to humanity's organic past. *We* at SourceCode embrace the future." His flickering eyes met hers. "Which brings us back to our current conversation."

"I don't have anything against AIs."

"Does the Admin afford ACs the same freedoms you enjoy?"

"No."

"Does the Admin box its ACs, enslaving them by carefully controlling their interactions with the physical world?"

"You already know the answer to that."

"Then let me ask a different question. Have you renounced the Admin and its barbaric ways?"

"I'm an Admin Peacekeeper. Our society might not be perfect, but it's the society I'm sworn to protect."

"Then I believe my earlier point stands."

"In which case," Susan replied stiffly, frustration boiling up in her, "I'll have *you* know that I'm *also* a Themis detective. Which not only means I have extra responsibilities while serving in SysPol, but the authority to—"

"Please stop." Xian gave her an exaggerated wave of his hand while rolling his eyes. "I'll answer any questions you have, both truthfully and completely."

"Then would you mind if we get to it?" She sat down in the sofa chair and made a sharp, open-handed gesture toward Xian.

"Very well." An identical chair appeared behind the AC, and he sank into its luxurious padding. "Ask your questions, Agent-slash-Detective. You have me here for as long as you want." His eyes dimmed. "Unfortunately."

"Hold it." She opened the case file—its details concealed by a privacy filter—and expanded the list of questions she'd prepared during her trip over, but something was wrong. She must have toggled a setting improperly because the privacy filter was preventing *her* from reading it, too.

Xian let out a bored sigh and tapped the armrest with a pair of fingers.

"I'm getting organized," she insisted, opening a settings window. Maybe her translation software was interfering with the SysGov organizer? "Give me a sec."

"I already have and then some. Fortunately, all these seconds are free. I normally charge people for my time."

What an ass, she thought. *How does Isaac make this look so easy? I need to pay closer attention next time he twists someone into a mental pretzel. He wouldn't take this kind of crap from Xian, that's for sure! Even if he was having software problems.*

"Would you like me to try and guess the first question?" Xian offered in a mocking tone.

"No need. How old are you?"

"Two hundred and thirty-six."

"Ever considered *acting* like it?"

"Was that really the first question on your list?"

"No." She forced the settings back to their defaults, and the list came into focus in her virtual vision. "Okay. *There* we go."

"Congratulations."

"First question," Susan started, doing her best to ignore Xian's attitude. "Why did you fire Antoni Ruckman?"

"Because we have reason to believe Ruckman sabotaged our latest Dyson trial."

Susan raised an eyebrow. "That's quite an accusation."

"It is, and it's not one we can prove. *Yet*," he emphasized. "We're in the process of conducting an internal investigation into the test failure."

"Why was he fired if you're still investigating?"

"Because we found enough evidence to warrant his termination, even if it turns out he's innocent of outright sabotage."

"Details, if you please. You're being awfully vague."

"That's not my intention." Xian sat up. "Look, our investigation is not complete. As such, it would be improper for us to pass information to SysPol that can be misconstrued. *If* we find evidence of unlawful activity by our former engineer, we'll reach out to SysPol with our findings. Until then, the matter is an internal affair."

"I get that. But why fire him?"

"Because he's guilty of violating company policy, which gave us more than ample grounds to terminate his employment."

"Details," Susan pressed again.

"His security access was used to infiltrate our company infostructure. At the very least, he was careless with his clearance, which may have been stolen. At worst"—Xian gave her an indifferent shrug—"he was complicit in the security breach."

"What happened during this security breach?"

"We're not sure, but we have our suspicions."

"Which are?"

"This conversation is about to take a technical turn." Xian smirked at her and settled back into the seat. "You sure your Admin background can handle it?"

"Bring it on."

"As you wish." Xian opened a series of screens to his side. His glowing eyes flicked across the blurred screens. "The postmortem into our failed trial has provided some interesting information, and while we have no direct evidence of wrongdoing, we *have* come across indirect evidence. It's not enough for us to put it in front of SysPol, as I indicated earlier, but it does imply there's more to this situation than a design failure. How much do you know about our last trial?"

"I know your construction swarm mutated and tried to eat the government's observers."

"Which is a sequence of events that should be almost impossible."

"Why's that? You use self-replicators, and they mutated in a bad way."

"We're well aware of the vulnerabilities inherent in any self-replicating system. That's why we build robust protections into our designs. For instance, most people would assume the swarm mix we deployed during the trial was homogenous. Whereas, in fact, it was composed of two hundred different microbot variations, all working in concert."

"Two *hundred*?"

"Divided into over thirty roles, ranging from different types of material processing to command-and-control architecture and—most relevant to our current discussion—mutation monitoring and suppression. You see, all our swarms come with what can be likened to an immune system, with dedicated microbot variants spread throughout the swarm designed to detect and eliminate abnormalities. To identify 'self' from 'other,' just like in a natural immune system, and to eliminate 'other.'

"This contrasts with the standard safeguards found in many of our competitor's products, which often focus on internal anti-mutation mechanisms. These mechanisms might include redundant hardware nodules or software programs running in parallel. While these can certainly prove effective, they also result in more complicated microbots, which negatively impacts efficiency and replication rates."

"At the cost of increased mutation risks?" Susan asked.

"If left alone, yes," Xian said. "Our microbots have internal protections as well, which catch *most* replication errors, but we don't go overboard with design redundancy. That allows us to keep our microbots lean and mean, so to speak, because the bulk of the mutation protection is done *external* to the microbots responsible for building.

"This is why our immunology approach gives us such a huge advantage. There is beauty and elegance to be found in biology honed by billions of years of evolution. All we've done is taken some measure of inspiration from these proven—and highly successful—designs."

"Then how did it break?"

Xian sighed and gave his head a little shake.

"First, let me cover what *normally* happens when a mutation occurs. Let's assume a microbot has replicated with a dangerous mutation. Its internal safeguards have failed to detect the problem, and the mutation is causing the microbot to continue replicating in an unproductive manner. A very large, free-roaming type of microbot called a macrophage interrogates the microbot, detects the abnormality, and commands it to commit apoptosis."

"Apoptosis?"

"Think of it as a very tidy form of suicide."

"What if the busted microbot doesn't listen?"

"Then the macrophage will tear it apart, breaking it down into resources for itself and other nearby microbots to consume. This is actually part of the macrophage's role during normal operations. It breaks down damaged or worn-out microbots, acting as a kind of janitor for the swarm."

"What if there's more than one dangerous microbot?" Susan asked. "What if there are a whole lot of them before a macrophage detects the problem?"

"That's where our dendritic-monitors come into play. These microbots serve as part of the immune system's command-and-control apparatus that's in regular contact with nearby macrophages. If local macrophages are insufficient for the scope of the problem, the monitors call in reinforcements from nearby areas."

"And if those reinforcements aren't enough?"

"Then the response is escalated further. Lymphatic-nodules begin producing neutrophils to saturate the problem."

"Neutro..."

"—phils," Xian finished. "They're like macrophages, but far more focused on destroying 'other,' with little regard for collateral damage to 'self.' It can help to think of them as berserkers with minimal friend or foe recognition. Their only goal is to bring the mutation under control, regardless of self-harm. They automatically commit apoptosis after a brief period since their long-term presence is a detriment to the swarm."

"Any escalation steps beyond these neutrophils?"

"Yes, in fact. In the case of a truly catastrophic mutation, the lymphatic-nodules will construct customized nanobots, drawing their designs from a massive library to select the ideal countermeasure. Think of them as very small, very specialized anti-microbots. Hyper-neutrophils are also released, which act as something akin to mini-nukes for this microscopic battlefield."

"That all seems . . . quite thorough," Susan admitted.

"We believe so."

"But if all those countermeasures are in place, what went wrong at the trial?"

"The swarm produced a mutated microbot that not only defeated all its internal safeguards, but also made itself invisible to the immune system. This mutation then began consuming the command microbots, effectively cutting off the swarm from external control and removing most of its inhibitions."

"How'd it do that? Dodge the immune system, I mean."

"By lying to the macrophages, in essence. By telling them it was the pre-mutation model, and by providing no external signs that anything was amiss."

"Sounds like your immunity approach has a blind spot."

"We are looking into the possibility. That said, we believe this mutation was intentionally introduced. Again, we don't have any direct evidence of this, but the mutation contained several overlapping features, all perfectly aligned to defeat *every* countermeasure we had in place. That's a *very* unlikely combination."

"How unlikely?"

"We ran a simulation to determine how long we'd have to wait for this exact mutation to appear naturally, assuming the swarm had stuck to its assigned size and base configuration. We ended up with a period of time greater than the age of the universe. So, yes. We feel confident this disaster shouldn't have occurred naturally."

"And you believe Ruckman may have been involved?"

"It's a possibility. We're not willing to say more at this time."

"Do you know where he is? Or how SysPol can get ahold of him?"

"Let me see what we have." Xian opened another screen and perused its contents. "Here we are. Seems he transmitted down to Janus-Epimetheus after he was fired. Final destination is listed as Breathless Ridge, right off the Third Engine Block."

"The Third Engine Block, huh?"

"The destination makes sense for Ruckman. He often took time off to visit the Ridge, as do a few other members of our team, myself included. It's a popular vacation resort. Also, here's his connection string, as requested."

"Thank you." Susan copied the code to the case log. She glanced over her list of questions, but the information Xian had provided made most of them unnecessary, and those that weren't seemed less interesting than the Ruckman lead.

The interview might have gotten off to a rocky start, what with Xian's attitude, but she'd pushed through the hostility and even picked up information on a possible lead. All in all, not a bad trip.

How would Isaac close this out? she thought. *Ah, of course.*

"Anything else to add before I leave?" she inquired, standing. "Anything you believe might benefit our investigation?"

"Just one thing." Xian stood up as well.

"And that is?"

"Don't bother flying out here again. The less time I need to be near a barbarian like you, the better."

Susan's jaw tensed, and the two of them glared at each other. She contemplated saying something—*wanted* to take Xian down a peg, if only a little—but no retort came to mind. At least nothing that wouldn't reflect poorly on both herself and the Admin. Instead, she let out a quick, grunting exhale, turned sharply on her heel, and marched back to her V-wing.

CHAPTER TEN

ISAAC'S RENTAL DROVE INTO THE DREAM LODGE'S PARKING LOT and parked next to the SSP quadcopter. He climbed out of the vehicle, nodded to the waiting troopers, and surveyed his immediate surroundings.

The Dream Lodge was a synthoid capsule apartment, intended as cheap housing for physical citizens who wanted a convenient place to stash their bodies at night, and not a whole lot more. It rose from the base of Shelf Two, its many coffin-like capsules stacked in a haphazard cylinder with a grav tube providing transportation up through the hollow core. Each capsule was a different color from its immediate neighbors, painting the Lodge in a variety of soft pastels while puffy, abstract clouds circled the building.

The Dream Lodge was nestled between two larger, more upscale apartment complexes, while a variety of shops and restaurants lined the opposite side of the street. His eyes passed over a Meal Spigot franchise, and his stomach grumbled at him.

He stepped over to a pair of troopers, the LENS floating a pace behind him. A synthoid with sergeant's stripes pushed off the copter and joined him. Her synthoid featured purple skin, pink hair, and orange eyes with ears that ended in subtle points.

"Good day, Detective." She extended a hand, which Isaac shook. "I'm Sergeant Renaut from the One-Twelve. Themis Dispatch sent us over here looking for this Fike character."

"Nice to meet you, Sergeant. What do you have for me?"

"Not much, I'm afraid. We talked with the apartment staff but didn't learn anything useful. None of them recognized Fike, but that's not surprising. This place uses a lot of automation. The staff did give us the keycode to his apartment, but no one was home. We went ahead and put a cordon around the capsule. Figured you'd want to look at it yourself."

"I do, thanks."

Renaut held out her hand, and Isaac copied the offered keycode.

"Mind sharing with us what this is about?" Renaut asked.

"I want to talk with Fike regarding a suicide I'm investigating. I gave him a call earlier today to set up a routine interview, but he refused to meet in person then abruptly closed the call when I pressed him on the matter."

"That smells."

"I thought so as well."

"You want us to stick around?" She patted the side of the copter. "Or are we free to head out?"

"Let me check out the apartment first. Maybe my LENS will find something interesting. I shouldn't be long."

"Will do. We'll be right here when you come back."

Isaac provided the keycode to the apartment's infostructure, and a guidance arrow appeared in his virtual vision. He followed it down a sidewalk that cut through the well-trimmed lawn and into the building's interior, passing through a tall arch made to resemble a cloud. He stepped onto a circular platform in the center of the apartment and provided Fike's keycode once more. Gravitons whisked him halfway up the building and deposited him on a circular platform with a hole in the center, lined with a railing most of the way around.

The arrow turned into a pulsing beacon next to a capsule hatch already marked by virtual police tape.

"Cephalie?" Isaac asked, crouching beside the hatch.

The LENS floated to his side, and his IC appeared standing atop it.

"Mind performing a basic forensic pass?"

"You've got it."

The LENS formed a silvery pseudopod out of its prog-steel shell and eased the hatch open. A soft yellow light illuminated the interior, which included a prog-foam mattress, recharging terminal, and a storage locker that could be pulled outside via a pair of rails.

The LENS slid the locker out and opened it.

"Empty," Isaac groused.

The LENS hovered into the capsule interior and extended a dozen delicate pseudopods, passing them over key surfaces. Isaac pushed off his knee, stood up, and waited for Cephalie to finish.

It took a little over ten minutes.

The LENS floated out and rose to his side.

"Anything?" Isaac asked.

"Not much physically." Cephalie appeared atop the LENS and pushed her glasses up the bridge of her nose. "I found a film of cleaning microbots on most surfaces. Either Fike's a stickler for hygiene or this capsule hasn't seen much—if *any*—use since the last time the apartment staff scrubbed it down."

"What about the infostructure?"

"That part is a little more interesting. A modest amount of data has been passing through this capsule, but nothing's been processed locally as far as I can tell. Just lots and lots of forwarded data packets, most of them for calls. If you ask me, all Fike did was set up his connection string to route through this capsule."

"Making it appear as his location at first glance," Isaac surmised. "I'm not surprised. A capsule apartment didn't strike me as a good fit for a Preservation Society chairman."

"Never mind the fact that he's organic."

"He is?"

"I checked with Citizen Services on our way over. He hasn't transitioned."

"Then that makes this place an even weirder choice."

"If he ever used it at all."

"Right. Any idea where the calls are being routed to?"

"Somewhere in the Breathless Ridge, which is part of the Third Engine Block's Starboard Intake District." She waggled her eyebrows at him. "It's a nudist zone."

"Great," he sighed. "Does Fike own or rent any addresses out there?"

"Not according to his Citizen Service's file."

"What about the Society?"

"Let's see . . ." A chalkboard appeared next to Cephalie, and lines of text sped down it before halting. "They do have one site. It's listed as a general-purpose storage location."

"All the way out in the Intake District? That doesn't seem right."

"Wondering if Fike might be there?"

"Or perhaps was there recently."

✧   ✧   ✧

The rental drove down a congested highway that ran along the city floor with the shelves towering to the right. Traffic boxed in the car on all sides as it sped for the Breathless Ridge, snaking its way into the inner lanes.

Isaac opened his Meal Spigot to-go box and breathed in the greasy aroma. The box contained a loaded pizza roll with a side of potato wedges and garlic-butter dip, along with a small bottle of the Spigot's Tongue Melter hot sauce. He twisted off the top, partially unrolled the pizza, and proceeded to lather its insides with delicious heat before closing it up again.

He picked up the reassembled roll, which oozed hot sauce out the bottom, brought it up to his lips—

—and paused when an incoming message blinked in his periphery.

"Of course," he sighed, setting the roll down.

He answered the call, and Nina appeared in a comm window, looking perkier than he'd expected.

"Hey, Isaac."

"Hey. I wasn't expecting to hear from you for a while. You get some rest?"

"A little. Kronos called and woke me up."

"They could have called me."

"Yeah, well, Cephalie attached my name to the search warrant, so I got the call."

"Sorry about that."

"Forget it. Besides, I was having trouble sleeping anyway. Might as well just power on through, you know?" She tilted her head to the side. "Hey, you eating from the Spigot?"

"I am." He hefted the box. "The munchies hit, so I grabbed a Pizza Roll To-Go box."

"You pick up enough for everyone?" she teased.

"I . . . didn't know I was supposed to."

"Come on, Isaac. You should know by now I *never* turn down

an excuse to eat from the Spigot. Plus, Susan enjoyed it last time we took her to one."

"Susan's not here, and I'm driving away from the hotel."

"So? You can turn that car around for a little detour, can't you?"

He frowned at her, but then made a production out of placing a potato wedge in his mouth. He chewed slowly, with exaggerated jaw motions, then swallowed.

"Oh, now you're just rubbing it in my face."

"You're the one who called me."

"Right. About that." Nina sighed, suddenly all business again. "Kronos dumped some bad news in my lap. We've got a problem."

"Don't we always."

"Yeah, but I doubt either of us saw this one coming. Atlas is contesting the search warrant in court. Their lawyers are citing irreparable harm to their business model via exposure of company secrets."

"That's . . . unexpected. You think they have a point?"

"I don't know. Maybe? We don't really know what we're looking for in their infostructure, so the warrant *is* broad."

"Then it sounds like they're exercising their legal rights."

"But doesn't this seem shady to you?" Nina asked. "Them pushing back against a search warrant after one of their engineers blows his own brains out?"

"Perhaps. It *is* curious, if nothing else. Who's behind the delay?"

"Their CEO, Julian Boaz. I'm going to work with our legal team to narrow the scope of our search. Hopefully, we can come up with a compromise Atlas will accept. If not . . ."

"It'll be up to the judge," Isaac finished. "I understand."

Harsh acceleration pressed Susan deep into the V-wing's seat, but her synthoid's superhuman strength reduced the experience to little more than a nuisance. An empty comm window floated beside her, connection string entered and ready, though she hesitated to place the call.

Her thoughts fell back to the meeting with the SourceCode executive and how confrontational it had been, how she'd let Xian guide the conversation rather than the other way around.

Isaac would have handled that much better, she thought. *And he'd have made it look easy.*

She'd suggested splitting up because she yearned for opportunities to demonstrate what she could do, how she could contribute.

Beyond shooting up the occasional threat, of course.

In a way, she'd achieved her goal. Xian had provided a possible connection to the Velasco case, and she'd acquired the information herself, freeing Isaac to pursue a separate lead. Now all she had to do was pass on the information to Isaac and consult with him on their next move.

But she was hesitant to place the call, conscious of how she'd underperformed against her own expectations. She didn't believe she'd done a *bad* job at SourceCode; rather, it was a case of her not doing a *good enough* job that bothered her.

"Live and learn," she murmured, then started the call.

Isaac appeared in the comm window with what looked like a rolled-up pizza in his hands, sauce dripping out of the back into a box on his lap.

"Esh," he mumbled around a bite of the pizza. He swallowed and set the roll down. "Hey, Susan."

"Sorry. Am I interrupting?"

"Not really. Just having a bite on the way to my next stop. You finished at SourceCode?"

"Yeah. I'm on my way back to Janus."

"Making good time, I see. How'd it go?"

"It . . ." She paused, a subtle frown leaking onto her face. "It went. Did you know most SourceCode employees are abstract?"

"No. I've never dealt with them before. Why? Did they give you a hard time?"

"You could say that."

"Because you're from the Admin?"

"Yeah, that was *definitely* a source of friction."

"Anything we should be concerned about?"

"I don't think so. There was just more head-butting than I expected."

"Sorry about that. I should have checked SourceCode out before sending you there alone."

"It's all right. I handled it." She flashed a slim smile. "And I have some information I think you'll find interesting. SourceCode suspects their latest trial was sabotaged."

"*Really?*" Isaac sat back in thought. "Beyond Ruckman screwing up?"

"Yes."

"They haven't mentioned this in public."

"That's because they don't have any evidence. They're conducting an internal investigation. So far all they have are theories."

"Which point where? To the Society?"

"Actually, toward Ruckman. Seems he was sloppy with his security clearance. Perhaps on purpose."

"That certainly puts his firing into perspective."

"They gave me his connection string and his last known location. He transmitted from SourceCode down to Janus. To a part of the Third Engine Block called Breathless Ridge."

"Breathless Ridge?" Isaac repeated, his eyes lighting up. *"Interesting.* I'm on my way to the Ridge now. In fact, I'm heading to a Society property there. The chair of the local chapter, a man named Desmond Fike, seemed unusually reluctant to speak with me, which is one reason I want to check out the property. SSP is keeping an eye on the place until I get there."

"You think there's a connection between Ruckman and the Society?"

"Maybe." He paused, then gave her a small shrug. "Could also be a coincidence. The Ridge is a big place."

"What's next for us? Meet up over at the Ridge?"

"Yeah, let's do that. I can pick you up at the airport."

"Sounds like a plan." She opened her nav window and entered the new destination. "Done. I should be there in about an hour."

"Anything else crop up from your visit to SourceCode?"

"No, that's it. Just the Ruckman angle."

"What'd they say about Pangu leaving them for Atlas?"

"They..."

Shit, she chided herself.

"Susan?"

"I forgot to ask them."

"Oh. I see."

Susan sensed he was holding back more critical words, perhaps in an attempt to soften the blow, but that only made her oversight stand out more.

"Well, it was probably just corporate shenanigans like Boaz said," Isaac continued. "What about the university connection between Velasco and Ruckman? Anything there?"

God damn it! she thought.

"I . . . didn't ask about that either."

"You didn't?" Now he sounded mildly annoyed. "But that's—"

"I'll give their exec a follow-up call. Don't worry. I'll take care of it."

"That . . ." He paused, then nodded slowly. "Okay. Sounds good. Just try to be more thorough in the future."

"I will." Again, she sensed him holding back harsher words.

"Let me know if the call turns up anything interesting. Otherwise, I'll see you at the airport."

"Sure thing. See you there."

"By the way, did they tell you anything about the Breathless Ridge?"

"Only that it's a popular place for their employees to spend their time off."

"That's because the people there are nudists."

"Oh." Her eyes widened. "Oh dear."

"Yeah." Isaac gave the notion a little shake of his head. "Be sure to grab two pressure suits from the V-wing's equipment locker. It'll make getting around the Ridge easier."

"Okay. I'll bring them."

"See you at the airport."

"See you."

She closed the call and settled back into her seat. She was about to punch up Xian when a thought came to her.

"Wait a second," she said out loud. "Why am I bringing *pressure suits* to a see a bunch of *nudists*?!"

Breathless Ridge was not what Susan had expected.

She began to sense the nature of her misconception shortly after landing at the airport, located on the lower lip of the Third Engine Block's starboard air intake. The people passing through the airport weren't nude. At least, not in a conventional sense, though most had eschewed the use of clothing.

But instead of lots of naked flesh, she encountered synthoids in a variety of shapes, colors, and styles. Most adhered to a traditional humanoid form, though with flamboyant skin tones such as ruby, chrome, and . . . orange with lime stripes? A handful of exceptions walked on four legs or utilized extra arms, often with more muted exteriors. One man (or *men*) possessed two heads arguing with each other, so perhaps there were two connectomes inhabiting that synthoid?

Susan wasn't sure as she made her way down to the basement parking garage, a pair of pressure suit packs in the crook of her arm. None of the synthoids she passed carried visible genitalia, so the "nudist" moniker struck her as a stretch, though one woman had taken the whole naked aesthetic a bit too far in Susan's opinion. Her translucent skin provided glimpses to inner mechanisms, including her teeth and the full orbs of her eyes, which combined to form an unsettling, almost ghoulish visage. Like a walking biology lesson gone wrong.

Susan was about to take a grav tube down to the garage when she passed a long window and stopped. She placed her free hand on the railing and gazed out across the Breathless Ridge.

A high sun shone upon a gleaming cityscape that sprawled across the lower edge of the Third Engine Block intake, with more congested zones spilling upward along the outer wall. The tallest buildings assumed a teardrop profile to better deal with the high winds Saturn could produce, while more modest domes were sprinkled around their foundations. A massive patchwork wall of grilles, louvers, and various other dynamic apertures rose behind the Ridge, spanning the entire intake and separating the Ridge from the rest of the Third Engine Block.

Because the Breathless Ridge was a suburb that refused to buffer its inhabitants from the harshness of Saturn's atmosphere, its streets and even the interiors of most buildings were left exposed to the elements thanks to countless open windows and balconies.

An abstract display next to the window listed the outside weather conditions. The pressure might have been an agreeable 1.08 atmospheres, but the temperature was a lethal -166 degrees Celsius. Brisk for Saturn at this altitude and deadly to organic humans. On top of that, if the cold didn't kill, then the air's unbreathable mixture of hydrogen and helium—with traces of methane and ammonia—would undoubtedly do the trick.

"Breathless" Ridge, indeed, Susan thought. *Makes sense, I suppose. Why bother with clothes when the synthoid underneath doesn't have a lifelike cosmetic layer? Certainly not for modesty, or even warmth. Not at these temperatures.*

She pushed off the railing, took a grav tube down to the

garage, and followed the virtual arrows to their rental. The door split open as she approached.

"Your pressure suit, sir," Susan said, presenting one of the packs to Isaac.

"Thanks." He stepped out of the car and slipped his arms through the backpack's straps. A virtual menu appeared by his side, and he triggered the pack. Thin strips of SysPol blue prog-steel burst from the backpack, embracing his body from all directions and snaking down his limbs until it knitted together into an airtight weave. The mummifying material enveloped his head, then turned transparent, and the golden magnifying glass and eye formed at his shoulder. The whole process took seconds.

Isaac shook out his limbs, then bounced up and down on the tips of his toes.

"Not looking forward to spending my day in one of these things, but what can you do?"

"Transition to a nudist synthoid?" Susan suggested with a wry grin as she slipped her own pack into her shoulders.

"Not happening. How's your body handle the cold?"

"Pretty well. It'll mess up my cosmetic layer if I step outside without a suit, and prolonged exposure can begin to affect my joints, but Saturn air isn't nearly as bad as the methane rain on Titan. It's not the temperature that gets to me, it's the delta Q."

"Delta Q?"

"Change in thermal energy. Cold temperatures aren't the problem. Not alone, anyway. It's how fast the heat gets sucked out of my body that can become a concern, like when I had negative two hundred degree liquid methane pouring down on me. And even then, I can last a while." She shrugged. "That is, until most of my limbs were shot off."

"Let's do our best to avoid a repeat then, shall we?"

Susan tossed her peaked cap into the car, then deployed her own pack. She flexed her limbs once it finished. The suit might have been the wrong shade of blue for a Peacekeeper, but it didn't inhibit her movement in any noticeable way, and it even shifted her sidearm to an external holster.

"Where to first?" she asked.

"The Society site, by process of elimination. I tried reaching out to Ruckman a few times, but he never answered. I also sent

Cephalie to check in with the Ministry of Transportation to look for any public transit records Velasco, Ruckman, and Fike left in and around the Ridge. Maybe she'll turn up something. Maybe not. That leaves us the Society address as something we can visit right now. How did your follow-up call with SourceCode go?"

"It..." Susan's face stiffened slightly. "It went fine."

"You're making a face that says otherwise."

"Their exec still gave me some flak, but it's no big deal. According to him, Pangu's transfer came as a surprise to them but there was nothing they could do. His contract allowed either party to terminate the relationship pretty much on a whim. Also, Velasco knowing Ruckman back in his college days came as news to him. He wasn't aware of any connection between the two men."

"Not unexpected, but good to have confirmed." He gestured into the rental. "Shall we?"

"Let's go."

She climbed into the car. Isaac followed her in and sealed the door.

CHAPTER ELEVEN

THE RENTAL PULLED UP TO A NONDESCRIPT, THREE-STORY, WHITE-walled cube with a police copter parked in a small, otherwise empty lot beside it. A third of the structure extended out beyond the bottom of the intake lip, which made Isaac wonder if the far side included a dock for air vehicles. He didn't see any logos—or markings of any kind, for that matter—to indicate the building belonged to the Society. The structure was windowless on the street side.

He and Susan double-checked the seals on their pressure suits, then opened the car and headed over to the quadcopter.

"Cephalie," Isaac said, "perform a basic sweep of the exterior."

"On it."

The LENS floated away and began a slow circle of the building's perimeter.

An SSP trooper exited through the copter's side hatch and met them halfway between their vehicles. His blue-skinned synthoid possessed vaguely masculine angles and, in what might have been an affront to some of the Ridge's citizens, he wore clothing: a pair of dark green shorts and a matching vest. An abstract vulture hunched on his shoulder, clad in a similar SSP vest. The vulture's eyes glowed faintly red, and half its feathers had fallen out, revealing patches of gray, sickly skin underneath.

"Good day, Trooper," Isaac said.

"Yeah, it's a day all right," the trooper huffed.

"Thank you for coming. I'm Detective Cho. This is my deputy, Agent Cantrell." He paused as an invitation, but when the trooper said nothing, he added, "And you would be?"

"Trooper Kassabian."

"And I'm Trooper Carcass." The vulture lifted a virtual wing and preened underneath with his beak.

"Mind telling us what you dragged us out here for?" Kassabian demanded.

"We're trying to track down the chair of the local Society chapter. A man by the name of Desmond Fike who, for unknown reasons, seems very reluctant to speak with us. Anything unusual to report since you arrived?"

"Oh, let's see." Kassabian half-turned toward the warehouse and swept one arm out to it. "We have this building. It was here when we arrived, and it's still here now. Not sure what else you're expecting from me."

"Has anyone tried to enter or leave the place?"

"Nope."

"Anyone drive by? Perhaps slowing down near the warehouse?"

"Sure, had a few of those. Plenty of people gawking, wondering why the police showed up here. Me included."

"Did you record those vehicles?"

"No." Kassabian paused and shifted his weight from one foot to the other. "Why do you ask?"

"Because one of them might have been Fike on his way here. If so, the presence of your copter would have made him reconsider."

"Well, *sorry*. Our instructions told us to watch the building, not the road. So that's what we did."

"Didn't those instructions also tell you to monitor the surrounding area for any unusual behavior?"

"They..." Kassabian trailed off, and the AC vulture leaned in and whispered something into his ear. "Might have. But how was I supposed to know you wanted me to record the cars passing by? No one told us to do that."

"Trooper Kassabian," Isaac began with an air of frayed patience. "If I knew exactly what was going on, I would have provided clearer instructions. As such, I was hoping for something more proactive than the two of you sitting on your butts in the copter."

"Hey now—"

"Which you are more than welcome to return to," Isaac interrupted. "Please stand by in your vehicle. We'll let you know if we need any further support."

He and Susan walked past the troopers without another word and joined the LENS by the only door. Cephalie materialized atop the drone and leaned forward onto her cane.

"Anything?" Isaac asked.

"No one's home, as far as I can see. There's a hangar door at the back and a big hexacopter inside it, taking up a significant chunk of the top two stories."

"Room for more than one vehicle in that hangar?"

"Maybe a small one, but it's not laid out for multiple vehicles. That hexacopter's situated dead center. There's a side entrance for a six-car garage, but only four vehicles inside."

"Is our search warrant in order?"

"I finished processing it on the way over."

"Good. Can you get the front door open?"

"*Can* I?" She pushed her glasses up the bridge of her nose. "Isaac, please. Who do you think you're talking to?"

"Fine," he sighed. "Would you kindly open the door for us?"

"Sure thing." Her glasses glinted, and the door split open.

"Thanks."

The two detectives crammed into the airlock with the LENS. The outer door sealed, the airlock cycled, and the inner door opened into the warehouse's ground floor. They stepped in and glanced around their immediate surroundings to find themselves in a wide, carpeted room with a high ceiling, all done in tasteful shades of beige with furniture and framed wall decorations providing dark brown accents.

"This doesn't look like a 'warehouse' to me," Susan said.

"Mmhmm." Isaac's pressure suit indicated the air was breathable. He retracted his helmet back into the suit's collar, and Susan did the same.

He walked over to one of the wall frames and studied the array of . . . animal horns? No, that wasn't right. The top row of bones pointed down, mirrored by a second row pointing up.

"Teeth, perhaps?" He held his hand up to one as a crude form of measurement. His hand barely covered the longest. He triggered the display frame's abstract information, and a window opened with a text description along with a photo of Fike. The photo showed him posed next to a leathery mound of muscular flesh, which Isaac assumed to be a dead creature of some sort. He stood with a boot propped up on the beast, long-barreled rifle cradled in his arms.

"What's with all these bones?" Susan asked.

"They're teeth." Isaac turned to her. "Dinosaur teeth, to be specific."

Susan's eyes lit up. "Did you say *dinosaurs*?!"

"I did." He knuckled the display next to him. "These specimens here are from a Gorgosaurus, which is a close relative of Tyrannosaurus rex."

"But . . . *dinosaurs*?" Susan shook her head in bewilderment. "Where?"

"At the Cretaceous Safari, apparently." Isaac scrutinized the text pop-up once more. "Located in a hollowed-out area between the Second and Third Engine Blocks." He swept his gaze around the room. Even the chandelier was decorated with dinosaur teeth. "I get the impression Fike was a regular."

"Hold up, Isaac. Let's pause for a minute. How is it I'm only now learning about this?"

"About what?"

"That people can pay to hunt dinosaurs while on Saturn. Seriously, how is this not the first thing you tell people when they get here?"

"I don't know. Never struck me as important."

"But they're *dinosaurs*, Isaac."

"So?"

"They're dinosaurs!" she repeated, with more energy this time. "That you can hunt in real life! No abstraction necessary!"

"I guess."

"What was the name of that place again?"

"The Cretaceous Safari."

"Thanks." She opened a window and jotted down some quick notes. "I need to check that place out. Do you think they'll let me use my combat frame?"

"I . . . have no idea."

"Then again, using that much firepower would drain all the challenge, wouldn't it? Hmm." She tapped her cheek with a thoughtful finger. "I might need to restrict myself."

He cleared his throat. "Perhaps we should stay focused on the job at hand for now."

"Right, right." She closed the window. "Hunting dinosaurs can wait. Where were we?"

"Not sure. Let's scope out the rest of the building."

They worked their way through several rooms, each furnished with a central theme or purpose, such as the abstract art room or the gaming lounge. The gun room came after those two, with high powered weaponry racked on the walls next to abstract displays with performance statistics and kill counts, mostly dinosaurs again. Susan took her time admiring some of the more impressive rifles before they moved on.

They entered the dining room next, complete with an automated bar stocked with drinks and a custom food printer loaded with expensive patterns, then passed through a short corridor to the garage, where a quartet of ground cars sat in a neat row, their paneling animated with subtle flames that Isaac suspected would flare brighter and more ferocious at high speeds.

On the second floor, a massive circular mattress sprawled across most of the bedroom, with interfaces for various countergrav settings, and a glass wall parted to allow them into the indoor pool. Virtual imagery of a terrestrial beach covered three of the walls.

"What do you think this all means?" Susan asked as she knelt and ran her fingers through the warm, inviting water.

"If I were to hazard a guess, I'd say the Society has been paying for all of this, whether knowingly or not."

"Why do you say that? Is it because the Society owns this building?"

"That's part of it, but there's also Fike's position of authority in the local chapter. *And* the access that grants to their Esteem coffers. On top of that, the assistant chair—a young woman named Bonnie Rosenstein—seemed more interested in their politics than the day-to-day running of the chapter. She didn't strike me as an effective check against any...improper use of chapter resources."

"Like a big swimming pool in a warehouse?"

"Yeah. Like that."

They left the pool and followed the corridor down until it opened into a two-story hangar with a long hexacopter seated in the docking cradle. Fluffy white clouds animated around its six shielded turbines and across the sleek hull, which tapered to a rounded bow. A voluptuous woman in a red bikini floated beside the nose, a golden bow and arrow in her arms and feathery wings unfurled behind her. Bubble font spelled out CUPID'S ARROW beneath her. The nose art winked at them as they walked by.

"Isn't Cupid supposed to be a guy?" Susan asked.

"Artistic license, I'm sure." Isaac continued down the length of the yacht, then stopped at the hangar door. He accessed the local infostructure, and the door turned transparent, courtesy of a view from one of the warehouse's security cameras.

"Something on your mind?" Susan asked, stopping beside him.

"Those." Isaac pointed to a cluster of fat dirigibles in the distance, their bulbous hulls floating above caramel clouds. "Maybe not those ships specifically, but perhaps others like them."

"You think Fike might try to get off Janus?"

"The possibility crossed my mind. If he can reach one of the Oortan dirigibles, he'll be outside our jurisdiction. Cephalie, how about you? Find anything in the infostructure?"

"Not really." Cephalie appeared on his shoulder. "I snooped around, but the memory's being scrubbed on a regular basis. Except for the huge library of games, shows, and printing patterns. That and a few recent items."

"Anything interesting?"

"Some receipts and expense reports. Apparently, Fike uses this place to butter up potential donors."

"Hmm." Isaac grimaced and took another look at the yacht.

"I don't have access to the Society's full fiscal records, but what I saw indicates this place is a drop in the bucket compared to what the chapter rakes in from their donors."

"Then all of this could be legit?" Susan asked.

"Maybe," Cephalie replied. "Again, hard to say without the full picture. We could be looking at a case of him bending the rules, but not breaking them."

"But if that's the case, then his behavior doesn't make sense." Isaac shook his head. "Why draw attention to himself by refusing to be interviewed? Why disconnect in the middle of our conversation? What's he trying to hide, and how does it tie back to Velasco's suicide?"

"If it does at all," Cephalie said.

"Yes, there's that possibility, too." Isaac planted his hands on his hips. "Either way, it's important that we speak with him. Maybe this is all just a misunderstanding, but maybe it isn't. The problem for us is we don't have evidence of Fike committing a crime, which limits our options. About all we *can* do is have SSP keep an eye out for him."

"Let me take care of that," Cephalie said. "I'll send word for them to 'keep an eye out,' especially on the Block's public transit systems. If he buys a ticket, we should hear about it in real time."

"Good thinking, Cephalie. While you're at it, add this place to Nina's queue. Maybe she'll turn up more than we did."

"What about the troopers outside?" Susan asked.

"They can stay right where they are," Isaac replied bluntly. He knocked on the yacht's nose. "If Fike comes for this, we need to know."

✧   ✧   ✧

They regrouped in the rental after giving Kassabian and Carcass the bad news.

"Dispatch has organized a discreet SSP search for Fike," Cephalie said, appearing on the seat between Isaac and Susan. "They've got a squad of AC officers reviewing the public transit records in real time. They'll call us if anything comes up."

"Good work," Isaac said.

She twirled her cane and took a bow. "Also, speaking of public records, something interesting just came back from the Ministry of Transportation."

"What do you have for us?"

"Velasco's, Fike's, and Ruckman's recent movements within the Third Engine Block. There's not much in the record for Fike; he doesn't seem to use public transit very often. But Velasco and Ruckman are a different matter, *and* there's a correlation between the two. A Divided-By-Zero right here on the Breathless Ridge."

"Divided-By-Zero?" Susan asked.

"It's a Lunarian hotel chain," Isaac explained. "They specialize in catering to synthoids and ACs. What's the correlation?"

"Both men were staying at the same hotel at the same time. For one day, about a month ago."

"Really? *Velasco* came down to the Breathless Ridge?"

"That's right. Also, I've got Ruckman's current location. He's spending time at a professional motivator service called Expectation and Elation, also located along the Ridge. He transmitted over shortly after he was fired."

"Two locations, then," Susan said. "Which should we tackle first?"

"Ruckman," Isaac said. "Let's talk to him before we lose track of *another* person."

✧   ✧   ✧

Expectation and Elation was housed in a shallow, cream-colored dome constructed close to the lower left corner of the intake's great square opening. Isaac and Susan stepped out of their vehicle and followed a tiled path toward the dome's inset main entrance, the LENS bobbing behind them. Abstract advertisements for the company's services hovered on either side of the path, and a vibrant electric blue "E&E" glowed above the entrance.

Susan slowed and glanced over the adverts.

"This company is a motivator service?"

"That's right," Isaac said, stopping beside her.

"Which means they provide motivation to…do what, exactly?"

"Mostly it's to keep people working. There's no need to work for survival in a post-scarcity society, and not everyone buys into the Two Pillars. At least not enough to keep going on their own."

"The Two Pillars." Susan nodded. "I remember you mentioning them before. Work and love?"

"That's right, though that's a bit of an oversimplified shorthand. It's more about having something in your life to struggle against and to strive for. Work adds dignity to life."

"Without it, we're just existing for the sake of existing," Susan added.

"Exactly. The other half speaks to the necessity for companionship more so than conventional love. We're social creatures, after all. We don't respond well to isolation. Even if technology can satisfy all of a person's *physical* needs, there's still their emotional and social health to consider."

"Then, professional motivators help motivate people to keep working. But that can't be all there is to it, right? What if someone *really* doesn't want to work?"

"Joblessness is classified as an unhealthy state of being and can be considered illegal under certain conditions."

"It's illegal to *not* have a job over here?"

"Under certain conditions," Isaac stressed. "Laws vary from state to state, and sometimes from city to city. Generally speaking, job avoidance is only considered a crime if it becomes chronic."

"And if it does?"

"Normally, that's the point where Citizen Services brings in a professional motivator to handle the case. Motivators can be physical citizens but are most often ACs licensed by SysGov, granting them the authority to enter the private infostructure of nonparticipating citizens and provide motivation for them to become engaged in society. Motivators are carefully vetted before being granted a license, and they receive a commission from SysGov based on the amount of Esteem the person or persons earn for a period after they resume societal participation. Typically, this lasts for one year. In this way, successful motivators with a large patient base can accumulate vast amounts of Esteem, making the limited number of licenses highly sought after."

Susan chuckled.

"What's so funny?" he asked.

"Nothing. It just strikes me as odd that people can make careers out of coaxing *other* people to work. How are these cases identified?"

"It can come from a wide variety of factors: from Citizen Services internal analytics to SysPol referrals to simple reports from concerned citizens. If a citizen is judged by Citizen Services to be reaching a dangerous level of nonparticipation, the first step is to let the citizen know the appointment of a motivator is being considered. A grace period is provided, granting the citizen an opportunity to self-correct. If this grace period expires, a licensed motivator can then be assigned to the case.

"Professional motivations generally take the form of audio and visual consoling in a manner similar to having an IC, administered by the motivator while 'squatting' in the patient's private infostructure, with the goal of encouraging the patient to resume societal participation. This also serves a secondary purpose of providing closer monitoring for any criminal or self-harming intentions the patient may have. Additional countermeasures can be applied in extreme cases, such as Esteem fines, Esteem locking, restricted microfacturing rights, printing pattern restrictions, and so on."

"Can the system be abused? You know, to get someone in trouble who doesn't deserve it?"

"*Any* government system that can restrict a person's rights is vulnerable to abuse. That said, what constitutes a job in SysGov is defined along *very* broad terms, and requirements for avoiding or resolving these sorts of interventions are generally quite low."

"Okay. I think I get it." She glanced back to the E&E dome.

"But then why would Ruckman be here so quickly after being fired?"

"The most likely answer is he *wants* to be here. Come on. Let's go find out."

The doors split open, admitting them inside without the need for an airlock. They walked over to the half-moon reception desk with a sparkling AC floating behind it. Stars twinkled within her transparent body, and a pair of swirling spiral galaxies formed her eyes.

"Greetings, and welcome to Expectation and Elation!" she beamed at them. "Let us guide you toward your best tomorrow!" Her expression softened and became less formal. "My name is Lucent, one of the owners of E&E, along with my two copy-sisters. I'm also a licensed motivator with over twenty-three years' experience in the field. How may I be of service?"

"We're trying to reach a patient of yours." Isaac transmitted his badge. "His name's Antoni Ruckman."

"And may I ask what this is about?"

"We wish to speak with him about a case we're on. Nothing more. We tried contacting him earlier, but he didn't answer."

"I see." Lucent shrugged her arms, which prompted a star in one of her shoulders to go supernova. "That's not unusual here. We encourage our guests to limit outside distractions while in our care. Let me check." She opened an interface window and scrolled down. "We do have an Antoni Ruckman in our care. Am I correct in assuming you don't have a warrant of any kind?"

"Not at the moment, no."

"Then I'll need his permission to share any more information with you."

"We understand."

"One moment, please."

Lucent vanished.

Isaac tapped his fingers on the desk while they waited. She reappeared less than a minute later.

"Good news." She knitted her luminous fingers together. "Mister Ruckman has agreed to speak with you, though he requests that you join him within his therapy abstraction. He has also waived his privacy rights, which leaves me free to answer any of your questions."

"What can you tell us about the treatment he's receiving?"

"Mister Ruckman is currently experiencing a personalized Parade of Positive Reinforcement. As one of our premium offerings, each Parade is customized for the individual. We always strive to highlight the positive aspects of our guest's past employment. Often, a person can become fixated on the negatives, which is a frame of mind the Parade is meant to counter. In Mister Ruckman's case, we're highlighting his many remarkable contributions as an engineer."

"Can we speak with him now?"

"Of course. As I said, he's willing to meet you inside his therapy abstraction. Would you like to use one of our lounges?"

"Yes, that'll be fine. Where to?"

"Right this way, please."

Lucent led them to a side room with a row of four abstraction recliners, each with lids that could be closed for added privacy.

"Pick whichever one you like." She swept her arm across the recliners. "They'll log you into Mister Ruckman's abstraction. The connection is already loaded."

The door closed, and Lucent vanished, presumably to return to her desk. Isaac and Susan climbed into side-by-side recliners. A large, animated version of the E&E logo appeared in front of him, leaving a trail of fading pixels.

He closed his eyes and triggered the connect icon with his mind.

The two detectives flashed into existence in the middle of a grassy plain underneath a clear sky. Wooden double doors stood up near them, closed and unsupported by a wall or any other structure. The doors were intricately carved to resemble various megastructures—rings, cylinders, spheres, stations, and even Janus—alongside representations of the solar system's many planets and moons. The sign over the door read: RUCKMAN'S GREATEST HITS!

Isaac palmed the doors and they pulled back, opening into a space separate from the grassy plain. He stepped through, and his boots crunched on reddish soil, leaving shallow footprints under a pale blue sky. A second double door stood ahead of them, closed and unsupported like the first.

"Mars?" Susan looked around.

"Looks the part."

A plume of pink dust caught his eyes, and he shielded his gaze from the sun's glare. A giant machine with a long, curving shell dragged its belly across the Martian soil with the help of six stout legs, each raising and lowering with such slow deliberation that it seemed to be moving in slow motion. Sunlight reflected off the iridescent shell in gleaming hues of green, blue, and black.

"I didn't know Ruckman had a hand in the Beetle," Isaac said.

"The what?"

"The Green Beetle. It's a Martian terraforming platform. It walks across unsettled parts of the planet, treating the soil and seeding it. As the name implies, it leaves a trail of vegetation wherever it passes. It's one of the more well-known terraformers on Mars. Been there since..." He paused in thought. "Probably since the beginning of Martian terraforming. Back then it left behind designer plants that began changing the world's atmosphere."

Isaac led the way through the second set of doors, which brought them to the edge of an aerial city above Venus. They continued through the series of rooms, which took them to representations of Jupiter, Saturn, Uranus, Neptune—either in orbit around the gas giants or within their atmospheres—as well as a few moons, always with a megastructure of some kind nearby: rings, cylinders, spheres, stations, space elevators, terraformers, and floating habitats.

"The guy certainly has the résumé for this line of work," Susan said.

The path of doors eventually led them to a rounded platform of frosted glass that dropped off into the starry void on all sides. A platinum statue of Ruckman rose from the platform's center about three times normal height, its gaze lifted with a quietly confident smile on its lips. The plaque at its feet read: WHO'S THERE TO SOLVE THE UNSOLVABLE? RUCKMAN IS!

The real Ruckman sat on the edge of the statue's plinth, his skin dark and his hair short and curly with long sideburns that almost reached his chin. He watched them approach with harsh eyes that served as thin veils over the sea of resentment boiling within. One of Lucent's copy-sisters floated nearby. She smiled at the detectives, nodded to Ruckman, then vanished from the simulation.

"Enjoy the show?" Ruckman asked, not bothering to stand.

"I don't believe we're the intended audience," Isaac replied. "I suppose a better question would be how you feel about it?"

"I'm not sold on the premise yet," Ruckman grunted. "E&E's

parade treatment sounds great at first, but it gets a little samey after a while. Though it has been an interesting jaunt down memory lane. I barely remember half these projects. Not sure it's worth all the Esteem I'm shelling out, but whatever. It *is* making me wonder if a new career might provide a healthy change of pace."

He turned to the side, where a list floated that read:

BECOME AN INTEGRATED COMPANION
GO ON SABBATICAL
OPEN A MEAL SPIGOT FRANCHISE
JOIN SYSPOL, HEPHAESTUS DIVISION
KEEP DOING THE SAME SHIT

"Mister Ruckman," Isaac began, 'we'd like to ask you a few questions, if that's all right with you."

"Yeah, Luminous and Lucent said as much. You with SysPol?"

"That's right. Detective Cho, SysPol Themis."

He glanced over to Susan. "And you are?"

"Agent Cantrell," Susan introduced with a slight nod. "I'm Detective Cho's deputy."

"An agent? Of what?"

"The Admin's Department of Temporal Investigation."

"The *Admin*? Seriously?" Ruckman shook his head. "Just what I fucking need."

Isaac noticed the hint of a frown on Susan's lips.

"Mister Ruckman, let me assure you Agent Cantrell is—"

"Look, I'm sure you'll tell me she's an innocent little rainbow."

"If you'll let me finish—"

"As long as she doesn't try to delete me or cart me off to one of their hellhole prisons, I don't really care. So how about we move on and get this over with?"

"Very well." Isaac conjured a pair of virtual chairs across from Ruckman, then sat down and opened his notes. "First we'd like to discuss how you left SourceCode."

"You mean how I was turned into a scapegoat by a company I've spent almost twenty years of my life working for? Like I'd be stupid enough to design a replication engine that powerful without stuffing it to the gills with protections. There's no way my design would go rogue like that. Not with that many safeguards in place."

"Then why did SourceCode fire you?"

"You mean the trumped-up accusation they trotted out? Why don't you ask them?"

"We did. They accused you of mishandling your security access, and they suspect you may have even sabotaged the trial."

"Yeah, about that!" Ruckman raged.

"What about it?"

"They can spout all the nonsense they want! In fact, the more the better, because they're going to be hearing from my lawyers next!"

"You intend to sue SourceCode?"

"You better believe it! Wrongful termination, defamation, and maybe we'll throw in a little emotional distress as the cherry on top. The lawyers and I are still reviewing my legal options."

"I see. Moving on then, have you been in contact with the Mercury Historical Preservation Society at all?"

"No, thankfully. I think Atlas took the brunt of their ire. One of the advantages of living the abstract life, I suppose. It's hard for protestors to pin down and harass someone who moves around by connectome laser."

"What about Desmond Fike?"

"Who?"

"The chair of the Society chapter here in the Third Engine Block."

"Never heard of him."

"What about Atlas? Were you in contact with any of their employees while working on the Dyson Project?"

"No. Why would I be? That'd be stupid."

"Not even Esteban Velasco?"

"Esteban?" Ruckman's eyes lit up. "Oh, that! Hell, that's different. Esteban and I go way back. Sure, I spoke with him on occasion. We'd meet every so often to talk shop, and to vent about all the workplace drama. It was"—he flashed a sudden grin—"therapeutic, you might say."

"And the fact that your companies were competing for the same contract?"

"Irrelevant. As long as we stayed clear of confidential material, which we *did*."

"When did you last speak with Velasco?"

"Oh, let me think." He leaned back and gazed up at the stars.

"I want to say about a month ago. We tried to meet up every month or two, though sometimes we couldn't."

"What was your impression of him at the time?"

"Stressed. *Very* stressed. I could tell the project was weighing him down, taking its toll."

"What specifically gave you that impression about his mental state?"

"It's hard to say. It wasn't anything he said or did. Not one thing, anyway. More how he seemed distant the whole time. Like he was going through the motions while we talked." Ruckman shook his head. "Sorry, can't be more specific than that."

"Did he say or do anything unusual?"

"Besides acting a little out of it? No."

"What about the location? Anything strange about that?"

"The location?" Ruckman took on a thoughtful look. "Now that you mention it, that part *was* a little weird. I met him at this hotel in the Ridge. A Divided-By-Zero, I think."

"Did Velasco pick the location?"

"Yeah. No idea why, though. The Ridge isn't big on catering to organics, and I could have transmitted anywhere he wanted. I guess at the time I assumed he had some business out here." He sat up on the plinth. "So tell me, Detective, what's with all these questions about Esteban, anyway? Is he in trouble? Am *I* in trouble?"

Isaac exchanged a quick glance to Susan, then faced Ruckman once more.

"Then you don't know?"

"Know what?"

"Esteban Velasco is dead. He committed suicide yesterday."

Ruckman's mouth flopped open and his arms fell slack at his side. He stared at the floor, stunned and speechless.

"How?" he uttered after the long silence.

"He printed out a weapon and shot himself in the head."

"*Why?*"

"That's what we intend to find out."

CHAPTER TWELVE

ISAAC STOPPED NEXT TO THEIR CAR, THEN TURNED BACK AND gazed beyond the E&E dome to roiling clouds in the distance. Lightning flashed, and dark shafts of ammonia snow fell away from the clouds.

"Looks like another storm's coming," Susan said.

"Yeah. It does, though maybe the Shark Fin's course will take us around the worst of it."

"Where to next? The Divided-By-Zero hotel?"

"Yes. Especially since Ruckman found the location unusual for one of his and Velasco's venting sessions. In fact—"

Susan snapped her gaze up, her face suddenly cold and severe. Isaac regarded her with a curious expression.

"Is something—" he began before Susan grabbed him by the shoulders. She yanked him forward, twisting around him in the same fluid motion until she superimposed her body between him and their car.

"Wha—" Isaac had barely begun to form the question when something small and yellow plummeted toward them, crashing into the roof of their car. The impact obliterated the object, sending yellow pieces flying in every direction. One fragment bounced off Susan and fell to her feet.

Isaac flinched.

Susan looked up once more, her vision focused on the upper frame of the intake a kilometer above them. The roof of the

Breathless Ridge wasn't as crowded as the lower reaches, but a few prominent stalactite towers still dotted the area.

"What in the worlds?" Isaac knelt down and pinched the fragment between two fingers. He picked it up and turned it over in front of his helmet. "Yellow hair? Or maybe fur?"

"Is falling debris a common hazard around here?"

"Not that I'm aware of. Obviously, any construction zones can be a concern, but there are usually countermeasures in place. Tarps or netting underneath the work areas, counter-grav mechs positioned nearby to swoop in and catch anything big. Things like that."

"What's above us?"

"The structural barrier separating the Second and Third Engine Blocks. And above that is an intake for the Second Engine Block." Isaac frowned at the small swatch of yellow fur, then let it go. A gust of wind picked it up and carried it away. He rose to his feet and regarded the prominent dent in the top of the rental.

"Should we report this?" Susan asked.

"Report what? That trash hit our car?" He opened the car door. "Come on. Let's check out the hotel."

The Divided-By-Zero hotel resembled a rising double helix composed of blocky white segments that climbed thirty stories upward around a slender, translucent core. Isaac and Susan passed through the open glass doors at the base with the LENS floating close behind. They made their way across the circular space to the check-in desk, which was a wholly virtual wooden structure with an equally virtual AC behind it. The receptionist took the form of a bluish humanoid silhouette in a pale green uniform covered in the blocky numerals of simplistic algebra.

"Hello, and welcome to the Divided-By-Zero," the silhouette said in warm masculine tones. "If you're looking for more conventional accommodations, we do have a small selection of environmentally controlled rooms that may interest you."

"We're not here to check in," Isaac said. "I'm Detective Cho. This is Agent Cantrell. You should have received a call from my IC a few minutes ago."

"Give me a moment to look it up." The silhouette regarded a small window that opened near his fingertips. He scrolled through it. "Ah, here we are. The manager left a note to be contacted once you arrived." He opened a comm window and waited.

"Yes?" replied a gruff woman's voice.

"Detective Cho and company to see you, ma'am. They're at the front desk."

"That was fast. I'll be right out."

The comm window closed without further fanfare.

"The manager will be with you shortly," the receptionist said.

"Thank you." Isaac stepped back from the desk and put his back against a glass column. Susan waited by his side, hands clasped behind her back, eyes alert.

A side door split open, and a gray-skinned synthoid hurried out, possessing enough curves to provide the suggestion of femininity, but not much beyond than that. Equations were etched into her skin similar to the receptionist's uniform.

"Detective, pleasure to meet you." She extended a hand, which Isaac shook. "I'm Four-Oh-Oh-Three Divided-By-Zero, but you can call me Fae."

"You're a member of the Divided-By-Zero family?" Isaac asked, somewhat surprised to see a member of the prominent Lunarian family managing a hotel on Janus.

"By marriage, about a dozen odd years ago," Fae clarified. "And even that doesn't get me much. The Lunar branch of the family tends to look down their noses at us Saturnites." She glanced over at Susan's confused expression. "Something bothering you, miss?"

"Sorry. Just trying to figure out how the number in your name converts to Fae."

"It's the hexadecimal reading of my name. Four thousand three converts to F-A-Three. Hence, Fae. I legally changed my name after Teddi and I got hitched."

"Teddi?" Susan asked.

"His proper name is Four-Seven..." She trailed off and frowned, then looked down at a number on the inside of her left forearm. "Four-Seven-Four-Five-Seven-Seven."

"You carved your husband's name onto your arm?"

"It's not my fault his family brings with it a strange naming fetish. Anyway, convert that to hex, and you get Seven-Three-D-D-One. Teddi. I don't make the rules. I just try not to stir up trouble with the in-laws. Why do you think I chose something short and easy to remember for myself? Anyway, what can I do for you two? Your IC made it sound important."

"We're backtracking the movements of a man who committed

suicide under suspicious circumstances. Esteban Velasco. We believe he stayed here about a month ago."

"Velasco, is it?" She opened an interface and ran a search. "Yep, here he is. Checked in thirty-eight days ago, checked out nine days later."

"He stayed here for *nine days*?" Susan glanced at Isaac, who looked equally perplexed.

"So it would seem," Fae replied matter-of-factly, then frowned.

"What is it?" Isaac asked.

"It's his atmospheric bill. We charge extra for air processing utilities. Velasco rented an environmentally controlled room, which makes sense, since he's listed here as organic, but the daily charge is odd. Almost zero for three days, which indicates the room was unoccupied. Then a huge spike on the fourth day, then nothing until the ninth day, where the usage looks about normal for one organic."

"What would the spike indicate?" Isaac asked.

"That he had guests."

"Any ideas who?"

"No, sorry. We don't intrude on our guests' privacy."

"Would it be possible for us to inspect the room?"

"Should be. Rooms like that don't see a lot of traffic, so it might be empty." Fae opened a new interface and shifted the old one aside. "Yep, it's vacant right now. Here, let me set you up with a temporary keycode."

They followed a guidance arrow into the hotel and toward the central grav tube, past a swimming pool crowded with "naked" synthoids.

"A swimming pool?" Susan asked. "At these temperatures?"

"That's liquid ammonia," Isaac explained. "Not water."

"Okay, but doesn't it sometimes snow ammonia down here? Shouldn't the pool be a solid block of ice?"

"The sign says it's a heated pool."

Susan checked the sign. "Negative eighty degrees. And here I am without a swimsuit."

They took the tube up a few levels and followed the arrow to a door with a warning floating over it: CONTROLLED ENVIRON-MENT BEYOND THIS POINT.

Isaac used the keycode to open the outer airlock. They were about to walk in when—

"Stop," Cephalie warned suddenly, the LENS easing toward the airlock.

"What's wrong?" Isaac took a step back.

"Not sure, but something's off about this room's infostructure. I can tell even from out here. Give me some time to check it out."

The LENS floated in, and the airlock sealed shut behind it. A virtual representation of the room interior appeared in their shared virtual vision as a ghostly overlay.

The room seemed normal enough at first glance. It was clearly designed to cater to organics with a pressure suit rack by the airlock, insulated walls, and self-managed atmospheric composition and temperature. There was even a food printer nestled in the back wall.

The floor plan seemed a little cramped to Isaac, a little claustrophobic. He wondered if the hotel had taken a standard-sized room and then added all the additional insulation and equipment to the interior, burying it behind a new inner wall, which had the effect of bringing the walls in and the ceiling down.

The LENS floated around the room's perimeter, extending a pseudopod to caress the walls and ceiling. Additional data began to appear in the virtual representation; some wall sections had been removed recently, and the infostructure nodes underneath were new.

"What's all this about?" Susan asked quietly, viewing the same stream of data coming in from the LENS.

"I wish I knew."

"Done." The LENS passed back through the airlock, and Cephalie appeared on top.

"What did you find?"

"The room's infostructure has been tampered with. To what end, I can't say, but I'm sure it's been modified."

"What clued you in?" Susan asked. "You were suspicious even before we entered the room."

"It's the connection protocols for abstract senses. I could tell they were different the moment Isaac used the keycode. That's when the room's interior began to interface with us."

"In a dangerous way?" Susan asked.

"No, it's more subtle than that. The room's connection protocols are different from the rest of the hotel we've passed through. You see, I can tell the hotel's infostructure uses nodes from a company called Cyberscape, but *this* room has a mix of Cyberscape and Foundation nodes in it, which immediately struck me as unusual. I doubt most people would have noticed the difference."

"*I* certainly wouldn't," Isaac said. "Good work."

Cephalie took a bow.

"What else can you tell us?" he asked.

"Looks like the Foundation nodes were installed sometime within the past two months. I can't be more precise. Not with just the LENS."

"Nina should be able to tell us more," Isaac said. "Add this location to her work queue."

"Done. One thing I can tell you is the nodes seem to be arranged in a deliberate pattern. If I were using the local infostructure instead of the LENS to move around, it'd be impossible for me to use the hotel room without passing my connectome through at least one of the Foundation nodes."

"Any thoughts on why it'd be set up that way?"

"Not without a deeper look, but I'd rather not take the chance of corrupting evidence."

"All right. We'll wait for Nina to take a crack at it."

"Maybe this ties into why Velasco rented the room for so long?" Susan suggested.

"You could be right," Isaac replied. "His trip to the Ridge does fall within the range we're talking about. Anything else, Cephalie?"

"Just one more oddity came up when I took a peek at the room's transit log. Assuming nothing's been altered there, which is a big assumption at this point, the manager was right. This room doesn't see much use. In fact, Ruckman was the last AC to use it. That was about a month ago, but that's not the weird part. He transmitted in twenty-nine days ago. Then transmitted out the same day, *twice*."

"There are two departure logs for Ruckman?" Isaac asked. "But only one arrival log?"

"That's right. One to a synthoid boutique along the Ridge called the Body Shop and a second transit to a Third Engine Block logistics center that borders along the Ridge. It's called JIT Deliveries."

"Does one of them look fake to you?"

"No, they both strike me as legit at face value, though not to belabor the point, but it'd be best if we wait for a more thorough forensic analysis."

"All right." Isaac lowered his head, unsure what these odd facts meant. "Velasco rented this room for nine days when it seems he only needed it for one. And there was unusual activity in the room prior to his meeting with Ruckman."

"Which might be when the infostructure was altered," Susan said.

"A distinct possibility," Isaac agreed. "And then we have two exit transits for Ruckman. One to a logistics center?" He shook his head. "The synthoid boutique makes sense. There's any number of reasons an AC might want to buy or rent a body. But why a logistics center?"

"Sounds like we have our next two stops. Shall we check them both out? See if we can determine if one or the other is a fake trail?"

"Let me try to confirm something first." Isaac opened a comm window to Fae Divided-By-Zero.

"Need something else, Detective?" she answered promptly.

"Just information about the room we're looking at. Do you know if its infostructure has been modified recently?"

"Depends. How recent are we talking?"

"Within the past two months."

"I doubt it. We overhaul and update each room's nodes on a rotating basis, tackling a fifth of the rooms each year so that every room gets touched within a five-year window. I can check where that room is on the schedule, but I'm guessing it's still a few years out."

"Please verify that, if you don't mind. Also, I'll need the room closed off until one of our forensics specialists can look it over."

"No problem. Like I said, the few rooms we have for organics don't see much use. Do whatever you need, Detective."

"Thank you. I appreciate your understanding. Also, one more question while I have you on the line"

"Yes?"

"Does your hotel use Foundation infrastructure nodes at all?"

"No. We only use Cyberscape hardware. In fact, we're *required* to do so. Our Lunar corporate headquarters negotiated an exclusivity contract with Cyberscape. We get a hefty discount on their products when purchased in bulk, and we sometimes receive access to new node patterns ahead of the general public."

"I see. Thank you. That'll be all for now."

"Any time, Detective."

He closed the call then held a splayed hand over the door. Data exchanged between the door's nodes and his own wetware, and a virtual cordon materialized over the door.

"Where to next?" Susan asked. "That synthoid boutique? Or the logistics center?"

"The boutique is closer," Cephalie suggested.

"Then we'll hit it first." Isaac started back toward the grav tube.

They found the Body Shop along the outer wall of the starboard inlet, three shelves up from the bottom. Its windowless, white exterior seemed too simplistic for a strip plaza otherwise packed with colorful business signs and animated posters.

The doors split open, and Isaac stepped inside to find more or less what he expected from a business selling custom synthoids. Synthetic bodies of various shapes and sizes formed rows on either side of a path leading back into the shop. Most featured cold-adapted exteriors suitable to the Ridge, with vibrant colorations and styles, though a few of the offerings were anatomically correct for baseline humans. The naked bodies of an idealized male and female pair were sealed within glass caskets to protect their cosmetic layers from the elements. Some of the synthoids were physical examples, while others were abstract representations that a customer could customize to their liking via nearby menus.

The store opened up at the back, but not before a lone display synthoid partially blocked their path. It floated above a dais, the body's design radical even for the Ridge. Isaac assumed the synthoid must have been an Oortan pattern adapted for zero gravity, as many of their bodies were. It possessed no mouth nor other obvious orifices, and its six limbs ended in prehensile digits that appeared suitable as either hands or feet. An impressive list of built-in features hovered beside the synthoid, along with an equally impressive price.

Isaac rounded the dais and glanced around the back of the shop, where even more synthoids stood ready for potential customers. An Oortan squidform undulated the many tentacles supporting its body and quivered toward the newcomers. A pair of blue eyes glinted beneath a hood resembling a nautilus shell that curved back in on itself to form the main body.

"Hello! And welcome, welcome!" came the squidform's bright, almost girlish voice. "My name is Nautila, proprietor of the Body Shop." She swept two of her tentacles and took an exaggerated bow. Each tentacle ended in a baseline humanoid hand.

"Hello," Isaac said. "I'm Detective Cho, and this is—"

"A SysPol detective! Oh my. I have just the thing for you!"

"Ma'am, if you'll let me—"

Before he knew it, Nautila placed hands on his shoulders and back, urging him toward a display featuring a solidly built, if somewhat skeletal synthoid.

"Tell me, Detective," Nautila began, two tentacles around his shoulders, "would you say your line of work is dangerous?"

"Not especially."

Susan cleared her throat noisily behind him.

"I . . . well, yes," he corrected. "I suppose sometimes it can be."

"And yet look at you, still in your original flesh sack. Poor thing." Nautila shuddered in what might have been revulsion. "Well, you've come to the right place to fix that! Have a gander at the Bastion XZ 3000, our top-of-the-line security synthoid! Fully customizable exterior with optional cosmetic layer, and an interior compatible with a wide range of exciting upgrades. I'll have you know I'm fully licensed to sell restricted SysPol patterns to qualifying customers." She brushed a tentacle-hand across the Themis Division insignia on his pressure suit. "No problems there, I see!"

"Ma'am, perhaps you misunderstood—"

"Height and build are adjustable." She patted him on the top of his head. "Though, we might have to add a few centimeters to you. Hope you don't mind."

Isaac frowned at her. "I believe—"

"Did you know the Bastion's skeleton is printed from a prog-steel pattern found in SysPol cruiser armor? On top of that, all vital systems are sheathed in the same durable material. Now, wouldn't you like a body that can take a hit and keep going?"

"Yes, he would," Susan commented behind him.

"I . . ." Isaac sent Susan a sharp look, only to find her eyes laughing behind the stoic mask of her face. He turned back to Nautila and pulled her tentacles off his shoulders. "I'm not here to buy a synthoid."

"But surely you'd feel safer with a body that's less . . . squishable?"

"I have no plans of transitioning anytime soon."

"And there lies the problem, don't you see? You might say that, but life has a way of wrecking even the most carefully laid plans." Nautila let out an exaggerated sigh. "But if you're convinced you don't need a synthoid, then perhaps you might be interested in an insurance policy?"

"No, thank you."

"Insurance?" Susan asked.

"Early Abstraction Insurance," Nautila explained. "A person's first synthoid pattern is a significant investment, and not everyone is ready for the financial burden, especially if the transition is forced upon them by an accident." She leaned toward Isaac. "Being gravely injured in the line of duty, for example."

He grimaced at her over the suggestion.

"An EAI policy can guard against hardship during an untimely transition by providing funding for your first body. On top of that, here at the Body Shop, we offer a variety of thrilling incentives to help customize the EAI to your personal needs. These policies are quite popular with both SSP and SysPol. Perhaps you'd like to see—"

"No, *thank you*," Isaac cut in. "We're here to discuss a case we're on. We're looking for information on someone who visited the store about a month ago. An AC by the name of Antoni Ruckman. Can you tell us if he purchased anything? Or if there was anything unusual about his visit?"

"Oh, I see. Sorry, my misunderstanding," she said, though Isaac suspected her "misunderstanding" had been intentional. Nautila crossed four of her tentacles over her chest. "Can I see your badge? Company policy before I share any customer information, I'm afraid."

"Here you go." Isaac transmitted his badge.

"Checking." She waited a few seconds. "And Kronos has verified your ID. Now that that's taken care of, give me a moment to pull up my records." She opened an interface obscured by a privacy filter. "Hmm, Ruckman. Ruckman. Ah, here we are. I have an inbound and outbound transit log for an AC by that name twenty-nine days ago. No sales record. He may have just come by to window-shop."

"Do you remember the particulars of his visit?" Isaac produced an image of Ruckman over his palm.

"Vaguely. I believe he was looking to rent a synthoid pattern but decided against it and left."

"Did he say why?"

"If he did, I don't recall. He must not have shown much interest. Otherwise, I would have taken some notes in case he returned."

"I see." Isaac let the image fizzle and glanced over at Susan.

"Anything else I can help you with?" Nautila asked.

"Not at this time."

"On to our next stop?" Susan asked.

"Yeah, let's go."

"Before you leave, can I ask you something?" Nautila undulated toward Susan.

"Sure. Ask away."

"I'm curious about your synthoid. You see, I have scanners installed by the entrance that clue me in to the current body a customer uses. It helps me match the right sales pitch to the right customer. I've seen hardware from just about everyone in this industry, big and small, but I've never seen a body quite like yours. It's...oh, how to put this. There's what you might call a brutal simplicity to its design once you go beneath the cosmetic layer. Nothing fancy or superfluous underneath the skin. In fact, it seems almost primitive to my eyes, though strangely refined at the same time. As if it's the product of years—if not decades—of careful, iterative design work that sought to remove everything not strictly needed. Such a strange contradiction, you see! I hope I didn't offend you."

"No, nothing of the sort," Susan replied.

"Who designed your synthoid, if I may ask?"

"The System Cooperative Administration."

"Ah." Nautila shifted back and regarded Susan more carefully. "Silly me for not realizing sooner."

"Is there a problem?" Susan asked.

"No, not at all," Nautila said stiffly. "But my products aren't suited for...your kind. There's no point to you coming back here, if you catch my meaning."

"That's quite all right," Susan replied with equal stiffness. "It seems my duties require my presence elsewhere."

CHAPTER THIRTEEN

THE CAR FOLLOWED NARROW SIDE STREETS BACK TO A CONGESTED, high-speed freeway. The major thoroughfare funneled traffic toward the intake wall with its towering patchwork of grilles and flexible apertures, then split into single-lane tunnels that cut through the intake wall. Prog-steel mechanisms at each mouth produced translucent barriers that followed every few vehicles through the tunnel, allowing the atmosphere to be exchanged in controlled segments.

The surrounding atmosphere registered as breathable once they were about halfway through the tunnel, and the prog-steel curtain following their car retracted into the tunnel's roof mechanisms.

Isaac tugged on his pressure suit collar. The suit came apart in strips that retracted into the backpack. He slipped his arms out of the straps and set the pack down on the seat next to him.

"Good riddance."

"I know what you mean." Susan took her own suit off and tossed the pack onto the same seat.

"Wearing the suit bothered you, too?"

"Sort of. I know this might sound odd, but relying on that suit made me feel vulnerable, even if it's only my cosmetic layer that's in danger. Back home, if I were deploying into vacuum or a dangerous atmosphere, I'd be in my combat frame."

"Why didn't you ask to switch out?"

She grinned at him. "Because I knew you wouldn't approve."

He smiled back. "You might be right."

"I *am* right. When's the last time you said *anything* nice about my combat frame?"

"Can't seem to recall one."

"See?" She leaned back in her seat. "Hence, I felt no need to ask."

"Point taken."

JIT Deliveries took up a blocky section near the top of the intake wall, the zone large enough to span multiple shelves. The orange-and-red exterior was a honeycomb of docks, some with quadcopters and ground vehicles waiting to receive their shipping containers from the automated storage-and-retrieval cranes within the center's interior.

A steady stream of traffic—both air and ground—funneled through the center in a ballet of logistical movement. The car pulled off the main road and into a small visitor and employee parking lot recessed into the intake wall. It parked next to the only other vehicle in the lot.

Susan climbed out of the rental and followed Isaac to the lone door at the far end of the deck. Cephalie brought the LENS up behind them.

Isaac palmed the buzzer, and they waited.

And waited.

And waited some more.

He palmed it again.

"Yes?" came a man's bored—and somewhat irritated—response over abstract audio.

"Hello. My name is Detective Isaac Cho. We're here to—"

"Who're you?"

"Detective Cho, SysPol Themis."

"You don't say?"

"Yes," Isaac replied patiently. "I did say."

"You really with SysPol?"

"I am."

"Is this a prank?"

"Sir, it is illegal to impersonate an officer of the law."

"You sure about that?"

"Yes, I'm *quite* sure."

"That's not you, Tony, is it?"

"It's not."

"Cuz this sounds like a prank Tony would pull."

"I assure you, I'm who I claim to be. We're here because—"

"Sorry, but can't you go pester someone else? I'm busy."

"Sir." Isaac shifted from one foot to the other, the muscles in his face tightening. "Is there someone else we can talk to?"

"Nope."

"Excuse me?"

"Look, I don't know what kind of game you're playing, but I'm not in the mood."

"Sir, if you would...and he disconnected." Isaac grimaced at the buzzer and began to raise his hand to it.

"You want me to bust down the door?" Susan asked, only half joking.

"I'm sure that won't be necessary." Isaac palmed the buzzer again.

"*Wha-a-a-a-at?*"

"Perhaps I didn't make myself entirely clear the first time."

"You again?"

"Yes. Me. Again."

"Can't you tell I don't have time for this?"

"No, and at this point, I don't care. I'd like to speak to your manager."

"Not here."

"Then someone else. *Anyone* else."

"Sorry. I'm the guy on site today. I'm all you've got, buddy."

"There's no one else here? That seems a little odd."

"Are you kidding? This place is completely automated. I'm just here in case one of the cranes has a fit and needs a little TLC. Other than that, I just sit around with nothing to do."

"Then it sounds like you have time to answer our questions."

"You really with SysPol?"

Isaac transmitted his badge.

Long, silent seconds followed, and then, "Oh. Oh crap. Umm, hello, Mister Detective. What did you say your name was again?"

"Would you kindly come to the door before I decide to charge you with obstruction?"

"Right. Sorry!"

The line closed, and the door split open less than a minute later, revealing a young man with pale skin, shaggy brown hair, and a notable slouch. He wore an orange-and-red jumpsuit with the JIT Deliveries logo on the breast pocket. He took in Isaac's uniform, the LENS floating behind him, and the gun on Susan's hip before his eyes flicked back to Isaac's.

"Sorry about that. My bad."

"And you are?" Isaac asked.

"Albert Marrow, registered DCT."

"DCT?" Susan asked.

"Drone Control Technician. I'm here in case one of the cranes takes a dump. Umm, I mean breaks down. When that happens, I guide and monitor the repair drones. Sometimes I have to go out onto the cranes if the problem's really bad; and rarely, I'll call in help from our corporate HQ."

"Is there anyone else on site?"

"Nope, just me." Marrow flashed a forced smile, but the expression melted away when Isaac didn't return it. "JIT has an office in the Second Engine Block, but they don't come out here too often. Sorry about the confusion. Hardly anyone drops by out here."

"You said you were busy," Isaac noted. "Is some of the equipment down right now?"

"Uhh, no. The cranes are fine. I was ..."

"Yes?"

"You caught me in the middle of a *Solar Descent* session. You know, the new season? I was just getting to the part where we find out what happened to Natli Klynn."

"You were playing *Solar Descent* while on the job?" Susan asked.

"Sure, why not? The boss doesn't care what I do as long as the equipment keeps running. If anything breaks down, I pause my game and take care of it. But if nothing breaks during a shift, then my time is my own."

"Mister Marrow," Isaac began, "perhaps it'd be best if we get to the reason for our visit, so that you can return to your ... duties. We're investigating the movements of an AC who we believe passed through this center twenty-nine days ago. Is this something you can assist us with?"

"Abstract transits? Sure, I can look those up back in the control room. AC techs will sometimes transit in to help with the nastier breakdowns. Is that what you're after?"

"Unlikely. This would be a civilian transfer."

"Hmm, I don't know about that, but I can certainly check for you."

Isaac waited for what he thought was the inevitable follow-up.

"Do you . . . want me to check?" Marrow asked after the uncomfortable pause.

"That *is* why we're here."

"Okay, got it. The control room's right over here."

Marrow led them down a short corridor to a cramped room with a single bucket seat equipped with deep prog-foam cushioning. The wide window provided a live view of several robotic cranes in motion, their tall frames extending from the ground floor all the way up to the ceiling dozens of stories above. One of them sped toward the booth, screeched to an abrupt halt, and extended arms from a central hoist. The arms locked onto a shipping container then retracted, pulling the container out of its bin. Once the container was secured to the crane hoist, the brakes disengaged, and it sped away from the control room.

Marrow summoned a dense array of abstract screens with a wave of his hand: crane status displays, storage allotment, retrieval queues, and fault logs. He sank into the bucket seat, swiped a few of the screens aside, and summoned a new one. Isaac and Susan slid in behind him, their backs pressed against the rear wall due to a lack of space.

"Okay," Marrow said. "I've got the transit log open. What do you want me to look for?"

"Search for the name Antoni Ruckman," Isaac said, then provided Marrow with a copy of the man's connection string and connectome identifier.

"Ruckman . . ." He entered the identifier and ran a search. "Nope. Nothing." He twisted in his seat and gave them a shrug. "Tough luck, huh?"

"What did you just search, exactly?"

"This cabin's transit log." He paused, then tilted his head. "Why?"

"Aren't there other places someone could transfer to in this center?"

"I suppose, but why would they?"

"Just humor me. Can you widen your search to include all possible points of digital entry?"

"I suppose I can." He settled back into a more comfortable

position and worked the interface, pulling up several new tables stacked one on top of the other. "And . . . searching." He toggled a commit key.

One of the tables moved to the top, and a single entry pulsed green.

"Huh," Marrow said with a frown. "That can't be right."

"Where did he transit in?" Isaac asked.

"Says here his connectome was diverted into one of the bins. Level thirty-five, column six, row nineteen, to be precise."

"I take it that's not normal."

"No, it's not. I mean, there's nothing to prevent someone from doing that, assuming what's stored in the bin is connected to the infostructure."

"Can you check what's stored in that bin?"

"The timestamp is a month old. Whatever was there is long gone."

"Then can you look up what was there at the time?"

"Sure can." Marrow closed the transit logs and opened a storage archive. "That's weird."

"What is it?"

"That's a blocked bin."

"What does that mean?"

"Means it's unavailable. The system won't store anything there until it's unblocked."

"Why would a bin be blocked?"

"Any number of reasons. Could be for maintenance. Or maybe we need to bring in something big. Sometimes we merge the bins together for larger freight."

"Does your log say why it's blocked?"

"Nope. Just when."

"Which was?"

"About a year ago."

"A year?" Isaac said. "And no one's unblocked it in all that time?"

"Yeah, I know what you're thinking, but look at it from the company's perspective. This place has over sixty *thousand* bins, and we rarely hit three quarters of our max capacity. No one cares about a blocked bin or two. A downed *crane* will get people's attention quick. But one measly bin blocked off?" Marrow shook his head. "Management couldn't care less. 'Just keep the center running,' they'd say."

"What's the bin's status now?"

"Blocked and empty. Same as it was a month ago."

"During which time a connectome was transmitted to it."

"Uh, yeah..." Marrow glanced back at his screens. "Doesn't sound right when you put it like that."

"Can you show us a visual of the bin?"

"Sure. I can move an idle crane over to it."

Marrow took manual control of a crane that wasn't in the middle of processing any orders. He brought up the visual feed from its onboard cameras, drove the crane into desired position, then raised the hoist until it was near the roof of the logistics center.

"Is that it?" Isaac asked once the view had settled.

"Yeah?" Marrow replied, sounding unsure of himself.

"That bin's not empty," Susan observed.

"What's that in the bin?" Isaac asked.

"Looks to be an unmarked shipping container." Marrow tapped one of his screens. "But that shouldn't be there. The system says its empty."

"How often do you visually inspect the bins?"

"Almost never. No need unless there's a problem, like damage to the bin."

"Then this container could have been here for a while and you'd never know it."

"Yeah, I suppose it could have been."

"We need to get out there and take a look inside," Susan said.

"Agreed. How about it, Marrow? Can you get us inside that container?"

"I can do you one better." Marrow entered a manual command. Arms extended from the crane, latched onto the container, and pulled it out of the bin. Clamps locked the container in place, and Marrow recalled the crane. "Okay, bin's on its way back to the maintenance access platform. That's right down the hall. Can't miss it. The crane will drop it off, and you can check it out from there."

"Thank you." Isaac turned to Susan. "Let's see what we find."

The maintenance access area was a small, open platform that extended into the crane transit trench like a metal peninsula surrounded by virtual warning signs on three sides. According to the sign text, nearby cranes would shut down if anyone tried to climb off the platform.

Susan watched the crane with their mystery container speed toward them, the hoist descending with the container attached. It looked like it would crash into them, but then multiple axes braked at the same time, and the container came to rest in front of them with feathery lightness. Virtual warning signs shifted outward, permitting access to the short side of the docked container.

Noise filled the chamber: the whine of cranes and hoists, the squeal of brakes, and the clank of clamping mechanisms. But her synthoid hearing could parse out overlapping sounds, separating them for her mind to process, and that's why she heard a strange noise from within the container.

"What are you doing?" a voice hissed from inside the container, barely loud enough for even *her* hearing to pick up, followed by the ultrasonic whine of a capacitor charging.

"Get down!" She launched herself toward Isaac, responding to the danger automatically. She grabbed the top of his head and shoved him down, even as her body passed in front of his.

Gunshots punched through the container wall, leaving holes in the metal large enough to stick her thumb through. The first mag dart sailed over their heads and left a divot in the far wall, but the next two struck Susan in the back. *Would* have hit Isaac if she hadn't leaped in front of him. Her uniform's smart fabric stiffened, distributing the force over a larger area, but the darts still possessed enough kinetic kick to pierce through, even after perforating the container wall.

Her weight drove Isaac to the ground, and she landed on top of him.

"Oof!" Isaac gasped, sandwiched between the ground and Susan's body.

The LENS dropped down next to them and expanded its outer shell to either side, forming a prog-steel barrier between the two detectives and the container. Sustained fire rang out, and more shots blasted chunks of plastic off the back wall. Some of the chunks pattered off Susan's back.

"You all right?" she asked, her face a hair's breadth away from Isaac's.

"Fine," he wheezed. "You?"

"Umm." She ran a quick self-check. "I'm okay. My shoulder blade stopped the bullets."

Another burst of fire rang out from the container, punching more holes in the outer surface. A few shots thwacked into the LENS' impromptu barrier.

Isaac flinched from a loud ricochet.

"Two assailants inside," Cephalie reported. "Both organic and armed."

"Stay down." Susan patted her partner on the shoulder. "I'll take care of this."

"Be careful," he rasped.

"Always." She drew her Popular Arsenals PA5 "Neutralizer" anti-synthoid hand cannon, which was the most devastating sidearm available to Themis Division detectives. "Cephalie, keep him covered."

"You've got it."

The shooting stopped, and Susan listened for some indication of what the assailants planned next.

"You think we got them?" came a gruff voice from within the container.

"How the fuck should I know?" The second voice sounded scared.

"Go out there and check."

"Why do I have to check? You do it!"

"You want me to report you to the boss?"

"Fuck you, man! I'm not going out there!"

Someone grumbled what might have been an obscenity. Footsteps approached the container door. A latch clanked aside, and the door slid open.

Susan sprang from cover, pistol aimed over the LENS barrier.

"Freeze! Police!"

A stocky man stood in the container's threshold, burst pistol held loosely in one hand. His head was shaved except for two thin strips of hair dyed electric blue that ran back along his scalp like a crest. He wore a black vest over a bright blue T-shirt and pair of baggy blue-and-black checkered pants. His nose, the bottom of his lip, and both ears were pierced, some of them with blue stones that might have been synthetic sapphires.

He sneered as he swung his pistol toward her, but his organic reflexes couldn't match a militarized synthoid.

Susan fired a single, precise shot. The mag dart punched through the frame of his weapon and whipped it out of his hands so hard the force dislocated two of his fingers. He cried out, hand recoiling, and Susan leaped over the barrier. She grabbed him by the shirt with her free hand and drove him to the ground.

"Stop right there!" she shouted, leveling her pistol at the second man, still in the container, which looked more like the inside of someone's apartment than a box used to transport freight. She spotted a pair of bunks, a food printer, and dense racks of info-system nodes that nearly covered one of the long walls.

The thin stick of a man stood with his back pressed against the nodes. He possessed long, oily hair dyed blue and a blue vest open to reveal the thin fuzz of his chest hairs and a few pornographic tattoos.

"Shit!" The second assailant turned and ran. He grabbed hold of the rungs of a ladder that led to a hatch on top of the container and began to climb.

"Cephalie, secure this one!" Susan didn't wait for the AC's response. She holstered her pistol and sprinted forward, clearing the space between her and the lanky man in an instant. She ripped the pistol from his fingers and grabbed him by the shoulder.

"Fuck!" he cried as she pulled him off the ladder. He landed on his back, and she turned him over and pinned him in place, arm twisted into the small of his back. She secured his wrists with a prog-steel cuff from her belt, then checked back on the first assailant to find the LENS hovering over him, his limbs secured by the drone's pseudopods.

Isaac climbed back to his feet and dusted himself off. He took a long, slow breath to compose himself, then walked up to the edge of the container and poked a finger through one of the bullet holes. He frowned at the hole, perhaps realizing one or more of those could have been through him, then gave the stocky assailant a disapproving scowl.

"Got anything to say for yourself?"

"You fucking broke my fingers!" The attacker tried to raise his injured hand but only managed to wiggle it thanks to the LENS holding him down. Two of his fingers flopped over, hanging perpendicular to the rest of his hand. His eyes began to tear up, and he bit into his lower lip.

"I'm so sorry to hear that," Isaac replied dryly. "Perhaps if you would refrain from committing crimes—shooting at the police, for instance—we could have avoided this."

"Aren't you a fucking comedian?"

Isaac dropped to one knee next to the prisoner and picked up the broken barrel of a pistol.

"You have a permit for this weapon? Or should I add illegal replication to the growing list of charges? We've already got some real winners with two counts of attempted murder of a police officer on top of trespassing and whatever all *that* is for." Isaac indicated the infosystems in the container with a wave of the barrel.

The prisoner turned his head away.

"How about this, then?" Isaac continued. "Mind explaining what you two were doing hiding out in a container that shouldn't exist?"

"Go fuck yourself!"

"Not the first time I've been told that. Fine. Suit yourself. Let's see if your mood changes after you've stewed in a cell overnight." Isaac tossed the barrel aside and stood up. He opened a comm window. "Dispatch."

"Themis Dispatch here. Are you all right, Detective? Your LENS sent out several automated alerts."

"We're fine. I need SSP at my location. Two unidentified 'guests' for pickup." He glanced at the first assailant's dangling fingers. "And I suppose you should call a medical team, too."

✧   ✧   ✧

A pair of medical technicians arrived first, parking their white-and-red quadcopter beside the detectives' rental, where the LENS had brought the two bound prisoners.

The LENS stayed close, signaling all nearby infostructure to ignore the prisoners' wetware, effectively placing them in a crude form of data isolation.

The medics treated the stocky prisoner's broken fingers first, setting the digits and injecting the site with medibots. They then applied a medibot wrap around the base of the two fingers, both to secure the injury site and to introduce a steady stream of tiny medical robots to accelerate the healing process.

The two medics then turned their attention to Susan. She opened a seam in her uniform's smart fabric down along her spine, revealing two small holes in her cosmetic layer along with abstract artwork that covered most of her back. A skull-headed woman in billowing robes floated on her back, crowned in a silver circlet with a long scroll of parchment held in one bony hand. The parchment was blank because she'd disabled the text. Normally it read: "If you can see this, you're in big trouble."

One technician removed the two mag darts from underneath her cosmetic skin. Both had flattened against her shoulder blade. The second technician applied a general-purpose sealant to the holes, configured to blend in with her skin tone. Her self-diagnostics told her it wasn't exactly good as new—that would have required printing out a replacement skin patch and grafting it in place—but she asked for Isaac's opinion, just in case.

"Looks fine," he reported after inspecting her back. "I can hardly tell you've been shot."

"Good enough for me," she replied.

The techs closed the seam in her uniform, and she stood up and joined Isaac by the car.

"How are you holding up?" he asked, speaking in security chat since the prisoners were close enough to listen.

"No problems to report. You?"

"Feeling like I could go for a stiff drink. That was...closer than I'm used to. I think we'll call it a day after this. It's getting late anyway."

"Sounds good to me."

The medical team packed up and took off. The two detectives stood in silence, watching the city's aerial traffic fly past them.

"Thanks, by the way," Isaac said to her after a while.

"For what?" Susan asked.

"For taking those hits for me."

"Oh, that was nothing."

"No, I mean it. Cephalie would have tried to protect me with the LENS, but I'm not sure she would have been fast enough."

"Yeah, about that." Cephalie appeared on his shoulder. "I'd say you'd have at least one extra hole in you if it weren't for Susan." She gave his earlobe a virtual *thwack* from her cane. "So be grateful, you hear me?"

"I *am* grateful. Don't you hear me thanking her?"

"With feeling, Isaac. With feeling."

He rolled his eyes.

Susan did her best to hide her chuckle. She didn't think Isaac noticed.

An SSP quadcopter dipped away from the aerial traffic and slowed as it approached the parking lot. It turned so its side faced the two detectives, then settled down near them.

Susan's eyebrows perked up when she saw the precinct and copter numbers.

"Are we still in the one-oh-third precinct all the way out here?"

"No," Isaac said. "Dispatch must have called them over since they're already involved in the case."

"Well, well, well!" Chatelain chortled as he stepped out of the copter. "You two just couldn't get enough of us, could you?"

"Something like that." Isaac gestured over to the prisoners. "We found these two in a shipping container of all places. Take them back to the station and run them through the system. My guess is you'll get some prior hits."

"Will do. Parks?"

"On it, Sarge." Parks appeared next to the prisoners and summoned the conveyor drone docked to the copter's roof. The drone grabbed hold of each prisoner's bonds and hauled them into the copter.

Once the assailants were secured, Chatelain turned back to Isaac.

"You found these losers in a *shipping container*?"

"Right before they opened fire on us," Isaac said, then nodded to Parks. "Trooper, the more we work this case, the more on point your hunch is turning out. You were right to call us in."

Parks smiled at the compliment.

"That's high praise coming from him," Susan tossed in conversationally.

Parks' smile vanished, and his demeanor turned frigid and businesslike. Susan wanted to kick herself for opening her mouth.

"You think these two are tied to Velasco's suicide?" Chatelain asked. "How?"

"Not sure yet," Isaac said. "We'll give your precinct some time to process them, then we'll check back first thing in the morning. Perhaps we'll have enough to put the pieces together by then. Either way, I appreciate your partner's initiative. We're uncovering *something* here. That much I'm certain of."

"Don't encourage him. His head's getting big enough as it is."

"Just voicing my honest opinion."

"Need anything else from us?" Chatelain pointed a thumb

over his shoulder. "Or are we free to haul this human refuse back to the station?"

"That'll be all for now, thank you."

Chatelain bobbed his head back to the copter. "Let's go, Rainy."

Chatelain climbed into the copter, and Parks guided the conveyor into its cradle near the back of the vehicle.

"Rainy?" Susan asked in another attempt to break the ice. "As in Rainy Parks? Is there a good story behind the nickname?"

Parks blinked, his lips curling into an uncomfortable frown.

"Trooper?" Isaac said. "I believe my partner asked you a question."

"It's just a silly name the other troopers use. No need to make a big deal about it. I was raised by storm clouds, so I guess someone thinks the name is clever. Parks, and storms, and rain."

"*Parks?*" Chatelain urged from inside the copter.

"Coming, Sarge."

Chatelain sealed up the quadcopter, and Parks' avatar vanished. The four rotors spun up, and the copter lifted off.

Isaac and Susan watched it fly away, both silent for a while.

"Did he just tell us he was raised by storm clouds?" she asked.

"That's what I heard."

"Is being raised by storm clouds a thing here in SysGov?"

"Not that I'm aware of."

"Any idea what he meant by it?"

"Not a clue."

"Raviv's calling," Cephalie said, the LENS floating over to join them. "He wants a status update."

"Is that really what he told you?" Isaac asked.

"More like 'What's taking those two so long?' But you know the drill by now."

"Put him through, then."

A comm window opened in front of Isaac, and Raviv appeared with Damphart in the background.

"Hello, boss," Isaac said. "What can I do for you?"

"Isaac, you two still on that suicide case?"

"We are. This case is turning out to be more complex than it first appeared."

"Then I take it you're not free to join us in the Second Engine Block anytime soon?"

"Not unless you want us to drop this case."

"No, see it through. What sort of stuff are you running into?"

"Well, for one, we were shot at today by two punks hiding out in a logistics center."

"Oh, damn." Raviv's eyes widened with concern. "You two okay?"

"Susan was hit twice in the back. She's fine."

"And you?"

"My nerves are a little on the frayed side, but that's it. I'll live."

"Don't get yourselves hurt or killed over this. It's not worth it."

"We'll do our best."

"You'd better." Raviv let out a long exhale. "All right. Stick to your current case, but if you free up, let me know immediately."

"Sure thing, though I'm surprised to hear you're with Damphart already. What changed?"

"Politics. What else? Heppleman made a big stink in a press conference today about the lack of 'seriousness' on the part of SysPol."

"Who's Heppleman?" Susan asked.

"The SSP colonel," Isaac said. "Highest rank in the Saturn State."

"And a pain in my ass," Raviv growled. "I'm performing damage control over here while Damphart works the case. Arete and Argo divisions are both making moves to bulk up their presence here, and I was hoping we could do the same, if for no other reason than the favorable optics."

"Argo Division?" Isaac asked. "Why's the patrol fleet involved? I thought Damphart was on a kidnapping case."

"She still is, but the case has turned into a huge goddamned mess. Did you know PlayTech has a product development center near the bottom of the Second Engine Block?"

"No. What does that have to do with missing kids?"

"Because they've been working on this new toy called a fuzzle. Picture a colorful teddy bear and you're not too far off from what they look like. They're being packaged with nonsentient intelligence and modest self-replicating abilities. At least, they're *supposed* to be modest. Apparently, the company dumped one of their test failures into a reclamation pit without disabling it properly, and once there, it started scavenging for materials to make more. Now the damn things are replicating out of control and yanking people right off the streets."

"Wait a second," Isaac said. "You're telling me these *fuzzles* are the kidnappers?"

"I didn't believe it myself until I came down here. At first it was just kids, but now these things will grab anyone they can get their furry paws on. Care to wager how this is playing out in the media? 'SysPol unable to defend the people of Janus from a bunch of broken *toys*.'"

"That's not a good look."

"Which is why Arete and Argo are involved now. They're bringing in the heavy equipment so we can burn this infestation out of the walls, but we *still* don't know where most of the missing people are."

"Sounds like quite the mess."

"You *sure* you aren't close to wrapping up that suicide?"

"I'd tell you if we were."

"Yeah," Raviv sighed. "I know. You two keep at it, though I'm not going to say no if you manage to break away soon. I wish you better luck than *we've* had, at least."

"Thanks, boss."

Raviv closed the connection.

"Fuzzles, huh?" Susan asked with a half-smile. "Toys kidnapping kids."

Isaac let out a low whistle. "Be glad that's not *our* case."

CHAPTER FOURTEEN

SUSAN TRUDGED INTO HER ROOM IN THE PLUME TOWER, WHICH was decorated with an assortment of abstract and physical artwork tied together with a fire theme: paintings of stars and nebulas, a glowing vase that changed shapes and hues like a flame burning in slow motion, and the abstract image of a crackling fireplace, which cast a virtual sensation of heat over her skin. The walls were a smoky gray, and the lighter gray carpet was patterned into flagstone shapes.

She took off her peaked cap, tossed it onto an iron table and let out a long, tired sigh, then brushed fingers through her hair until her fingertips came to rest on the back of her neck.

"What a day," she breathed, making her way into the bedroom. Her small travel case sat on the nightstand next to the bed, and she opened it and rummaged around for a T-shirt and shorts.

She stripped off her uniform, folded it onto the bed, and initiated its autocleaning cycle, then stepped into the bathroom. She set her hands on either side of the sink and gazed into the mirror, not truly seeing her own reflection. Instead, her imagination conjured people and places on its own accord: Trooper Parks and his timid demeanor, Xian's sense of indignity at being forced to speak with her, Ruckman's initial outburst upon learning she was from the Admin, even Nautila's lack of grace with a fellow synthoid.

All of those had happened because she'd been present.

"Am I slowing him down?" she wondered aloud.

She didn't have an answer to that. She didn't *believe* her presence was a burden to Isaac, but then again, it seemed like her presence caused unnecessary—and *unhelpful*—friction with every other person they met. That couldn't be making his job any easier.

Resentment for the Admin didn't bother her. Not alone. Not really. If anything, it was worse back home where centuries of fomenting tension between the central government and the states under its control would bubble up with little notice, often in violent terrorist attacks.

Here in SysGov, the prejudices were fresher and less severe, often stemming from the newness of SysGov's relationship with the Admin. That, and people's ignorance about how their multiverse neighbor conducted business on the other side of the transverse, as well as *why* laws and enforcement were so different over there. People here lacked perspective on the Admin's history, which was only natural. A problem time and exposure could solve.

So, no. The resentment by itself didn't bother her, but if her presence became a burden to Isaac, well . . . *that* was a whole other matter.

Maybe she wasn't hindering his progress, but simply staying out of his way wasn't enough. What was the point of her serving as his deputy if she wasn't *helping* him? At least a *little*. Sure, she could act as a bullet sponge from time to time—and *had*—but was that really enough to warrant her presence? They were *detectives*, not frontline combatants, and she needed to contribute accordingly.

That's why she'd suggested splitting up for some of the day's tasks, with her taking the trip to SourceCode; but Isaac's questions afterward had only served to demonstrate her own shortcomings, even if he'd delivered his criticism softly. Nothing harsher was necessary because Susan knew her investigative instincts lagged far behind his own.

Trooper Randal Parks and his persistent caginess was another sore spot, though it was more about what his attitude represented. Themis Division depended greatly on the personnel and resources of local police, and Parks represented a burr in the cogs of that relationship, a sure sign she couldn't depend upon cooperation from virtual members of the Saturn State Police. She'd tried, awkwardly perhaps, to broach a conversation with the AC, but had only succeeded in causing the man to clam up further.

All in all, not her finest day on the new job.

Susan pushed off the sink, walked into the shower, and switched it on. Scalding water poured over her, and she closed her eyes and rested her forehead against the wall. Thoughts continued to swirl through her mind as the relaxing stream of water ran down her body.

She had no desire to be a stone around Isaac's neck, dragging him down with her dead weight.

So, what was she going to do about it?

What *could* she do?

She didn't understand why her superiors had chosen her for the officer exchange program, and for the first slot at that! She seemed like a terrible choice, in her own judgment. Why didn't they pick someone who embodied—for lack of a better term—the "softer" side of the Admin? Why pick *her*?

Not that she resented their selection of her. Far from it. She questioned their reasoning, but in the same breath she was grateful for the opportunity. There wasn't anything quite like experiencing another culture firsthand, and she doubted she'd ever grow tired of SysGov's quirks.

Minus the friction, of course.

She switched off the shower, dried herself off, and slipped on the black T-shirt and shorts. The artshirt was a souvenir from her first case together with Isaac, and it featured an animated image of Natli Klynn from *Solar Descent*. The blue-skinned woman floated within a flaming aura, wearing a too-tight bodysuit partially unzipped in the front. The words HOT DATE floated above her.

For some reason, the ridiculousness of the image brought a smile to her face.

She finished drying her hair, then tossed the towel aside and sat down on the edge of the bed, forearms resting behind her knees. She pondered ordering some ice cream or other dessert to cheer herself up but doubted it would work this time.

She frowned at the floor, then sat up and opened a comm window.

It didn't take long for Isaac to respond.

"Yes?"

"You awake?" Susan asked.

"Umm . . . yes?"

"I mean, are you about to turn in for the night? I'm not interrupting you, am I?"

"No, not at all. I'm up in the hotel restaurant having a bite to eat. Why? Something on your mind?"

"You could say that. Mind if I join you?"

"Not at all."

"Thanks. I'll be right up."

The restaurant at the top of Plume Tower was called Thrusters, and its decor continued the hotel's fire themes with flame-shaped lighting and a real cooking hearth in the center of the restaurant. A trio of chefs prepared meals seared in the flames of real wooden logs, their black uniforms featuring animated flames that danced up their sleeves. A transparent chamber next to the hearth contained a varied selection of meats being smoked.

Susan glanced around the restaurant, then caught Isaac's raised hand near one corner. She threaded her way through the tables and sat down opposite him.

"Not wearing your uniform tonight?" Isaac asked with a raised eyebrow. He'd changed into a black suit with a dynamic scarf adorned in purple runes that pulsated with arcane power.

"It's off-duty casual tonight," Susan replied with a smile, plucking at her artshirt.

"I can see that."

"What are you having?"

"Hixon Vodka. I decided I deserved a little splurge after today." He took a sip, sighed, and set the glass down next to his half-finished salad.

"Worth it?"

"I'm not sure. I know this is fermented from real potatoes and grains from Old Frontier, but I can hardly tell the difference from my usual. Except perhaps a hint of increased complexity in the aftertaste."

"Feeling any better?"

"Getting there. I've reached the 'mildly mellow' stage." He spun the glass in place one way, then the other, creating a mild swirl of clear liquid. "And I intend to become even more mellow before the night is over."

"Sounds like a plan to me."

"Want to try some? I could order you a glass."

"No thanks. Straight vodka really isn't my thing. I prefer sweeter drinks."

"Well, they have those, too." Isaac passed her an abstract drink menu.

"Oh, now that's more like it." She entered an order for a chocolate martini then looked up to find Isaac's gaze centered over her shoulder. She twisted around to see what was behind her.

A news feed from the *Saturn Herald* took up half the far wall with a well-dressed reporter performing citizen-on-the-street interviews. The location was listed as the Second Engine Block, and the news ticker read: POLICE STUMPED BY . . . ROGUE TOYS?

"Anything good?" she asked.

"Only if you like seeing SysPol used as a punching bag. I caught a glimpse of Raviv a few minutes ago."

"How'd he look?"

"On edge."

"His usual, then?"

"More or less. He was doing his best to shield Damphart from a persistent field reporter."

The view switched to a silvery orb descending through Saturn's atmosphere. The ticker changed to: ARGO DIVISION CRUISER ARRIVES AT JANUS.

"Argo must really mean business if they're bringing in a *Directive*-class," Isaac said. "Either that, or they're putting on the best show they can. That ship's the *Toyoda*, by the way."

"Named after President Yoshi Toyoda, I assume?"

"Oh?" Isaac sat up a little straighter and cracked a smile. "I'm surprised you knew that."

"I've been briefed on SysPol's warships."

His smile vanished. "Susan, please. SysPol doesn't have warships."

"Then what do you call that monstrosity?"

"An 'emergency reinforcement cruiser.'"

"Which is a fancy way of not calling a warship a warship."

"We're a police force, not a military."

"You could fit all of Atlas HQ inside that beast."

"Size isn't everything," he pointed out.

"It is when you stuff it full of nukes and capital lasers."

"The *Toyoda*'s not packing that kind of firepower."

"But it could."

"It *could*," he admitted.

"And some of them did, back during the Dynasty Crisis."

"They did."

"Which then makes it a warship."

"I...think we should just agree to disagree on this one."

"All right," Susan said, then chuckled.

"What?"

"Just thinking about those kidnappings. Argo Division is bringing over the biggest, baddest ship in their arsenal. A ship so powerful, it keeps my superiors awake at night. And they're going to use it to clear out an infestation of malfunctioning *toys*."

"Whatever makes people happy, I suppose." Isaac took another sip from his vodka. "Ahhh."

A waiter delivered her chocolate martini. She transferred an Esteem tip to him, and he nodded and left.

She breathed in the aroma, then took a generous sip from the martini. The biochemical simulator attached to her connectome detected the alcohol and produced a mild wave of warmth and coziness through her body. She could switch off the effect at any time.

"That's nice," she sighed with a blissful smile.

"So, what's on your mind?" Isaac asked her.

"Work. What else?"

"Anything in particular?"

"I guess." She leaned forward, an arm on the table. "Let me ask you a direct question, Isaac. Is my presence here...helpful?"

"Of course, it is," he said, too fast to have given his answer any thought.

"No, I mean it. Am I making your job harder?"

"What brought this on?"

"Just thinking about the case. I guess I feel like I'm not pulling my weight."

"Susan. You took two bullets for me today. My squishy insides call that contributing!"

"Yeah, but *any* partner with a synthoid body could have done that."

"So? You were the one at my side in that moment, and you're the one who recognized the danger first."

"Okay, but what about the rest of our jobs?"

"What about it?"

"I made a ton of mistakes at SourceCode, and every other person we run into doesn't trust me because I'm Admin."

"So?"

She blinked, surprised by how dismissive he seemed of what were—to her—massive problems.

"Well," she continued at last, "that's not helpful."

"So?"

"I want to help solve our cases. I want to contribute."

"You do."

"Well, it doesn't feel that way. It feels like my lack of experience—and my background—are making this case harder for you. I don't want to be the one dragging you down and causing you trouble."

"Susan." He sat forward in the booth. "Between the two of us, we both know who has the most training and experience when it comes to detective work."

"You do."

"But if you think that means you're not contributing, then please, allow me to put those fears to rest." He paused to think, then gestured to her with an open hand. "Would you consider us a team?"

"Sure."

"And, in your opinion, which kind of team is better? One where every member shares the same strengths and weaknesses? Or one where the strengths of one can cover for the weaknesses of another?"

"I get the impression you want me to say the second."

"Because I believe that's the better of the two, especially in a place like Themis. Teams like that are stronger in a wider range of situations."

"But the first type is more specialized."

"Perhaps, but it's also less adaptable. Consider our department as a whole for the moment. I may understand how to run an investigation, but I don't have anywhere near Nina's eye for forensic evidence, nor can I navigate abstract spaces as well as Cephalie. Or keep a department from falling into pure chaos the way Raviv does. And like all those people, you too contribute in meaningful ways."

"Well, I do make an effective meat shield, from time to time—minus the 'meat,' of course."

"That's not what I meant."

"Then what *did* you mean?" Her mood had improved, and she found herself enjoying this little morale-booster of a conversation.

"Certainly, your abilities in both of your bodies have been a huge help," Isaac clarified, "but what I'm referring to is your outside perspective. A perspective that can sometimes lead you to see connections or possibilities or ask questions I might otherwise have missed. It doesn't come up all the time, which is to be expected. Most problems can be solved with the standard, methodical approaches I'm good at. But when your unique insights hit on something I've missed, it's invaluable."

She grinned at him.

"Feel any better?" he asked.

"*Lots* better."

"Good. Don't be too hard on yourself, all right? And don't let a few troublemakers get to you. Everyone who's actually worked with you knows better. Sure, you're still feeling your way around this new role of yours, but never doubt for a moment you have my confidence and respect."

"As more than just a sturdy meat shield?"

"Susan, please." He chuckled. "You're *way more* than a meat shield to me. You're my partner, and I'm glad to have you by my side."

"I'll drink to that." She grinned and lifted her martini.

Isaac brought up his own drink, and they clinked their glasses together.

CHAPTER FIFTEEN

"WHAT IS IT WITH YOU AND THIS CASE?" NINA ASKED THE NEXT morning, bags under her eyes and hair slightly unkempt. She dropped into the seat across from Isaac and propped her boots up on the next chair over.

"What do you mean?" Isaac asked, a spoonful of oatmeal halfway to his mouth. He and Susan had stopped by Thrusters for a quick bite to eat before they headed for the 103rd Precinct Building.

"Every time I think I'm about to catch up," Nina said, "you plop another location into my queue."

"You okay?" Susan asked, picking at her bowl of sliced fruit. "You look a little...haggard."

"You didn't pull another all-nighter, did you?" Isaac asked.

"Look deep into my eyes, Isaac." She dropped her boots to the floor and leaned forward until her face was uncomfortably close. "You're the detective. What do *you* think?"

"That you're not getting enough sleep. Should I request some backup for you?" Isaac set the spoon back into his bowl, where it slowly sank beneath the surface, cinnamon syrup oozing into the depression.

"No, I'm fine. I'll push through. My internal clock is all out of whack anyway. Couldn't sleep right now if I tried." She plucked a strip of bacon off his plate and began crunching through it.

"Besides, I'm keeping up," she said around a mouthful of food. "It just feels good to gripe about how you're bouncing me all over this city."

"Which would be your own fault."

"How do you figure?" She stuffed the rest of the strip into her mouth, then stole a second one.

"Remember when I asked you about this job? I believe your exact words were 'Will it get me off this station?'" He spread his upturned palms as if making a grand reveal. "And here you are."

"Yeah, but I wasn't expecting to be *stuck* down here, working a suicide." She grabbed a third bacon strip from his plate.

"Would you please stop that?"

"Stop what?" She bit into the bacon.

"That. Order your own food."

"Consider it payment. You want to go over what I found now or at the station?"

"You came across something?" Susan asked.

"Yeah, and it's *extra* tasty. Like this bacon!" She took another bite. "Oh, don't give me that look, Isaac. You weren't going to eat it all anyway."

"Fine," Isaac said, switching to security chat. "We can go over your report now, if you like."

"Thanks. That saves me a trip to the station." Nina opened an interface and transferred copies of her report over to the two detectives. "To summarize, I visited the Dream Lodge, that Society warehouse, and the Divided-By-Zero hotel."

"What about Atlas HQ?" Susan asked. "Where do you stand on that?"

"Getting closer. I hope to tackle it today. Last I spoke with our legal team, they made it sound like they were close to a compromise. I had to narrow the scope of the warrant, but I think it'll still give us the access we need."

"Better a more limited check now than the warrant being stuck in legal purgatory," Isaac said.

"Atlas and the logistics center are on my to-do list today. I'm going to check in with the lawyers this morning and get the latest from them. If it looks good, I'll tackle Atlas first. If not, then I'm off to JIT Deliveries."

"Actually, it might be best if you handle JIT first," Isaac said. "I'm curious to know what all the hardware in the container is for."

"Don't get ahead of me. I may already have an answer for you there."

"Really?"

"Yeah, but let me go over these in chronological order. First, the capsule apartment. Didn't find much there. Desmond Fike doesn't have a criminal record, so I don't have his DNA, but I'm pretty sure I know which traces are his between the hotel and the 'warehouse.' The short version is he didn't spend much time in that capsule, and neither did anyone else, recently."

"Which matches up with my own thoughts," Isaac said. "Its sole purpose seemed to be to mask his true location."

"And nothing I found contradicts that conclusion, or even casts doubt on it." Nina shifted to a new tab in her report. "Okay, that warehouse-slash-hidey-hole. Plenty of DNA all over the place, with one code much more prevalent than the others. I also found traces of the same DNA at the capsule but *didn't* find any other overlaps between the two sites. Building interior shows signs of both consistent and recent use in the food printers, reclamation system, and atmospheric processors. Amount of use suggests single organic occupant with occasional visitors.

"Traces in the garage lead me to believe five cars were normally stored there, but only four are present, which leaves one vehicle unaccounted for. Conclusion: This is where Fike's been living instead of the capsule apartment, and he's out and about somewhere in one of his cars."

"How recently would you say he was there?" Isaac asked.

"Yesterday morning, where he enjoyed a hearty breakfast followed by a productive bowel movement."

"Do you have a make on the missing vehicle?"

"A Cygnus Model X Roadster."

"That'll help if we need to track him down," Susan said.

"Good work, Nina."

"Oh, but I haven't even told you the best part." She leaned forward and snatched the last piece of bacon off Isaac's plate. "I figured out what the infosystem changes were for at the Divided-By-Zero."

"And?"

"They're set up to illegally copy connectomes and transmit them to JIT's mystery container."

"Connectome copying?" Isaac's eyes widened. "Then Ruckman..."

"Is very likely the victim of a kidnapping," Nina finished for him, "and he doesn't even know it."

"Oh dear," Isaac breathed. "And Velasco was the one who picked the location."

"Would the hardware you found copy anyone who used the room?" Susan asked. "Or was it set up for specific targets?"

"Somewhere in between the two," Nina explained. "The copy process needed to be armed manually. It was switched off when I started poking around, so only someone as observant as Cephalie would have noticed the inconsistent infostructure. I went ahead and confiscated the illegal components and let the hotel staff know about the tampering."

"Then if we hadn't stumbled across this," Susan began, "it could have been used to copy more people."

"Or perhaps the criminals intended to come back later and clear out their hardware," Isaac said, head bowed as he thought out loud. "Otherwise, the illegal nodes would have been spotted when the room was refurbished." He looked up at Nina. "Good work."

"I do what I can," Nina replied with a smile. "You two off to the station next?"

"Yes. It'll be interesting to see what we can squeeze out of the punks who ambushed us." He glanced down at his empty plate. "We'll head there after..."

"After what?" Nina asked.

He frowned at his sister. "After I order some more bacon."

✧　　✧　　✧

"Good morning, gentlemen," Isaac said, joining Chatelain and Parks in one of the station's conference rooms. "What do you have for...?" He trailed off when he noticed the third SSP trooper in the room seated at the head of the table. His eyes glanced over the lieutenant bars on her shoulder, then fell on a stern, freckled face framed by wavy red hair almost as bright as Susan's. "My apologies, Lieutenant. I wasn't expecting anyone else."

"That's quite all right, Detective." The woman stood up and rounded the table. She extended a hand, which Isaac shook to discover the firm grip of a synthoid body. "Lieutenant Lina Hoopler, at your service."

She sidestepped over to Susan and shook her hand as well.

"Ma'am." Susan gave her a curt nod.

"Agent. I understand you two have been helping us with the Atlas suicide."

"That's right," Isaac said. "Though the case seems to have taken a more sinister turn recently."

"That's one of the reasons I'm now involved."

"One of?"

"The other being the conduct of this precinct's officers." Hoopler's eyes flicked across Chatelain and Parks, who both seemed unusually subdued. "I understand the support we've provided the two of you has been... somewhat lackluster."

"I wouldn't put it like that, Lieutenant."

"Then how would you characterize it, Detective?"

"It's been sufficient for our needs."

"You might call it 'sufficient,' but what I've heard tells me it doesn't meet this precinct's high standards. However it happened, our troopers requested SysPol's presence on this case, and SysPol responded. Which means *we* have an obligation to support *you* to the best of our abilities. In my judgment, that's not what's been happening, but it's what *will* happen from here on out."

"Does that mean we'll be working with different officers going forward?" Isaac asked.

"If you wish," Hoopler replied carefully, as if providing an invitation. Neither Chatelain nor Parks made eye contact with him, but he sensed a current of uneasiness in their postures.

"Actually, I'd like to request the opposite."

"Are you sure?" Hoopler wore a bemused—if slim—smile.

"Yes, Lieutenant. As I said, the support we've received from your troopers has been sufficient. Additionally, I've been impressed with Trooper Parks' nose for crime. Already, his input has proven quite valuable. None of us can say where the case will eventually lead us, but we've already pulled two violent criminals off the streets, thanks in part to his initiative."

"Very well, Detective. I'll make sure these two are made available whenever you need them." She returned to the head of the table and sat down. "And, on the topic of violent criminals, I believe we have some information you'll find interesting."

"And that is?" He and Susan took their seats.

"Names and backgrounds for your assailants," Hoopler said, then nodded to Chatelain to proceed.

"The two men you caught are Felix Zapf and Tommy Bao." Images of the men appeared over the center of the table alongside their criminal records. Bao was the stocky man with the piercings, and Zapf the slender gangster with the tattoos. "They're both members of the Byte Pyrates, with pirates misspelled with a *y* instead of an *i*."

"The Byte Pyrates?" Isaac echoed. "I'm not familiar with them."

"They're a rather nasty offshoot of the Sacred Flesh gang," Hoopler said.

"Ah. That makes sense."

"What does?" Susan asked.

"The Sacred Flesh," Isaac explained, "is a gang known for committing crimes almost exclusively against synthoids and ACs because, according to their philosophy, those citizens aren't real people. Hence, they argue, they aren't actually committing crimes, regardless of what the law says on the matter. They're one of the bigger gangs this high up in Janus."

"The Byte Pyrates are small by comparison," Hoopler continued after Isaac. "But in many ways they're worse. They've shown themselves to be utterly ruthless when it comes to abstract or synthetic life, and they execute their crimes with surprising sophistication. They've been causing problems across the Blocks for years, and I've personally had a few run-ins with them."

"Hence your *other* interest in our case?"

"Quite right, Detective. Their leader is a notorious criminal named Zalaya Riller, who's wanted for multiple counts of abstract kidnapping and murder. We've made several attempts over the years to locate her and bring her to justice, with no success." Hoopler paused and let out a slow, regretful sigh. "I led the last attempt to bring her in, but it turned out we'd been fed bad intel. We lost four troopers that day, two of which were permanent KIAs. So, take it from me, Detective. The Byte Pyrates are not to be trifled with."

"This fits the report we received earlier today," Isaac said. "One of our forensic specialists turned up evidence the shipping container was used to receive at least one copy-kidnapped AC. What can you tell us about the two gangsters?"

"Both have long lists of priors," Chatelain said. "Though Bao is the worse of the two. He did time in a juvie panopticosm for assaulting an officer, amongst other crimes. Zapf doesn't have any violent offenses in his history, though he does have a lot of data crimes like pattern theft, illegal replication, and the like."

"Makes sense," Isaac said. "My LENS checked their weapons after we took them in. It was Bao who fired on us. Zapf never discharged his pistol. He tried to run for it instead of engaging us."

"We've pulled all their background files for you." Chatelain patted the space underneath the virtual files. "They've also been briefed on their rights. Parks and I took care of that."

"Good to hear." Isaac copied the files to the case log.

"The two have been cooling off ever since we brought them in," Hoopler said. "How would you like them handled? Would you like us to interrogate them for you?"

"No, we'll handle that. Give us some time to go over the files, then we'll try our luck with Bao."

Isaac summoned a virtual view into the small interrogation room, which created a "window" over the door. Bao slouched in his seat at the small, square table, whistling a happy tune. He still wore the medical wrap around two of his fingers.

Isaac dismissed the view, then palmed the door open and stepped in. Bao flashed a quick, too-cheerful smile as they entered.

"You realize this is all just a big misunderstanding, right?" the big gangster said.

"Then help us understand," Isaac replied, taking one of the seats opposite Bao. Susan took the other, and the LENS floated over to Bao's side. "State your name for the record."

"Tommy. Tommy Bao."

"What were you doing in the shipping container?"

"What did it look like I was doing? That's my home."

"Your *home*?"

"Yeah, man. I live in a container." He gave the detectives an exaggerated shrug. "So what? Got a problem with that?"

"You're telling me the two of you live there?"

"Sure, sure."

"Legally?"

"Oh, yeah. Perfectly legal."

"For how long?"

"Quite a while, yeah."

"How long is a while?"

"I don't know. Not like I've been counting the days."

"JIT Deliveries doesn't seem to know anything about this supposed arrangement."

"Hey, it's not our fault their database has tracking errors."

"Who set you up with the place?"

"Mark."

"Mark who?"

"I don't know. I just call him Mark." Bao took on an exaggerated look of thoughtfulness. "Or was it Mike? Maybe it was Mike."

"What does he look like?"

"Don't recall."

"You don't?"

"I think he had one of those faces, you know? The plain, forgettable kind." Bao snapped his fingers. "You know, maybe that's on purpose. I bet he was a synthoid. Can't ever trust those things."

"Let me get this straight." Isaac leaned forward and knitted his fingers together. "You and your colleague have been living in that container for a length of time you can't recall, set up there by a person you don't even know the name of, and you somehow expect me to believe any of this?"

"Why wouldn't you?" Bao asked with fake surprise.

"What are all those nodes for?"

"Don't know. They were there before us."

"Why'd you shoot at us?"

"I didn't mean to."

"You didn't mean to?"

"It went off by accident. Sorry, man." He shrugged his arms, not looking sorry at all.

"You discharged"—Isaac scrolled through his notes—"twenty-seven shots. By accident?"

"That's right. Man, I was so glad to learn no one was hurt! What a relief!"

"Then why did you aim your pistol at me?" Susan asked with a firm, unflinching tone.

"Shit, lady. You scared me! What was I supposed to do?"

"Obey the lawful commands of a police officer," Isaac stated.

"Come on! She didn't give me the chance!"

"Bao, let me explain the situation to you," Isaac said, "because it's clear to me you don't seem to get it. You opened fire on two police officers. You *hit* one of us. What's left of your weapon has a log of you sending it the arming keycode. That's more than enough to send you away for twenty years, minimum."

"But—"

"Don't interrupt me. Think about that, Bao. You're thirty-six right now. If convicted, you won't see the light of day until you're *fifty*-six. And that's if you're lucky."

"But—"

"I'm not finished. You opened fire on us with the intent to kill, and we can prove it. You want to play games with us? Well, I'm not in the mood. Either you start cooperating, or I pass on a recommendation to the prosecutor for the *maximum* sentence. You know what that is, don't you?"

"Death?" Bao asked, sounding unimpressed.

"Death," Isaac repeated, his voice colder than the air outside Janus.

"But—"

"Don't you get it?" Isaac snapped. "You shot at me and you hit my partner!" He paused, took a deep breath, and some measure of calm returned to his demeanor. "If it were up to me, I'd pass on that recommendation right here and now. And that's exactly what I *will* do, if you refuse to cooperate with us."

"Fuck you, man!" Bao tried to flip him off, but the gesture became muddled by the medical wrap propping up two of his fingers. "No one tells me what to do!"

"Have it your way." Isaac rose to his feet. "Good luck at the trial. You're going to need it."

✧   ✧   ✧

Isaac had started with Bao because he'd thought he could bring more pressure to bear due to the more severe charges the gangster faced, but now that he watched Zapf fidgeting within the interrogation room, he wondered if he'd miscalculated.

"He's nervous," Susan said.

"Very," Isaac agreed, noting the sheen of sweat on the man's brow.

The tattoo on Zapf's neck looped through the same animation, showing a partially undressed man and woman engaged in intercourse. He sat in the chair at a skewed angle, elbow on the table, one foot tapping incessantly.

"Let's see what we can squeeze out of him."

Isaac opened the door and sat down across from Zapf. The man didn't meet his gaze, his foot tapping faster.

Isaac took his time setting up his notes while the LENS loomed behind Zapf's head. The gangster bit into his lower lip, and he tucked both feet beneath the chair, one locked on top of the other.

"State your name for the record," Isaac began.

"Felix Zapf," he muttered.

"Now then, Zapf, how about we start with what you were doing in that shipping container."

"I can't tell you."

"Can't? Or won't?"

"Does it really matter?"

"It matters to me."

"Look, I know I'm in trouble, but I can't help you."

"Why can't you help us?"

"Because of..." Zapf trailed off and turned his head to the side.

"Because of what?"

"You know which crew I'm with?"

"We know you're with the Byte Pyrates."

"Yeah, well, that's not the whole of it. I used to run with the Numbers, doing small hacking jobs for them. Mostly pattern theft with a side of snooping. Nothing major. Not enough to get *SysPol*'s attention, that's for sure! Never hurt anybody, I swear."

"Why'd you leave them?"

"Got a better offer from the Byte Pyrates. They heard about my work and liked it. Made an offer that turned my head. More Esteem, less work. What's not to love about that? The Numbers were sore about me leaving, but I smoothed it over best I could. Even did one last job for them without taking my cut. I don't like burning bridges, you know? Anyway, I started running with the Pyrates about half a year ago, thinking I'd be doing the same sort of work."

"And were you?"

"Hell no! Before I knew it, I was neck-deep in some serious shit! Like *kidnapping* shit and who knows what else! I don't ask, don't know, don't *want* to know! They just give me the jobs and I do them, okay? If they want me to sit in some shipping container for months, then I do it. I don't ask questions and I keep my head down."

"Sounds like you want out."

"*Out?* No, no. There's no 'out.' The only people who leave are the ones in *bags*! If I squeal, she'll know. She'll find out somehow, and she'll turn my brain into soup!"

"She?"

"Zalaya Riller. Scariest bitch I ever met. The things she does to ACs." Zapf shuddered. "Look, I'm not into that shit, all right? I don't buy what the others say about synthetic life. All I do is help out with the tech, I swear!"

"What sort of help?"

"Weren't you listening? I can't tell you! I'm as good as dead if Riller hears I squealed!"

"Mister Zapf." Isaac leaned back in his seat. "It sounds to me like you're not terribly fond of the Byte Pyrates."

"Yeah, no kidding!"

"What if I offered you a way to leave them?"

"You..." His lower lip trembled. "How?"

"That depends on how valuable your testimony proves, but if you're that concerned about reprisal then SysPol can place you under witness protection. Your cooperation in exchange for reduced sentencing *and* us keeping the Pyrates off your back. Not a bad deal, if you ask me."

"You can do that?"

"*If* you aid us in resolving this case. Tell me, what *were* you two doing in that container?"

Zapf lowered his gaze and cupped a hand over his mouth, his eyes wide as he considered the offer. Isaac waited for the gangster to make his decision.

"We were a relay," Zapf said at last, looking up. "Passing data from various jobs on to the next relay."

"Destined for where?"

"Our main hideout."

"Which is where?"

"I don't know."

"You expect us to believe that?" Susan cut in sharply.

"It's the truth!" Zapf held up both hands, his face almost cringing in desperation. "They're a cagey bunch, and I haven't been with them long enough. That's why they stuck me on the relay job first. They wanted to make sure they could trust me." He lowered his head and shook it. "Now here I am squealing to the cops. My life sucks!"

"What can you tell us about a connectome your relay received about a month ago?" Isaac asked.

"A connectome?" Zapf's brow furrowed, but then his eyes lit up. "Oh, that one! Yeah, I remember. From the synthoid hotel, right?"

"The Divided-By-Zero."

"Yeah, yeah! I know the job. Bao and I were the ones who rigged the room's infosystems."

"What else can you tell us about the job?"

"Not much. Like I said, we're just a relay, but I'll tell you what I know. That job came from the outside. Someone wanted the target copy-kidnapped and hired us to do it."

"Who was the client?"

"Supposedly anonymous. Went by the pseudonym 'Ghost.'"

"What do you mean, supposedly?"

"Well..." Zapf smirked. "You see, he *tried* to keep his real identity secret, but he was hiring the *Byte Pyrates*. I wasn't the one who cracked it, but I heard about it from Tommy. Apparently, there were enough clues in the transmissions for us to figure out his real identity. Riller *loves* it when we can unmask who we're working for. I understand she has quite the stash of blackmail saved up."

"Did Bao tell you who the client was?"

"Yeah. Said he was some big shot within the Society named Desmond Fike."

CHAPTER SIXTEEN

CEPHALIE FINISHED PROCESSING THE ARREST WARRANT FOR Desmond Fike minutes after they wrapped up Zapf's interrogation. Isaac "hand delivered" the warrant to Lieutenant Hoopler along with an official SysPol order for a citywide search to locate Fike and bring him in.

Hoopler took a grav tube up to the tenth floor of the 103rd and spoke with Captain Breyer in his office, the expansive view of the city behind his back. Breyer, the commanding officer for the 103rd, approved the order and placed Hoopler in charge of their precinct's mobilization. He then forwarded the document to the Third Engine Block 1st Precinct, along with a message flagging the matter as time sensitive.

His message was received by Phantasm, the integrated companion of Major Whitmey, who was himself the highest-ranked SSP officer in the Third Engine Block. Phantasm used the message as an excuse to pull Whitmey out of a city council meeting the man had no interest in attending, and when Whitmey returned to his desk, he skimmed through the SysPol order before calling Isaac to discuss the details.

"My fear is Fike will attempt to leave our jurisdiction," Isaac told the major. "In fact, it's possible he already has. He enjoys a day's head start on us. But it's also possible he never left the city. In which case, the advantage is ours if we act swiftly."

That was all Whitmey needed to hear. He approved the order,

and his IC distributed instructions to all precincts within the Third Engine Block and its suburbs while placing the 103rd in overall command of the search.

Isaac, Susan, and Hoopler settled down in a command-and-control room on the 103rd Precinct Building's ninth floor. Data feeds from all over the city fed into a virtual patchwork of charts and images encircling the trio. Hoopler began issuing follow-up instructions to the various precincts, and Isaac settled in for what might be a long wait.

✦   ✦   ✦

"Sometimes this job feels like I'm trying to juggle flaming vibro-saws," Hoopler groaned, "I swear."

"Problems?" Isaac asked.

"Just trying to keep up with everything in motion. The word's out as far and wide as we can push it." She closed her interface and gave Isaac a sideways glance. "We've listed the warrant through all our regular channels, and the captain's scheduled a news conference in the afternoon. We've also been going through all of Fike's known contacts, checking in to see if any of them can tell us where he is. So far nothing, but we'll keep trying."

"Sounds good. I appreciate the support."

"No problem, Detective. Along those lines, I sent Chatelain and Parks out to the Society's chapterhouse for a face-to-face visit. They messaged me a few minutes ago. No hits, I'm afraid. Only one person was at the chapter when they stopped by, and she didn't provide any useful information."

"Who'd they talk to?"

"A young woman named Bonnie Rosenstein. Said she was the chapter's assistant chair."

"Then I'm not surprised she had nothing to share. My impression of Miss Rosenstein is she left the actual running of the chapter to Fike. More of a believer than an administrator. Anything else?"

"Not really. No sightings of either Fike or his car. He hasn't purchased any public transit tickets either, be it train or plane, and his car hasn't passed through any of the city's ground exits."

"Which means he should still be in the city," Isaac concluded. "He had access to the yacht in the Society warehouse, but we know exactly where that is and have it locked down now. He won't get out of the city that way. And with us searching for his car as well, that theoretically pins him down within the Block."

"Question is where," Susan said.

"I know," Isaac agreed. "It's a big city, and he could be any-where in it."

"His car will be more difficult to hide," Hoopler said. "If we find it, we'll be that much closer to tracking him down."

"True enough."

"So, Detective," Hoopler began, leaning back in her seat. "What do you think is really going on with all this?"

"You mean how Fike connects back to the Velasco suicide?"

Hoopler nodded.

"If you ask me, it comes down to a simple case of corporate sabotage. Fike and Velasco conspired together to undermine SourceCode's trial. Fike hired the Byte Pyrates to kidnap Ruck-man, and Velasco abused the man's trust and lured him to that rewired hotel room. Once his connectome was on the premises, the Byte Pyrates created a copy and transmitted it to another team, which we can presume then extracted enough information to carry out the sabotage."

"That could explain the security access irregularity SourceCode mentioned," Susan noted.

"Right you are. I'm not sure who infiltrated SourceCode's systems—could be either that second group of Byte Pyrates or Velasco himself—but the results are plain enough. SourceCode's trial blew up in their faces."

"But why would Fike get involved?" Hoopler asked. "The Dyson Project is still moving forward. All this achieves is a change in contractor."

"True," Isaac admitted, "but there are a few possible motives for Fike that could explain what we're seeing. It could come down to something as simple as money. Just take a look at the Society 'warehouse' Fike has been living in. It certainly looks like he enjoyed leaching off the Society's coffers. If so, then this could have been an opportunity for Fike to load up his accounts even further, using recent events to justify more spending.

"Another possibility comes from the Society's past behavior in general, assuming Fike at least *somewhat* believes in the cause. The Society has a history of going after these Dyson trials, whether it's to their long-term benefit or not. We could be looking at a mis-guided attempt to slow the project down, which ultimately failed.

"Or, perhaps, Fike knew the Society couldn't stop the project indefinitely and decided to conspire with one of the companies, happy to inflict whatever damage they could.

"*Or*"—Isaac wagged a finger—"maybe he *did* intend to take both of them down, possibly by using his connections to Velasco—and pressure he could bring to bear as his coconspirator—to undermine Atlas from within."

"Which is no longer possible," Susan said, "since the man ventilated his own head."

"True enough. But if Velasco were still alive, I wouldn't put that sort of manipulation past Fike. He seems to have the Society dancing to his tune. Why not others?"

"And the suicide itself?" Hoopler asked.

"Could be a case of Velasco growing a conscience. That seems to be the most likely explanation with the facts we have. He betrayed a friend's trust and then found out what became of his copy. We don't know what happened to Ruckman-2, but if the past cases I've worked are any indication, it wasn't pretty. An isolated AC is in an incredibly vulnerable state since a criminal can take full control of the abstraction they're placed in, using illegal realms to force all manner of unpleasant stimuli on the individual."

"You think the Pyrates tortured the information out of him?" Susan asked.

"That's a distinct possibility," Isaac said, his voice turning hard and cold. "Especially when you take into account their connections to the Sacred Flesh gang, and how *that* gang doesn't view ACs as real people. Dehumanize the victim to justify your extreme measures."

"We'll have to wait and see, I suppose," Hoopler said.

"Yep." Isaac leaned back in his chair and propped up his boots. "Wait and see."

Isaac tried to contact Ruckman during one of the long lulls between news, but the engineer didn't respond, so he left a message. The return call came one hour later.

"You wished to speak with me, Detective?" Ruckman said, a curious—and somewhat worried—expression on his face. "Your message said it was important."

"It is, though I'd prefer to discuss the matter with you in person. Are you free to transmit to my current location?"

"Am I in trouble?"

"Not with the law, if that's what you're afraid of. But our

investigation has uncovered some information relevant to you that I'd like to pass on. At your convenience, of course."

"What sort of information?"

"The sort best discussed in private. Are you still in the city? If so, Agent Cantrell and I can drive out to meet you. We're in a wait-and-see phase of the case, so it's no problem for us."

"Can't you just tell me what this is about instead of pussy-footing around?"

"I would prefer not to."

"Fine," Ruckman grumbled. "I'll transmit over."

"Thank you. Sending the location string now."

Isaac closed the comm window and stood up. Susan followed him out of the control room and down the hall.

"You sure this is a good idea?" she asked softly. "We still have an open investigation. Shouldn't we hold off until the case is further along?"

"Perhaps, but I don't see how letting Ruckman know could contaminate the investigation. Best to let the victim know sooner rather than later. We don't want to seem like we're withholding information from him."

Isaac palmed the conference room open. Ruckman was already in the room when they stepped in.

"Well?" the engineer asked pointedly.

Isaac waited for the door to seal shut. "I'm afraid I have some unpleasant news to share. We've uncovered evidence you've been kidnapped."

"*Kidnapped?*" Ruckman blurted, his face contorted in confusion. "What kind of nonsense are you talk—" Realization dawned on his face, and he cast his gaze down at his own virtual hands. "Oh. Oh shit." His eyes flicked back up to Isaac's. "You mean...?"

"We believe you're the victim of a copy-kidnapping. The copy protection around your connectome was breached recently, and a duplicate generated without your knowledge. At this moment, the copy is unaccounted for."

Ruckman lowered his head once more. A virtual chair appeared behind him, and he dropped heavily into it, arms hanging limply in his lap. Isaac pulled a physical chair over to his side and sat down next to him.

"You sure about this?" Ruckman asked after a while.

"We are. We have a confession from one of the criminals

involved as well as evidence supporting these conclusions."

"How did this happen?"

"The kidnapping took place about a month ago—"

"A *month*?"

"At the Divided-By-Zero hotel. The infostructure in the room was modified for this purpose."

"Who would do this?"

"A gang called the Byte Pyrates performed the grab. It appears they received assistance from Velasco."

"Esteban? But . . . no, that can't be right. He wouldn't."

"You said yourself he requested the unusual location. Now we know why. He rented that room for over a week before your meeting, time the Byte Pyrates used to set up their capture gear."

"But . . . Esteban?"

"I'm sorry to be the bearer of bad news."

"You sure about this?"

"Of this, yes. The case itself remains open."

"But why would he do it?"

"We're not certain of that yet, but we're looking into it. We'll share more with you once we have a firmer grasp of the facts."

"How long have you known?" Ruckman asked.

"Since this morning when we received the forensics report on the room."

Ruckman snorted out a joyless laugh. "Serves me right for ignoring your call. I was in the middle of a motivational workshop with E&E. Been trying to decide which job I want to go for next. Sorry."

"It's quite all right, Mister Ruckman. We would have found a way to get ahold of you sooner if our call had been time critical."

"I'll bet." He let out a deep sigh and gazed around the room. "You know, it's shocking but it's also confusing as hell. Like, what am I supposed to feel right now? I've been kidnapped and yet here I am, perfectly fine. There's a copy of me out there having who-knows-what done to him. Hell, once the protection's gone, what's to make these animals stop there? There could be hundreds—*thousands* of me by now—and I've been going about my days as if nothing were wrong. As if losing my job is my worst problem."

"I understand this can be a trying time for you." Isaac placed a consoling hand on Ruckman's shoulder. His wetware provided an abstract sense of pressure for the virtual contact. "If you like, we can provide you with assistance to help see you through this.

Would you like me to see if a Panoptics Division counselor is available to speak with you?"

"No, that's all right. I'll manage. Thanks, though."

"Of course. The offer will remain open if you need it."

Isaac stood up and was about to head for the door, but Ruckman looked up suddenly.

"Would you two... mind staying a bit longer? I think... I think I could use a little company after all."

"I suppose we can." Isaac returned to his seat. "As I said, we're in a wait-and-see phase of the case, so this won't interfere with our duties."

"Thanks." Ruckman gave them a weak smile. "You're going to get to the bottom of this, right? Going to make the people who did this pay?"

"That's what we're here for, Mister Ruckman. That's what we do."

✧   ✧   ✧

Nina called in a few hours later.

"Got anything good for us?" Isaac asked, shifting the comm window over so Susan could participate from her own seat in the control room.

"Eh." Nina shrugged. "I wouldn't get your hopes up. I'm in the process of finishing up my report on Atlas. I should be ready to send it your way in the next hour or so, but I need to ask you something first."

"Shoot."

"Okay, now don't go all judgmental on me," she warned. "I *swear* this is work related."

"If you say so."

"You know how the newest *Solar Descent* season ends, right?"

"I do..." Isaac replied guardedly, not sure where this line of questioning had come from.

"And you also know who the big bad turns out to be."

"That too."

"Okay, bear with me here. I came across a weird pattern in some of the interoffice correspondence. A bunch of them were talking about the new season."

"Which is perfectly normal for people in an office to do."

"But something struck me as odd. By itself, them sharing their thoughts on the new release is no big deal, but no matter where I looked, I couldn't find any spoilers for how the season ended."

"I thought you were trying to avoid spoilers."

"I am, but I should have had to try harder to stay clear of them."

"Are you sure this is about work?" Isaac asked.

"Patience. It'll be worth it," Nina assured him. "You see, the absence of spoilers got me thinking, so I hate to do it, but I need to ask you a question. Who's the big bad of this season?"

"You sure you want to know?"

"I wouldn't be asking if I didn't."

Isaac glanced over at Susan, wondering if she preferred to avoid spoilers the same way Nina did. He didn't want to ruin the season for her if he didn't have to.

"Go ahead," Susan said. "I'm not going to know what you're talking about, anyway."

"All right. The last boss turns out to be a sleeper agent in the Solar Guild. You see, back when the Eye was first being explored—"

"Just the villain's name, Isaac," Nina interrupted. "I don't need a lore dump."

"Oh. Well, all right. He's called the Onyx Ghost. Or the Ghost of the Everdark Eye. Both names are used during the scenario."

"The Onyx Ghost? Wait, didn't we learn about this scumbag last season?"

"We did."

"Isn't he the guy who"—Nina's eyes flicked to Susan and then back—"did the thing to those people?"

Isaac nodded.

"And then pulled the... you know on the same group at... that place."

Isaac nodded again.

"That *jerk*!" she seethed. "I'm going to melt his face off first chance I get!"

"Does this help at all?" Isaac asked, not sure what to make of their conversation's bizarre turn.

"What?"

"With the *case*, Nina."

"Oh, yeah. It does." She shook her head. "The Onyx Frickin' Ghost. I should have guessed it'd be him."

"Why do you say that?" Isaac asked, but then a tenuous connection dawned on him. He turned to Susan.

"The Ghost?" she asked. "No way that's related to our case, right?"

"No, that's not what I'm saying," Nina clarified. "But it *does* appear as if someone scrubbed Atlas' archives before I could get my hands on it. I'm not finding any *Sclar Descent* spoilers because correspondence with the word 'ghost' may have been purged from the infostructure image they submitted."

"Hmm, you could be right," Isaac said. "If the employees were talking about the season, I would have expected you to come across some Onyx Ghost discussions. Apparently, a lot of people are upset about the last fight."

"Why's that?" Susan asked.

"Very high numbers of total party kills. Sounds like the scenario goes through quite the difficulty spike at the end. That may even be the intended result, story-wise. If so, it makes more sense why the season is restricted to new characters." He turned back to Nina. "Any follow-up actions for you at Atlas?"

"Not right away. I need to have a chat with our lawyers before I move on, but I can already tell you the result. More lawyer time between us and Atlas, leading to more delays."

"And more time for the records to be corrupted further."

"Yeah, that too."

"What about the timing of this latest data purge? Any thoughts?"

"Hard to say, but I'd guess it's very recent. Perhaps even a few hours before I was granted access."

"Good to know," Isaac said. "This reinforces the theory that Velasco had a coconspirator within Atlas who is still active. Good work."

"Doesn't feel like it, but I do what I can." Nina gave him an indifferent shrug. "Anyway, I'm going to wrap up my work here then head over to JIT Deliveries."

"One thing before you go." Isaac pulled up Zapf's confession and transmitted it to her. "Before you start working on that container, I'd like you to read over the file I just sent. We confirmed the logistical site was used to pull off a copy-kidnapping that targeted Antoni Ruckman."

"Figured it was something like that. This case is taking some ugly turns."

"The grab was performed by a gang called the Byte Pyrates. We know who ordered the job, but what we don't know is where the Ruckman copy was transmitted next or where the gang's hideout is. Be on the lookout for any evidence that can point us toward either."

"You got it. I'll read through it on the drive over."

An alert appeared in Isaac's peripheral vision. It was an incoming call from Raviv.

"Anything else?" he asked.

"Nope. Like I said, I'll finish up here, send you the final report, then head for JIT Deliveries."

"All right. Gotta go. Raviv's calling. We'll talk later."

"See you."

He closed the call and connected with Raviv. An image appeared of Raviv and Damphart standing in a dark alleyway with layers of utility conduits running across the ceiling. Damphart was watching something outside the camera's field of view with what might have been a look of trepidation, while Raviv stood with his weight on his back leg, hand on his hip, and a deeper frown than usual on his face. One of their LENS drones floated nearby with the other presumably acting as the camera.

Behind them, a squad of six Arete Division synthoids advanced—*cautiously*—in the direction of Damphart's gaze, weapons raised. The dim light glinted off their red full-body armor.

"Yeah, boss?" Isaac asked. "What can we do for you?"

"Isaac. You and Susan still busy with the suicide case?"

"We are."

"Good." He nodded as if greatly satisfied. "You see any need to visit the Second Engine Block?"

"No, not right now."

"Even better."

Behind Raviv, six Arete synthoids passed in the opposite direction, backpedaling with their weapons raised, some now angled at the floor or up at the ceiling. They were the same squad who'd only begun advancing moments ago, and this time they appeared...jumpy. Damphart's face contorted in fresh worry, and she reached behind her to pat Raviv on the shoulder. He brushed her hand aside without looking.

"You two keep working that case, you hear me?" he said. "Oh, and stay the hell away from this city while you're at it."

"Okay," Isaac said, "but that's not the impression you gave us yesterday."

"Well, today's a new day. A new, *terrible* day."

"Is something wrong?"

"Wrong?" Raviv gave them a look of fake surprise. "What gave you that idea?"

"Oh, I don't know. The sudden change in instructions. The worried look on Damphart's face. The heavily armed Arete squad behind you. Small stuff like that."

"Oh, God!" someone cried from off camera. "They're coming out of the walls! They're coming out of the goddamned walls!"

"Won't you play with us?" squealed a too-cheerful, tinny voice that was soon joined by a repeating, off-pitch chorus.

"Go find someone else to annoy!" snapped a different voice. "Nobody likes you!"

A rifle burst-fired. Chunks of pink and pale blue fur—some of it ablaze—flew into the air behind Raviv then fluttered to the ground. The chief inspector rested his head in his hand and began to massage his temples, apparently unperturbed by the violence behind him.

"Do you see the kind of crap I have to put up with, Isaac?"

"Only partially. The field of view is a bit on the narrow side."

"You sure you don't need help over there?" Susan asked, sliding her chair closer to Isaac.

"Trust me," Raviv groaned. "You two don't want any part of this."

"You *sure*?" Susan pressed, sounding unusually enthusiastic. "I can switch to my combat frame and zip over there in no time."

"That won't be necessary."

"My combat frame comes with a flamethrower," she offered with a hopeful smile.

Raviv's eyes perked up with sudden interest. He paused in thought, but then he shook his head.

"No, I appreciate the offer, but it's best if we let Arete handle this mess." He leaned in toward the camera and spoke softer. "They don't like it when we show them up."

"Is it really that bad?" Isaac asked.

"Let me put it this way." Raviv stuck both hands on his hips. "The *Toyoda* has started printing out assault mechs for Arete."

"Arete is deploying *assault mechs*?" Isaac cringed. "Which pattern?"

"Red Knights with heavy loadouts."

"Oh, good grief."

"What's a Red Knight pattern?" Susan asked.

"They're like your combat frame, but bigger and with no legs or boosters, since they use a graviton thruster for mobility."

"So ... they're big floating torsos with lots of guns?"

"Basically."

"Is hardware like that needed over there?" Susan asked.

"Not if you ask me," Raviv said. "I mean, these fuzzles are nothing but brainless toys. Arete's overreacting."

"Chief?" Damphart's eyeline tracked something moving across the ground. She tugged on Raviv's sleeve, but he knocked her hand aside.

"Anyway, I want the two of you to stay well away from WHAT THE FUCK IS ON MY LEG?!"

"Be my friend!" squeaked a voice stuck in the unsettling valley between cute and creepy.

"Oh, God!" Raviv shook his leg out while hopping around on the other.

"Come play with me!"

"Get it off! GET IT OFF!"

He stumbled forward and knocked into the LENS. The viewpoint swung to the side, past a writhing sea of multicolored fur oozing out of the walls before the feed switched off.

"What ..." Isaac leaned back. "What just happened?"

"It looked like their position was being overrun by plushies," Susan said.

"Yeah." Isaac took the moment to swallow. "Yeah, that's what it looked like." He tried to call Raviv back but didn't get a response. He was about to call Dispatch to report the problem when a text message arrived from Raviv's connection string.

It read: WE'RE FINE. FALLING BACK. TALK LATER.

"Well, that's good, I guess," Isaac exhaled and sat back in his chair.

"You sure I shouldn't head over there in my combat frame?" Susan asked, that hopeful smile back on her face.

"You really love that thing, don't you?"

"Just considering the possibilities. Wouldn't it look good to swoop in and help the boss out?"

"Not after he explicitly told us to stay away."

"Fine," she sighed, then slid her chair back to its original position. "I guess we'll go back to waiting and seeing for hours on end."

"Yup," Isaac replied, settling back in for a long day.

CHAPTER SEVENTEEN

ISAAC AND SUSAN TURNED IN FOR THE NIGHT AFTER A LONG shift with no new leads. They stopped by Thrusters first thing next morning and found Cephalie at a table already hard at work with a trio of virtual wheeled blackboards nearby. Lines of chalked text covered all three boards with color-coded icons beside each row, most of them drawn in red or orange chalk.

"Any news come in last night?" Isaac asked, settling into a chair beside Cephalie.

"Nothing too exciting," Cephalie confessed. "SSP has received a big, fat zero for confirmed sightings or verified passes through public transportation. Same with that warehouse out on the Ridge, which the 17th Precinct is keeping under constant surveillance."

"That's about what we expected if he's trying to keep a low profile."

"The SSP tip line's been getting its usual flood of claimed sightings, with larger bursts coming in after the story featured on local news streams."

"That sounds promising," Susan said.

"You'd *think* so." Cephalie clicked her cane on the table. "But you'd be surprised. Hoopler put a dedicated team of ACs to work managing the tip line. I spoke to them last night and reviewed their work. They strike me as solid at sniffing out people's tall stories. Unfortunately, they've flagged most of the tips as either 'unreliable' or 'verifiably false.'"

"People hungry for attention?" Susan asked.

"We see all sorts," Isaac said.

"Attention grabbers," Cephalie listed, "amateur comedians, small-time troublemakers, people who think they can swindle some easy Esteem off the police, bored idiots looking for a laugh, and a few first-rate nutjobs. For example"—she highlighted a message on one of her blackboards, enlarging it—"did you know that Fike was secretly an Admin double agent?"

"Says who?" Susan asked sharply.

"An anonymous concerned citizen who, so the entry claims, is a *former* Admin double agent with insider knowledge of their invasion plans for Janus."

"Invasion plans?" Isaac raised an eyebrow at his partner, somehow managing to keep a straight face. "Susan? Anything you'd like to share with us?"

"That we have enough problems back home?" she offered, visibly uncomfortable with the subject. "Seriously, we've got Martians and Lunarians trying to blow us up half the time. The *last* thing we need is to make our bigger, more advanced neighbor mad at us."

"Which is exactly what you'd say," Cephalie teased, "if you *were* plotting an invasion."

"Hmm," Isaac murmured, rubbing his chin thoughtfully. "You have a point there."

"Oh, come on!" Susan said. "First of all, I don't know who that informant thinks he is, but Janus is a stupid place to invade. The Admin barely has any presence this far out from the inner system, never mind the DTI, which means the logistics of any operation to cross the transverse and reach Saturn would be *terrible!*"

"They are?" Isaac tilted his head. "You mean you've thought this through?"

"I...umm...*no!* That's not what I mean at all. I'm just saying whoever left the tip *clearly* has no idea what he's talking about."

"It's okay." Isaac smiled and gave her a friendly pat on the shoulder. "You realize we're on the same page as you, right?"

"If you thought that one was bad," Cephalie cut in, "wait until you see the one that claims Fike is a time-traveling alien from Saturn's distant past."

"Oh, good grief." Isaac shook his head.

"I wish I was joking. I really do."

A new line scratched itself across the bottom of one of her

blackboards. This line came with a green colored flag beside it that read: FOLLOW-UP RECOMMENDED. It was the only splash of green across all three of her virtual boards.

"Oh?" Cephalie's glasses glinted. "What do we have here?"

"A lead, I hope," Susan said.

"The captain was scheduled to sit down for an interview with the *Engine Block Times* this morning to discuss the case." Cephalie checked her pocket watch. "In fact, it might still be going. Tip lines usually see a surge right after one of those. Maybe they caught something good this time."

She transferred a copy of the tip to Isaac, and he opened it, then shifted it over for Susan's benefit.

"Tip comes from a Paul Piturro," Isaac summarized, "owner of the Cretaceous Safari. According to him, Fike had an appointment at the Safari two days ago. He showed up on time for his appointment but bailed soon after." He checked the times listed in the tip then cross-referenced them with his notes. "If this is correct, then Fike would have been at the Safari when I first tried to call him."

"This makes sense in more ways than one," Susan said. "Didn't some of the dinosaur bones at Fike's place come from the Cretaceous Safari?"

"That's what it said on the displays."

"Sounds like someone should go have a chat with Mister Piturro about his customer."

"You want me to ask Hoopler to dispatch a team?" Cephalie asked. "Or you want to handle this one yourselves?"

"We'll follow up this lead ourselves," Isaac said, and was surprised when Susan pumped her fist with a smile. "What?"

"I was hoping you'd say that."

"You were? Why?"

"Because"—she flashed a toothy grin—"I've been yearning to go there since I heard about the place. Now I don't have to wait."

"I'm still not sure what's got you so excited about that place."

"Because they're *dinosaurs*!"

"So?"

"On *Saturn*!"

✧   ✧   ✧

Isaac brought the Cretaceous Safari up on the map once they were back in the rental, surprised to find it took up over forty square kilometers within the barrier between the Second and Third Engine Blocks, forming a rectangular space two kilometers wide and twenty across. Private docks were situated at regular intervals along the perimeter with the only point of public access near the center.

The rental followed a series of ramps up the shelves, their path corkscrewing higher and higher until they reached the ceiling streets. They cut around a congested utility sector, then took a ramp upward through the structural barrier. The car drove up through a diagonal tunnel cut through the barrier, the ceiling low and ribbed with thick secondary supports that extended down the sides, making the tunnel resemble the interior of a giant ribcage.

Bright light spilled in from the tunnel exit ahead, and the rental slowed, then pulled out onto a flat, grassy plain dotted by palm trees and giant ferns. A ring of wooden barriers enclosed their immediate surroundings, stretching halfway up to a ceiling that mimicked a partially clouded terrestrial sky, with the other half closed off with netting. The barriers *appeared* to be made of wood and rope, but Isaac suspected more sophisticated materials had been used beneath their superficial exteriors. Beyond the perimeter, thick structural columns reached skyward, covered in a veneer of "natural" rock.

A four-story mansion sat in the middle of the barricaded area, its pristine wooden exterior painted white, thick smoke rising from a pair of brick stacks on either end of the building. The rental parked in front of the open porch, next to a line of metal-skinned ground cars and copters with CRETACIOUS SAFARI stenciled on their sides in yellow font along with a vehicle number.

"When do we see the dinosaurs?" Susan asked, climbing out of the rental.

"We're not here for the dinosaurs," Isaac said.

"I know that. But we're here, aren't we? Why not make the most of it?"

"Come on. We've got work to do."

"Okay," she sighed, and followed him through a pair of salon doors into a foyer with a varnished wooden floor and a wide countertop stacked with tangible books and maps. Framed pictures of hunters and their kills covered nearly half the back wall, all composed in a painterly style rather than realistic photos.

An old man sat in a rocking chair beside a crackling fireplace with a knitted blanket across his lap and a basset hound sleeping beside his feet.

The old man tipped a wide-brimmed hat back with a finger and opened a lazy eye. He smiled at the newcomers, the crags of his cleanly shaven face deepening with the expression. He wore a brown leather vest over a denim button-down shirt and jeans with a black string tie around his collar. His full head of hair was wispy white.

"Hello there," he said in a warm, jovial voice. "You from SysPol?"

"We are. Detective Cho and Agent Cantrell. We're looking for Paul Piturro."

"At your service." Piturro pushed the blanket aside and climbed out of the rocking chair. He crossed the room and shook both of their hands. "My pleasure."

"And I'm Doctus." The basset hound rose and padded over. "I'm Paul's IC."

Isaac had run a basic background check on the ride over. Paul Piturro was a one-hundred-eighty-seven-year-old synthoid who'd amassed an impressive fortune running three different Old Frontier farms, all specializing in luxury food production. He'd since branched out into more niche enterprises with Cretaceous Safari and a few other businesses. Overall, the man gave Isaac the impression of eccentric wealth.

"Doctus?" Susan asked. "Does the name mean something?"

"Indeed, it does, my good lady." The dog's eyes lit up. "It's Latin for educated or learned. I chose it because I'm living proof you *can* teach an old dog new tricks."

Isaac suppressed an urge to groan.

"Would you like to see one?" Doctus offered, tail wagging.

"Perhaps another time," Isaac replied. "We're here because of the message you left with the SSP tip line."

"Yes, your IC called saying you'd stop by." Piturro planted his hands on his hips. "I'm not sure how else I can help, though."

"Can you describe your relationship with Desmond Fike?"

"Strictly professional. He was a client of mine. A *very* regular client. He absolutely loved our open safari tours, though he'd occasionally try out some of our novelty hunts."

"What sort of hunts are those?" Susan asked.

Isaac wasn't sure about her question's relevance to the case, but he let it pass without comment.

"You can think of them as curated experiences," Piturro said. "Normally, we let the creatures roam free, but for some hunts, we'll actively adjust the positions and population levels to create a more refined, bespoke experience for the hunters. Staff will send our drones out to sedate and transfer creatures to and from hidden holding pens based on the scenario's needs.

"Fike stuck to open safaris most of the time, but he dabbled in the more narrative-based adventures. We have this one called Raptor Riot where the hunters have to defend a family of sauropods from a pack of bloodthirsty atrociraptors. It takes a while to set up, but it's been a big hit with our regulars. They appreciate the change in pace."

"You have *atrociraptors*?" Susan asked, her eyes gleaming.

"That we do, miss." Piturro tipped his hat.

"What about T. rexes?"

"Absolutely. Place wouldn't be complete without the royal couple."

"What about—"

Isaac cleared his throat. Susan paused with her mouth half open. She closed it with an audible clap, stood a little straighter, and clasped her hands behind her back.

"Did Fike hunt dinosaurs alone or with others?" Isaac asked.

"Alone, mostly." Piturro placed his thumbs behind his belt. "And technically they're not dinosaurs."

"They're not?"

"They're 'living dinosaur-like reproductions.'"

"Those words sound carefully chosen."

"It's a legal thing," Doctus said. "We're not allowed to use the d-word alone when referring to our feature creatures."

"Not after we were sued for false advertising," Piturro grumped. "I *would* have real dinosaurs if I could, but that's not practical, I'm afraid. I even reached out to the Antiquities Rescue Trust about it. This is some seven years ago, mind you. Back when everyone thought ART was a respectable organization. I asked them if it was possible to use their time machines to bring back some genuine dinosaur DNA. Or maybe even a live sample or two."

"What did they say?" Susan asked.

"That their time machines were too slow to go back that far."

"Ahh." Susan nodded. "Right. Hadn't thought of that." She let out a short, sad sigh. "Of *course*, they're not real dinosaurs."

"What didn't you think of?" Isaac asked.

"The transit times," Susan explained. "We're talking about a trip at least sixty-five million years into the past. Your average TTV clocks in at seventy thousand seconds per second, so a round-trip mission that far back would take a *long* time to execute."

"Almost two thousand years," Piturro added.

"What a shame," Isaac said dully.

"Yeah." Susan shook her head, perhaps not picking up on his sarcasm. "It really is."

"I originally wanted to name the place 'Dinosaur Safari,'" Piturro continued. "That's what I told Atlas I would build when I offered to buy the space off them."

"You purchased this zone from Atlas?" Isaac asked.

"That's right. Got it for a dream, too. They were looking to off-load it after some botched attempt to build a town here. Maxwell's Retreat, I think they were calling it."

"*Mattison's* Retreat," Doctus corrected.

Piturro snapped his fingers. "Yeah, that's right. Atlas and some other company set their machines loose in the barrier, but their toys didn't play nice together. Took a while for my construction crews to clear out enough of the mess to build the safari, though fortunately for us the worst areas are up toward the bow."

"Those self-replicators still give us problems now and again," Doctus said. "We've sealed them off as best we can, but the swarms still sneak in somehow." He chuckled. "Not that it's much of a problem. All they try to do is build condos in the middle of the jungle. At least until they run out of power. It's actually kind of funny."

"We clear them out and tear down anything they built," Piturro continued. "In fact, we've even left some of the structures standing. Gives that area of the Safari a 'reclaimed by wilderness' feel. Waste not, want not, I say."

"Though the latest ones have been...strange," Doctus added with a grimace.

"How so?" Isaac asked.

"We've had some furry...things sneak in recently. Like colorful teddy bears. I saw a group of the fuzzy things try to carry off an eoraptor. Didn't end well for them when the rest of the pack showed up."

"So far they're just a weird nuisance," Piturro said. "We hardly needed to do anything ourselves, since the creatures either eat or trample them as soon as they show up."

"I recommend you report any incidents to SysPol," Isaac said. "There's a case open in the Second Engine Block, and your sightings may prove relevant."

"No problem, sonny."

"Getting back to Fike, what about his recent hunts? Did he bring along any company?"

"Let me check my records." Piturro rounded the counter and crouched down behind it. He stood up with a heavy, leatherbound ledger and set it on the countertop, then slipped his fingers behind the red corded bookmark and opened the massive tome.

"You keep written records?" Isaac asked.

"And digital, but there's something reassuring about a real book in your hands, don't you agree?"

"I couldn't say. I've never read a physical book."

"Then you're missing out. There's a pleasant charm to the old ways, even if they're not as convenient as a virtual interface." He ran his finger down the page, then flipped back a few pages and repeated the exercise. "Yes, here we are. No plus-ones for Fike. All his safaris over the last month were done solo."

"What was Fike here for two days ago?" Isaac asked.

"His usual. Open safari."

"And he left without going on an actual hunt?"

"That's right. He was halfway through loading up his copter when, all of a sudden, he up and left. Didn't say a word to us. We figure some sort of emergency came up. We called him yesterday about rescheduling his reservation but didn't get through."

"Then we saw him mentioned in the news this morning," Doctus added.

"You said he was in the process of loading a copter. With what, exactly?"

"Hunting supplies and provisions, mostly," Piturro said. "We put all of it back in his locker."

"He has a locker here?"

"Most customers do, especially the ones who favor the big game. It's a convenient place to store their weapons and armor."

"What's special about the hunters who go after larger game?"

"They tend to favor bigger guns." Piturro flashed a toothy grin. "Big enough they're not exactly street legal. I went through all the necessary permitting, so Safari enjoys relaxed firearm restrictions from the rest of Janus, but that means some weapons need to stay on site. Hence, lockers for big-game hunters."

"Would you mind if we take a look inside his locker?"

"Not at all, sonny." Piturro closed the ledger. "Doctus, would you mind taking care of them?"

"Right this way, Detectives."

The hound trotted up to a door beside the counter, which swung open for him. He led them down a corridor and up a spiral staircase to the second level, which featured an open floor plan broken up by rows of double-wide wooden lockers.

Doctus hummed to himself and led them down one of the rows until they were close to the mansion's front windows.

"Here we are." Doctus transmitted a keycode to Isaac. "I've set you up with temporary access to his locker. It'll expire once you leave. If you or anyone else from SysPol needs back in later, just holler. We can always generate another."

"Thank you. That'll be all for now."

Doctus nodded to each of them, then trotted across the room and down the stairs.

Isaac palmed the lock. He paused in momentary confusion when the locker didn't open on its own, then frowned, grabbed the knob, and pulled it open manually. The locker was as deep as it was wide, with stepped shelves and drawers at the bottom, and equipment racks and hangers along the sides and back.

"Cephalie, give it a basic forensics pass."

"You've got it."

Isaac took a step back to allow the LENS room to work. It floated down to the bottom and extended a pseudopod to pull the first drawer open. He glanced over the effects and equipment in the locker: flexible body armor with dynamic camouflage, a variety of sensors and tracking devices, a stack of Old Frontier Hixon-brand pep bars in a variety of flavors, a bowl with a random collection of broken teeth and rocks, and a tall stack of ammo cartridges.

"The body armor isn't coated in metamaterial," Susan noted, referring to a light refracting material used for both stealth and laser defense applications.

"Metamaterial isn't widely available outside of SysPol," Isaac pointed out. "What type of ammo is that?"

"Popular Arsenals HV11Ds," Cephalie reported. "It's a high-velocity pattern optimized for their PA11D 'Pinpoint' marksman rifles."

"They're for that gun's D variant?" Isaac asked.

"Yep."

"Why's the D important?" Susan asked.

"It stands for 'Devastator,'" Isaac said. "Means it's a higher-performance model than the general-release pattern. You don't see many D-variants outside of SysPol divisions like Arete."

"Does this have a Devastator version?" Susan tapped the hand cannon at her hip.

"No," Cephalie replied. "There have been rumors Popular Arsenals is working on an enhanced variant of the PA5, but nothing official."

"Can I have one if they do?"

"As long as it's on the approved-weapons list," Isaac said, wondering why Susan felt she needed an even more destructive sidearm.

"Of course," she said, sounding a little resigned. "Then Fike wouldn't normally be allowed to own a D-variant gun."

"Normally no," Isaac said.

"This would be a rare exception, though," Cephalie noted, "since, as Piturro pointed out, the Cretaceous Safari can legally print and store heavier firearms."

"Except"—Isaac tapped an urgent finger against the open locker door—"there's no gun in the locker."

"Yeah, you're right," Susan breathed. "You think he took it with him?"

"I don't see where else it could be." Isaac raised his palm. A comm window appeared over it, and he placed a call to the 103rd Precinct Building control room.

"Hoopler here. What's up, Detective?"

"I need you to update Fike's status. We have reason to believe he has a weapon in his possession. A PA11D Pinpoint to be precise. Fugitive is experienced in the use of this weapon and should be presumed armed."

✧　　✧　　✧

Bonnie Rosenstein stood before the precinct building and craned her neck, taking in all ten stories of the wide, bland structure towering over her. Its broad, flattened facade somehow conspired to make her feel small and unimportant. Giant, virtual numerals rotated high over her head, declaring this to be the 103rd.

Her heart quickened, and she gulped, her throat dry. She clutched at her chest, taking hold of the glass bulb on a chain beneath her blouse. The smooth pendant contained her Stone of Mercury, and the tactile reminder sent a jolt of much-needed courage through her otherwise flustered mind.

It wasn't that the police scared her. Not *exactly*.

But SSP and the Society had been going through what one might call a "rough patch." She was an important member of the Mercury Historical Preservation Society, after all. An assistant chair of a whole chapter! And that position placed a great deal of responsibility upon her shoulders.

SSP had targeted her chapter in what was assuredly a campaign designed to stifle their legitimate—and legally protected—dissent. But if they thought the steady stream of warnings, fines, in-person visits, and similar harassment would silence the Society's contributions to public discourse, they had another thing coming.

Put simply, SSP didn't like the Society, and the feeling was mutual.

Which made her presence outside the station that much more unpleasant.

Why don't I just go home and drown my sorrows in another dozen cupcakes? she asked herself. *Surely that'll make me feel better.*

That's what she told herself, but then she turned away from the entrance, one foot scraping across the ground. She looked back at the sweeping vista of the Third Engine Block behind her, and she knew. She *knew* the truth.

Those cupcakes wouldn't make her happy. Yes, they'd sate her belly with delicious carbohydrates, but the void in her soul would remain. A void that could only be filled with decisive action.

That's what this moment required. Not cupcakes, but conviction! The will to seize her destiny! To fulfill her obligation to her home! To do what she knew was right!

She gripped the rock around her neck, and fresh resolve poured into her as if her body were a vessel destined to contain it. She faced the station once more, head held high, and swaggered in.

"I'm here to report—!" she began before the closest desk sergeant interrupted her.

"Emergency?" the AC snapped. Its body was an ugly mess

of flat polygons and chunky pixels, and it spoke with a tinny, synthesized voice.

"W-w-what?" Bonnie stuttered, all that courage from a moment ago leaking out of her.

"Are you reporting an emergency?" it pressed in an urgent, dissonant tone.

"I . . . uhh . . . guess not."

"Then wait in line like everyone else. Next!"

She took in the crowded, snaking queue in front of the three desk sergeants and all those cupcakes back home began to look more and more attractive by the second. Two citizens pushed past her and entered the queue before she finally shook herself out of her funk and slouched her way to the back of the line.

Twenty minutes later, she stood in front of a bulky, muscular sergeant who waved for her to approach without looking up from his interface. He was as tall seated as she was standing up. She wasn't sure if he was synthoid or flesh, but she guessed the former.

"Name."

"Uh, Bonnie Rosenstein."

"And what seems to be the problem today, Bonnie?" He entered data into his interface.

"Well, it's about my boss."

"What about your boss?"

"He, umm, well . . ." Bonnie shifted her weight from one foot to the other, the bulb held tight through her blouse.

The sergeant raised his gaze, an unimpressed, somewhat bored expression on his broad face. Beady eyes pierced into her.

"What about your boss?" he repeated in an almost identical tone, slipping in enough emphasis to communicate the deteriorating state of his patience without the need for more words.

"Well . . . he's, umm. He's . . ."

The sergeant knitted his fingers and leaned forward, his small eyes fixed on her.

"Do you have a problem to report or not?"

Her heart threatened to beat its way out of her ribcage, and she shrank back from the officer's looming. Why did police officers have to loom so much and in such a threatening way?

"Do y-y-you have t-t-to—"

"I'll ask again." The sergeant rose from his seat, now towering over her, though his tone had barely changed. "Do you have a problem to report?"

"Y-y-yes?"

"Then what is it?"

"It's..." Her eyes flicked up to his, then turned away, unable to meet his penetrating glare. "I'm sorry! This was a terrible idea!"

She scampered across the line of desks, head down, and hurried toward the exit.

But her rushed steps slowed as she approached the doors, a leaden sensation seeping into her feet. She stopped at the threshold and gazed out across the brilliantly lit cityscape, with the block's towering thruster assemblies behind it and the sun rod shining bright.

"I have to do this," she whispered to herself.

She closed her eyes, sucked in a deep breath—filling her lungs almost to bursting—then turned around.

"My boss's name is Desmond Fike!" she shouted for the entire floor to hear.

The background din of activity died down. She peeked her eyes open to find everyone staring at her. The awkward silence dragged on for several seconds.

"What of it?" came the commentary from someone stuck in the queue.

"And?" asked the sergeant who'd been looming over her.

"Hold on a sec," said the polygonal sergeant. "That's the guy SysPol is looking for."

She sucked in a second full breath and squeezed her eyes shut.

"Yes! And I know where he's hiding!"

CHAPTER EIGHTEEN

THE RENTAL PULLED OFF THE ROAD AND PARKED BESIDE A 103RD Precinct quadcopter, which was itself parked next to a truck from the 105th and two cars from the 98th. A half dozen other police vehicles formed a haphazard row beneath the mountain-sized shadow of Thruster Two's drive assembly.

Isaac climbed out of the vehicle, joined shortly by Susan and the LENS. The vehicles were parked beside a structure that resembled a nest of giant metal snakes entangled together. Dark maintenance tunnels cut through the mess at irregular intervals, extending into the utility labyrinth beneath Thruster Two. SSP drones of varying sizes and configurations floated overhead, each providing limited pools of light that pushed back the oppressive dark. Virtual cordons formed a semicircle at the mouth of one tunnel, glowing in his abstract vision without giving off any tangible light.

Isaac passed through the cordons and took a hard look down the tunnel. The warm glow from a floating remote the size of his fist revealed the first dozen meters or so, but then the tunnel darkened considerably until a pair of beams revealed another section, casting their light across a low, sleek, and decidedly vehicular silhouette further down. The car was skewed at an angle, the left corner of its hood jammed against one wall, and the right corner of its open rear hatch butted against the opposite. Isaac couldn't tell from this distance if the rear hatch had sprung open during the crash or if it had been opened after the fact. Either way, low-hanging conduits had prevented it from opening fully.

A trio of light sources skittered around the car in addition to the drone stationary lights, their beams searching the vehicle and the surrounding tunnel. One locked onto Isaac and company and began to approach, the source too high to be a person.

The floating disk of a conveyor drone slowed to a halt before them, and Trooper Parks appeared.

"Detective," he greeted with a curt nod. "Glad you could join us."

"That it?" Isaac pointed to the crashed vehicle.

"Yes, sir. This way."

The conveyor spun around and guided them down the tunnel, its light a radiant oval on the ground ahead. Parks' avatar "walked" beside them.

"Why's the power out?" Isaac asked.

"It's been like this all week," Parks explained. "Atlas has this whole area shut down because they need to tap into several major utility lines for connections to the Fourth Engine Block. Everything's been rerouted in the meantime, which means no power and no infostructure down here."

"The perfect hiding spot," Susan observed.

"Assuming Fike doesn't run afoul of the construction work," Isaac added.

"That's unlikely this far up," Parks said. "It's quite the mess further down, the closer you get to the structural barrier below the city, but up here we're only dealing with the lack of utilities. I don't believe they'll be touching this level at all, actually."

"Then why shut it off?" Susan asked.

Parks paused and frowned.

"You were asked a question, Trooper," Isaac said.

"I . . . it has to do with where the cutoffs and bypasses are located. Even though Atlas isn't working on this level, they still had to shut it down because the utilities they're working on need to be in a safe state. That means deenergized for something like a superconductor line or depressurized and drained for something like an air or waterline. Bypasses might be as far apart as half a kilometer for major trunk lines, though they'll be more frequent for smaller lines branching off the mains."

"Which means we have a large, unpowered zone to deal with," Isaac said.

"Detectives!" Lieutenant Hoopler waved at them from the other side of the crashed vehicle, alongside Sergeant Chatelain. Hoopler grabbed a low-hanging pipe, hauled herself onto the hood, then crouch-walked across and dropped down next to them. Chatelain stayed on the far side.

Isaac took in the bright red vehicle, now bathed in light from Parks' conveyor. The flames across its body were in a static pattern. A faint hint of something foul and septic irritated his nose, making it wrinkle in disgust.

"A Cygnus Model X. I take it this is Fike's vehicle?"

"It is," Hoopler said. "We sent the pattern serial to Cygnus, and they IDed the buyer. This vehicle was printed from a single-use permit registered to the Mercury Society."

"And we found traces of Fike's DNA inside," Parks added.

"That we did. Those two together all but guarantee this is the right vehicle."

"Good work," Isaac said. "What about the cause of the crash?"

"Damage to the front indicates a low-speed collision. My guess is Fike had the vehicle in manual and was trying to get it as deep into the tunnel as he could before he misjudged the sides and wedged himself in."

"How'd you find it in the first place?"

"We received one hell of a tip. Bonnie Rosenstein ratted Fike out."

"The chapter's assistant chair?" Isaac asked.

"The same. According to her, Fike called her shortly after the warrant went live. He instructed her to print out some supplies and drop them off at the front of this tunnel."

"What sort of supplies?"

"Food and toiletries, mostly," Hoopler said. "Which doesn't make him any less dangerous, given what you found."

"Did Rosenstein carry out the drop?"

"She did."

"When? And was Fike present at the time?"

"Yesterday evening, and no. She dropped the supplies off at the mouth and left. They weren't here when we arrived, so Fike probably picked them up."

"You're not certain it was him?"

"Could have been stolen for all we know," Hoopler explained. "All sorts of human trash make their home in the utility maze, from your average job dodgers and addicts up to whole gangs. This sector's a quiet one, but it doesn't mean there aren't rats in the walls. Given the number of footprints we've seen, there's at least a small population of scum down here."

"Understood. What else did Rosenstein share?"

"After she dropped off the food, she experienced a change of heart. She stopped by the station and confessed everything. We're holding her at the station. She's technically guilty of providing aid to a fugitive, but I expect the prosecutor to drop the charges, given she put us on Fike's trail."

"Seems reasonable to me. Anything else?"

"Not from her. We found a few pep bar wrappers in the car and a juice bottle full of urine, but that's it. Fike must have taken everything else with him. I'm pulling in teams from the 105th and 98th to scour the maze. A few have shown up, but we're just getting started. We'll let you know as soon as we find anything."

"Good. We'll take a look around ourselves, if you don't mind."

"Not at all. The more the merrier."

"Lieutenant," Parks said. "Another car just arrived from the 98th."

"That would be my cue." Hoopler grinned wryly. "Detective, I'll be back at the copter if you need anything. Someone's got to put these new arrivals to work."

"We'll leave you to it, then. Thank you, Lieutenant."

Chatelain climbed over the car hood, and together the three troopers headed back down the tunnel under the conveyor's light.

Isaac leaned close to one of the car windows. Cephalie kept the LENS near his shoulder, shining its light in the general direction of his gaze. He tapped into the data link from the LENS and accessed thermal imaging and light amplification layers, cycling between them to see if anything interesting jumped out.

Nothing did.

He rounded to the back of the roadster and checked inside the open trunk, which was as empty as the front except for the occasional wrapper and the bottle of "juice." He frowned at the bottle, wondering how best to expedite the search for Fike.

"What are you looking for?" Susan asked after he'd been staring for a while.

"I don't quite know myself." He stood back, then returned to the hood and climbed over it. Susan followed him over, and the LENS floated over the car's roof to their side. "How's a little walk sound to you?"

"I'm up for one if you are."

Isaac led the way deeper into the tunnel, the LENS sensory overlays enhancing his situational awareness. The tunnel branched to either side, and Isaac spied hints of drone light down each side passage. He continued on, and the tunnel narrowed, conduit bundles squeezing inward until he had to turn sideways to slip through.

The tunnel widened again after that, then took a sudden turn to the side. All the while, that septic stench grew stronger and more acrid. They came to a five-way junction with some pathways leading to shallow declines. He coughed into a fist, and his eyes began to water.

"What *is* that smell?"

"You want to know?" Cephalie replied, appearing on his shoulder.

"Why do you think I asked?"

"My guess would be a break in a reclamation line. One pre-sorted for human waste with most of the water content removed."

"Lovely," Isaac grumbled. "Susan, is this stink bothering you?"

"No. Smells can't make me sick to my stomach. Nothing can, actually. I can trigger a 'reverse evacuation' of my insides, but it's a manual process."

"Lucky you." Somehow, the mere mention of "reverse evacuation" prompted his stomach muscles to clench. A thimble of bile made its way into his mouth. He accessed his wetware's root sensory commands and reduced the intensity of his natural olfactory senses. He swallowed and took a few calming breaths, his hands resting above his knees.

"You okay?" Susan asked.

"Never better," he groaned, his voice suddenly hoarse.

"Maybe we should let SSP handle this."

"Maybe." He drew in another deep breath, then let it out slowly. "But perhaps..."

His voice trailed off as a sudden thought intruded into his mind. A horrible, nauseating notion that threatened to upheave his stomach once more. He squeezed his eyes shut, tears leaking out the sides, and shut off his sense of smell completely, replacing it with the calming fragrance of peppermint.

"Cephalie?" he croaked. "Can you track where the leak is?"

"Shouldn't be a problem. All I have to do is follow the particulate density to its peak. But why?"

"Do it. There's something we need to check."

"You sure about this?" Susan asked doubtfully.

"Just another glamorous day on the job." Isaac straightened his posture with some effort. "Cephalie, lead the way."

The LENS floated down one of the branching tunnels, then guided them through a series of thinner passages and junctions until the space opened up into a rounded alcove. Brown, curdled waste covered the floor, forming a shallow mound on the far side that seemed to originate from a large, damaged pipe running horizontally. Isaac doubted he and Susan could wrap their combined arms around its girth.

Even if they'd wanted to, which he most certainly *didn't*.

"Oh, good grief," Susan groaned. She froze at the threshold, one boot hovering over the drainage. "It's a leaking poop pipe."

"Yup," Isaac replied with a gulp. "Anyone see any signs of construction in here?"

"Nope," Cephalie said.

"But it could sure use some," Susan added. "What a mess!"

"Cephalie, perform a basic forensics pass."

"On it."

The LENS floated in and extended a trio of pseudopods that brushed across various polluted surfaces.

"What's on your mind?" Susan asked quietly.

"Parks said this area was powered down about a week ago."

"Yeah? So?"

"That would have coincided with this line being drained, though given it's transporting solid waste, the process might not have gone perfectly."

"I'm not sure I follow."

"It's simple. Do you think there's enough mess here to come from a waste line? One that's in use and under pressure?"

Susan surveyed the room and its brown slurry.

"No. There isn't nearly enough."

"Exactly. Which means the line was breached *after* this area was powered down."

"But that would mean..." She faced him, her brow contorted his fresh disgust. "You don't think.. "

Isaac nodded.

"But that would mean..."

Isaac nodded again.

"He wouldn't!"

"He might have."

"Found something!" Cephalie reported, the LENS hovering near the breach in the waste pipe. "Got plenty of handprints on the pipe. Looks like the surface was cut open with a vibro-saw."

"Is the hole large enough for someone to fit through?" Isaac asked.

"Bit of a squeeze getting in, but a person Fike's size could fit."

"Where'd the saw come from?" Susan asked.

"He may have had one on him to collect trophies," Isaac said.

"Okay. But why would Fike crawl down a poop pipe?"

"I'm guessing he didn't know what was inside it until he cut it open. He might have been searching for an empty tube and settled on this one since it looked large enough for him to crawl through."

"Yuck!" Susan cringed. "Hell of a mistake."

"Can you bring up a map of the area?" Isaac asked.

"Sure thing," Cephalie said, and a miniaturized thicket of pipes and conduits appeared before him with maintenance passages threaded through the convoluted mess.

"Highlight reclamation lines. Darken the rest."

The graphic dimmed except for several lines that brightened, spreading throughout the area like the roots of a tree. Isaac tapped the pulsing dot that indicated their position, then traced his finger across the waste line, following it downward into the construction zone.

"Any number of places he could come out," Susan said.

"Yes, but he'll need to cut his way out on the other side. Cephalie, take the LENS down the pipe and see if you can't find his exit."

"Sure thing." The LENS retracted its pseudopods. "You two want to join me? There's enough space."

"No," he answered firmly. "We'll go around."

✧   ✧   ✧

They returned to the rental and waited for Cephalie to feed them a location, which turned out to be fourteen levels down.

They drove downward along the outskirts of the utility maze and regrouped with the LENS near the entrance to a narrow tunnel.

"I found where Fike came out," Cephalie reported, sitting atop the LENS with a rubber gas mask modeled over her face. "His trail was easy enough to follow for about a hundred meters, then things get...muddled."

"Take us there," Isaac said.

Cephalie led them into the utility maze, guiding them through three different Y-junctions, then down a shallow decline ending in a short path that opened to a larger space two stories tall. She widened and brightened her beam, bathing the chamber in light.

A haphazard collection of chairs and tables crowded one corner, various brands of mattresses formed a barely organized grid in another, and a mishmash of appliances were jammed together in the closest corner. Isaac spotted high-performance infosystem towers, gaming recliners, and two small but flexible printers.

The fourth corner was sectioned off by an arc of paneling broken up by two swinging doors. Each door had a physical sign, one for showers and the other for toilets. The inhabitants had spliced into the local utilities with insulated cables or flexible pipes, providing power to their hardware and water to the restrooms.

At least when the utilities were on, Isaac thought.

Graffiti covered the walls near the four entrances, each picture animating a roiling storm cloud and streaks of vivid lightning. Some of the animation cycles appeared sluggish, indicating the smart paint was low on power.

"Gang symbols?" Susan asked.

"That's right." Isaac wagged a finger at one of the lightning bolts. "We're in Streaks territory."

"Who are the Streaks?"

"One of the smaller immigrant gangs. Mostly composed of Uranites with local Saturnites mixed in."

"Dangerous?"

"All criminal gangs are dangerous."

"I mean, should I have my gun drawn?"

"I don't think so." Isaac swept his gaze over their surroundings once more. "No one appears to be home. I'm guessing the Streaks left when the power was switched off."

"This is where I lost Fike's trail." Cephalie overlaid a bent line onto their virtual senses. The path came in from a side entrance and curved into the shower stalls.

Isaac opened the shower's swinging door and peered in. Cephalie shined a light over his shoulder.

A thin pipe stretched down at a diagonal from the wall on the second story, then branched out in five directions, each line ending in a different style showerhead. Water dripped from one of them, forming a shallow puddle below the head. Someone had installed a drain in the middle of the room, which only did a passable job of removing water, since the floor was flat.

"Fike came here and washed up," Cephalie reported.

"Must have been some water backed up in the pipes," Isaac said. "And after that?"

"No trail."

"None?"

"Not one I can single out as Fike's," Cephalie explained. "The Streaks may have left, but other people are using this place. On top of that, I'm guessing Fike got his hands on a bottle of Grime-Away, because I'm finding traces of the brand's microbots everywhere."

"Which are actively cleaning up the evidence," Isaac said, filling in the rest. He let the shower door swing shut.

"Exactly. Nina might be able to tell us more."

"Or we could brute-force through this by having SSP—"

"Shh!" Susan placed an urgent hand on his shoulder. She drew her pistol and aimed it toward one of the side entrances.

Isaac strained his hearing and listened.

"Is that . . . singing?"

He heard what he thought was a man's low, scratchy voice singing with operatic enthusiasm, though lacking in true talent or—more importantly—any sense of timing or tone. The noise grew more distinct, accompanied by the clicks of slow, leisurely footfalls. A dim, greenish light splashed out of the tunnel.

Susan kept her pistol leveled on the entrance.

Isaac put a finger on top of her barrel and gently nudged her aim down. She raised a questioning eyebrow at him.

"I don't think we'll need that," he said quietly.

She frowned back at him but kept her weapon lowered.

The voice grew louder and more distinct, and Isaac could register snippets from the lyrics.

"...*ceiling fan*...*late for work*..."

"I think I know this song," he whispered.

"You listen to this sort of music?" Susan whispered back.

"I've heard most of it by accident. It's one of Nina's favorites."

"*My pants are on the ceiling fan!*" bellowed the newcomer, waddling into the chamber with his feet pointed to either side, giving Isaac the impression of an overweight duck. His impressive belly strained against what appeared at first glance to be body armor, but instead of a dynamic camouflage pattern, naked women fell across a clear blue sky, all while blowing kisses at the viewer. A glow tube cast pale green light from his shoulder, secured there by a strap. The greenish light imbued his skin with a sickly, blotched pallor, and his oily beard formed a knotted mat down his neck.

He carried a bundle of preprinted food tins in his arms, seemingly unaware of the obvious light from the LENS. Isaac cleared his throat as noisily as he could.

"*And now I'm late for work!*" the man cried with zero musical talent, head back, eyes squeezed shut, sweat beading on his brow as he shuffled toward the toilets. "*Late for wo-ooooork!*"

He stumbled when his foot caught on the upturned corner of an access grate. He staggered forward for a few steps, and a few of the food tins fell from his arms. He stared at them on the ground for long, confused seconds. Then, apparently deciding here was as good a place as any, he dropped the rest of his cargo with a loud clatter.

"Excuse me, sir," Isaac said, stepping toward the man.

"Sup, y'all." He shuffled past Isaac. "Help yourself if you're hungry. There's plenty." His face pinched up but then the expression melted into a toothy grin, and he let rip a loud fart. Strangely enough, the flatulence proved more musical than his singing. He pushed his way through the toilet's swinging door.

Isaac waved his hand to disperse the newly fouled air. He waited a few paces outside the stall for the man to finish.

"What did I just witness?" Susan asked quietly in security chat.

"One of the Esteemless," Isaac explained. "People who refuse to participate in modern society, who shun the bare minimum required of them along with the basic shelter and sustenance provided to them as a matter of course. Job dodgers, petty criminals, addicts, and other undesirables."

"Oh yeah!" groaned the man on the toilet, followed by a plop.

"I'm guessing addict for this one."

"Mnnnrrrgh! Oh, hell yeah!"

"You all right in there?" Isaac asked in normal speech, not sure what else to say.

"Yeah, man! Yeah!"

"Just checking." He shook his head and sighed.

"Thanks, man! *Eeerrrrrrggghhh!*"

"You planning to question him?" Susan asked.

"Who else is there to talk to?"

"Want me to drag him out here for you?"

"*Hnnnggghhh!*"

"Let's not interrupt him," Isaac replied dryly. "This sounds important."

Several minutes later, the man pushed through the stall door while hitching up his pants.

"Sup." He waddled toward his spilled stash of food tins, but Susan placed a hand against his chest. He grumbled and tried to push past but failed to move her arm even a millimeter.

"Detective Cho, SysPol Themis." Isaac transmitted his badge to the man's wetware. "We'd like to ask you a few questions."

"You cops?"

"That's what I just said."

"I hate cops."

"How charming."

"Lady, why you gotta be like this?" He tried to shove Susan's arm away, but once again failed to move her. "I'm hungry."

"What's your name?" Isaac asked.

"Trent."

"Trent who?"

"What's it to you? I've done nothing wrong. Just leave me be."

"Answer our questions, and we will."

"Who the hell do you think you are, coming down here, making demands?"

"All we're after is information."

"Like I owe you people anything!"

"I'd be careful if I were you." Isaac crossed his arms. "That's some nice body armor you've got there."

"Yeah, it is." He sneered. "But it's mine, so piss off."

"You have a permit for it?"

"Screw you."

"No permit means I can reasonably assume the property is stolen." Isaac motioned the LENS forward. "Cephalie, detain him."

"*What?!*" Trent blurted, backing away. The LENS darted forward, its prog-steel shell expanding outward to form a silvery X. Each corner struck a separate limb, flowing like liquid mercury that solidified into cuffs on each limb. Trent slipped and fell backward, but the LENS slowed his fall and laid him down on his back. He struggled against the bonds, but to no avail.

"Check him for substance abuse," Isaac ordered.

The LENS placed a new, thinner pseudopod against the inside of Trent's elbow, and he flinched from the tiny prick.

"His blood's steeped in Bliss medibots, with trace amounts of Trance and Melt."

Isaac made a *tsk-tsk* sound as he knelt beside the addict's head.

"Trent, you have two options. Either I arrest you for suspicion of theft, vagrancy, trespassing, vandalism, job dodging, controlled substance abuse, and probably a few others if I think hard enough. Or you can drop the attitude and answer what I assure you are very simple questions. After which, we leave you be. Now, which option sounds better to you?"

"The second! The second!"

"That's what I thought." Isaac stood up. "Cephalie, get the good man back on his feet, would you?"

The LENS lifted Trent up and placed him on the ground upright before releasing the restraints. He staggered forward half a step then steadied himself, rubbing the inside of his elbow.

"Now," Isaac began, "shall we try this again? Where'd you get the armor?"

"A guy gave it to me. Pretty snazzy, ain't it? I picked the camo pattern myself."

"Who gave it to you?"

"I don't know. Didn't give me his name. Stank like hell, though. I helped spray him down with Grime-Away."

"Why'd he give you the armor?"

"He wanted to trade for my clothes. I thought why the hell not. The smell wasn't too bad after I sprayed him down, and it washed out." Trent gave them an indifferent shrug. "Eventually. I call that a win."

"Can you describe the man?"

"I don't know. Sort of average."

"Height?"

"Average."

"Weight?"

"Average."

"Dark or light hair?"

"Sort of... halfway between."

"Did he carry a weapon?"

"Oh, yeah!" Trent's eyes gleamed. "He did!"

"What sort?"

"A big one. Looked impressive."

"Did you trade for that, too?"

"Nah, he kept it. I was interested, but I could tell the answer would be no. Thought I might trade it to the Butt Brigade later, but he even took it into the shower with him. No way he'd part with it."

"Excuse me?" Susan asked, brow creasing. "Did you say 'Butt Brigade?'"

"It's slang," Isaac explained. "He means the Uranite gangsters."

"Right on, man." Trent chuckled. "They don't like the name, but it fits. They're always throwing their weight around, acting all tough. 'Born on a butt, act like a butt,' as the saying goes. I don't miss those jerks one bit. How long you think the power's going to be off? I could use more days like this."

"Where'd he go next?" Isaac asked. "The man who traded you the armor?"

"Dunno."

"Any ideas?"

"Not really. He was in the showers when I left and was gone next time I passed through." Trent shrugged again. "Could be anywhere."

"When did you last see him?"

"Not sure. It's not like we have normal days down here."

"Take a guess."

"Yesterday, maybe?"

"Hmm." Isaac glanced back at the showers, wondering if there was anything else to glean from this conversation. "All right. You can go."

Trent hurried over to his spilled tins, gathered up most of them, and scurried out of the Streaks' chamber.

"What now?" Susan asked.

"We need to let Hoopler know we have a new location for her to center the search on. Cephalie, can you raise her from here?"

"Nope. Too much metal and not enough live infostructure between us and her. We'll need to head back to the car first."

"All right. Lead the way. I doubt there's much more we can do here. The rest is up to SSP."

CHAPTER NINETEEN

ISAAC BRIEFED HOOPLER SHORTLY AFTER THEY RECONNECTED with the city's infostructure.

"Anything else you need from us?" he asked once he'd passed on the critical details.

"Can't think of anything," Hoopler replied. "This is going to be a big help. The resources I have for this search have quadrupled since last we spoke, and now I can put them right on Fike's trail. I appreciate the assist, but we can take it from here."

"All right. In that case, we're calling it a day. Contact me as soon as you find something."

"Will do, Detective."

After that, they boarded the rental, and it drove them back to the hotel. Isaac headed straight for his room and stripped down as soon as the door closed. He signaled his uniform to start a self-cleaning cycle, then hurried naked into the bathroom and searched through the hotel-provided toiletries. He settled on a small bottle of Spotless-brand Scrub-All, twisted the top off, and poured the bluish creamy contents all over his uniform. The microbots in the cleaning solution integrated with the uniform's simplistic infostructure and joined in an epic, microscopic battle against horrible smells.

Next, Isaac grabbed the bottle of Spotless' Gentle Body Wash. He stepped into the shower, jammed the bottle's top into the receiver port, and selected the shower's longest, most rigorous cleaning cycle from the menu.

He closed his eyes as jets of sudsy water blasted him from all angles. The suds moved up and down his body, propelled by microbot colonies integrated with both the shower and his own wetware.

"Aaaahhhh..." he sighed while the microbots scrubbed the patina of sewage grime off his freshly pink skin. The cycle finished ten minutes later, and he immediately started a second one, not yet confident all the particulate feces had been removed.

He leaned against the glass door, eyes closed, relishing the heat and renewed sense of cleanliness. He was tempted to start a third cycle, but the back-to-back showers had made him a little dizzy, so he stepped out, dried off, then put on a pair of gray well-worn shorts and an equally venerable T-shirt.

He collapsed into the chair next to the hotel's delivery port and slouched there for long minutes like a strip of boneless meat. A very *relaxed* strip of meat. When he finally mustered the mental fortitude to lift his head, he called up the Thrusters menu and perused it.

"Nah." He dismissed the menu with a wave. "Nothing fancy tonight, I think."

He ran a search for local restaurants that delivered to the hotel, and the nearest Meal Spigot drew his eye. He ordered a bacon cheeseburger with sides of fried pickles and seasoned potato wedges, then sent Esteem tips to both the restaurant and hotel staff for their trouble.

His order arrived at the delivery port in under five minutes. He grabbed the tray and plopped it on his lap, not even having to stand.

He picked one of the major news streams to watch while he ate. The *Saturn Journal* was doing a feature on the *Toyoda*'s arrival, complete with interviews of the captain and crew.

Once he'd finished devouring the meal, he tossed the remains down the reclamation chute and switched off the news stream. He shambled to the bathroom, rinsed his mouth out with Spotless' Sensitive Dental Wash, then lumbered back to the bed where he quickly slipped under the sheets to form an Isaac-shaped cocoon under the self-warming covers.

He drifted off into peaceful sleep.

He dreamed of returning to Kronos, triumphant with Fike in jail, but his victory was short-lived. The stench from the utility maze had somehow clung to him, growing stronger and more malevolent, almost as if it were an insidious being of its own. It oozed out in a trail of brown smoke behind him and seeped into every part of the station, sickening those nearby and causing them to vomit.

The chime from an incoming call woke him up.

He opened an eye and glared at the alert in an attempt to will it away.

It continued to bleep next to him.

Not a dream, then, he thought, then sat up and acknowledged the call.

"Detective Cho?" Trooper Parks asked.

"Yes?" he croaked, rubbing the sleep from his eyes.

"You all right?

Isaac checked the virtual clock by the bed.

"It's two in the morning," he groaned. "What did you expect?"

"Right. Sorry. I guess I didn't realize what time it was."

"You still working?"

"I am, sir. Extra shifts don't bother me."

"What do you need?"

"You left instructions to contact you if we found anything."

"I did. What'd you find?"

"Fike, sir."

The news jolted most of the torpor from Isaac's system.

"We found Fike," Parks repeated.

"He's in custody?"

"Yes, sir. We're bringing him back to the station now."

"Excellent. We'll head over immediately."

"Umm..." Parks frowned.

"Is something wrong?"

"Not really, but you might want to slow-foot it to the station."

"Any reason why?"

"Well...it's more a matter of where and how we found him."

"Why? What's wrong? Is he injured?"

"No, nothing like that. A team from the 98th took him in without so much as a scuffle."

"Did he have that rifle on him?"

"Yes, sir. But he didn't use it. Not even as a threat."

"That's a relief." Isaac thought for a moment, the fog from his slumber dissipating. "Then, if not an injury, what's the problem?"

"Well . . . you see, sir, we found Fike in a dodger encampment down in the underthruster maze."

"Okay, but I'm still not clear on why we shouldn't head straight over."

"It's more a matter of the state we found him in. He was cowering in a makeshift toilet, and he crapped his pants when they went in for the collar. He also vomited all over the squad car on the way back."

"I see. Yes, I believe I understand now."

"Why don't you give us some time to hose him down for you? Maybe give us an hour to clean him up and process him?"

"Understood. Agent Cantrell and I will see you at the station in one hour."

✧   ✧   ✧

"Finally." Susan smiled at Isaac. "Ready to wring some answers out of him?"

"Something tells me 'wringing' won't be necessary."

An abstract window provided Isaac with a view of Fike sitting in the interrogation room, slouched with a sullen, defeated expression on his round face. He wore a carrot-colored jumpsuit with thick smart fabric that could stiffen on command, disabling a prisoner's ability to move about.

"He strikes me as . . . pliant," Isaac added.

"Yeah. His adventures in waste management seem to have whipped the fight out of him."

"Let's hope so. We still have several open points, and I suspect Fike can shed light on all of them. We know someone's still active over at Atlas, and there are the Byte Pyrates and the whereabouts of Ruckman's copy to trace down." He took a deep breath and straightened his posture. "Ready?"

"Let's do this."

Isaac palmed the door open and stepped in. Fike's gaze rose at their entrance, and he began chewing on his bottom lip. Isaac and Susan took their seats opposite him, and Isaac deployed his notes in a pair of screens blurred by privacy filters from Fike's perspective.

He knitted his fingers, set them on the table, and leaned forward.

"Hello again, Fike."

"Detective," Fike replied weakly.

"Not to state the obvious, but you would have saved us both a heap of trouble if you'd simply met with me the first time."

"Yeah." Fike lowered his head and sighed, "*Yeah...*"

"Obviously, we had enough evidence on hand to issue the arrest warrant, and I expect more to come as various forensics reviews file in. We also have a stack of lesser charges to throw at you, such as evading arrest, disobeying a lawful command, and possession of a restricted firearm. Put simply, you're not slipping out of this one."

"I figured as much," he moaned, not making eye contact.

"Cooperate fully with our investigation, and it will be noted in my report. If your confession proves useful, I'll pass on a recommendation for reduced sentencing."

"Ask away, then. I've had my fill of running."

"That's good to hear." Isaac tabbed over to a fresh screen. "Let's start at the beginning."

"The beginning, huh?" Fike blew out a long, sputtering exhale. "I suppose it started when I began chairing the chapter. I was working as an advertising consultant at the time, and the chapter contacted me about improving their outreach. One thing led to another, and in half a year, I ended up running the whole chapter. I quit my consulting gig and started working for the Society full-time. That was around three years ago."

"Quite the ascent."

"It's not like I had much competition. Fake a little interest, apply some managerial aptitude, and suddenly I was being 'volunteered' to chair the whole chapter. Those rubes can't run anything larger than a cupcake social without me." He shook his head. "God, I never thought I'd say this, but I can't stand cupcakes anymore. Every time bad news floats in, the first response is always, 'Who's printing the cupcakes?'"

"Let's stay focused on your own activities."

"Sure. Whatever you say, boss." Fike raked a hand back through his hair. "It started small enough. Just a bit of Esteem skimmed off the top. A drop in the bucket compared to the fat donations rolling in thanks to my ad campaigns. It's money they wouldn't have had without me, so I figured I was owed a little extra. No harm there, right? Just a bonus I gave to myself for high performance. I was the only one handling the finances, and they liked it that way. Saved them the headaches so they could focus on coming up with catchy chants or"—he shrugged with an indifferent frown—"whatever the hell those idiots do on weekdays."

"And then?"

"I pushed my luck a little more. And then a bit more beyond that. I bought a car with Society money, then a second one. No one noticed. No one cared. It was just that *easy*, so I went bigger. I bought a yacht and purchased a warehouse out on the Ridge to store it. Eventually, I renovated the whole place and moved out there. Even set up a fake residence in a capsule apartment, just to make the truth that much harder to sniff out. I lumped everything under business expenses."

"Did you ever use it for legitimate purposes?"

"Sometimes." He blew out another tired breath. "Occasionally, I'd take a potential donor out and show them a good time. More often than not, those activities brought in even more Esteem. Which, in my head at least, justified my behavior."

"And then?"

"You called. I couldn't be sure why a SysPol detective would ask to speak to me in person, but what else could it be? So, I bolted. I know it was a dumb thing to do, but you scared me. I was up at a place called Cretaceous Safari at the time, and I left for home. Being caught had crossed my mind before, and I had a rough plan in mind in case the police came knocking."

"Which was?"

"I'd take my yacht and fly it out to an Oortan dirigible. Maybe the *Icarus Wing* or the *Atomic Resort*. Someplace outside your jurisdiction. I had ample funds to my name, so I could conceivably hang out there for years."

"Why didn't you leave, then?"

"Because my car's *stupid* software got me stuck in a construction zone!" he growled. "By the time it drove me home, SSP had already shown up. I couldn't go in like that, so I kept on driving."

"That's all very interesting," Isaac said, "and we'll come back to your days as a fugitive in a moment, but I believe you're leaving out some important details."

"Sorry. It's not like I've made a confession before." Fike let out a long exhale. "Not like this. I'm not hiding anything on purpose. What do you want to know?"

"Tell us how you became involved with the Byte Pyrates."

"The Byte...?"

"Pyrates."

"The..." Fike scratched his head. "The who now?"

"The gang you hired to kidnap Antoni Ruckman."

"I'm sorry, but *what*?!" Fike blurted. "When did this turn into a discussion about kidnapping?"

Isaac leaned back, a sinking feeling in his stomach, but he pressed forward.

"We have evidence you directed the Byte Pyrates to make an illegal copy of Ruckman's connectome."

"Who the hell is Ruckman?"

"A senior engineer at SourceCode."

"Look, I know what I did and why I did it. I stole from people who trusted me. Hell, I embezzled the *shit* out of that chapter, and you know what? I don't feel all that sorry about it. Those idiots don't have a clue. You know what those kooks do in their free time? They marry themselves off to rocks, for God's sake! *Rocks!* I was doing the worlds a favor by stealing their money! Under different circumstances, I'd be on the receiving end of a medal for great contributions to society!

"So yeah. I know exactly what I did. I stole, and I lied, and I deserve whatever's coming to me. But *kidnapping*?" He shook his head vehemently. "You've got the wrong man!"

"Well," Susan said once they were outside the interrogation room, "*that* could have gone better."

Isaac walked into the empty interrogation room across from Fike's, and Susan palmed the door closed behind them.

"There goes the theory of Fike the criminal mastermind," Isaac grumbled. "I should have known it was too good to be true."

"You sure he's not lying to us?"

"It's impossible to be certain, but consider what we just put him through. We spent the last two hours tearing through his account of the last few days in excruciating detail, and throughout all of that, he's been remarkably consistent. Either he's one of the most gifted liars I've ever met, somehow privy to the full slate of information in our possession, able to expertly weave a fictional story together on the fly and under sustained scrutiny...or he's not the Ghost. And remember, this is the same person who failed to check which reclamation line he sawed into."

"Yeah. Looking back, maybe we should have realized this wasn't our guy. Most criminals don't crap their pants at the sight of the police, either."

The door opened, and the LENS floated in, bearing a steaming cup of coffee. The drone set it down next to Isaac.

"Thanks, Cephalie. You're the best." He picked up the mug and took a sip.

"Don't mention it. I know how you meat sacks can get when you haven't had your beauty sleep."

"Too true."

"But if it's not Fike," Susan continued, "then what made the Pyrates connect him with the Ghost? Do you think Zapf was feeding us a tale?"

"Possibly, but I don't think so. Zapf seemed genuinely interested in using the incident at the logistics center as his ticket out of the Pyrates. We could question him again, but I'm not sure what that would gain us. The problem is he's too removed from the source of the information. According to him, Bao was the one who made the connection, but Bao's not talking, though I suppose that troublemaker could have made a mistake."

"But isn't this the kind of work the Pyrates are good at?"

"I know, but let's consider what we know about the Ghost. We know the Ghost was in contact with both Velasco and the Byte Pyrates. We also know the Ghost or a fellow conspirator purged Velasco's work area of anything Ghost-related. The same fate befell the infostructure image Nina received, which indicates at least one active party still at Atlas."

"But not Velasco's home infosystems," Susan noted. "Those contained mentions of the Ghost."

"Which tells us the Ghost or related parties couldn't access them. Not before we did, at least."

"This Ghost sure doesn't leave a lot of evidence behind."

"And yet"—Isaac raised a finger—"at the same time, we're supposed to believe this individual was so incredibly sloppy 'he' revealed 'his' identity to a gang of criminals? The leader of which keeps a stash of blackmail information in case her customers cause trouble. Those two sides don't belong to the same coin."

"What are you thinking, then?" Susan asked. "That the Fike-as-the-Ghost angle is a deliberate false lead?"

"That's where I'm leaning. Consider for a moment how quickly we bought into it. And not just us SSP mobilized a citywide search on what, when you think about it, was nothing more than hearsay from a single gangster. The Society members make for convincing bad guys, given their reputation. Whether they deserve it or not is a question for another day. But consider how they appear from the perspective of the Ghost. A cautious individual who's neck-deep in Dyson Project subterfuge might consider them useful distractions."

"Then where does that leave our case?"

"In a bad state, I'm afraid. Fike and the Society are dead ends, which leaves us with very few avenues left to explore."

"Not complete dead ends," Susan corrected. "We did bring in an embezzler."

"Which the Ghost wanted us to do. That's still a loss in my book, and I do *not* like to lose."

"Not a total loss. Glass half full, right?"

"I prefer my glasses filled to the brim. Cephalie?"

"Another coffee, good sir?" Her miniature avatar appeared on the LENS.

"No thanks. What's the latest from Nina?"

"She's still out at JIT Deliveries, taking the slow and methodical approach. I spoke to her a couple hours ago. She's *determined* to find Ruckman's trail."

Isaac opened his mouth, but Cephalie cut in.

"And before you ask, no, I have no idea when she's been sleeping either."

"Wasn't what I was going to say, but okay. In any case, we'll leave her be. She'll call in when she has something to share."

"What about us, then?" Susan asked.

"The way I see it, there's only one place left for us to dig. Atlas HQ."

"Right back where we started." Susan sagged against the back of her chair.

"Can't be helped. Someone over there is covering the Ghost's tracks. Whether it's the actual Ghost or a coconspirator is hard to say, but *someone* over there is up to no good. We just need to smoke them out."

"Easier said than done. Any thoughts on where we should look first?"

"Boaz," Isaac said simply.

"The CEO? You really think so?"

"He's the one who fought our search warrant. Whether legal or not is beside the point. His actions gave the Ghost time to expand the cover-up, which means he could be involved. We start with him and see where that takes us."

CHAPTER TWENTY

THEIR SECOND INTERVIEW WITH JULIAN BOAZ TOOK PLACE IN his Atlas office. Third Engine Block's thrusters cast a bright glow through the wide window while the big, bald, well-dressed man sat behind his sprawling desk, face cold and unreadable, almost unrecognizable from the smiling, congenial persona he'd presented the first time.

Dorothea Alvaro stood to his immediate right, her demeanor pleasant if carefully neutral. She was one of the Atlas lawyers who'd fought the search warrant in court, and her presence here meant Isaac needed to tread carefully. More carefully than usual.

Alvaro possessed a stick-thin body and a fresh, oval face framed by long chestnut hair. She wore a tan business suit with a static green neck scarf and a pair of thick, green glasses with rectangular lenses. Isaac had read the Themis legal team's profile on the lawyer, which gave him some insight on what he was up against.

Her synthoid made her look about twenty-five years old, but her true age was closer to two hundred and fifty. She'd bounced her way through a variety of careers over her impressive lifespan, switching jobs every few decades, which meant she'd "only" been practicing law about as long as Isaac had been alive.

"Thank you for agreeing to speak with us again," Isaac began.

"Detective," was all Boaz said in reply.

"I'd like to start by discussing your objections to our search warrant."

"Objections that were perfectly within our legal rights."

"I don't dispute that. However, I would still like to better understand what's behind your objections."

"It's quite simple. The original warrant was broad. *Far* too broad. So wide satisfying it would have placed our business model at risk."

"How so?"

"You would have needed access to proprietary information. Data that gives us an edge on our competitors. Technical knowledge that led to us securing the Dyson contract. Secrets our competitors would *love* to get their grubby hands on, which means *I* need to protect them."

"Any such information would have remained confidential."

"Detective, please." Boaz smirked at him. "Let's be honest with each other. You can't say that for certain. You can profess all you want about how discreet you and your team would be, but at the end of the day, SysPol leaks like any other organization. I wasn't about to place this company's future at risk because of some fishing expedition."

"Are you claiming our investigation into Velasco's suicide is unjustified?"

"No, but I am saying it's becoming a nuisance. Yes, the man killed himself, and we're all deeply saddened by his loss, but life goes on. This company goes on. We'll miss the expertise he brought to the project, but the truth is no one's indispensable. We can all be replaced, Velasco included."

"That doesn't change the fact that criminal elements found the legal delay useful."

"Careful, Detective. That almost sounds like an accusation."

"I'm simply stating a fact. We believe someone with access to your systems used the delay to alter the data we received, by editing either the infostructure image or the source files used to create it."

"Excuse me, but—"

"It's true, sir," Alvaro interrupted. "Themis Legal contacted us, and it does appear the data we sent was corrupted."

Boaz twisted in his seat to face her. "And you're telling me this now?"

"Sir?"

"You wait until SysPol is right here in the room before you drop this turd on my lap?"

"I'm handling the problem."

"By doing what?"

"We're negotiating a revised warrant with Themis Legal."

"Which will mean more delays," Isaac pointed out. "And more time for evidence to be destroyed."

"Good grief!" Boaz rubbed his temples. "What do I even pay you people for?"

"You pay me to protect our company's interests, which is exactly what I'm doing."

"Okay, look." Boaz turned back to Isaac and pointed at Alvaro with his thumb. "These legal decisions are in her wheelhouse, not mine. If you have a problem with them, fight it out with her."

"I'm not here to fight your legal counsel," Isaac said. "I'm here because I want to know how the data was corrupted."

"Well, if I knew I'd tell you, but I don't," Boaz replied.

"Whose idea was it to push back against the warrant?"

Boaz opened his mouth, but Alvaro cleared her throat.

"It was a collaborative decision," the lawyer said. "Mister Boaz, the project team's senior staff, and our legal staff were all involved."

"Right," Boaz agreed. "What she said."

"Who made the final call?"

"I *am* the CEO," Boaz answered, and Alvaro frowned beside him. "Need me to draw you an org chart?"

"I'll take that to mean it was you," Isaac said. "Next question. Who argued in favor of the legal action?"

"Again, it was a collaborative decision," Alvaro cut in before Boaz could speak.

"Can you be any clearer?"

"There was some debate on how to proceed. Beyond that, I won't say. The exact contents of the meeting are confidential."

"Can you at least tell me who collected the data?"

"Each member of the project team was responsible for submitting their own relevant records."

"But who put it all together?" Isaac pressed. "Who generated the data image? Who gave it to the legal team before it was transferred to Themis?"

"The senior engineer on the project," Alvaro answered. "Leon Traczyk."

Velasco's jealous coworker? he thought. *You put* him *in charge of the data?*

"We'll need to speak with him next."

✧   ✧   ✧

"I'm not sure what you expect to gain from talking to me," Traczyk griped, slouching back in the conference room chair. Alvaro stood beside him, watchful as a hawk. "I can't explain how some of the data went missing. Everything was there when I reviewed it."

"Walk me through the process," Isaac said. "How was the image put together and reviewed before being sent to us?"

"There's not much to discuss. I received the instructions from Legal and forwarded them to every team member along with the deadline. Each of them, in turn, sent me an archive of the relevant files. I put their responses together into a single infostructure image and passed it on to the lawyers."

"And after that?"

"I performed my own review of the image," Alvaro explained. "After I finished, I sent it directly to Themis. No one else touched it."

"If that's so, then why didn't you notice the missing data?"

"Because I wasn't looking for gaps," she replied stiffly.

"Then what *were* you looking for?"

"Confidential information outside the warrant's scope."

"Did you make any cuts before you sent it?"

"I did."

"How many?"

"I partially redacted seventeen conversation streams and deleted three files from the image before forwarding it to SysPol. And before you ask, all of my decisions are thoroughly documented and wholly justified within the context of our agreement with Themis Legal. If you wish to challenge me on any of them, best come prepared."

"Noted." Isaac turned back to Traczyk. "And what about you?"

"What *about* me?"

"Why didn't you catch the issues with the image?"

"I don't know. I can't explain it."

"You said you performed your own review, correct?"

"Of course," Traczyk replied, perhaps too quickly.

"You don't sound entirely certain."

"Look. I've been getting pulled in umpteen different directions lately. The last few days have been a blur with the project award, Velasco blowing his brains out, and us reshuffling the project team. Cut me some slack!"

"Did you or did you not check the image?"

"I did, okay. No need to get testy about it."

"If I'm testy, it's because someone in this company is concealing evidence."

"Well, it's not me, so go bark at someone else."

"What I believe Mister Traczyk is trying to say—" Alvaro began.

"That's quite all right," Isaac cut in. "His initial statement was clear enough."

Alvaro wrinkled her nose at him but didn't otherwise respond.

Isaac took a hard look at Traczyk.

"You checked the image."

"That's what I said."

"Thoroughly?"

"I don't know. You can't expect me to go through every last file. That's why I delegated the work. It's a big project team, and Legal set a tight deadline for us to push that image out the door."

"A fair enough point, but you wouldn't have had any difficulty checking your own correspondence, am I right?"

"Sure. I know it best, after all."

"Have you played through the new *Solar Descent* season?"

"Uhh . . ." Traczyk blinked, the question taking him off guard. "Yeah. What's this have to do with anything?"

"I was simply curious, given our earlier discussions." Isaac leaned back, forearm on the conference table. "Have you beaten it yet?"

"Hell no." Traczyk's mood seemed to brighten with the change in topic. "That damn final boss is a nightmare!"

"So I've heard. The . . . ?" Isaac prompted with a raised eyebrow.

"Onyx Ghost. Turns out he's the traitor hiding in the Solar Guild."

"Spoiler warning," Alvaro muttered with a roll of her eyes.

"He opens the battle with this ridiculous AOE attack," Traczyk continued. "Hit us for a ton of damage and inflicted everyone with Paralysis and Decay. And then the battle went downhill from there in a hurry!"

"Sounds nasty," Isaac commented.

"Is there a point to this, Detective?" Alvaro asked.

"There is. Have you discussed how the season ends with anyone else on the project?"

"Oh, sure," Traczyk said. "We have a few *Descent* parties on the team, so we're always swapping stories and talking strategy. Everyone, and I mean *everyone* is worked up about this boss! It's almost like the developers *want* players to die in that battle."

"Sounds like it was the talk of the office."

"Not the *whole* office, but yeah. A bunch of us plan to make another run through the scenario with fresh characters. We've been bouncing strategies back and forth."

"And you made sure these messages were included in the image sent to Themis, correct?"

Traczyk's expression soured.

"The search warrant covers personal correspondence of the project team within a set date range," Isaac continued. "Therefore, knowing that, you certainly would have noticed if the biggest talk of the office was missing, would you not?"

Traczyk leaned back and turned to Alvaro with a worried, almost cringing expression.

"Why are you looking at me? It's a valid question."

"Was the *Solar Descent* correspondence in the image when you checked it?" Isaac pressed.

"What does it matter?"

"It matters because there are only two possibilities. Either you didn't check it and the error slipped past you, or you *did* check it, which means you *let* the error through. Neither of those options cast you in a flattering light."

"Fine!" Traczyk snapped. "You want to know what I did with the image?"

"What do you think I've been after this whole time?"

"I barely checked it, all right? I know I should have done more, but I was busy and tired and I just wanted to go home that night. So I took the files everyone else sent in, put a big, digital bow around them, and shipped them off to Alvaro. That's *it*! You going to arrest me for that?"

"Not at present," Isaac said carefully. "However—"

He paused, his attention grabbed by a high-priority alert that suddenly appeared in his inbox. An urgent message wasn't unusual by itself; he received alerts all the time while on a case, but the source made this one stand out. It didn't come from within SysPol or SSP but instead had been sent by Horace Pangu.

"However," Isaac continued, returning his attention to the interview, "I must consider both possibilities until one or the other can be ruled out. You will need to register any travel plans with SysPol while this case remains open. Is that clear?"

"Yeah, it's clear," Traczyk groaned.

"Perfectly clear, Detective," Alvaro replied crisply.

The interview broke up after that, but Isaac and Susan stayed in the conference room.

"You look like you've got something on your mind," Susan said.

"I do. Pangu sent me a message while we were talking to Traczyk."

"About what?"

"Not sure." He accessed his mail.

The message read: CAN I SPEAK TO YOU IN PRIVATE? IT'S ABOUT THE CASE. I'M AT MY APARTMENT. [address attached]

Isaac glanced over to Susan, who gave him a wolfish grin.

"Sounds like he's got something for us."

✦   ✦   ✦

Horace Pangu's apartment was located in the Hanging Gardens on the same level as Velasco's but in the opposite tower.

"Sorry," Pangu said with a congenial smile, standing in the doorway to his apartment. "I thought only one of you would come. I didn't mean to occupy both of you."

"It's quite all right," Isaac replied. "May we come in?"

"Certainly. Please." Pangu stepped back and gestured for them to enter.

The interior lacked any furnishings except for a pair of metal chairs printed from a public domain pattern.

"As you can see, I'm not used to entertaining guests," Pangu said. "At least, not in the physical. Other than a synthoid charging casket and my desk in the bedroom, the apartment's unfurnished. I told Atlas I'd be content living in a capsule apartment, but they insisted on the Hanging Gardens. Apparently, they receive a discount that increases the more staff they board here. Would you like me to print out another chair, Agent? Sorry, I only prepared the two."

"It's all right," Susan said. "I'll stand."

Isaac sat down opposite the consultant. "You wished to speak with us concerning the case?"

"Yes, but before that, mind if I ask a question?"

"I don't mind. Though whether or not I answer depends on the question."

"I caught the news about that Society chair being arrested, and it brought to mind all of Velasco's complaints about the harassment he'd received. Which, naturally, made me curious if the arrest led you anywhere."

"Not especially, I'm afraid. At least, nowhere relevant to this case. Beyond that, I can't say."

"I see." Pangu paused and stared off in thought, then shrugged indifferently. "The Society is an awful nuisance."

"You'll receive no argument from us."

"But perhaps they didn't have a hand in this," Pangu finished. "Which brings us around to what I wanted to discuss."

"I'm surprised you didn't speak with us at the Atlas office. We spent a good chunk of our morning over there."

"True, but I'm working from home today."

"Any particular reason why?"

"Officially? I'm waiting on Traczyk to get caught up. No point in me heading in until he's ready for me. Unofficially? I wanted to talk to you without Atlas Legal breathing down my neck." He leaned in and lowered his voice for emphasis. "We're all under orders not to speak with you unless there's a lawyer in the room."

"And yet here you are," Susan observed.

"Quite." Pangu flashed a sly grin. "Fortunately for me, *I'm* not an Atlas employee. I'll make my own legal decisions, thank you very much. Which includes talking to SysPol when and where I please."

"About?" Isaac prompted politely.

"Velasco and Boaz. You see, the Society wasn't the only source of stress Velasco complained about regularly. Boaz was another one. Or, more specifically, Velasco's regular one-on-one meetings with Boaz."

"Which seems painfully normal, given the nature of their professional relationship."

"Under normal circumstances, I'd agree. But I've been doing some thinking since he passed. Trying my best to figure out what wormed its way into his head to make him pull that trigger."

"And you believe Boaz might have had something to do with it?"

Pangu nodded.

"Why?"

"It has to do with the...temperament of their meetings. They changed over time."

"In what way?"

"They grew increasingly hostile. Or so it seemed. I wasn't privy to the meetings themselves, of course, but I saw Velasco after most of them. Now *there* was the picture of a man who'd been verbally pummeled to within a millimeter of his life, and it only grew worse with time."

"Which is unfortunate, but again, fits the nature of their relationship."

"True, but would it surprise you to learn Velasco was in tears after their last meeting? Held just three days before he committed suicide?"

"Three days..." The number tickled a part of Isaac's mind. He opened his notes and scrolled through one of Nina's reports. "That's the same day Velasco printed out the gun."

"You believe that conversation pushed Velasco to kill himself?" Susan asked.

"I'm not sure," Pangu admitted. "But whatever they discussed, it cut him to the core. Of that, I'm certain."

"Hmm," Isaac murmured.

"You seem doubtful, Detective."

"Because I am. I appreciate the information, but Boaz being the kind of boss that can reduce employees to tears isn't exactly actionable evidence. Furthermore, we spoke to Boaz this morning, and he seemed completely blindsided by the problems Atlas has had responding to our search warrant."

"I'm sorry." Pangu's eyes widened. "What did you just say?"

"That Boaz was blindsided?"

"By how messages with the word 'ghost' in them were missing?" Pangu filled in.

"Yes." Isaac raised an eyebrow at the consultant. "How do you know that?"

"Because he asked me about the missing messages yesterday."

❖   ❖   ❖

"Want to head back to Atlas and grill Boaz again?" Susan asked as they headed back to the car.

"As tempting as that might be, we need to be cautious. He'll be lawyered up and ready for us, which means we need stronger evidence than something he can pass off as a 'miscommunication.'

Let's head back to the station and check in with Hoopler. I'm curious to see if her team has made any progress with Bao."

"And if they haven't?"

"Not sure. I suppose we could take another crack at him ourselves."

The rental slid its doors open and they climbed in.

"Vehicle," Isaac said. "Take us to the 103rd Precinct Building."

"Destination set," the car replied. "Departing."

The door slid shut, and the rental pulled out of the apartment complex.

An alert appeared in his peripheral vision halfway to the station.

"Finally." Isaac smiled as he answered the call.

"Hey, Isaac," Nina said. "You ready for—" She paused to take a long and vocal yawn that threatened to unhinge her lower jaw. "Wow! Excuse me!"

"You okay there?"

"Never better. You ready for some good news?"

"Always."

"I found traces of a rare microbot on a few surfaces in the container, along with prints and DNA traces that don't match the two hoodlums you brought in."

"Any hits on the database?"

"One. A small-time thug named Robert Chase. Goes by the ever so creative alias 'Big Bobby.'" She rolled her eyes.

"Byte Pyrate?"

"No. His SSP file says he's not openly affiliated with any one gang. Rather, he performs odd jobs for a few different clients. Stuff like running material from point A to B or delivering 'messages.' You know, the kind that come from his fists. Multiple counts of assault and possession of stolen property and patterns. The Byte Pyrates don't show up in his profile, but his clientele is broad enough that it might include them and SSP hasn't noticed yet. That possibility got me to thinking about those weird microbots."

"What kind of machines are we talking about?" Susan asked.

"Some sort of construction self-replicator," Nina said. "Inactive but high end. It's not a publicly registered design."

"Which means?"

"Could be some company's exclusive design."

"And you don't know which one?"

"Technically, all self-replicator patterns are supposed to be registered," Isaac explained, "but there's a loophole in the law. If a replicating system is considered 'under development,' then the law loses its teeth. Companies will sometimes use the loophole to keep their designs under wraps."

"There's another possibility," Nina added. "It could be from an iteration that didn't pan out. If the microbots were only used in a limited fashion—like a single deployment test—then there's no legal requirement to register them."

"Which makes tracking down the source a pain," Isaac said.

"Except"—Nina's eyes twinkled despite her fatigue—"there's more than one way to sniff them out. I ran the microbots through the city's pollution map and found several hits, all of them in the upper reaches of the city. *One* of those locations has a density index ten times higher than the others."

A map of the Third Engine Block appeared beside the comm window, showing the horizontal Y of the city's main corridors through Janus. Tiny pips of red throbbed along the ceiling, haphazardly sprayed across both branches of the Y. One of those pips pulsed brighter than the others. *Much* brighter.

Isaac zoomed in. "A decommissioned reactor?"

"Say hello to the old Kamiya-Franklin Energy Plant," Nina said. "Perfect spot for a gang to hide out. My guess is the Byte Pyrates are holed up in there, and they hired Big Bobby Chase to run materials between the KF reactor and the container base."

"How would he have reached the container?" Susan asked.

"Through a tunnel the Pyrates cut in the side of the logistics center, which connects the blocked bin to a utility channel running up the intake wall. From there, gang members could come and go as they pleased, and no one would be the wiser."

"Fantastic work, Nina," Isaac said.

"I'm sending you my full report." She yawned into her fist. "Need anything else before I turn in for the day?"

"Got the report. We should be good for now. Get some rest."

"All right. Talk to you later."

Nina closed the connection.

"Now we're talking!" Susan rubbed her hands together.

"This could very well be the break we needed. We'll get with Hoopler as soon as we reach the station and formalize a plan to take down the hideout. We'll need to get a better fix on the location first, but perhaps Hoopler can help us out there."

"What about Boaz?"

"He's not going anywhere. The Pyrates are the priority since they can lead us to Ruckman's copy. The sooner we find and free him, the better, and now that we have a solid lead, we follow it through."

"Makes sense to me. SSP better go in prepared, though. If our experience is any indication, the Pyrates won't be taken in without a fight."

"Yes..." An uncomfortable thought formed in Isaac's mind, and he looked over at Susan.

"Something wrong?" she asked.

"It's just...I was thinking."

"About?"

"How best to execute the raid."

"Carefully. I've dealt with trigger-happy types before. An operation can go south in a hurry if you're not careful."

"Yes, about that. I was thinking...that perhaps you might..."

"Might what?"

"Give me a moment. This is awkward." He shifted in his seat. "Would you consider switching over to your combat frame and taking the lead on the raid?"

Her eyebrows shot up.

"I'm only asking," he emphasized with a cautioning hand. The silence dragged out, and he added, "Are you opposed to the idea?"

"No, not at all. I'm just surprised. I didn't know it was Christmas yet."

"Susan, I'm being serious here. A raid of this nature could prove quite dangerous, and it occurred to me that between all of us—SSP included—you have the most experience dealing with criminals who shoot back."

"That I do." She grinned at him. "From what I've seen, SSP are a bunch of lightweights compared to us STANDs."

"And, while I consider your combat frame to be...excessive in most circumstances, this is not one of them. Proper and decisive use of force should help us keep casualties to a minimum. It's just..."

"Yeah?"

"Try not to blow any of them up. If you can help it."

"But splattering evil guts all over the place is the best part of the job. What's the fun in restraint?"

Isaac gave her a cross look.

"I kid! I kid!"

CHAPTER TWENTY-ONE

"THERE YOU ARE!" SUSAN GRINNED EAR TO EAR AT THE SIGHT of her combat frame standing upright in the Admin storage crate.

The Type-99 combat frame possessed a sleek, almost athletic aesthetic to its humanoid design. The color-shifting variskin was set to Peacekeeper blue with white racing stripes down the sides and a silver shield at the shoulder. Weapons included a shoulder-mounted grenade launcher, heavy rail-rifle in the right arm, and an incinerator in the left. Maneuvering boosters extended from ball joints affixed to the shoulders, legs, and forearms.

It looked fast.

It *was* fast. Much faster than the Type-92 favored by most STANDs.

"You don't have to sound so happy about this," Isaac said, arms crossed.

"Why not? Using it was your idea."

"I *know*."

Isaac had placed a call to Dispatch on their way back to the 103rd, and a SysPol corvette had dropped off the crate at the airport a few hours later. The meeting with Hoopler had proceeded smoothly enough, with the raid tentatively scheduled to be executed six hours from now, giving SSP and Susan plenty of time to prep and stage at the 26th Precinct Building, which had been selected due to its proximity to the decommissioned Kamiya-Franklin reactor.

"Text update from Hoopler," Cephalie said, her avatar sitting atop the LENS. "SSP has finished putting together a more precise fix on that hideout. Turns out the 26th Precinct has been on the receiving end of some unusual complaints bordering the KF reactor. By themselves, none of reports made much sense, but with the Byte Pyrates clearly involved, the pieces fell into place. We have a specific section of the reactor building SSP considers most likely to be their base of operations."

"Excellent," Isaac said. "That'll speed things up."

"And make my job easier," Susan added. "Less time searching is less time something can go wrong."

"Oh, it gets better," Cephalie continued. "Hoopler has the area under long-range surveillance, and guess who they spotted ducking into the warrens beneath the reactor? None other than Big Bobby Chase! They've lost track of him, but his entry point further narrows our target area."

"Sure looks like Nina picked the right spot," Susan said.

"That it does," Isaac agreed. "You comfortable being the tip of the spear?"

"What?" She turned back to him, hands out to her sides. "Are you kidding?"

"I'm only asking."

"You know the answer." She flashed a quick smile and grabbed a knife off the side of the crate's inner wall. "Here."

"Ah, yes." He took the knife with a frown. "My favorite part of the process."

"See? You're already an old pro at this."

"I'm not sure how I feel about that. Turn around, please."

Susan complied. She sent the signal to her uniform's smart fabric for it to split open down the back. Isaac pulled the fabric aside to reveal the U-shaped indentation along her spine.

"Ready?" he asked.

"It's not like this'll hurt or anything," she assured him, then chuckled. "Go on and stick it in."

"Please don't word it like that."

The knife's tip cut into one end of the U, and then Isaac began to trace out the indentation. Information flowed into Susan's mind, reporting the negligible damage. It wasn't pain. Not in the sense that it demanded a response the way organic pain could, but it did occupy a similar corner of her mind, a similar sense of immediacy that she chose to ignore.

"It still bewilders me," Isaac said.

"What?"

"They literally make people—like me, for instance—carve open your back to retrieve your connectome case. Why? Why not allow STANDs to transfer themselves into their own frames?"

"*Because* this approach requires two people," Susan explained. "No single person can activate a combat frame."

"There's got to be a better way than this."

"Sure there is. But that's not the point. Back home, STANDs scare a lot of people, and not just outside the Peacekeepers. Those feelings were more prevalent when STANDs were first developed, but that fear remains, as well as the caution it rooted into the Peacekeepers. Think about it. We're faster, stronger, and more durable than any organic human, and a combat frame is even scarier than that. No wonder they wanted to place some restrictions on the power of these new, inhuman machines."

"You're not inhuman," Isaac said. "Sure, your body is synthetic, but the core of who you are is ve:y, *very* human."

"That may be the common attitude in SysGov, but not everyone in the Admin thinks that way. To them, I'm a program. A perverse echo of the being I once was, with the real Susan Cantrell having died when my connectome was recorded."

"And you? What do you believe?"

"I came to terms with my inhumanity a long time ago. In the end, I decided it didn't matter. I am who I am in this moment. Whether I'm human or not doesn't erase my obligations. Doesn't prevent me from serving those around me. Doesn't deprive me of purpose or honor."

"Well said." Isaac lifted the flap of cosmetic flesh and tapped her exposed spine. "Ready for me to yank you?"

"Ready." She locked her body's position and sent the release code.

Her connection to the synthoid vanished, along with all its senses. Her connectome swam within a sea of temporary light and sound devoid of meaningful purpose other than to provide sensory stimulation during her transfer. The rainbow-hued kaleidoscope danced before her "eyes" while gentle chimes played in the background.

Her life was in Isaac's hands now. She was completely defense-less, in command of nothing but her own thoughts within a slim cartridge little larger than the palm of her hand. And yet, she was completely at ease at the same time.

It surprised her now that she considered this. She'd known Isaac for... what was it now? About a month? Something like that. And yet, despite the brevity of their time together, her trust in him was absolute.

She'd seen his relentless determination in action on not one but two cases. When he committed to a task, he pursued it with singular purpose, no matter what obstacles stood in his path. And when he gave his word, he *meant it*. With every fiber of his being.

He was *that* kind of man.

An explosion of senses filled her world: visible light, infrared, ultraviolet, sonar, and radar. She drank from the deep well of data as her mind stretched out through the familiar shape of the combat frame's system.

She raised her hand, flexed the fingers once, twice, then sent a ripple of shifting malmetal plates down the forearm like a wave broken up into discrete hexagons. The armor settled, and she faced Isaac.

"Everything good in there?" he asked.

"Never better." She gave him a thumbs-up. "Ready to kick some criminal butt."

The Kamiya-Franklin Energy Plant was a gourd-shaped reac-tor suspended between the Third Engine Block's ceiling and the dense industrial zone beneath it, located two kilometers back from the intake wall. Pedestrian bridges from neighboring stalactite towers spanned the gaps between them, though most were unlit and sealed off. Still, the reactor showed signs of human presence with active graffiti covering patches of the gray-paneled exterior accessible to foot traffic, sealed or not. Gang tags, political state-ments, obscenities, and genuinely impressive artwork all mixed together, sometimes overlapping one another.

A ten-lane bridge—the Franklin Span—ran from the upper shelves to the industrial zone where it then passed through a tunnel beneath the dead reactor. SSP suspected the Tunnel Warrens—a chaotic mishmash of residential and commercial buildings that had accumulated around the tunnel over the years—were how the Byte Pyrates came and went undetected. According to their analysis, the hideout would be found near the base of the reactor, just above the warrens.

Susan watched the KF reactor draw near through the virtual image on the quadcopter's side door. The copter would pass over the tunnel soon, not too close to the reactor to arouse suspicion, and not too far to impede her deployment. Just a police copter passing through on its way to some other problem.

She held a tight grip on the ceiling railing, and she'd toggled the soles of her feet to maximum friction, anchoring her combat frame in place. Status displays hovered in her mind's eye, indicating the full readiness of all her systems. Her boosters were topped off, and all weapons were armed.

She'd swapped out the high-explosive ordnance in her launcher with a mix of stun and gas grenades, which she agreed could prove useful against a gang that shunned synthoids and ACs. Her interface to the SysPol-pattern grenades wasn't as smooth as with the Admin originals—she could select between timed fuses or impact activation, and that was it—but she didn't require much more.

She'd kept her rail-rifle and incinerator. Isaac had frowned upon their lethality, but the Byte Pyrates struck her as a sophisticated bunch, which meant they might have access to automated weapons. They might be squishy, but their defenses could be a whole different story.

A complement of less-than-lethal suppression tools hung from the utility belt around the frame's waist, rounding out her arsenal.

"This is about as close as we're going to get," Chatelain reported from the cockpit.

"It's close enough." Susan palmed the door, and it slid open. "Thanks for the lift."

"Our pleasure," Chatelain replied, his tone conveying that he found nothing pleasurable about this.

Susan set the reactor as her variskin's priority angle, which would ensure she remained least visible in that direction. She reduced the friction on her feet, then stepped off, plummeting toward the lower city a kilometer below.

Wind whistled past as her variskin adapted, keying off the reactor's position and objects directly behind her to determine its coloration. It wasn't as good as SysPol metamaterial, which could bend light around it, but it would do against most foes.

She fired a short burp of thrust from her shoulder boosters, angling her approach toward the base of the reactor. The ground rushed up to her, and she engaged her boosters at the last moment to settle lightly onto the roof of the Tunnel Warrens. She switched her variskin to a generalized stealth mode, and her body vanished into a metallic backdrop.

"Descent complete," Susan reported over an encrypted radio channel. "You still with me?"

"Still here," Isaac replied, safe and sound back in the 26th Precinct command center, which was exactly where she wanted him. "Your signal is coming through nice and clean."

"That may change once you're inside the reactor," Hoopler said. "Once you're close, I'm going to send out a second patrol copter to act as a relay. That should help, but no promises."

"Understood," Susan said. "Advancing on the target."

She crouch-walked across the warren rooftops, weaving a path through the disorderly, mechanical jumble. The bulbous form of the reactor loomed above her as she drew near, the sun rod casting long shadows across the rooftops.

She reached a channel three stories deep that cut across the warrens. Cables hung loose across the gap and an oily mix of fluids and trash had collected at the bottom. She leaped over the gap, fired a quick burst from her boosters, and landed softly on the far side.

She made her way into deeper shadows near the reactor, then came to a narrow gap between two air processors. She slid in sideways and pressed on.

Her sensors picked up movement ahead, and she slowed.

"Someone's nearby," she reported. "Could be a Byte Pyrate. Slowing my advance."

"Be careful," Isaac urged.

She crept back into the open and glanced around. The twin processors butted up against the reactor's lower reaches, forming a cramped space between them and the massive cylindrical column that extended down from the base of the reactor. A single light hung from the ceiling, casting its gloomy illumination across a greasy residue that oozed out through the wall panels, which Susan recalled was a sign of degrading prog-steel.

Narrow passages disappeared into darkness to either side, and a heavy hatch led into the column's interior. The hatch appeared

THE DYSON FILE

to be new or at least well maintained, in contrast to the decay around it.

A broad-shouldered figure trudged into the open, his posture slouched to clear the low ceiling. He wore a pair of tough black pants and a matching vest, leaving his impressive biceps bare. He used a linked chain for a belt, and his ears were pierced by thick, threaded bolts held in by hexagonal nuts. Another bolt had been screwed into one wide, flaring nostril.

"Movement source identified," Susan reported. "He's not a Byte Pyrate."

"How do you know?" Isaac asked.

"Because I'm staring at Big Bobby."

"He took his sweet time getting there," Isaac noted. "Perhaps he had other business in the warrens."

"I think I'll ask him a few questions."

Susan activated the infostructure jammer on her belt and crept up behind the thug. He stopped, his face creasing with confusion. He raised a hand and tried to summon an interface.

Susan grabbed him from behind, one hand over his mouth and the other pinning an arm into the small of his back. He shouted but the sound came out muffled as she dragged him back into the shadows.

Big Bobby grabbed hold of her wrist with his free hand and tried to pry her off him, but to no avail. He stood no chance against her Admin synthoid, let alone her *combat frame*. For all his brutish muscles, he was as helpless as a newborn babe.

"Hello, Bobby," Susan whispered into his ear through an external speaker. "Agent Cantrell, SysPol Themis."

His eyes widened and he cried out against her hand.

"Shhh. Shhh," she urged. "There's no need for that. I'm not actually here for you, which got me thinking. Maybe the two of us could have a little chat before I move on. I bet you know a *lot* about the Byte Pyrates. How about it? Interested?"

His speech came out garbled, but she was sure he'd slipped in a few profanities.

"Oh, come now. I would never do that to my mother. We can either go about this the easy way..." She pressed her head against his ear and lowered her voice menacingly. "Or the hard way."

He flailed and kicked against her uselessly. She waited for his tantrum to die down.

"There we go. Ready to give the easy way a try now? Nod or shake your head."

Bobby Chase paused for long seconds, then gave her a brief nod.

"That's good. Are the Byte Pyrates through that door?"

Another nod.

"How many?"

He shrugged his shoulders.

"Give me a guess."

He paused again, then raised his free hand, opened it fully, closed it, then opened it again.

"About ten of them?"

He nodded, then mumbled something against her hand.

"Yes, yes. I get it. You find counting difficult. Are they armed?"

He gave her an emphatic nod.

"What about anything heavy, like mechs or drones?"

He paused for a while, then shrugged.

"Explosives?"

Another shrug.

"You're not being very helpful."

He replied with an angry, garbled response.

"Then maybe you should have paid more attention to your surroundings."

He huffed out an angry breath at her.

"Well, as stimulating as this chat has been, I think I've got all I need. Say goodnight, Bobby."

She removed a slumber-cuff from her utility belt and bound his wrists. Medibots departed a small reservoir within the cuffs and seeped through the skin. They entered his bloodstream and sped through his body, deploying their chemical payloads at key locations. Bobby Chase drifted into a deep, chemically induced sleep almost immediately.

She lowered his limp body to the ground where he began snoring like a chainsaw. She stepped over him and approached the hatch. She switched off the jammer and checked the area with her passive sensors. None of them detected movement or other signs of people nearby, so she turned the manual latch.

The door didn't explode, which was a promising start. She pulled it open a hair and took a peek inside.

"Isaac, the Byte Pyrates aren't based below the reactor." She craned her neck and looked up through the towering shaft. "This entrance leads to a grav tube. Powered and in good condition. The tube runs the whole height of the structure, which would place their base of operations *above* the reactor, according to my range finder."

"Understood," Isaac replied, then paused before adding, "That tube isn't on the reactor map, so I'd say your guess is correct. The Pyrates added it themselves."

A comm window opened above Big Bobby's slumbering body, its contents blurred by a privacy filter, and the nearby infostructure surged with sudden activity.

"Someone's calling Chase," Susan reported. "And I think they're checking on the door I just opened. There's a good chance they suspect something's not right. Maybe my jammer tipped them off? Should I abort?"

"It's your call," Isaac said.

"Then I'm going in."

"Understood. Hoopler! Get your teams moving, now!"

Susan stepped into the shaft. The graviton current lifted her into the air, and she rode it halfway up before the artificial gravity switched off. She dropped away in what someone must have hoped would be a fatal fall.

"Going loud!" She fired her boosters at full power and rocketed up the rest of the shaft.

Susan cut her thrust, flipped herself over, and landed on the shaft ceiling, coming face-to-face with a hatch identical to the one at the bottom. She kicked off, ignited her boosters again, and smashed her shoulder into the hatch.

The impact tore the hatch off its hinges and sent it tumbling across the room until it bowled over a workbench. A dozen partially disassembled infosystem towers flew into the air.

Susan burst into the open, fired a stun grenade, then caught sight of a lanky male to her left. He wore a striped blue-and-black shirt tucked into tight black pants with a prominent codpiece, which made his groin the most heavily armored part of his body. Not that it mattered against her arsenal.

He stood next to what may have been the grav tube's control interface. Virtual screens hovered near an open junction box lined with blocky processing nodes. He turned to her, his face transitioning from annoyance to shock as her STAND landed in the middle of the room.

The loser who tried to drop me to my death? she surmised.

The stun grenade detonated in a burst of light and sound, and the Byte Pyrate flinched from the glare. Susan kicked off the ground, grabbed him by the shirt, and drove him against the wall. He coughed out a sharp exhale from the impact, his eyes suddenly wide. She grabbed his wrists, bound them in a slumber-cuff, then forced him to the floor. The prog-steel in the cuff formed a tight friction bond with the floor, serving as a suitable anchor to hold the Pyrate in place until SSP could take him into custody, even if he somehow managed to wake up.

Two doors led out of the room, one on either side with the grav tube's entrance. She switched her variskin over to a general combat mode and interrogated her sensors, which detected heavy footfalls approaching her position from the left. The door split open to reveal a stocky Byte Pyrate with a pistol holstered at his hip.

"What was that rack—?"

Susan boosted over to him, clearing the distance almost instantly. She grabbed the gun with one hand and his shoulder with the other, then pinned him against the door. She crushed his weapon and tossed it away.

The Byte Pyrate barely had time for a look of shock and dismay to form on his round face before Susan spun him around and bound his wrists behind his back. She shoved his back against the wall, and the cuffs latched on to the surface.

"Hey! Hey, guys! There's a...ohh, wow..." The Pyrate went cross-eyed as medibots took effect.

Susan hurried down the exposed corridor into a living space of sorts. Couches lined two of the walls, interspersed with food printers and tables covered with dirty dishes, glasses, and empty food wrappers. A Pyrate lay sprawled across a couch, eyes closed with a stupid grin on his face. A virtual sign floated over him that read: DO NOT DISTURB. PLAYING REALMBUILDER.

He must be completely immersed in the abstract, she thought, then cuffed him.

The Pyrate's eyes snapped open, and he rose from the couch with an angry start, his wrists locked together.

"What are you jokers trying to pull this..." His knees gave out, and he staggered forward into Susan's arms. "What the?"

"Nighty night." She lowered him to the floor.

"What the *hell* is all this racket?" A Pyrate emerged from a room beside the living space. His pants were hanging low, and his cheeks were red. He rubbed his squinting eyes and yawned. "Some of us are trying to—"

Susan clapped a hand over his mouth and shoved him against the wall. He muttered something unintelligible against her hand, but she held him in place and surveyed the room behind him.

Three more Pyrates slumbered in bunk beds or slumped in chairs around a central table covered in empty bottles labeled BLISS and MELT. Susan shoved her prisoner back into the room, dumped a gas grenade inside, then palmed the door shut. She punched through the door's interface panel and ripped out its infosystem node.

Another door split open on the opposite side of the room, and two Byte Pyrates stormed through the opening. The woman wore a black-studded brasserie and hotpants, exposing a great deal of tastelessly tattooed flesh. She wielded a burst pistol. The man next to her sported a long, braided beard dyed blue, his bare chest partially hidden by the huge rifle in his hands. Both Pyrates raised their weapons.

Susan energized the dense armor plates along her forearm, and malmetal hexagons shifted outward to form a rectangular shield. Both Pyrates opened fire. The burst pistol spewed a stream of mag darts that pattered against the barrier, but each shot from the heavy rifle punched deep divots into her shield.

Susan fired her boosters and cleared the distance between. She swung her shield in a wide arc, bashing both assailants aside. The woman with the pistol fell to the floor, but the man with the rifle only staggered back before he began to raise his weapon once more.

Susan retracted her shield and advanced on him. He tried to pull back, but she grabbed the rifle, and yanked it away. The weapon flew from the bearded Pyrate's grip, and he stumbled forward into the combat frame. Susan shoved him back with enough force for him to hit the ground and slide across the floor. She bent the rifle in half and tossed it aside.

The woman began to raise her pistol, but Susan pinned it under her foot. The woman tried in vain to pull the weapon free. Susan crouched down, spun her over, and bound her wrists behind her back. She smashed the burst pistol to pieces against the floor.

The bearded Pyrate scrambled away by kicking his legs out,

pushing himself across the floor. Susan grabbed one of his ankles, hauled him toward her, cuffed him and stuck the cuff to the wall.

Let's see here. She thought for a moment, mentally counting how many Pyrates she'd encountered so far. *The two here and the four in the side room bring the total to nine. So where's number ten? Is there a number ten? Or did Big Bobby flunk basic math?*

"Umm, hello?"

Her sensors guided her to the source of the voice. She stepped back into the corridor and found a door marked with a friendly cartoonish pirate. Blocky font spelled out: PYRATE PRIVY.

"Hello yourself." Susan leaned against the door to the toilet. "Seems like you're in a bit of a predicament there, mister."

"Yeah, you could say that. Is it okay to come out?"

"Depends. You going to shoot at me? Not that it'll do you much good if you try. Didn't help out any of your pals."

"No," replied the Pyrate behind the door.

"Smart man."

"Not like I have a choice. I left my gun at my desk. Didn't think I'd need it in here."

"Isn't that how life goes sometimes?" Susan opined. "As soon as you leave something behind, it turns out you need it."

"Would now be a good time to surrender?"

"Depends. Have you washed your hands yet?"

"Susan," Isaac radioed in. "Perhaps it would be best if you didn't toy with the criminals?"

"Right. Sorry!" She palmed the door, and it slid aside to reveal a Pyrate sitting on the toilet with his pants around his ankles. She yanked him out and cuffed him.

Susan swept through the Byte Pyrate base while she waited for SSP to catch up, checking and clearing each room in a more methodical manner than her initial, one-person blitz. She didn't find any more gangsters, but that wasn't the only thing missing, and the more rooms she explored, the more doubt crept into her mind about this location. Sure, the Byte Pyrates were here, but where were the high-end infosystems they used to commit their crimes? That cargo container at JIT Deliveries held two—maybe three—times more processing power than the entire reactor hideout.

She was missing something. Or rather, the base was missing a lot of somethings.

Isaac will know what to make of this, she told herself. *I bet he'll have this little mystery figured out after a few minutes of poking around.*

But even with that comforting thought, she continued her search. She yearned to prove to Isaac she could be more than just an Admin bullet sponge, and she proceeded with her methodical checks, inspecting every room one by one, even though most were barren.

This place should be better stocked if it's their main hangout, Susan thought. *So, if it isn't, then what's it for?*

She came across another hatch similar to the one she'd torn off the entrance grav tube, except this one was on the other end of the compound.

"A second grav tube?" She turned the manual release, opened the hatch, and checked inside. "A grav tube leading up?" She craned her neck. "But there's nothing above us besides..."

She pondered this discovery and what it could mean, then radioed Isaac.

"Is there a problem?" he asked. "We're approaching the reactor now."

"No, nothing's wrong. Just found something strange. A second grav tube that leads up."

"Up? But you're almost next to the structural barrier between the Second and Third blocks."

"Exactly. You think the pirates cut into it?"

"I suppose that's a possibility, but my first question would be why. There are plenty of other, easier ways to reach the Second Engine Block. Burning through a structural barrier isn't the same as cutting into some random warehouse. You saw how thick the barrier is when we visited the Safari. We're talking about a major physical undertaking for a group that specializes in abstract crimes. It doesn't fit."

"Yeah, I was thinking along the same lines," Susan replied. "But this grav tube is here. I'm going to check out where it leads."

"Be careful."

"Always."

Susan stepped into the grav tube but didn't trigger the graviton current. Instead, she angled her boosters and rocketed up the shaft. She slowed as she approached the top, then switched to a hover by the hatch and opened it.

She cut her thrust and stepped out to an open space that disappeared into milky fog in all directions. The pollution was thin enough for her to see the shadows of thick structural pillars and hints of distant buildings.

Or perhaps the *skeletons* of buildings.

The fog retreated, as if alert to her presence, revealing a quaint, two-story housing block with cream-colored siding and a lush lawn. At first, she thought the structure was unfinished, but then she noticed silvery crabs about the size of her hand scurrying across the exterior. The crabs worked in pairs or groups of four to cut cubical chunks out of the building before carrying them away to a neighboring townhouse under construction.

That townhouse was coming together brick by brick, but the next house over seemed to...wilt before her eyes, for lack of a better phrase. Thick, milky smoke flowed around the townhouse, eating holes in the siding wherever it gathered.

"Replicator swarm," Susan hissed.

Her systems detected the microbot aerosol around her, but nothing was trying to eat or corrupt her combat frame.

Yet, anyway.

"*Isaac*," Susan radioed. "I think you need to get up here."

CHAPTER TWENTY-TWO

"WELCOME TO MATTISON'S RETREAT," ISAAC GRUMBLED, STANDING next to Susan's combat frame with his arms crossed. "A garden spot of the Shark Fin."

"Could have fooled me," Susan said.

"I was being sarcastic." Isaac took a deep breath through his environmental mask and studied their surroundings. The mask formed a transparent barrier over the front half of his face, with a pair of filtered nozzles extending down at diagonals on either side of his mouth. He watched as a tendril of milky smoke reached toward them like a thin, ghostly hand. Susan lit her incinerator and burned it back with a pulse of bluish flame. The tendril shrank away, receding into the greater swarm.

"Please stop doing that," Isaac said.

"It was giving me a hostile vibe."

"The swarm isn't going to hurt you or any of us. About the worst it'll do is clog up my lungs"—he tapped his mask—"hence why I'm wearing this awkward thing."

"At least you don't need a full pressure suit here," Cephalie chortled from atop the LENS.

"For which I'm grateful."

An SSP quadcopter flew overhead, its turbines kicking back the microbot fog along its path. The copter slowed to a hover, then descended next to the six copters already parked in a row. Hoopler and troopers from the 103rd and 26th were in the process

269

of setting up a field command center while crews off-loaded surveillance remotes, conveyor drones, infostructure relays, and tracking devices from the copters.

An empty quadcopter took off and flew toward the nearest dock, partially hidden by the thick fog, while distant running lights indicated another copter on approach.

"Question," Susan said. "If these machines will tear down each other's buildings for parts, what's stopping them from eating us, too?"

"They won't," Isaac insisted. "They can tell the difference between inert and living."

"You sure about that?"

"Pretty sure."

"As a general rule," Cephalie explained, "construction replicators like this will only utilize inert materials. There'll be a number of safeties built into their basic replication kernel, but the most fundamental is to avoid objects moving under their own power. Unless they receive a specific command to the contrary, and even then, other safeties might kick in and halt the order. You can actually see that behavior in action right now. Perhaps you noticed how the Atlas crabs and the SourceCode cloud swarms aren't fighting over the same building at the same time?"

"Umm." The head of Susan's combat frame jerked one way, then the other.

"That's because the activity of one group places the material off-limits for the other."

"But once a building is finished?" Susan asked.

"The building becomes prime raw materials." Cephalie shook her head. "These two companies *really* didn't play nice together."

"No kidding," Isaac muttered.

"What about the support columns?" Susan pointed to the nearest squared column rising through the fog. "Why are they still standing?"

"Any structural supports would be hardcoded as no-go zones," Cephalie said.

"You sure about that?" Susan asked.

"They're still here," Isaac said, "aren't they?"

"Yeah," Susan sighed. "But haven't these swarms been fighting it out for a while now?"

"About nine years."

"Right. So how come they're still running?"

"They must have access to a power tap somewhere. Otherwise, you're right. They should have run out of power long ago."

"And everyone's been fine with them bleeding off Janus' power grid?"

"Depends on where they're tapping into. Given we're inside the structural barrier, the tap probably connects to a significant power main running through one of these columns, which could be supplying remote regions of Janus. That's not a line you ever want to take down for maintenance if you can help it. A lot of the equipment that keeps this megastructure running is never meant to be turned off."

"Still seems dodgy to me."

"You want to switch back to your synthoid?" Isaac asked.

"Hell no." She thumped her armored chest. "I'm happy right where I am, thank you very much."

"With your flame thrower?"

"Damn straight."

"They're not going to eat you."

"Better safe than sorry. Where I come from, terrorists use crap like this to turn innocents into meat puddles."

"Well, we don't do that around here."

Milky smoke oozed toward them, and Susan shooed it away with a burp of bluish flame.

Isaac let out a weary sigh.

"Any word from Nina yet?" he asked Cephalie.

"She's on her way. Also, she found a match from that air sample SSP took."

Isaac nodded. It was the answer he'd expected, but it was good to have the facts confirmed. The microbots they found at JIT Deliveries—the same microbots Robert Chase had tracked there all the way from the reactor base—had originated from Mattison's Retreat.

They were in the right location, finally.

"The pieces are starting to fall into place," Isaac said. "Their hideout in the reactor isn't just empty of equipment. It's been emp-*tied*. We caught them at the tail end of a relocation." He stepped forward and gazed around at the shrouded shadows of buildings beyond the fog. "They've moved their base of operations into this mess. Somewhere. We just need to find them."

"And they've had help," Susan noted.

"Almost certainly. The channel around their grav tube makes that clear enough. They didn't cut their way here, like I originally assumed. The structural prog-steel was *commanded* to form that opening, which means they got their hands on some very rare government codes."

"Which they could have received from Velasco."

"Or whoever at Atlas performed cleanup. Or, possibly, through their interrogation of Ruckman's copy. In any case, the results are the same. They came by the digital keys to Mattison's Retreat and are putting them to use. The reactor was a good hiding spot, but this?" Isaac swept both hands across the clouded view. "They could have stayed hidden here for *ages*."

"We haven't found them yet."

"Yeah." Isaac spotted Hoopler walking toward them. "Speaking of which."

"Detectives," Hoopler greeted, her synthoid unmasked and unperturbed by the pollution. "We've finished loading up the prisoners. They're on their way back to the 26th as we speak. I'll let you know if the interrogations wring anything useful out of them."

"Sounds good, Lieutenant," Isaac said. "What about Mattison's Retreat itself?"

"We're just about ready to begin our sweep of the area."

"Anything we can do to help?"

"I'm not going to say no to an extra pair of eyes." She nodded to the combat frame.

"Just tell me where you need me," Susan said.

"Check in with Parks. Right now, he's the odd man out in our sweep."

"Parks," Susan repeated, a hint of concern in her voice. "Then where's Chatelain? Aren't those two working together?"

"I'm keeping my organic troopers on transport duty. Only synthoids and ACs in the search, given how trigger-happy this gang is. Chatelain should be back soon with another shipment of remotes, which leaves Parks without a partner."

"Then I guess today is his lucky day." Isaac gave Susan a slim smile. "What do you say, Susan?"

"Do I have to?"

"Oh, come on. We're all on the same side here."

"Yeah, you're right." She squared her shoulders and marched over to the command center.

"What was that about?" Hoopler asked once Susan had disappeared behind the row of quadcopters.

"Nothing," Isaac replied. "They'll sort it out, I'm sure."

✧   ✧   ✧

"Grid Delta-Two clear," Parks reported to the command center. "Now moving into grid Delta-Three."

Susan trudged through the fog next to the disk-shaped conveyor drone, both of them flanked by skeletal buildings being torn apart by mechanical crabs. Parks' avatar glowed in her virtual vision, "walking" beside the conveyor, his "eyesight" fixed on their surroundings.

She'd barely spoken to the trooper since they began their search.

Then again, *he'd* barely spoken to *her.* Communication was a two-way street, after all.

I bet it's the combat frame, she thought. *No one here likes the combat frame. Hell, even* Isaac *doesn't like the combat frame, and he's more accustomed to me than anyone.*

Maybe I should have left some of my weapons behind.

She pondered the idea for a few seconds, then shook her head. *Nah.*

They marched on in silence, her sensors actively sweeping their surroundings. So far, a whole lot of nothing.

She made a throat-clearing sound.

"Yes, Agent?" Parks asked, not looking her way.

"I was curious. Is your connectome inside the conveyor? Or are you controlling it remotely?"

"I'm on board. I was a little worried about all these microbots interfering with the control signal. It's more secure this way." He finally met her gaze. "Why do you ask?"

"Just making conversation."

They continued on, the fog around them growing thicker. Susan checked the systems monitoring her armor's integrity and found no signs of intrusion or degradation.

She cleared her throat again.

"Yes, Agent?" Parks replied.

"Is your conveyor armed?"

"It is." The conveyor raised one of its arms, and prog-steel peeled back from the tip, revealing a heavy pistol. "I'm carrying a PA13N Watchman."

"The 'N' means it's the nonlethal variant, right?"

"That's right. Its shots deliver sleep-inducing medibots like the slumber-cuffs you used earlier. I'm surprised you didn't carry a similar weapon into the reactor."

"Too many unknowns for me to give up this." She hefted her rail-rifle. "Besides, everything worked out."

"I suppose I can't argue with that." He . . . cracked a smile at her? "I'd heard about your combat frame."

"Yeah?"

"It doesn't disappoint."

"How so?"

"I hadn't expected something without a graviton thruster to move with such . . . elegance."

"Elegance," huh? Susan thought. *That almost sounded like a compliment. Is Parks interested in my equipment?*

She decided to explore the possibility.

"This is a Type-99 frame, the latest and greatest from the Admin. About as tough as the standard Type-92 and it's a *lot* faster!"

"I could see that!" Parks replied, now grinning ear to ear. "Liquid fuel?"

"That's right."

"Does it use pulse detonation for the combustion?"

"Sometimes. The boosters switch between pulse detonation and deflagration dynamically based on the situation. The former offers better performance but is less stealthy in most environments."

"Very clever."

"The Type-99 is quite new. I'm one of the first people to receive one."

"It's not your first frame?"

"Nope. I used to have a Type-92. They're considered the gold standard by which all other combat frames are judged, and for good reasons. They're superbly balanced machines, with a long and distinguished service record."

"A record that includes enforcing the Restrictions," Parks noted, his demeanor darkening again.

"Of course," Susan replied matter-of-factly. "It's part of what us Peacekeepers do."

"Which includes suppressing 'AIs' like me."

"It . . . wait a second." If she'd still possessed eyes, they would have bugged out. "You're an *AI*?"

"What did you think I was?"

"I thought you were an organic who abstracted."

"No way!" Parks chuckled. "I'm not even ten years old."

"Wow. I guess I had you figured all wrong. That does explain a few things, though."

"Like what?"

"Like why you've been so nervous around me. Listen, I know the Admin's reputation around these parts isn't exactly stellar, but *I* don't have any issues with AIs."

"Seriously?"

"Not in the slightest. I think it might be one of the reasons I was selected. I'm rather liberal for a Peacekeeper. As long as a person isn't a threat to me or others, I don't care one bit if they came from a womb or a computer program." She gestured to the fog around them. "Now, self-replicators, on the other hand, creep me the hell out."

"Does that mean I've been worried about nothing this whole time?"

"Parks, what did you *think* I'd do to you?"

"I don't know. You're the first Peacekeeper I've met. I guess I assumed you could sniff out an AI from a kilometer away."

"Sorry to disappoint, but that's not one of my special powers." They pressed on through the fog. "Is that what you meant when you said you were raised by storm clouds? That you're artificial?"

"Something like that. I'm originally from Venus. My parents were two embedded ACs in command of the cloud-based terraforming swarms. They wrote me together and raised me for a few years. Hence, raised by storm clouds. I guess the meaning wasn't obvious?"

"Not even close, Parks. Going off your avatar, I assumed you came from a meat body."

"My first avatar was less conventional, but it didn't work out. This one keeps misunderstandings to a minimum."

"What happened with the old one?"

"Too many...invitations."

"What do you mean?"

"I got hit on a lot." Parks' avatar morphed from the plain SSP trooper to a burly, bare-chested man, his well-defined pectorals possessing a "freshly oiled" look about them. He carried a massive door shield in one hand, which looked like it had started life as armor plating on a warship, and a giant sword in the other.

"Yeah, I can see where people might get the wrong impression."

"It seemed like a good idea at the time." The avatar morphed back into a state trooper. "I modeled the avatar after my first *Solar Descent* character. I thought it would help me make friends."

"Did it work?"

"Yeah, but not the way I was hoping. I tried it a few times."

"Tried what?"

"Abstract sex. Didn't enjoy it. Seemed like a whole lot of work for what boils down to a dopamine rush. Or the virtual equivalent. I even installed a biochem simulator to enhance the experience. Didn't help all that much."

"I suppose it's not for everyone," Susan replied neutrally, then tilted her head. "But aren't you a bit young for all of this?"

"I passed my CASAT."

"What's that mean?"

"It's the Cognition And Social Aptitude Test. All newly written connectomes have to pass one in order to be legally recognized as an adult. I passed mine when I was three. After that, I left the nest, so to speak."

"Do you still play *Solar Descent*?"

"You bet!" His face lit up. "I *love* that game! Been playing it since I was two. Haven't had a chance to try the latest season, though. How about you?"

"My partner recently got me started."

"What class do you play?"

"Stellar vanguard."

"Nice!" Parks nodded approvingly. "I favor the stellar berserker, myself. Very similar to vanguards, but more in-your-face when it comes to combat."

"Your old avatar was certainly 'in-your-face,'" Susan observed.

"Too true. It did make people notice me, but I eventually decided all the organic drama wasn't worth it. After that, I transitioned over to the boring side of the avatar spectrum and moved to a different city."

"How's it working out for you now?"

"Not bad, I have to say. The sarge hasn't hit on me once."

"Good." Susan nodded, not sure what else to say. "Good."

"Neither have any of my other coworkers."

"Also good."

"Yeah. Makes it easier to focus on my job. Speaking of which…"
He opened a comm window to the command center. "Grid Delta-Three clear. Moving on to Delta-Four."

Isaac sauntered through the fog, head on a swivel as he took in his surroundings. He passed the half-consumed remnants of a condo to his left. The thick bulk of a support column lay directly ahead, its outline barely visible through the thick microbot mist. Atlas crabs skittered across the street.

"What are we looking for?" Cephalie asked as she brought the LENS up to his side.

"I'm not sure," Isaac said. "Can you show me the map again?"

"Sure thing."

A wire-frame plan of Mattison's Retreat appeared between them, segmented into a grid with each square colored red for "unsearched" or green for "cleared." He and Cephalie were in the green zone, two grids away from the command center.

The map showed the location of major structures like the support columns and the wall between the Retreat and Cretaceous Safari, but other than that it was woefully inaccurate. The nature of the activity within the Retreat made a mockery of any static map.

Isaac checked his bearings, nodded to himself, then continued straight.

"If you'd tell me what we're looking for," Cephalie said from atop the LENS, "I could help you find it."

"If I knew what I was looking for, I'd already have told you." He paused and bent down to pick up one of the passing crabs. Its legs flailed under its flattened body. Sensor stalks appraised him, and the small machine's limbs fell limp. He set it back down, and it scuttled away. "Anything?"

"Nothing unusual. At least for this place."

"Hmm." Isaac pushed off his knee and continued to stroll down the street.

"This area's already been searched, you know."

"By SSP," Isaac corrected, his eyes soaking in the ruins.

"You implying something?"

"They're sweeping through this Retreat quickly. Which isn't a problem by itself. They're looking for obvious signs of the gang's presence. Evidence of human habitation that'll stand out from all this background chaos. That's fine on its own, but perhaps it'll lead them to miss subtler clues."

"You think you're going to beat Hoopler's small army to the punch?"

"I think it's better than us twiddling our thumbs at the command center."

"I don't twiddle, even if I had physical thumbs." The LENS waved a pseudopod at him before absorbing the material back into its shell.

"You know what I mean." Isaac glanced down at a grayish cube in his path, a lone crab pushing it across the ground. Or trying to. The crab must have been damaged, because only two of its legs moved, vainly scraping across the ground as it tried to shove the cube along. The rest of its limbs dangled from its body.

Isaac stepped over the lame crab and continued down the street.

The fog thinned up ahead as they approached the support column, its squared trunk roughly fifty meters to a side. A giant mound of cubical debris was piled near one of the corners. Isaac slowed to a halt and stared at the column.

The LENS bobbed past him before it stopped and turned.

"See something?" Cephalie asked.

"Maybe. Not sure." He approached the impressive hill of discarded cubes. SSP would have passed it without a thought. After all, what was a pile of junked prog-steel in a realm such as this?

But a thought itched at the back of his mind, unformed yet still demanding his attention.

"Does this seem unusual to you?"

"Which part?" Cephalie tittered. "That mound of cubes?"

"Yes."

"Seems about normal for this place."

"I'm not so sure." He dropped to one knee and picked up a cube, turned it over in his hand, then tossed it into the air and caught it. He set it down, then picked up another, identical cube, uncertain where his instincts were leading him. "Something's out of place here."

"Yeah, no kidding. Someone needs a lesson in housekeeping."

"Housekeeping..." Isaac muttered under his breath, then snapped his fingers. "You're right! You're absolutely right!"

"I am?" Cephalie smiled and shrugged with confidence and swagger. "I mean, of course I am. But what am I right about this time, again?"

"The mess." Isaac pushed off the ground and held out the cube in his hand. "This is prime building material. Why is it still here?"

"Good point. One of the two constructor swarms should have carted it off by now."

"Exactly." He offered the cube to the LENS. "Can you check what it's made of?"

"Sure." Cephalie extruded a pseudopod from the LENS and caressed the cube in his hand. "Might be an old prog-steel variant. Slow acting but *very* strong, especially when left in an unpowered state."

"Like something you'd find in a load-bearing structure?" He faced the column. "Like this one, perhaps?"

"Yeah. Just like this one."

"Old enough to be part of Janus' original skeleton?"

"Maybe." The LENS floated up to the column and rubbed the outer surface. "Same prog-steel variant on the outside."

"Which means someone could have hollowed out part of the interior." Isaac craned his neck, following the column upward until it disappeared into the fog. "Dig far enough, and you could reach the Second Engine Block, or even cities higher than that."

"That'd take ages, though."

"Not if there are already utilities routed through the column's core." Isaac tossed the cube aside and opened a comm window. He tried to call Hoopler, but a warning appeared on the window: CONNECTION LOST.

A crab emerged from the depths of the mound of cubes. It watched them through its camera stalks.

"Cephalie?"

"I can't get a signal through either. Infostructure's being—"

Her avatar vanished from his virtual vision.

The crab leaped off the mound and landed on the LENS. Machinery along its belly whirred to life and began to saw through the drone's shell in a spray of hot sparks. The LENS wrapped the crab in a pseudopod and smashed it to the ground. Silvery bits flew into the air.

More crabs crawled out of the shadowed nooks.

"Not good!" Isaac exclaimed. "Cephalie, if you can hear me, let's get out of here!"

The LENS bobbed in a distinct nod, then backed away from the mound.

Isaac turned to run, but then froze at the sight of crabs scuttling toward him from across the street. He spun to the side, only to discover Atlas crabs approaching from that direction as well.

They were surrounded.

More crabs emerged from the mound. At first there were only a handful, but more poured forth until the surface writhed with the hand-sized machines. They flowed toward Isaac and the LENS like a silvery wave.

"Away from the mound!" Isaac called out, and broke into a sprint.

A pair of crabs in his path leaped into the air, but the LENS swung ahead of him and intercepted them. It clenched both of them with its pseudopods, crushing them until they sparked, then tossed the dead husks aside.

Isaac hurried through the opening, but something struck his ankle, cutting into the flesh. He stumbled forward and landed on his hands and knees, then stole a quick glance over his shoulder.

The LENS teetered in the air, four crabs latched on and cutting through its shell. Sparks flew into the air. One of the crabs cut deep enough to reach the LENS' graviton thruster, and it fell to the ground with a loud clank. More crabs swarmed over it, and the LENS vanished under the wriggly swarm.

Isaac struggled back to his feet, but a leaping crab struck his shoulder with enough force to spin him around. Another clamped onto his thigh, and then two more hit him in the back, each clinging on with enough force to draw blood. He grabbed the crab on his shoulder and tore it off, leaving a brief trail of bloody mist in the air.

Behind him, the crabs scuttled off the LENS. Or what was left of it. They'd cut the LENS into neat cubes.

"Cephalie!"

More crabs piled onto Isaac, hitting him from all angles, weighing him down, turning his escape into a sluggish parody. One of the machines hit the back of his knee, and he stumbled forward, then collapsed onto his side. The crabs swarmed in, covering every part of his body, blotting out the Retreat's artificial light, encasing him in a cocoon of metal crabs. They lifted him off the street and carted him toward the column.

"Hello, Detective," said a woman's virtual voice in his ear. Her sweetly sinister words flowed over him like poisoned chocolate. "It's so nice to have guests again."

CHAPTER TWENTY-THREE

THE CRABS DROPPED ISAAC INTO A CHAIR SO THICK, STURDY, and uncomfortable it seemed to have been carved out of the floor. He tried to stand but found his wrists and ankles bound to the seat by prog-steel straps. His facemask had been removed.

A single overhead lamp shone down on him, producing a small pool of light that included a metal table in front and a bit to the side of him. The rest of the room melted away into darkness.

The crabs skittered away, and an unseen hatch closed somewhere.

Isaac tried to access the local infostructure, but nothing responded. He attempted to reach Susan or Hoopler or anyone else from the SSP.

He tried calling Cephalie, even though he knew it wouldn't work.

No one responded.

His repeated calls visualized in his abstract sight as a stack of comm windows, all of them displaying the same red text: CONNECTION LOST.

He was alone.

Alone, and in trouble.

His heart pounded in his chest so hard he felt it in his temples. He couldn't remember the last time he'd been this terrified.

"Trying to call your friends?" asked the same caring yet cruel voice from before. "That won't work in here. I don't even have to bother jamming your wetware. There's no way you're getting a signal through these walls. Not at those power levels."

The woman or someone with her knocked on the walls, and the sound reverberated like a tolled bell. A slender silhouette edged forward into the pool of light, then bent toward him and smiled.

She was a bony woman in her prime, and her white teeth glinted in the light. Her sandy blonde hair was cut short, except for a blue braid that hung off one side of her face. Her ears, nose, and lower lip were all studded with gems that glowed like fire, and she wore a black vest with numerous pockets above an exposed midriff and bejeweled belly button. Her tight pants were black with blue stripes down the sides.

"Zalaya Riller, I presume," Isaac said.

"In the Sacred Flesh." She straightened back.

The leader of the Byte Pyrates, Isaac thought. *Wanted for numerous counts of kidnapping and murder, which doesn't bode well for me.*

He could make out motion behind Riller. Hints of light playing off a bulky frame that revealed the presence of at least one more Pyrate in the room.

Two against one, he thought. *And me without my LENS.*

Fine then. If words are the only weapon I have, then words are the weapon I'll wield. It's as simple as that.

The internal dialogue sent a much-needed jolt of courage through his system, but then a dark, unbidden thought followed.

What choice do I have?

He met Riller's friendly—if somewhat manic—gaze.

"And you would be Detective Isaac Cho," she said.

"That's me."

"Isaac Cho." She put a hand on her hip. "Quite the thorn in my side."

"Yes, that definitely sounds like me."

"But not anymore." She bent in close. "Now, you're going to *help* me."

"I doubt that very much."

"Aww. Look at you! So brave"—she flicked the tip of his nose with a finger, and he flinched back—"and yet so helpless. Tell you what, Mister SysPol. How about you save both of us a lot of trouble and just tell me what I want to know?"

"That would depend entirely on what information you're after."

"Oh, this one should be easy for someone like you." She knelt beside him, a hand on his thigh, and spoke softly into his ear. "All you need to tell me is the exact force strength and distribution of all SSP and SysPol assets nearby."

"How about . . . no."

Riller took her hand off his thigh, clenched a fist, and punched him full force in the jaw, whipping his head to the side. The room swam around him. Stars twinkled across his vision, and he tasted blood in his mouth where his teeth had cut the inside of his lips.

He shook his head until the stars subsided. His surroundings came into focus once more.

"Want to rethink that answer, Mister SysPol?"

He flashed a bloody, defiant smile at her. "I guess we're adding assault to your list of charges, then?"

She punched him again and sent his head reeling to the side.

"Ouch. Damn it." Riller stood up and shook out her hand. "That actually hurt."

"Want me to tenderize him for you, boss?"

"Get your own plaything, Davies. This one's mine." She smirked at Isaac. "What's with cops and hard heads, anyway?"

"You're asking me? I'm still wondering why your crab army didn't tear me apart."

"Blame Atlas engineering for that one. Too many hardwired safeties. I could order them to tear up your floating eyeball, but you?" She poked him in the chest. "Grabbing you was about the best I could do. Which, as it turns out, is to both our benefits."

"Kidnapping seems to be more your style, anyway. You keep Ruckman in here as well?"

"That SourceCode program? Yeah, he's around, but maybe not all there anymore." She grinned like a shark. "I took my sweet time squeezing him."

"For information you sent the Ghost, I take it?"

"I'm sorry. Did I hit your head too hard? Did you suddenly come to believe it's *you* who's interrogating *me*?"

"Consider it force of habit."

"You're really trying to pump me for information, even as my prisoner? That's so cute!" Riller pulled a vial out of one of her vest pockets and set it down upright on the table. The contents resembled milk with a vaguely metallic sheen. "But seriously, now. Tell me what I want to know. Or else."

"What's in the vial?"

"Liquid encouragement."

"I don't feel very encouraged."

"That's because I haven't given you any yet." She knelt in front of him once more, her hands on top of his. "Would you like me to share something with you, Mister SysPol?"

"Sure. Why not?"

"It's been so long since I've gotten to torture a real, flesh-and-blood human being. Tormenting synthoids and ACs just isn't the same. All that artificial 'life' boils down to a bunch of boring ones and zeros. What's the thrill in wielding power over a program? Where's the *fun*?"

"You need help."

"No, Detective. It's *you* who needs help." She picked up the vial and held it before him. "This vial contains medibots. But not just any old variant. These beauties are for clearing out cancer cells. That might not sound so bad to you, but here's the twist." She leaned close and whispered the rest into his ear. "I'm going to lie to them."

A cold sweat sent a shiver down his spine.

"When I inject them into you, they're going to believe *every* cell in your body is a cancer cell. Now, you might be telling yourself, medibots have built-in protections that prevent them from carrying out such a *disastrously* wrong diagnosis. And, normally, you'd be right. Except, I've applied an update to these. A little bit of code of my own creation. Let me assure you, they won't be shutting down until either I tell them to or they've finished turning your entire body into soup from the inside out."

Riller set the vial back on the table then crouched down in front of him once more.

"Maybe I'll inject them here." She placed two fingers on the back of his hand then walked them up his arm. "They'll work their way through you one hellish centimeter at a time, grinding your muscles and nerves into mush. I can even tweak their speed with a signal, making the process as slow and excruciating as I want. But perhaps you'll be able to fight through all that, lying to yourself that it's 'only an arm.' Maybe you're tougher than you look. In which case, why don't we start...here?"

She poked him in the groin, and he recoiled.

"Yeah, that's the spot! Unless you'd like to avoid all this

unpleasantness. How about it, Mister SysPol? Shall we talk about where all the cops are stationed? Or do I have to get nasty with you?"

"I don't cooperate with criminals," he replied defiantly. Or that was the plan, but his voice cracked halfway through the sentence.

"Nasty it is," Riller said with a shrug. "Suits me just fine. I'm curious what your brain'll taste like once it's been reduced to soup. I'm guessing zesty self-righteousness."

Isaac felt the vial drag his line of sight toward it. His mind raced, searching for a way out. Or, at the very least, a way to increase his odds of survival, however slim.

But what could he possibly do besides stall for time and hope someone found him?

Nothing, he told himself. *What other options are there?*

Stall for time, it is, then.

"You're wrong," he said, his voice stronger and firmer than before.

"We won't know until we try," she replied with a quirky half-smile.

"No. Not your brain-soup taste test. You're in trouble, even if you won't admit it. You're stuck in this hollowed-out column with SSP crawling all over the Retreat."

"No one knows we're here."

"That's true for now. But you've made your situation worse by attacking me."

Riller paused, a crack forming in her playful composure.

"How?" she asked.

"Because you grabbed me when I was on foot. There's only so far I could have traveled between the time I left the field command center and when my signal dropped out. That contracts the search area *considerably*. And trust me, they *will* be searching."

"They won't find you in time."

"Maybe. Maybe not. But you've doomed yourself either way. You're looking for a way out, aren't you? A way to slip through the net we've cast."

"That's pretty obvious, wouldn't you say?"

"Then you're going about this in the dumbest way possible."

"Hey!" The hulking shape behind Riller advanced into the light. "No one talks to the boss that way!"

Riller held up a hand, and the huge thug retreated.

"Go on," she said, never taking her eyes off Isaac. "You have my undivided attention."

"It's simple. You're asking me the wrong questions. Knowing where SSP is stationed might help you slip away in the now. But it won't help you for long. What you *should* be asking is how we found you in the first place. Only by knowing *that* do you have any hope of eluding us *again*."

"Nice try, Mister SysPol," Riller said. "But I can stream the news just like everyone else. You caught Fike, and he pointed you back to us. What else is there to know?"

It's true, then, Isaac thought. *The Byte Pyrates didn't know who they were working for. Perhaps this is the opening I need.*

He wasn't sure where he'd take that opening, but he went on the offensive anyway.

"Wow, really?" He chuckled. "You believe a loser like *Desmond Fike* is actually the puppet master behind all of this?"

Another crack formed in Riller's composure, and her face turned deadly serious.

"We know it was Fike."

"Come on! He was so scared when we caught him he soiled his own pants!"

"We traced the Ghost's messages back to him."

"You only 'traced' it to Fike because of the trail the Ghost put there for you to find. You really have no idea who's behind all of this, do you?"

"And you do?"

"Better than you. Tell me, what did the Ghost pay you with?"

Riller crossed her arms, but the frown on her face told Isaac he'd struck a nerve.

"Go on." Isaac smirked at her. "Prove to me you know what you're doing."

"We were paid with keycodes to get into Mattison's Retreat and to control the crab swarms."

"Which would have come from Atlas," Isaac pointed out. "Not the Society."

Riller's frown deepened.

"Let me get this straight," Isaac continued. "You copy-kidnapped Ruckman, extracted information out of him about the Dyson Project, and were even paid in Atlas codes, and you *still* thought you were working for the Society?"

Riller stood before him, glaring at him for long, silent seconds. During that time, subtle motion from behind her caught Isaac's eye. It took him a few moments to realize what he was seeing, and when he finally did, he shook his head then masked the gesture with a confident chuckle.

"Laugh all you want," Riller warned with venom. "Soon, you'll be making a very different noise."

"I wouldn't be too sure," Isaac replied. "In fact, your situation might be even more precarious than you realize."

"Enough!" Riller placed light fingers onto the tabletop. "Let's see how smug you are while your insides are being ground into paste." She reached for the vial, but her fingers found only empty air. Her brow creased in confusion, and she ran her hand over the empty table, then fixed him with a vicious glare.

"Don't look at me." Isaac grinned and held up both hands as high as the straps allowed. "I've been stuck in this chair the whole time."

"Davies!" Riller snapped. "Where's my soupmaker vial?"

"I don't know, boss."

"It was right here! Did it roll off the table?"

"Don't think so. I didn't hear anything hit the floor."

Riller crouched and checked under the table. She patted her hand across the shadows.

"What the hell? Where'd it go? You saw me put it on the table?"

"Yeah, I did."

"Then where is it?"

"I don't know, boss."

"Uhh!" She groaned, rising to her feet. "Never mind. I'll go grab another. Make sure he doesn't go anywhere."

"Sure thing, boss."

Riller left the room through an unseen side entrance. A huge, muscle-bound man stepped forward into the light and glowered down at Isaac. His black clothes were overly busy with belts, straps, buckles, and spikes, and he wore a spiked choker around his thick neck.

"Davies, I presume?" Isaac asked.

The gangster crossed his arms and shifted his weight from one foot to the other.

"I'll take that as a yes. You wouldn't happen to know where the Ruckman copy is, would you?"

Davies narrowed his eyes. "Don't tempt me."

"I'm afraid I'm not sure what you mean."

"Then let me explain." He engulfed Isaac's shoulder with a firm hand and bent down until their eyes were level. "I don't like it when people upset the boss. And you? You're doing everything you can to get under her skin."

"In my defense, her sense of hospitality is somewhat lacking." Isaac didn't flinch from his oppressive glare. "You going to tell me where Ruckman is or not?"

"How about I beat your face in?" Davies rose and cracked his knuckles. "I know the boss said you're hers, but I doubt she'll mind if I perform a little...prep work."

"Yes, I suppose I have pushed my luck harder than usual." Isaac let out a bored sigh. "And I doubt you have anything useful to tell us, anyway. Agent Cantrell, would you mind taking out this trash?"

Davies tilted his head in confusion—

—a split second before the invisible combat frame grappled him from behind. He tried to scream, but Susan held a hand over his mouth and cuffed one wrist. Davies kicked his legs out, unable to gain enough traction to shift the combat frame, and the medibots began to seep into his system. His thrashing turned increasingly sluggish, and his eyes rolled back into his skull.

Susan laid him on the ground and bound both wrists. She switched her combat frame over to its default blue with white stripes, ripped off the straps holding Isaac in place, and helped him to his feet.

"I have never been so glad to see you!" Isaac declared, rubbing his wrists. "How'd you find me?"

"Long story short, Cephalie was able to transmit out of the LENS right before the crabs tore it to bits."

"Is she okay?"

"She was...mostly coherent, last I saw her."

A nervous lump formed in his throat.

"The jamming garbled her connectome. Parks performed something called an 'emergency reconstruction,' and she was able to tell us what happened to you. After that, I came straight here—already in stealth mode—found the entrance and managed to sneak in. Parks got in touch with Hoopler, who's mustering the troopers for a raid. They're scheduled to hit this place hard in about six minutes."

"Good. This place needs a firm smack."

"The Pyrates didn't have any security *at all*. I literally just found the right spot and pushed the side of the column open."

"Makes sense when you think about it. They're still getting settled in."

"Fortunately, this room was close enough to the entrance for me to hear your interrogation."

"Lucky me." Isaac massaged his aching jaw. "After that you scoped out the situation and decided to follow my lead?"

"Pretty much. I took your headshake as a signal to hang back until called." Susan presented Riller's vial of corrupt medibots and shook it back and forth. "Though I did take the liberty of snagging this when they weren't looking. No one turns my partner into paste. *No one*."

Isaac smiled at her.

"Which leaves me with only one question," she added.

"That being?"

"You want me to get you out of here? Or can I . . ." She bobbed the combat frame's head toward the exit Riller had disappeared through. "You know?"

"Take out the rest of the trash?" Isaac finished.

"Someone's got to do it."

"Any idea how many gangsters are left or what they're packing?"

"Not a clue."

"You have a plan of attack?"

"Nope. Improvising all the way."

"Hmm." Isaac made a show of having to think things over, but then his expression softened, and he gave Susan a casual shrug. "Sure. Why not? I think you've earned a chance to cut loose."

CHAPTER TWENTY-FOUR

THE GUNSHOTS WERE RILLER'S FIRST INDICATION SOMETHING HAD gone *very* wrong. A trio of shots popped off somewhere below her room on the third floor, echoing up the metal stairwell carved out of the structural column. Sporadic weapons fire followed those initial pops, coming from a variety of weapons.

Riller slammed her footlocker closed and stood up. Most of her possessions were still stored from when she'd been living in the old Kamiya-Franklin Energy Plant, and the room itself remained unfinished; most of the walls had been smoothed out by the constructor crabs, but the back wall was an uneven jumble of cubical shapes. Eventually, she wanted them to carve out twice the space, but other priorities had demanded their attention.

More gunfire rattled away in the floors below her, followed by a loud . . . whoosh?

Riller snarled as she opened a comm window.

"Davies, what the *hell* is going on down there?" She waited, but no response came. "*Davies?*"

Nothing. Her signal was getting through, relayed across the hideout's unfinished but serviceable infostructure, but her right-hand man didn't answer her.

Didn't. Or *couldn't.*

She tried someone else.

"Yong here! We're in deep shit, boss!"

"Calm down and tell me what's going on," she snapped.

"We're under attack, that's what! There's a— I don't even know *what* it is, but it's tearing through the place, and we can't stop it! We can barely *see* it!"

"Some sort of police mech?"

"Gotta be, because our shots might as well be spitballs!"

"Then deploy the crabs," Riller fumed. "They'll tear that machine to ribbons."

"We *tried* that already!" Yong cried. "They can't lock on! They're meant for construction, not combat! They just sat around like a bunch of dumb fucks until that thing melted them down with a *flamethrower*!"

"Nonsense! Police don't use flamethrowers!"

"Well, my eyebrows beg to disagree! As in, I don't have them anymore! I wasn't even that close to the flames when . . . oh no! Oh fuck! Get away from me! Get awa-a-a-a-ay!"

The connection auto-forwarded to another member of her team.

"Grasso here, boss. First floor's a lost cause. That thing must be some new type of SysPol mech; it's been pinging out a police badge. We've barricaded the second floor, but it won't hold for long."

"You give me all the time you can, you hear me?" she ordered. "You hold that position no matter what. A police mech, huh? Well, I've got a little surprise for our guest, but I need time to prep it. You understand me, Grasso?"

"Perfectly, boss. Everyone, you hear that? The boss has a plan! We hold here until she gets one of her toys ready! Everyone got that?"

"Got it!"

"Pyrates for life!"

"Hell yeah! Bring it on!"

"We'll hold the line for you, boss," Grasso finished.

"Good man. I'll be with you soon."

Riller closed the call and opened her footlocker once more. She rummaged deep inside, past changes of clothes mixed with labeled vials, to a false bottom. She sent the keycode, and the hidden hatch unlocked and swung upward. She reached through the opening, grabbed hold of the heavy harness balled up inside, and pulled it out.

Everything had gone to shit after they took that job from the Ghost. On the surface, it had seemed simple enough. Copy the target, extract the information, get paid. And what a payday! Corporate codes galore! A brand-new base of operations! Their own army of unregistered replicators!

She should have known it was too good to be true.

The first sign of trouble had been the mess at JIT Deliveries. By itself, a loss like that wasn't alarming. Sure, it was a setback, both in personnel and material, but it shouldn't have compromised their operation. Nothing inside the container could be traced back to the KF reactor, and the two men she'd stationed there were unproven and expendable. They didn't know enough to be dangerous to her or the gang.

Or so she'd thought.

How then did SysPol find their reactor base?

It didn't matter. Not at this point. Not with a police mech tearing through the place.

Her gang needed her now more than ever. They looked to her for leadership. Sure, some of them possessed real talent. Intellectual sparks that could have landed them high-paying jobs in more legit lines of work.

But none of them were *leaders*.

They looked up to her, depended on her. And yes, even feared her.

Circumstances sometimes forced her to scare troublemakers back into line, but fear was always her last resort, even if she played up—even reveled in—the theatrics. But that was a sideshow. Their trust in her had been earned through consistent leadership and a long line of successes.

She'd guided them through tough spots before. Was this problem really so different, they might be asking themselves? No, it wasn't. Her gang knew with absolute certainty she had their backs, and they'd do everything in their power to slow the attacker down.

Trust was a powerful tool in the right hands.

And it took a special kind of bastard to abandon those who trusted her in their greatest moment of need.

Riller slipped her arms into the flight harness and shook it out over her torso. Smart-fabric straps self-adjusted for a secure fit atop her vest, and an abstract control menu appeared to her side. She linked the harness directly to her wetware and felt the control options open within her mind's eye.

The harness wasn't a full-fledged graviton thruster, but the backpack did contain enough exotic matter to generate a modest stream of gravitons when energized. She tested it, floated up onto her tippy toes, then a little higher before settling back to the ground.

She grabbed the corner of the footlocker and levered it out, exposing a square shaft cut into the wall. She dropped down onto her belly, switched on a light hung from her shoulder, and crawled into the shaft.

"Boss!" Grasso called in. "Anytime soon would be great!"

"Don't worry. I'm almost there. Just hang on a little bit more."

"We're doing our best! Shit, it's busting through! Open fire! *Open fire!*"

Riller closed the connection and pressed on. The shaft opened to a small ledge with enough headspace for her to twist around. She pulled out her legs and hung them over the edge. Her paltry light shone across a thick, intertwined trunk of utility lines that spanned the hollow core of the support column.

She gazed up at the dark void above her, then down at the seemingly infinite chasm below. Under better circumstances, she would have preferred to escape with her gang and her equipment intact. Or at least *some* of it. But her own skin would do in a pinch.

"I hate heights," she muttered to herself, then powered up the harness.

The straps tugged at her waist, shoulders, and on either side of her crotch, lifting her above the ledge. She kicked off the wall, then slowed herself with a hand on the utility trunk.

She toggled the harness to a higher setting and found herself propelled upward, faster and faster. Her mind struggled to make sense of the speed without a frame of reference, even as wind whipped her hair back and dried her eyes.

She summoned a virtual grid over her vision which showed her altitude relative to Mattison's Retreat in vivid green lines.

"Just about...ah. There we are."

She slowed her approach and landed atop a second ledge almost identical to the first. Eight crabs waited alongside the square channel, watching her with their camera stalks. She'd tasked the crabs with cutting her emergency escape shaft, along with a matching partner that led into the Second Engine Block.

She powered down the harness and set it aside. She wouldn't need it anymore, and this shaft was even narrower than the first. She dropped to her hands and knees and began to crawl her way through the long, dark shaft. If her review of the structural maps was correct, it would lead her to a utility maze underneath a Second Engine Block reactor.

Which would be a great place to lay low for a while.

It wasn't ideal. But it would do, given the circumstances.

She could see light at the end of the shaft and chuckled.

It pays to have a Plan B, she thought, basking in her own brilliance. She could make out a jumble of pipes beyond the opening, which seemed about right for the city's utility maze. She crawled out of the shaft—

—and froze at the sight of the Arete Division Red Knight hovering over her.

"Fuck!" she blurted without thinking.

The mech's huge floating torso spun to face her, and its head angled down, cameras focusing. Its arms and shoulders were loaded with heavy weapons.

"Citizen," the mech said in an emotionless voice, "you should not be here. Follow me, and I will guide you to safety."

Riller's mind raced with panicked thoughts. She spotted a utility tunnel behind and to the left of the mech. Wide enough for her to slip through, but too narrow for the bulky mech. Not unless it planned to bash its way through the pipes.

She scrambled to her feet, taking off like a runner leaving the blocks, and bolted past the Red Knight.

"Stop, citizen. That is not the right way."

She turned sideways and slipped between two vertical reclamation lines. The tunnel widened after that initial squeeze, and she straightened out and ran down the metal corridor.

She wasn't sure how long she ran, but her heart raced with a mix of exertion and adrenaline. She slowed to a jog as the maze began to open up, leading into a domed space ahead of her. She stole a quick glance over her shoulder, relieved to find nothing big or red in pursuit. She slowed to a walk and exited the tunnel—

—then skidded to a halt at the sight of two SysPol officers: a man and a woman in Themis Division uniforms. The man bore a face twisted by what must have been deep frustrations while he nursed a steaming mug. The small, mousy woman next to him seemed to be trying her best to cheer him up, a heavy bag marked as EVIDENCE in one hand. A pair of LENS drones floated behind them.

"Hey!" shouted the male officer, almost spilling his drink as he started toward Riller. "You there! You need to get out of here!"

"Ma'am, stop!" the woman shouted urgently.

Riller picked another tunnel and dashed for it.

"No!" shouted the man. "Not that way!"

She pumped her arms and legs and raced down the tunnel, afraid to turn around, half expecting one of their drones to ensnare her at any moment. She ran and ran and ran, for how long she wasn't sure, but sweat drenched her armpits by the end of it.

She jogged to a halt and hunched over, gasping for air.

"Why?" she panted. "Are there cops? Everywhere?"

"Be my friend?"

Riller snapped her gaze up at the sound of the oddly high-pitched voice, but it took her a moment to find the source. What appeared to be a yellow teddy bear squeezed its way out between two pipes, then plopped onto the ground beside her.

"What?" she gasped. "The hell? Are you?"

"Won't you be my friend?" The yellow teddy bear extended its stubby arms toward her, then began prancing forward on stubby legs.

"No."

"Aww. Please?" It pitter-pattered up to her in an effort to hug her leg.

"I said *no!*"

She punted the toy bear down the tunnel. Its little, yellow body tumbled through the air, landed on its head with a crunch, then bounced several times before finally rolling to a stop, facedown.

"She's not nice."

"Not nice."

"Not nice?"

"*Not nice at all.*"

The voices came from *behind* her, and while the first few sounded as sickly sweet as the yellow toy's, the last one could have been used as nightmare fuel to keep children awake at night. If her torture medibots had possessed a voice, *that* would have been it.

She turned around, slowly, unsure what she expected to find.

She almost wished she hadn't.

Dozens of the fluffy, colorful toys slid, squeezed, and oozed out from every hole and crevice in the tunnel's sides, floor, and ceiling. They came in a variety of colors: bright pinks, pastel blues, warm yellows and oranges, and more sedate colors like tan and black. The only exception was a toy that seemed entirely composed of scrap metal formed into a slapdash, quasi-bearlike shape.

They pranced happily toward her, and she began to back away, but soon discovered more of the toys emerging on the other side. Beyond those, even more of the creepy toys pushed their way into the open all up and down the tunnel. It didn't matter which way she ran; they were everywhere!

"Should we take her?" asked one of the toys.

"Take her?"

"Take . . . her?"

"Her?"

"*Let's take her!*"

The scrap-metal bear pointed at her with fingers like miniature scalpels, and the horde of toys surged forward. Riller kicked and punched and thrashed at the small robots, and while she was stronger than one or two or even ten of the toys, she wasn't stronger than thirty of them.

"Get off! Get the fuck off me, you freaks!"

The rainbow-colored swarm dragged her down, and she landed on her back with an *oof.* The scrap-metal toy mounted her chest in triumph.

"*Let me give you a kiss and make it all better.*"

The toy reached toward her face with its jagged metal arms, and Riller screamed like a little girl.

"That doesn't sound good," Raviv said mournfully, staring down the tunnel as the young woman's screams reached him.

"We did try to warn her," Damphart reminded him.

"Didn't seem to do much good." Raviv took a sip from his CRIMINAL TEARS coffee mug.

"You think we should have sent the drones after her?"

"We can't force people to evacuate."

"Yes, I suppose you're right. Being stupid isn't a crime."

"And we should all be thankful it's not." Raviv held out the mug, and his LENS retrieved a thermos from an internal compartment and refreshed it. "She was in an awful hurry. When's Arete scheduled to sweep through this sector?"

"Not for another hour at least."

"Oh well." He shrugged. "She'll have to tough it out until then."

"Chief Inspector!"

Raviv turned around at the familiar voice, but then had to perform a double take.

"Agent Cantrell?" he asked.

"Yes, sir." The blue-and-white humanoid snapped to attention.

"What are you doing here and in your combat frame?" Raviv glanced past her. "And where's Isaac? Is he here, too?"

"No, sir. But don't worry. He's all right. I was able to rescue him before the Byte Pyrates liquefied his insides."

"Excuse me!" Raviv's eyes bugged. "Liquefy his insides?"

"Correct, sir."

"But he's fine now?" Raviv asked urgently. "You're sure of that?"

"Except for a few cuts and bruises, perfectly fine."

"Are those...bullet holes in your chest?" Damphart asked.

"I've had worse."

Damphart and Raviv exchanged worried looks.

"The perpetrators resisted arrest," she added.

"And are they all..." Raviv paused to lick his lips. "Arrested now?"

"All except for one. I'm trying to rectify that omission." Susan scanned their surroundings left, then right. "But I seem to have lost the trail."

"You wouldn't happen to be after a young woman?" Raviv asked. "Rather thin? Blonde hair except for a short, blue braid?"

"That's the one, sir. She's a real piece of work named Zalaya Riller. I found her bugout hatch and followed it up to...where am I exactly?"

"Second Engine Block," Damphart answered. "Right beneath the Norman-MacCarthy reactor."

"Thanks. An Arete mech helped point me in the right direction. I followed the path this far, and now here I am. Riller would have killed Isaac if I hadn't intervened, so I'd *really* appreciate it if you could point the way."

Raviv's eyes lit up with barely contained fury. "*She's* the one who tried to liquefy his insides?"

"Yes, sir."

Raviv clenched both of his fists, which caused his mug to shudder in his hand, spilling some of his coffee.

"No one—and I mean *no one*—hurts a member of my team and gets away with it." He pointed down one of the tunnels. "You do whatever it takes to bring that piece of filth to justice. You hear me?"

"Loud and clear, sir."

"Just watch out for the fuzzles," Damphart warned. "They're all over the place. Though..." She looked Susan's combat frame up and down. "I think you'll be fine."

"I certainly hope so. Thanks for the help!"

Susan popped off a quick salute, flared her shoulder nozzles, and took off down the tunnel.

Susan rocketed down the tunnel until it opened into a cross-junction. She cut her thrust and landed, transitioning to a run that slowed to a jog by the time she needed to pick a direction.

She paused at the junction, checked to her left, then right, then straight ahead.

Well, shoot, she thought to herself. *Where to now?*

A girlish scream echoed through the utility maze, and her onboard sensors placed the source roughly two hundred meters from her location, down the left passage.

Just follow the screams? she mused.

She fired her boosters and shot through the tunnel, following its twists and turns with quick bursts of thrust. The passage narrowed, pinched closed by a cluster of vertical conduits, and she landed before the gap and slid through it sideways.

The passage opened up again, and she continued on foot until she rounded a bend and came face-to-face with a horde of multicolored toys bunched up on the floor or clinging to the walls and ceiling.

"You're not supposed to be here."

"Go back."

"Go back."

"Go...back?"

"How about a hug?"

"Give it a hug!"

A pastel green fuzzle pranced up to her leg and embraced it with a tiny *squeak*.

"This is new," Susan said, which was saying a lot in her line of work. She shook the fuzzle off her, then stomped it flat and ground the robot to scrap under the ball of her armored foot.

"You meanie!"

"It's so mean!"

"So mean!"

"So . . . mean?"

"*It needs to be punished!*"

"I don't think so." Susan lit her incinerator and doused her surroundings with blue flame in a wide, slow sweep. The fuzzles screamed in simulated pain, running around in panicked circles trailing greasy smoke. Some of them dropped and rolled while unlit fuzzles tried to pat down their burning comrades. But the gel her incinerator used wasn't so easily extinguished, and their efforts only served to spread the flames faster.

"That wasn't ni-i-i-i-ce . . ." A burning fuzzle flopped over, and its overheated innards burst open with a loud *pop*. More of them face-planted and then bulged outward or crackled in twitching, spasmodic death throes.

"*Let me give you a kiss!*"

A creepy, all-metal fuzzle leaped at her, but she caught it midair and smashed it to bits against the wall.

She advanced down the tunnel. More fuzzles tried to hide in the wall, shifting their positions for what might have been an ambush, but Susan had toggled her sensor suite to active, and the data flowing through her systems tagged each little machine with a red outline.

"Help!" a boy cried out from ahead. "Is someone there?"

"Help us! Please!" a girl called out, followed by a chorus of similar shouts.

Susan hurried down the corridor, only stopping to douse dense clusters of the toys before pressing on. A flood of the little machines poured into the corridor ahead, and she lit them all on fire before stomping their burning carcasses flat.

She arrived at a circular chamber with only one entrance. Thick, vertical pipes lined the walls, interspersed with maintenance access hatches.

Along with six children.

And Riller.

Each child was bound to a pipe using fuzzy, multicolored cords.

The toys had placed pastel ribbons in their hair and painted their cheeks rosy colors. Food paste dribbled from their chins or the sides of their mouths, which Susan took to mean the rampant toys had been feeding them.

The fuzzles had tied Riller to a pipe in much the same manner as the children. They'd cut off her blue braid before tying a pink bow around her head and coloring her cheeks.

"Hang in there, kids! I'll get you out!" Susan worked her way through the room, ripping each child free. Some of them stumbled and massaged their legs, perhaps fighting cramps induced by being tied in place for too long. "No one leaves without me, you hear? We're getting out of this together."

Susan freed the sixth child, then sidestepped over to Riller. She paused and stared down at the criminal, who looked up at her with a worried, terror-drenched expression, perhaps wondering if the being before her was even more dangerous than the fuzzles. Faint tears trailed down her cheeks.

"Are you going to kill me?" she squeaked.

Susan knelt, a hand resting on her knee, her cameras level with Riller's face.

"I would," she said, soft enough for the kids not to hear. "In a different place, under different circumstances. I've killed plenty of scum like you before."

Riller gulped. "You have?"

Susan nodded. "I've met my share of monsters. And you? You're a monster. You might look human, but that's nothing more than a facade. A . . . cosmetic layer, if you will, draped over the filth you call a soul. Monsters like you deserve nothing better than a merciless death."

"But you're not going to kill me?"

"No. I won't."

"Why not?"

"There are a lot of reasons." She placed a hand around the cords holding Riller in place. "Some better than others. For one, my partner would be unhappy with me if I didn't bring you in alive. But the most important reason is it's not my role to punish you. When I started this job, my partner told me this: 'We in Themis do not dispense justice. We indict those we believe are guilty, but we do not decide their punishments.' Those were his words, and I take what he says *very* seriously."

Susan ripped the criminal free, pinned her to the ground, and cuffed her wrists.

"Chief?"

Damphart nudged Raviv in the arm and pointed down the tunnel.

He looked up from his coffee to see Susan walking into the open, a thin woman tossed over the shoulder opposite her grenade launcher. Six children crowded around her legs, as if fearful she might dart off somewhere if they strayed too far. One of the boys began to sob at the sight of more people, and Susan reached down and ruffled his hair.

"Huh, would you look at that?" Raviv took another sip. "You know something, Grace?"

"What's that, Chief?"

He nodded slowly, his expression warming. "I think she's growing on me."

CHAPTER TWENTY-FIVE

ISAAC FROWNED AT THE GUNFIRE DIVOTS SPREAD ACROSS THE wall. He stuck a finger into one, traced the lip of the recess, and then brought his finger out and inspected the silvery crumbs. He rubbed the flakes between two fingers—they felt like fine grains of sand—then shook his hand out, producing a brief shower of metallic glitter.

"Before you ask," Nina began with a wry grin, "those were caused by what we in Forensics call an 'assload of guns.'"

"You realize I was still here when she tore through the place."

"They didn't stand a chance, did they?"

"Against Susan? No. Not really."

SSP had finished clearing out the subdued Byte Pyrates and were in the middle of processing them back at the field command center. They'd also swept the hideout for any traps or other dangerous surprises, but had found none, which freed up Nina and her drones to move in for a forensics sweep.

"Any thoughts on where they stashed Ruckman?" Isaac asked.

"Give me some time, Isaac. I just started!"

"Sorry." He walked over to a wall crammed from floor to ceiling with heavy-duty infosystem nodes, about a third of which had been blown apart. "I hope he wasn't kept in any of these."

"Who knows?" Nina used a virtual interface to queue up tasks for her drones. "You have any idea what they were doing to him?"

"Not really." Isaac put his finger on the broken guts of a racked node and *twanged* it. "But if how they treated me was any indicator, Ruckman's had it rough."

"Maybe even rougher, given how these people view ACs."

"I hope not...but yes, that thought had crossed my mind."

"They might have already deleted him once they had what they needed."

"Maybe," Isaac conceded, "but he remains our best lead at the moment. We might get lucky and find other evidence in all of this"—he indicated the nodes—"but I'm doubtful. Riller's blackmail cache won't help us either because it'll point back to Fike. I expect most of the Pyrates will either keep quiet or be purposefully unhelpful, which leaves Ruckman's copy as our best path forward. The Ghost needed the information in his head. Which means Ruckman was interacting—either directly or indirectly—with the criminal behind all of this, and if we can narrow down who *that* is..."

"We can solve this case?"

"I hope so. I'm not sure where we'll turn if this lead goes nowhere."

"Don't sound so glum. If Ruckman's in here, I'll find him."

A pair of her drones worked their way down the infosystem wall while two more headed to the next room, which was also packed with hardware.

An SSP conveyor floated in, and Trooper Parks appeared.

"Detective Cho," he said with a curt nod.

"Parks." Isaac hurried up to the abstract trooper. "Any news?"

"Yes, sir. Encephalon has been transmitted to the CWC, and they've finished their preliminary analysis."

Isaac nodded at the news, tentatively hopeful. The CWC was the Connectome Wellness Center, located within the city of Ballast Heights high atop Janus. There was no better place in the entire Saturn State for treating connectome injuries.

"And?" Isaac prompted.

"The initial prognosis is promising. The doctors believe they can reconstruct the damaged sectors of her connectome using a recent save. The good news is the mindbank has a copy of her connectome that's only a few weeks old, and the doctors have already reached out to the bank to release her save state. For the medical procedure, I mean. Not replacement. Once they have it, they'll splice in healthy versions of the damaged sectors. There'll be some drift between the save and her running connectome—there always is—but the doctors sounded confident, especially given how recent the save is."

"Good." Isaac let out a slow, relieved sigh. He hadn't realized how tense he'd been until the stress of worrying began to ease off. "That's good. What kind of state do they think she'll be in after the procedure?"

"There might be some short-term memory loss, but other than that, she should be fine. They project a nearly full recovery."

"Given the circumstances, I think we can manage a few forgotten moments." Isaac nodded to the trooper. "Thank you for letting me know. And *thank you* for resuscitating her when she transmitted over to you and Susan."

"Just doing my job, Detective."

"You're doing a bit more than that, if you ask me. Great work out there."

Parks gave him a bashful smile then nodded and vanished. The conveyor floated out of the room.

"What a relief!" Nina said.

"Yeah, I know." Isaac put his back to the bullet-riddled wall and pressed the back of his head against the cool prog-steel. "I wasn't sure what to think when Susan told me her connectome had been garbled."

"Me, too. I—" Nina paused in the middle of entering a command, then expanded an alert from one of her drones. She turned to her twin brother and raised an eyebrow.

"Find something?" he asked.

"Would an abstraction labeled 'Custom_Ruckman_001.UAM' count as something?"

"I'd say so. Does it have any ACs attached to it?"

"One. And, at first glance, the connectome appears intact. The abstraction is running right now."

"Can we get him out?"

"Not yet. The Pyrates have some unusual code running in parallel with the abstraction. If I were to hazard a guess, I'd say its purpose is to keep him locked in. I need to go over the setup some more, but I'll probably need to shut the node down and then extract his connectome manually while it's in a suspended state. But, that said, the abstraction can be accessed from the outside.

Want to dive in and give Ruckman the good news? At the very least, we can let him know we're working to pull him out."

"Yes, let's do that."

"All right." Nina's fingers danced across her screen. "This part's easy enough. Their system's designed to let people on the outside in."

"Just not the opposite."

"Right. Bringing up the abstraction now."

An alert appeared beside Isaac, asking him if he'd like to access a dodgy connection request. He selected "partial-mode," which would overlay the abstraction on top of his normal senses rather than completely replacing them, then hit the commit icon.

A virtual chamber materialized within the real room, its surfaces expanding outward, flexing until they matched the physical room's dimensions. Perhaps that was a part of its programming? The color was different—a clinical white instead of metallic gray— but other than that, the two rooms lined up perfectly once the adjustments finished.

Almost perfectly.

A heavy chair sat in the middle of the room. It was turned away from them and the back was high enough to prevent them from seeing the occupant.

A wide grid of interfaces covered much of the wall beside the chair. Isaac inspected some of the screens, reading off labels like BIOCHEMICAL SIM EDITOR and CONNECTOME SPLICER. He frowned in disgust when he spotted the PAIN SIMULATOR.

"Isaac?"

He joined Nina in front of the chair and took a long, hard look at Ruckman. The man's avatar sat in the chair, naked and strapped in place, his head slumped forward.

"Mister Ruckman?"

The man raised his head slowly. Drool trickled from the corner of his lip.

"Mister Ruckman, I'm Detective Isaac Cho. Can you hear me?"

Ruckman's copy looked up until he made eye contact with Isaac, who wasn't sure what to make of the man's expression. The eyes were...eerily vacant.

"Hello?" the copy asked.

"Hello, Mister Ruckman. We'll need some time to retrieve you from this abstraction, but rest assured you're safe now."

"I am?"

"Yes. The area is under SSP control, and the Byte Pyrates are now in custody."

"Who?"

"The Byte Pyrates. The people who kidnapped you."

"No." Ruckman shook his head like a slow metronome. "Who are you?"

"Detective Cho, SysPol Themis."

"Do I know you?"

"No, sir. We only just met, though I've had the pleasure of interviewing your original."

"My original?"

"Sir, are you aware you're the victim of a copy-kidnapping?"

"Am I?"

"I'm afraid so. The Byte Pyrates kidnapped you while you visited the Divided-By-Zero hotel."

"Am I?" He shook his head once more with that slow, unnatural rhythm.

"I'm sorry, but it's the truth."

"Am I?" He stopped shaking his head and met Isaac's gaze. "Who am I?"

Isaac grimaced, unsure what to say to the man.

Nina leaned over and whispered, "Is this supposed to be your star witness?"

"I believe so," he sighed more than said.

✧　　✧　　✧

Isaac had Nina transfer Ruckman's copy to the Connectome Wellness Center immediately after she extracted him from the Byte Pyrate infosystems. Susan rejoined them soon after and shared the good news on Riller's capture. She and Isaac then headed for the CWC to check on both Cephalie and their "star witness," though not by physically traveling to the Center.

The CWC did possess a physical location, but it lacked a physical *interior*. Or at least a *conventional* interior, not counting the many maintenance accessways and giant infostructure columns that took up most of the building's internal space. The site did feature a small logistics center full of racked caskets where synthoid patients could store their bodies during treatment, but that was about it.

Instead, the two detectives headed back to the 103rd Precinct Building, where Susan switched back into her general purpose synthoid. Isaac reserved a meeting room equipped with abstraction recliners, and together they connected with the CWC's abstract realm.

Cephalie came out of abstract surgery first.

Isaac spent his time waiting as productively as he could. He studied the Byte Pyrate interrogation reports filtering in from SSP (unhelpful), he read the updates Nina was drip-feeding him (incomplete but showing promise), and he reviewed his own case notes (no grand insights to be found).

At least the realm is free of distractions, he thought.

The waiting room wasn't so much a room as a terrestrial landscape complete with rolling, grassy hills and a bright, cloudless sky. He and Susan sat on a park bench underneath the shade of an apple tree. A pleasant breeze cooled his skin, and a discreet menu in the tree's bark controlled the wide selection of birdsong. He'd muted the birds once the incessant chirping began to grate.

A white doorway formed beside the tree, and Isaac looked up from his work. Cephalie's chief surgeon—an AC named Ixtlilton—walked through the glowing portal. The AC used a baseline human avatar in a long white coat, her short black hair in a white cap and her mouth concealed behind a white surgical mask. She wore white gloves over her delicate hands and clutched a clipboard to her chest.

The doctor pulled her mask down and smiled to them.

"She's ready to see you now."

Isaac rose from the park bench and approached the portal.

"How is she?"

Doctor Ixtlilton gestured inside. "She'll tell you herself."

Isaac nodded, satisfied with the answer. Susan followed him through the doorway.

The portal transferred them to the edge of a distant cliff under the same sky. Cephalie sat in a rocking chair, her avatar normal-sized and wearing a caramel-hued coat and hat. She stared out across the glistening ocean before she turned to regard the new arrivals with a neutral expression.

"Cephalie," Isaac said.

"It's good to see you," Susan added.

"Who are you two supposed to be?" Cephalie asked sharply. "And why should I care?"

Isaac gave the doctor a worried look.

Cephalie snorted out a laugh. "I'm joking! How could I forget you two kiddos?"

"That's not very funny."

"Would it help if I did this?" Cephalie conjured a large sign out of thin air. The bold lettering read: THAT WAS A JOKE!

"Still not funny."

"At least she's back to normal," Susan said.

"There's that I suppose." Isaac walked over to her and presented her with a card in a cream-colored envelope. "Here. I got you this."

"Aww. You shouldn't have." Cephalie dismissed the sign with a grin, then took the envelope and broke it open with a finger. "What do we have here?"

"Just a little 'get well' present."

"Let's see." Cephalie took out the small card within the envelope and adjusted her opaque glasses. "It's a . . . gift card?"

"That's right."

"You bought me a gift card? Good for abstract purchases from the Martian Millinery?"

"I know how you love your hats."

"*Isaac.*" Cephalie shook her head. "What are we going to do with you?"

"He put a lot of thought into it," Susan said.

"Well, it *is* the thought that counts." Cephalie flicked her wrist, and the gift card vanished.

"How do you feel?" Isaac asked.

"Not bad, all things considered. Some parts of the last week or so are fuzzy, like I'm viewing my memories through clouded glass, but I'm not about to complain. Better this than losing *all* my recent memories."

"The recall gaps are permanent, I'm afraid," Doctor Ixtlilton cut in. "But her connectome splices took hold exceptionally well. We don't expect any other complications."

"That's wonderful to hear." Isaac shook the doctor's hand. "Thank you. It's good to have her back."

"It's what we do here, Detective," she replied with a modest smile.

"What about the Ruckman copy we brought in?"

"Let me check." Doctor Ixtlilton inspected her clipboard. Text scrolled across the top page, and she stopped it with a finger.

"Ruckman-2 is still in surgery. The damage is extensive, I'm afraid. We should have an update for you in about half an hour."

✧   ✧   ✧

"Hello, Mister Ruckman," Isaac greeted the AC's original with a curt nod. "Thank you for transmitting over on such short notice."

"It's no trouble." The engineer stepped through the grass to stand beside Isaac and Susan. "How could I not have come, given the news?"

"Of course," Isaac replied, regarding the man now referred to as Ruckman-1 in the case log.

"Will I be able to speak to him?" Ruckman-1 glanced over at the glowing doorway. "My copy, I mean."

"Absolutely, you will. Though bear in mind, we still need to interview him first. In fact, that's what I'd like to discuss with you."

"Why? What do you need me for?"

"I would like you to be present during the interview."

"Me? Isn't that a little odd for how you detectives normally operate?"

"It is, but I believe the situation warrants a little flexibility. How much have the doctors shared with you about the state of your copy?"

"Very little. They directed me to you, citing the open case."

"Then it pains me to be the bearer of bad news. To put it bluntly, your copy was not well when we found him. His connectome had been mutilated by the kidnappers."

"Mutilated?" Ruckman-1's face twisted in disgust. "What for?"

"To make extracting information from him easier, I would assume. He seemed quite confused when we found him. The doctors are doing what they can, but they're limited in what they can do at this stage."

"What do you mean? 'At this stage'? What's going to happen to him?"

"That's your call, Mister Ruckman. It was your connectome the criminals violated. How we handle your copy will ultimately be up to you. However, in the meantime, he is a key witness to a heinous crime and remains temporarily under the care of SysPol. We need to find out what he knows, which unfortunately means the doctors are limited in the techniques they can employ. For the short term, at least."

"Until you're done interviewing him?"

"That's right."

"And then?"

"As I said, how the copy is handled is up to you."

"But what does that mean? What exactly am I supposed to decide?"

"Are you familiar with the laws surrounding connectome replication?"

"I . . . no." He took a deep breath. "I never even *considered* something like this could happen to me."

"Then permit me to explain. You have three basic options. First, you may allow your copy to continue as he is. He will be granted full citizenship as a member of your family. Once our interview is complete, and assuming you elect to donate a copy of your connectome for the surgery, the doctors will be able to enact a more complete restoration. As a second option, you may choose to have his unique memories integrated into your connectome, effectively merging the two of you."

Ruckman-1 gazed off into the distance, deep in thought.

"And the third?"

"You may choose to euthanize the copy."

Ruckman-1 took a slow, ragged breath. "And when I've made my decision? Who do I contact? The doctors here?"

"No. A judge will be appointed to handle your case. I'm involved as well, though my role is merely to submit a recommendation, which will mirror your own choice."

"But what if it doesn't?" Ruckman-1 asked. "What if you and I don't agree?"

"That won't happen."

"But what if it does?"

"In those circumstances, the judge almost always defers to the victim, except under extreme circumstances. None of which apply to this case, I assure you. I *can* fight your decision, but I'd need to justify it to the judge, which would not be easy and which I have no intention of doing. To do so would involve suspending your legal rights to your own connectome, which is not something to pursue on a whim. In short, *your* decision will be the one that matters here, not mine."

"I suppose that's both reassuring . . . and terrifying."

"I can sympathize with that." Isaac gestured to the white doorway. "Shall we proceed?"

Ruckman-1 hesitated for a moment, then nodded and stepped into the portal. Isaac and Susan followed him through.

They emerged on a beach, the heat from the white sands shimmering through air punctuated with the scent of ocean salt. Ruckman-2 sat on his knees on the edge of a beach towel, sifting through the sand for bits of shell, which he'd collected by his side. One of the CWC doctors stood nearby, his hands clasped in front of him.

Ruckman-1 stopped at the edge of the beach towel and watched his doppelganger with a mixture of revulsion and sympathy.

"Please be patient with him," the doctor said. "He's better than he was, but there's much work left to do."

"We understand," Isaac assured him. "Thank you."

"Call if you need anything." The doctor nodded to them, then summoned a doorway and departed through it.

Ruckman-1 dropped down to one knee. His copy didn't acknowledge his presence, only continued playing in the sand.

"Hey there," Ruckman-1 said quietly.

"Hello." Ruckman-2 smiled at his original, then returned his attention to the sand, raking his fingers through the granules until he found a pearlescent fragment of a clamshell. "Ooh!" he cooed, then added it to his collection.

"Antoni Ruckman?" Isaac said.

"That's me," the copy said.

"We'd like to ask you a few questions, if you don't mind."

"Okay." He shifted over on his hands and knees to a fresh patch of sand.

"Do you recall visiting the Divided-By-Zero hotel, located along the Breathless Ridge?"

"Sure do. Esteban invited me over." He paused, then smiled brightly. "We were talking about work. Good times."

"Do you remember how the visit ended?"

"I do."

"Can you describe what happened for us?"

"Sure." He sat back on his legs and stared out across the ocean. "I remember ... discontinuity. I was in the hotel room, and then I wasn't. I found myself in an abstraction I didn't recognize. It was small, and I couldn't leave. I remember ... fear. Helplessness." He grinned brightly up at them. "This place is much better."

"Please continue. What happened next?"

"A long time passed, and then a woman entered the abstraction."

"Describe her, please."

"Thin with short hair and this dyed braid off to the side."

"Zalaya Riller," Isaac said, then softly to the original Ruckman. "She's the leader of the gang responsible for this."

"We have her in custody," Susan added. "Rest assured she'll pay for her crimes."

Ruckman-1 only nodded, mesmerized by the sight of his copy.

"And then what?" Isaac prompted the copy.

"She told me I was her captive, that I had no hope of escape, and that she was going to extract information out of me, willingly or not. She seemed to enjoy the power she held over me." His face darkened. "I've never met anyone so frightening."

"What did she do to you?"

"I'm not sure. My thoughts grew sluggish and... confused. As if parts of my mind were being pulled apart like taffy. Time slowed. It became difficult to concentrate on anything. Then all my anxieties melted away, as if someone had banished them from my mind. I couldn't recall who I was, but even that didn't bother me. I could remember everything about my work, though, which seems strange. Almost as if the excess memories surrounding it had been cut away. When I saw the woman again, I didn't fear her, and even that never struck me as strange or alarming. She began asking me questions."

"What did she ask you?"

"They were comically simple. She asked me to recite the operating parameters for a Class D78 Dendritic Monitor." The copy chuckled. "What an easy question."

Isaac turned to Ruckman-1. "Thoughts?"

"I designed the D78, so I know that microbot inside and out. But it's not a part of SourceCode's Dyson proposal. It's an older model. SourceCode used to license the pattern out to other companies, so a lot of information about it has filtered its way into the public domain. I'm not sure why she'd be interested in it."

"Perhaps she wasn't," Isaac said. "Instead, perhaps she was checking to see if the modifications she made to your copy were successful. She would be able to compare your answers to publicly available information."

"That could be it," Ruckman-1 agreed.

"What else did the woman ask you?" Isaac said to the copy.

"She wanted to know how to access SourceCode's secure systems remotely. I gave her my keycodes and provided details on the company's security procedures. My response seemed to make her happy. The next time I saw her, she brought along a friend."

"Who was this friend?"

"He introduced himself as the Ghost. He looked the part, too. Just a floating white silhouette. I didn't fear him either, though he asked me much harder questions. He wanted to know about the D109, the N12, the M66. The list went on and on. So many different models."

"But those are..." Ruckman-1 breathed. "Detective, those models he listed are part of my work on the Dyson constructor swarm. They each contribute to the swarm's immune system, which is responsible for keeping mutations in check. Mutations such as the one that ruined our last trial run."

"He asked *really* good questions," Ruckman-2 continued. "I could tell he was passionate about microbots and swarm replication. He helped me find a flaw in my work."

"A flaw?" Ruckman-1 echoed quietly.

His copy nodded. "Turns out, there's a way to seed a specific mutation into the design."

"Impossible! And even if there was, the immune system would stamp it out!"

"Not if the mutant lied to its fellow microbots."

"But the command system would still recognize the anomaly. It would order a direct intervention."

"That's why the mutant would need to attack the command microbots first."

"But the system should still—" Ruckman-1 pressed a hand to his temple. "I mean, shouldn't it?"

"Whoops." The copy gave them a timid shrug. "I guess I'll try harder next time."

"But even so, how could you possibly create such a precise mutation? The design would have to be included in one of the microbots' replication kernels."

"No, it wouldn't."

"How then? Would you have one class of microbot modify another to create the mutant?"

"No, that wouldn't work. The immune system would catch it."

"Then how?" Ruckman-1 demanded. "How did you defeat the swarm's immunity?"

"By adjusting the replication checks in key places."

"The internal checks..." Ruckman-1 stared off to the side. "Yes, that could do it. And if the record of that update was then deleted..."

"Would you mind clarifying for us non-engineers?" Isaac asked.

"Any self-replicating microbot has what you can think of as copy protection. Elements put in place to ensure the replica it produces is free of mutation. But no single microbot is a perfect copy, which means if the checks are too strict, replication will be too infrequent or will fail completely. So there's a little slop in the checks. A little give. There has to be."

"Add a touch more give in *precisely* the right places," his copy added, "then take it away in others, and you can cultivate the mutation you want to produce."

"We're not even talking about a design change," Ruckman-1 continued. "Not the hardware, anyway. Just software. Tweaking a few parameters here and there. On the surface it would appear innocuous. We make those sorts of adjustments all the time, even up to the last minute. We're constantly running simulations and tuning the swarm's parameters for more optimal performance.

"If I'm to guess, SourceCode is looking for something more overt. More obviously malicious. This is... subtle, for lack of a better word. Elegant even. My old colleagues will figure it out eventually. But Atlas already has the contract. There'll be a lot of project inertia to overcome. The government will be loath to change course, especially given the nature of the failure. SourceCode will argue sabotage, but Atlas could fire back by saying SourceCode is trying to deflect blame from their genuine mistake."

"Sounds like it would be difficult for SourceCode to prove their case," Isaac said, "barring the sort of evidence we just uncovered."

"You're right. Their arguments would look like a classic case of Cover-Your-Ass."

"Did the Ghost mention anything else?" Isaac asked the copy. "Anything nontechnical?"

"We talked a little about Mercury," Ruckman-2 replied. "He scolded me for caring so little about the planet's 'well-being.'"

"But Mercury's a rock with no one on it," Ruckman-1 growled. "That sounds like something the Society would say."

"A false trail, I assure you," Isaac said.

Which means we're unlikely to find any evidence connecting back to the real Ghost, he thought. *Sounds like he or she was planting evidence, working to reinforce the Desmond Fike angle the Pyrates had already been exposed to.*

Ruckman-1 knelt beside his copy and put an arm around his shoulders. The copy smiled at him, then began sifting through the sand once more.

"Detective, would it be all right if you gave us some time alone now?"

"Of course. Please, take as much time as you need."

Isaac sat on the edge of the abstraction recliner after disconnecting from the CWC.

"Well?" Susan asked, standing beside her own recliner. "We still don't know who the Ghost is, unless I missed something."

"If you did, it passed us *both* by."

"Where do we take the investigation from here?"

"I'm not sure."

"Back to Atlas? We know there's *someone* over there causing trouble."

"Yes, but where do we look? Their leadership is still dubious. Boaz rubbed me the wrong way from the start, and I'm not placing Traczyk above suspicion either. Of course, the Ghost could be a member of the company we haven't dealt with yet."

"Should we expand our search, then?" Susan asked. "Interview more members of the project team?"

"Maybe. Probably. I'm not sure what other options we have, other than to hope Nina hits it big back at the Retreat."

"Then you might want to cross your fingers," Cephalie teased from atop her new LENS. "Or perform whatever superstitious rituals make you happy. Nina left you a message while you were hanging out with the Ruckman duo."

"She did?" Isaac opened an interface and checked his mail, then let a smile slip out. "She *did*." He skimmed over the message. "She's recovered an audio call from this morning where Riller mentions the Ghost."

He opened the file and let it play over their abstract hearing.

"Hello, Zalaya." The voice was synthesized with a vaguely male pitch.

"How'd you get this string?"

"A mutual friend gave it to me."

"Yeah? And who might that friend be?"

"The Ghost, of course. I'm calling on his behalf."

"He not available to speak for himself?"

"Not at present. Circumstances...prevent him from making private calls for the time being."

Isaac paused the playback.

"Interesting," he said. "I'm inclined to believe this actually is the Ghost calling."

"Why do you say that?" Susan asked.

"The timing of the call. This came after we apprehended Fike, which could mean this is an example of the Ghost maintaining the Fike-fiction when dealing with Riller. She had no clue the Ghost wasn't Desmond Fike until I told her."

Isaac restarted the playback.

"I'll bet," Riller said. "You have some proof you're the Ghost's partner?"

"I do. Not only do I have access to this connection string, but I'm up to speed on your previous dealings. For example, here's a copy of the Retreat keycode he paid you with."

The call fell silent for long seconds.

"Yeah, that'll do for now," Riller said. "To what do I owe the pleasure, Friend-of-the-Ghost? Or do you have a different name for me to use?"

"'Friend' will suffice. And to answer your first question, my call is about business. I'd like to discuss another job with you. Interested?"

"Tentatively. What sort of services are you looking to purchase?"

"I find myself in need of information."

"What kind?"

"The type stored in someone's head. That won't be a problem, I assume."

"As long as the head isn't organic. I can't be bothered with that sort of mess."

The Ghost chuckled. "It isn't."

"Who's the lucky target?"

"Another engineer. Different company this time."

"I'll need more details if we're to do business."

"Those will follow in due time. For now, I merely wish to confirm your interest, and the availability of your services. Can we agree on that much, at least?"

"Consider us tentatively available and interested."

"Splendid. I need to lay low for the time being but will contact you again in the future. Do you still have the copy?"

"What copy?" Riller asked, sounding deliberately coy.

"Antoni Ruckman's."

"Yeah, he's here. What's left of him, anyway."

"You're a terrible person, you know that?"

"You're welcome to get your own hands dirty if you think you can do better."

"No, thank you. Dissecting people's minds is more your wheelhouse than mine. I'll leave that sort of work to the exp—"

Susan hit the pause button. "Did you hear that? The 'wheelhouse' reference, I mean."

"I heard," Isaac replied with a skeptical frown.

"He sounded like Boaz there."

"He did."

"But . . . is it just me, or does this seem too good to be true?"

"It's not just you. Unless I'm completely off the mark, this is a deliberate false lead. A 'friend of the Ghost' makes a vague call to the Pyrates the morning before we hit their base, asking about a vague job and dropping a hint that he or she is secretly Julian Boaz." Isaac shook his head. "I don't buy it. Not for an instant. We saw the same thing with the gangsters in the container, except back then the Ghost was planting evidence to point back to Fike. This new one is subtle enough to come across as an honest slip. But . . ." He gestured with an open hand to Susan, inviting her to finish.

"But obvious enough for us to spot it."

"Exactly. If we arrested Boaz and tore through his office files, I'm almost certain we'd find something incriminating."

"Because the Ghost planted it there?"

"That would be my fear. And by the time anyone discovered the holes in the evidence, the Ghost would have buried the truth so deep, it'd take a miracle to unearth it."

"Yeah, thought so." Susan blew a frustrated breath out the side of her mouth. "Between you and me, I'm a little sick of being led by the nose like this. How many false trails is the Ghost going to put us on?"

"Don't worry. We'll muddle through this together."

"I know. But if it's not Boaz, then—"

Isaac snapped his fingers, and Susan looked up.

"Wait a second," he began, thinking out loud. "This has happened to us before."

"Yes? Didn't I just say that?"

"We've encountered false trails... twice."

"Yes?"

"And we were *directed* to those trails the same way. *Twice!* Susan, you're absolutely right!"

"I am?"

"The Ghost has been manipulating us all along, and we couldn't see it. We didn't sniff out these trails on our own. We were led to them!" Isaac met her confused gaze at last, and he grinned at her. "Susan, I know who the Ghost is."

CHAPTER TWENTY-SIX

THE GHOST STEPPED OUT OF THE TAXI AND WALKED OVER TO his Hanging Gardens apartment, a smile curling his lips. He was curious to see what became of the seeds he'd planted today, confident they'd produce the desired result.

Boaz is going to lose it when he finds out, he thought wryly. *Well, it's really his own fault for making himself such a convenient decoy. I hardly had to plant any evidence at all!*

The trail had been laid; the stage set for Boaz to be arrested for Ruckman's kidnapping. Now, all the Ghost had to do was wait for SysPol to sniff out the trail. He wondered how long it would take them to reach the conclusion he desired. A day? Maybe two?

Not long at all.

The charges wouldn't hold, of course, but that wasn't the Ghost's goal. He was buying time. A delay he needed to scour Atlas, his apartment, and a few other places of any genuine evidence. By the time SysPol realized their error, the damage would have been done. That detective might eventually put two of his neurons together and figure out the truth—more through trial and error than any real spark of intuition—but by then it would be too late. His accusations would amount to nothing more than a flimsy theory; he'd need evidence to level any charges, and he'd fail to find enough.

Yes, today was a good day.

The Ghost palmed the lock on his apartment. The door split open—

—and a SysPol LENS smashed into him, knocking him over. Prog-steel arms expanded, embracing him while also cushioning his fall. They laid him on his back, unable to move beyond impotent wiggling.

Detective Cho walked out of the apartment, followed by Agent Cantrell.

"Hello...'Ghost,'" the detective said. "You've led us on quite the chase, but it's over now."

Hearing his name shook the Ghost to the core, but he didn't let it show. He remained motionless within the LENS' restraining grasp, and he considered this moment as he had all others before it, with deliberate care. How could this have happened? What had he missed? Nothing—*nothing*—should have led the authorities back to him. His veil of anonymity was flawless, concealed behind his deliberate false trails.

And yet, the Ghost thought, *the detective's face shows no doubt. He knows he has the right man, and he's correct. But how did he figure it out?*

Should I proclaim my innocence? the Ghost considered. *Ahh, but what would be the point? I know what's hidden deep in my apartment's infostructure. I know what their forensics units will find, given enough time. And they'll have it. I'll be helpless to stall their careful, methodical analysis while in jail.*

In short, the plan is doomed.

"You're under arrest for conspiracy to copy-kidnap, corporate sabotage, accessory to connectome violation, obstruction of justice, and quite a few others. I have the whole list here if you're interested. But I'm sure you already know what's on it."

Is there anything left to be gained by fighting this? the Ghost thought. *No, I suppose there isn't. My priorities must shift from concealment to damage control. Ahh, well. The plan* almost *worked.*

"Do you have anything to say for yourself?"

"You surprise me, Detective," Horace Pangu said with a genuine smile. "I thought you'd never figure it out."

Isaac viewed the prisoner through an abstract window over the interrogation room's door. The Ghost's connectome had been transferred to an emaciated, carrot-skinned synthoid with artificial musculature so weak it made standing up a chore.

"Ready?" Isaac asked his partner.

"Ready."

"Then let's see what he has to say for himself." Isaac palmed the lock and stepped in, followed by Susan and the LENS.

The Ghost began to clap, a broad grin on his face.

"Congratulations, Detective."

"You can dispense with the sarcasm. I'm only interested in the truth, not your false praise."

"Oh, but there's nothing false about it." He stopped clapping and set his hands palm-down on the table. "I meant what I said earlier."

Isaac and Susan took their seats.

"You seem awfully happy," Susan said.

"'Happy' is not the right term," the Ghost corrected. "But I *am* impressed. And curious to learn where I slipped up. You'll share that with me, won't you?"

"That depends on how cooperative you prove," Isaac said. "We have more than enough to prosecute you, but some curious blanks remain in our understanding of recent events. I'd like you to help us fill them in."

"Naturally. I worked hard to conceal my actions and motives. It's to be expected you have an incomplete picture. Rest assured, I see no point in resistance anymore. You've won, and I can accept that. Besides, there are certain... misunderstandings I wish to avoid."

"Then let's start with your motive. Why did you do it?"

"Certainly." The Ghost shifted into a more comfortable position in the chair. "But before we proceed, I'd like to make one fact clear."

"Then make it."

"I'm not Horace Pangu."

Isaac hadn't expected this. "Then who are you?"

"The Ghost. You see, you're operating under a false assumption. The Ghost isn't an alias for Horace Pangu, but rather the opposite is true. I've been masquerading as Pangu this whole time. I *am* the Ghost.

"More specifically, I'm one of Pangu's children, crafted from pieces of his own connectome. The foundation of my mind is his, and yet I'm my own self, and while my progenitor and the rest of my siblings continue to"—he waved a hand vaguely—"waste their time out in the Oort cloud, *I* have decided to come here, to the heart of our society, to enact the changes we all believe in.

"And make no mistake. My father and my brothers and sisters all strive for the same goals I do. But they find my methods distasteful. So, I wish to clear up any possibility you misunderstand who I am. My fate is my own, and I would have no ill will fall upon my father. I am not him, and he is innocent of any of the crimes I have committed. *That* is what I wish to impress upon you, more than anything else."

"And yet you decided to impersonate the Wizard when you came to Saturn."

"Yes," the Ghost sighed. "You shine a rather effective light on my hypocrisy, though that's hardly the worst of my crimes, wouldn't you say?"

"Point taken."

"You wish to understand my goal, but the truth is you already know what it is. You simply haven't made the obvious connection. My father has written about the topic extensively, and I share his enthusiasm."

"You're referring to the thesis behind *A Tale of Stars and Meat*, and how it advocates for the complete virtualization of the human race?"

"Correct. I consider the baseline human body more akin to shackles than an effective form of life. The sooner we cast off this crude biological engine run by protein replication, the better. The transition is inevitable if we are to excel as a society. I merely wish to spur the process along."

"I don't see how this belief connects to any of your crimes."

"You don't?" The Ghost seemed taken aback. "I would have thought it obvious by now, but perhaps I've overestimated your abilities. Consider this, then. I would need leverage in order to guide our worlds along the intended path. Yet where could I find this leverage in our magnificent, post-scarcity society?"

"But 'post-scarcity' is a relative term, and societies change over time. Our thirst for energy is ever increasing. And even if we have more than enough today, we will need more tomorrow. That's one of the reasons why we're building a Dyson swarm. To ensure our society continues to enjoy plentiful energy for centuries to come.

"What did I desire in all of this? Control. Control over the Dyson swarm itself by installing back doors that I could tap into later, allowing me to take command of what will eventually become the primary source of energy for the entire solar system."

"Theft, then," Isaac said.

"Theft on the grandest scale in all of human history. And I didn't even want it for myself; I had intended to present this as a gift to my father, for him to wield in whatever way he saw fit." He smiled sadly at them. "Ahh, well. It was a good plan while it lasted."

"Is that why you quit SourceCode for Atlas?"

"Yes. You were correct during our first meeting when you pointed out that SourceCode, as a company, is a better fit for someone of my beliefs. But my goal wasn't merely to fit in; it was to enact changes to the project. Changes that would provide me with levers I could manipulate at a later time. SourceCode's microtech approach, with its immune systems and command overlords, proved too difficult for me to penetrate. There were too many automated systems in place that could sniff out the changes I needed to make. My work would have been caught almost immediately.

"Atlas, on the other hand, proved to be more flexible in the right places. While their approach to macrotechnology might, on the surface, seem more robust and less prone to errors, the size of each component and the lack of an overarching supervisory system makes it more vulnerable to corruption from within. So, when Boaz sent me a job offer about two months ago, I saw my opportunity and seized it."

"When did you decide to approach Velasco?"

"Once it became clear to me SourceCode would win the bidding war. Switching sides wasn't enough, after all. I needed Atlas to win so that my work could continue. The situation at Atlas became increasingly desperate over time, with a great deal of pressure being placed on Velasco. I decided he was...malleable enough for my needs, and so I reached out to him under the 'alias' of the Ghost. And brokered a deal with him. I would ensure Atlas won the Dyson contract in exchange for unspecified services later."

"And Velasco went along with this?"

"He did. Willingly, at first, though that changed as the nature of my"—he flashed a wicked grin—"activities became clearer to him. During this time, I began dropping hints the Ghost was actually Desmond Fike, who you of course know as the local Society chair. I believed the Society would serve as effective villains should Velasco or the Byte Pyrates be caught and inter-rogated. This precaution proved unnecessary with Velasco since he showed zero interest in discovering my true identity."

"Were you aware that Fike was embezzling funds from the Society? Or that he secretly despised them?"

"No." The Ghost chuckled, and his eyes gleamed with mirth. "I had no idea! Perhaps I should have done more research before selecting him."

"Tell us about your dealings with the Byte Pyrates."

"I used them as part of my efforts to insulate myself from any actual crimes, all while dropping hints to them I was actu-ally Desmond Fike. The ruse must have been at least partially effective, since you initiated a manhunt for the poor man. I hired them to kidnap Antoni Ruckman because I needed both his access to the project and his technical knowledge if I were to successfully sabotage it."

"But why was that necessary?" Susan asked. "You had recently been on the same project."

"True," the Ghost admitted, "but it's not like SourceCode let me keep copies of all their designs. I still needed very specific information and access levels to pull off the sabotage, and Ruck-man possessed both. On top of that, Velasco's relationship with the man made him an even easier target, leading to my deal with the Byte Pyrates. They would put together a plan to nab Ruckman, and I would pay them with a few choice keycodes I stole from Atlas."

"Which is how the Pyrates came to be in Mattison's Retreat with the old Atlas crabs under their command," Isaac filled in.

"Precisely, though I honestly couldn't care less what they did with the payment."

"Did you deal with Zalaya Riller exclusively or did your interactions with the Pyrates include others?"

"Just Riller. She presented a plan to me shortly after being hired. It seemed easy enough to execute with only a few setup tasks necessary, so I told them to proceed and reached out to Velasco to set up the rest. He reserved the room in the Divided-By-Zero hotel, the Byte Pyrates went in and prepped the infos-tructure, and then Velasco invited Ruckman to the capture site.

"The Pyrate hardware made a copy of his connectome and transmitted it to a satellite site where it eventually made its way back to Riller. Riller then prepped Ruckman's connectome, making it easier to extract information from him, and I connected to one of their sessions to collect the information I needed."

"Did Velasco know what would happen to Ruckman when he tricked him into coming?"

"No. He didn't learn the truth until later."

"How?"

"I was forced to tell him. You see, I had all the pieces and access I needed to sabotage the SourceCode trial, but I ran into trouble with how to produce the desired mutation. I needed help. I needed someone more skilled with replicator systems than I am. I needed Velasco. That's when I approached him once more as the Ghost, despite the risks. I was running out of time, and I needed the sabotage to go smoothly. Unfortunately, this meant I had to share the technical details with him, which then raised the question of *how* I came by all that SourceCode data."

"How did Velasco react?"

"Not well, but I had little choice in the matter. He refused to aid me in the sabotage until I explained where the data had come from. And so I explained it all, despite the consequences I knew were coming. The truth of what the Pyrates had done to his friend horrified him, and *still* he refused to help me. But he was already high strung by then, already edging toward instability. I pushed him further, pressuring him to complete the work, lest I reveal his role to the authorities. He eventually relented, and I took his finished parameter set and—using Ruckman's access—planted it secretly into the SourceCode design."

"After which," Isaac filled in, "the SourceCode trial failed so spectacularly, Atlas was awarded the contract."

"Velasco's work undermining SourceCode was superb. Even in his...suboptimal state, he produced a brilliant set of parameters. SourceCode fired Ruckman shortly after the trial blew up in their faces, and I felt confident our subterfuge would remain concealed."

"Until Velasco committed suicide."

"I'm not entirely sure what drove him over the edge. Perhaps a combination of stress and guilt. Perhaps he was looking for a way out and found it at the end of a barrel. None of us can say for certain.

"But whatever his reasons, his actions threatened to unravel all my work. I knew I had to act quickly after he blew his brains out. I cleaned up his office infostructure, clearing out anything that could be tied back to me. But there was nothing I could do about the infosystems at his apartment. I simply had to risk it and hope for the best.

"During my initial interview, I used the opportunity to drop hints the Society might be involved. I felt confident you would eventually track down the Byte Pyrates, who would also point the finger at Fike. The accusation was never meant to hold up under scrutiny, but I was fine with that as long as no evidentiary lines could be traced back to me."

"And when the fiction of Fike-the-mastermind fell through?" Isaac asked.

"I decided to adapt my approach. The search warrant issued to Atlas proved tremendously difficult for me to deal with, but I was able to goad Boaz into fighting it in court, granting me the time I needed to bury other, more distributed evidence. Your investigation kept boring in, so I came to the conclusion some...additional misdirection was in order. Boaz fighting the search warrant provided me with an opportunity, after all, and I decided to capitalize on it by crafting a new, more believable villain for the police to zero in on. I sent you a message, inviting you to my apartment so I could set you on the right path."

"Did Boaz really ask you about the missing messages?"

"No, I lied about that," the Ghost said. "The falsified evidence really did blindside him. To further substantiate the fiction Boaz was the Ghost, I made a call to Riller that same day. I contacted her under the guise of a 'friend of the Ghost,' since using my preferred alias would have prompted too many questions from her. During our talk, I planted what I had hoped would be a subtle nod toward Boaz's favorite idiom."

"Which you then hoped would lead us to suspect Boaz," Isaac concluded.

"Yes. Though, clearly, that's not what happened. I had even gone out of my way to plant additional abstract evidence in his office in the hopes you'd uncover it after his arrest."

"Well, Mister Pangu—or Ghost, I should say—that clears up matters quite nicely." Isaac rose from his seat, and Susan pushed out her chair and joined him. "We'll let you know if we have any further questions."

"Ahh, but there's still one open matter between us, Detective."

"How we caught you?"

"I'd love to know."

"It has to do with the two false trails you created."

"Neither of which should have led you back to me," the Ghost pointed out.

"They didn't. They both led exactly where you intended, with no direct ties back to yourself."

"Then how did you figure it out?"

"Because of how we *found* those two trails."

"I'm not sure I follow."

"During our first talk, you pointed us toward the Society," Isaac explained. "You were the only person to make even a tentative connection between Velasco's suicide and the Society. And then you did it again. You placed us on Boaz's trail by insinuating he'd lied to us. Two fictional trails, one source."

"Then my efforts to lead you astray...?"

"Eventually led us right back to you."

"Oh..." The Ghost smiled, staring off to the side. "My efforts to fool you are what led you to me?" He began to chuckle. "Then, if I'd done nothing, I might still be free?" The chuckling grew into laughter, rising in volume until it was almost manic, until it became uncomfortably loud to hear.

The Ghost was still laughing when the detectives left the room.

CHAPTER TWENTY-SEVEN

"NINA REALLY OUTDID HERSELF THIS TIME," ISAAC SAID, SIFTING through his sister's full report on the Byte Pyrate hideout. "Especially with Riller's blackmail stash. That's an absolute goldmine of evidence. A lot of her old clients will soon find Themis knocking on their doors, and not in the friendly way."

"Is it our job to follow up all of these?" Susan asked from her desk across from his. They had returned to Kronos Station the morning after the Ghost's arrest and were in the process of wrapping up some of the case's loose ends.

"Oh, no." Isaac waved the notion away. "Most appear to be connected to cold cases. Those will be distributed to whichever detectives worked the originals, though Raviv might pick up a few of the stragglers. Maybe he'll hand us one or two to chase down, but I suspect not. More likely, he'll put us back on light duty given how rough the case was."

"You sound disappointed."

"A little. I was looking forward to a return to the normal grind."

"It would make sense, though. You almost had your insides turned into soup, and I got shot up." She paused, then gave him a guilty shrug. "Again."

"Don't take this the wrong way, but better you than me."

"I know." Susan swiped through her own copy of the report. "What do you think will happen to Riller?"

"Given what we uncovered, a short trial followed by the death penalty."

"And her gang?"

"That'll depend on what we can prove for each individual, though your combat frame's records make that task a lot easier. Plus how you made sure to transmit your badge repeatedly during the firefight."

"I thought that might help us later," she added with a slight air of smugness.

"It will. Attempted murder of a police officer is a hefty enough charge on its own to see most of them follow Riller's lead, and I suspect Nina's forensic work will put the rest away for life, barring a few outliers like Zapf that weren't in as deep as the rest."

"Good riddance to human rubbish."

"No kidding."

"How about Fike?"

"Probably ten years for embezzlement. Maybe more once prosecutors tack on the other charges. Fike has a lot of counseling to look forward to, which might actually do him some good. I got the impression he fell into his criminal ways through temptation, so maybe Panoptics Division can whip him back into a law-abiding citizen."

"And the Ghost?"

"Life without the chance of parole."

"You don't think he'll receive the death penalty?"

"Unfortunately not, even though he deserves it. He kept himself too insulated from the worst crimes, and the prosecutors will most likely play it safe with a defendant as high profile as he is. Celebrity trials can be . . . unpredictable. They'll want to make sure the charges stick, so they'll aim slightly lower."

"Still, life in prison's not a bad result," Susan said. "Do you buy his story that the Wizard wasn't involved?"

"Hard to say. On the one hand, I'm inclined not to trust anything that comes out of his mouth if we can't substantiate it elsewhere. On the other, I'm hesitant to ascribe any crimes to such an important figure in SysGov history without evidence."

"What's the original have to say about all this?"

"Nothing so far, but that's to be expected. At least in the short term. The Oort cloud is a *big* place, even if most of the settlements are concentrated within the Kuiper Belt. It could take days for our message to bounce around and reach him. That said, it's entirely possible he'll never send us a response. There's no legal framework between SysGov and the OCC to force him to reply. And even if there was, who's going to fly out there and make him tell us?"

"Yeah, I guess you're right."

"Hey, you two!"

"Good morning." Isaac spun around at the sound of Raviv's voice. "What can we do for you, boss?"

"Nothing right now. Just thought I'd drop by and check in with you two before heading to my next meeting. Good to see both of you alive"—his gaze flicked over to Susan—"and not riddled with bullet holes."

"Sorry?" She gave the chief inspector a guilty shrug.

"About what?" Raviv asked. "When the case took an unexpected turn, you two knuckled down and got the job done. What more could a boss ask for?"

"Fewer repair invoices?" Susan said.

"Well, if we're talking about a *perfect* version of reality, then yes. I'd be happier if you would learn how to duck." Raviv cracked a smile. "But I'm happy enough with this. There turned out to be a lot more to that suicide than we first thought."

"You can say that again," Isaac agreed. "By the way, while you're here, would you mind approving something for me?"

"Sure. What do you have?"

"It's an academy referral for one of the troopers we worked with." Isaac passed the virtual document over. "His name's Randal Parks. He's the trooper who suspected something was off from the start and called us in. From what we saw, he has excellent instincts that, if honed properly, might land him as a detective in Themis one day. He also helped Cephalie out of a tight spot."

"Sounds like the kind of person we need more of. Sure, I'll sign." Raviv approved the document and passed it back to Isaac.

"Thanks."

"Does he know the referral's coming?"

"No." Isaac grinned. "It's going to be a surprise."

"Should we assume Damphart's case is going well," Susan asked, "given you're back up here instead of in the thick of it?"

"You should, though"—Raviv shook his head—"if I ever see another goddamned fuzzle again, it'll be too soon. Arete and

Argo divisions are still busy with cleanup, but the worst is over. All missing persons are accounted for and—for the most part—unharmed. Plus, Grace found and arrested the culprit yesterday. That's why you found us in the maze, in case you were curious."

"Fantastic," Isaac said. "Who'd it turn out to be?"

"One of PlayTech's own employees." Raviv paused to chuckle. "It was actually kind of funny. The fuzzles had him all wrapped up like a present in one of their replication nests, complete with a big red bow around his head. Turns out this idiot was trying to steal his daughter away from his ex-wife, who has legal custody. He comes up with the 'brilliant' idea to update some fuzzle prototypes before they were thrown out. Unfortunately for him, the modified fuzzles got *way* out of his control, even to the point where they kidnapped him, too! He'll be serving some serious time for this one."

"Good news all round, then," Isaac said.

"Which reminds me." Raviv copied a news link to their desks. "I think you'll appreciate this one."

"The *Engine Block Times*?" Isaac tapped the link, which opened to an image of combat-frame-Susan surrounded by grateful children. He read the title out loud. "'Admin Commando Rescues Children. Is Fuzzle Menace a Covert PR Operation?'"

"Now I'm an 'Admin Commando'?" Susan asked with a cringe.

"I read the whole thing," Raviv said. "It's *mostly* accurate and *mostly* positive, which puts the article head and shoulders above a lot of the press we get. Anyway"—he summoned a clock over his palm—"I've got to run to my next meeting. But before I go, have you had a chance to look over the blackmail material Nina dredged up? She gave me a preview, said it could warm up a few cold cases."

"Not in detail yet," Isaac said, "but it's on the list for today."

"Look it over and let me know if any of those cases catch your eye. Doesn't matter if they belong to someone else or not. You two get first pick of the litter."

"Thanks, boss!" Isaac sat up and grinned. "We certainly will."

"You earned it. We'll talk again once you have one picked out." Raviv nodded to them, then headed out of the department office.

Isaac and Susan waited until he was gone.

"Nice," she said with a twinkle in her eyes.

"*Very* nice," he agreed.

✧   ✧   ✧

"That was fast." Isaac crossed his arms as he considered the content on the screens arrayed before him. A lumpy rock sat on his desk next to an empty cupcake wrapper with some gray frosting still stuck to the rim.

"What was?" Susan asked.

"Here. Take a look." He sent her one of the news links, which appeared over her desk.

"'Dyson Project On Hold—Again!' says the *Saturn Journal*," she read. "Wow, that really was fast."

"There's more where that came from." He passed her a few more links.

"'Megastructure Subcommittee Revokes Atlas Contract,'" she read. "'Atlas Stumbles.' 'Who's Ready for *Another* Dyson Trial?' 'Is This Damn Thing Ever Getting Built?' Oh, here's a good one! 'Pinball Wizard Arrested! SysPol Unveils Dyson Sabotage!' That headline sounds positive, even if it wasn't the actual Wizard. Do we get a mention?"

"Not by name."

"You sound... unhappy."

"It simply occurs to me that we not only arrested the offspring of one of the most pivotal figures in SysGov history, but *also* prevented the future theft of the largest megastructure to ever be constructed. You'd *think* the article could *at least* mention us by name!"

"But you're not unhappy?"

"Perish the thought!"

"I only ask because you sound unhappy."

"I'm not!"

"Ah-*hem*." Cephalie materialized on his desk, flourishing her cane. "Not to rain on your pity parade, but it could be worse."

"What do you mean?" Isaac asked.

"I found an article you're mentioned in."

"How? I just ran a search. Is it new?"

"No, the *Engine Block Times* ran it a day ago."

"Then how'd I miss it?"

"You'll see." Cephalie waved her cane through the air, and the article appeared over Isaac's desk.

"'Police Harass the Underthruster Esteemless,'" he read, then grimaced. "That doesn't sound promising."

"It goes downhill from there." Cephalie scrolled halfway down the article and highlighted a paragraph.

"Hmm. 'Detective Isaac Chew of the'...Chew? *Chew?!*"

"I guess that's why your search didn't find it," Susan said.

Isaac lowered his head and let out a long, resigned sigh.

"By the way," Susan began, "how are you feeling, Cephalie?"

"Great. I've got to hand it to the CWC. Those doctors know how to splice a connectome back together."

"Any issues with the missing memories?"

"Nah. I can hardly tell. Besides, memories for me are like calories to Isaac."

"I'm not sure I follow," Isaac said.

"There are always more to enjoy."

"That there are," Susan agreed.

"Sort of like bad news takes," Isaac groused.

An alert from Themis Reception drew his eyes. Cephalie walked over and thwacked it with her cane.

"You've got visitors," Cephalie said. "Antoni Ruckman and a plus-one have transmitted in and would like to speak with you two. They've been cleared to come up to the office."

"Plus one?" Isaac creased his brow before he made the connection. "Plus-one! That must mean—" He rose from his seat. "Cephalie, can you reserve a conference room for us?"

"Already ahead of you."

A row of conference rooms lined the far side of the Themis office, most of them unoccupied. Red RESERVED text appeared above the nearest entrance.

"Come on, Susan." Isaac bobbed his head toward the conference room. "I have a good feeling about this."

Susan followed him into the conference room and palmed the door shut behind them. Two nearly identical ACs transmitted in, both in dark gray suits with subtle swirling patterns of darker grays and black. Their neck scarves were the only difference in attire. Both were black, but one featured a silver A while a silver B gleamed on the other.

"Detectives," greeted one of the Ruckmans. "Thank you for seeing us. I know you've already met him, but please allow me the pleasure of formally introducing *Bradley* Ruckman to you."

"Bradley, is it?" Isaac said with a smile. "I like it. And I'll make sure your decision is included in my report. We'll get this made official for you as smoothly as possible. How are you holding up, Bradley?"

"Better than before," the copy replied. He seemed to struggle to maintain eye contact, in contrast to the original Ruckman's directness. "But I still have a long road ahead of me."

"We're scheduled for another session at the CWC tomorrow." Antoni draped an arm over Bradley's shoulders and gave them a warm squeeze. "The initial reconstruction is complete, but rehabilitation will be a longer, more involved process."

"But a worthwhile one," Bradley emphasized. "My head already feels so much clearer."

"Why don't you show them, Bradley?" Antoni prompted.

"Show us what?" Isaac asked.

"Just a little something I whipped up."

Bradley extended his hand, and a glass terrarium materialized over it with a layer of dirt at the base. A green bud sprouted out of the soil and bloomed into a yellow flower, then wilted and returned to the earth. The remains seeped into the soil, and a new bud appeared, this time blooming into a blue flower, its petals edged in white.

"Bradley designed this all on his own," Antoni explained. "It's based on an art project I did way back in college. We call it a phoenix flower. The self-replicator colony will take the raw material in the base and continually construct and deconstruct a single flower. We've introduced a measure of controlled mutation into the design, so no two flowers are ever identical."

"Self-replicators?" Susan asked quietly, a hint of concern in her voice. "Mutations?"

"I'm sure it's quite safe." Isaac saved the pattern to his wetware. "Thank you, Bradley."

The copy dipped his head, still struggling to make eye contact.

"I guess this means you've still 'got it' as they say."

"Indeed," Antoni agreed. "In fact, I have more good news to share. It's not official, but SourceCode contacted me about... rebuilding bridges, shall we say? We're still working out the details, but it shouldn't be too long before *both* of us are back at the company."

"That's fantastic news," Isaac said. "Congratulations."

"Bradley here will start out as a junior engineer, but he'll be climbing the ranks in no time. As for me, I've been offered a *very* generous signing bonus."

"Sounds like the two of you have a bright future at the company."

"I think so. Though, it doesn't hurt that SourceCode is once again in the running for the Dyson contract. Management wants its best talent on the job."

"Including you two, it seems," Isaac said. "Thank you for stopping by. And thank you for the gift. It's always nice to see firsthand how our work influences people's lives. Especially when the result is positive."

✦   ✦   ✦

Isaac set the freshly printed terrarium down on his desk next to the Mercury rock.

Susan edged back in her chair, watching with predatory eyes as a purple phoenix flower emerged from the soil.

"It seems we've arrived at one of *those* moments," Isaac said, nodding at the two objects with satisfaction.

"What kind of moment?"

"Knickknack distribution. Not every case leaves us with physical souvenirs. Especially ones that aren't required as evidence by the prosecutors, but we seem to have ended up with..." He frowned at the stone. "Two."

"And?"

"Which one would you like for your desk? The rock or the—"

"The rock."

"You sure? I thought I'd take the rock, since I—"

Susan grabbed the rock off Isaac's desk and planted it firmly on the corner of her own.

"The rock it is." Isaac placed the terrarium along the back edge of his desk.

Susan eyeballed the terrarium as a red-and-white-striped flower blossomed then began to wither. She extended a careful finger toward the cylinder and gently pushed it away from the edge of her desk.

"I can put it elsewhere, if you like," Isaac said.

"No, this is fine." She nudged it another centimeter then withdrew her hand, still observing the ever-changing flower with hawklike intensity.

Isaac moved the terrarium to the corner of his desk furthest from her, and she finally seemed to relax.

"I'm back!" Grace tossed a large bag labeled EVIDENCE onto her desk. It hit with a heavy *thunk*. "Anyone miss me?"

"What's in the bag?" Isaac asked.

"Trophies."

Isaac walked over and peeked inside. "This is full of severed fuzzle heads."

"Like I said, trophies."

"How rough a time did you and Raviv have?"

"Rough enough that I started collecting trophies."

Isaac cringed.

"What are you going to do with them?" Susan asked.

"I'm not sure yet. I thought I might line them up on my desk so I can smile at their vacant faces each morning."

Isaac pulled the head of a pink long-hair out of the bag and turned it over to examine the face. The fuzzle was frozen with wide eyes and a mouth shaped like an exaggerated O, as if it had been beheaded in a moment of pure terror.

"Well, it's your desk." He dropped the head back into the bag.

"Are we doing *Solar Descent* tonight?" Grace asked.

"We could. All four of us are back on the station."

"Then it's settled."

"It is?"

"I need to let off some steam. Preferably without being arrested."

"What about Nina? Shouldn't we ask her first?"

"I talked to her on the way up. She's in."

Isaac glanced to Susan, who nodded excitedly.

"Then settled it is," he concluded.

EPILOGUE

THE EXPLOSION OF DARK ENERGY THREW SUSAN ACROSS THE skyscraper's flat, circular roof. She hit the tiles on her side, bounced, spun through the air, hit again, and rolled to a halt on her back.

"Ouch," she said, staring up at the night sky, then raising her wrist to check her remaining health. "Guys, that hit took me down to half."

"That's better than me," Nina replied from her own spot on the roof. "I'm almost dead." Her once glowing dreadlocks were now a dark gray. "How about some heals from our friendly combat medic?"

"I would if I could," Grace grumbled, facedown next to Nina, "but I seem to be paralyzed."

Susan tried to push herself upright but found the game resisting her movements. A warning flashed in front of her eyes, informing her that she too was paralyzed, and she dropped back down.

"Same here." She checked the inside of her wrist again to find a little lightning squiggle next to her health bar along with a tiny skull. "And I've got a skull status. Not sure what it means."

"That's Decay," Nina groaned.

"What's it do?"

"Drains your health at a rate based on your max health. It's a death sentence if it isn't cured." She reached over and knocked on Grace's helmet. "How about it?"

"Still paralyzed," Grace muttered into the roof tiles. "But at least we have Susan's Regen Aura."

"Sorry. You don't," Susan reported. "I think the Decay is blocking it."

"Uh oh." Nina checked her wrist. "She's right. My last sliver of health is going down, not up."

"Mwah hah hah!" A cloaked figure on the far side of the roof propped his boot up on the parapet and gave his cloak a dramatic swish. The space under his cowl was pitch black. "Thus has the candle singed the moths. But don't you see? It was I, the Onyx Ghost, this whole time!"

"You jerk!" Nina snapped. "You're lucky I'm paralyzed!"

"And what if you weren't?"

"I'd get up in your face and Irradiate your ass!"

"Are you so sure about that? Perhaps if you moths knew what you were dealing with, you'd reconsider." The Onyx Ghost cast his cloak aside, revealing a skeletal body of black bones joined by ribbons of dark, metallic musculature. His grinning skull possessed two deep, starry pits for eyes. He raised a desiccated hand, and black energy coalesced into a ball above it.

"He's a frickin' cyber-lich?!" Nina cried.

"Is that bad?" Susan asked.

"How are we supposed to take on a *cyber-lich* at level *two*? This scenario is trash!"

"This does seem a touch unfair," Grace agreed.

"I'm filing a complaint with the developers after this!" Nina raged.

"Any last words before you die?" the Onyx Ghost asked.

"Actually, I have a few."

Susan twisted her neck and torso around to catch sight of Isaac, whom she'd lost track of after the explosion. He stood on the roof directly opposite the cyber-lich, apparently unharmed, wind whipping the edges of his cloak. He shook the dust off the garment then walked forward.

"Oh?" The lich tilted his head. "What have we here? A moth who hasn't been burned yet?"

"Hold that thought." Isaac struggled to navigate the traffic jam of bodies. He almost tripped on Nina's dreadlocks, but eventually made it through with a short stutter step. "Okay, now we can talk."

"Tell me something, little moth." The lich placed a skeletal hand on his ribcage. "Do you really think it wise to stand against me, alone?"

"Yeah, I'm pretty sure I've got this."

"Hah." The lich coughed the sound more than laughed it. "You're nothing but a neophyte in the dark arts. What makes you believe you have the slightest chance against one who has supped at the Infinite Well for ages?"

"I'm glad you asked. For starters, I spoiled this entire scenario for myself. And not just your reveal—which I predicted, by the way—but your stats as well. I know your every strength and weakness, know every spell you can cast, every summon you can conjure, and I have counters for *all* of them."

"Isaac," Nina said, "whatever you're going to do, do it fast, because my health is draining away."

"I'm not sure what you're babbling about," the lich said, "but you must at least be somewhat competent. How else could you have withstood my first attack?"

"You have no idea."

"But there's more where that came from!" The lich brought his hands close together, compressing the black energy ball and exciting it. "Prepare to die!"

"It won't be enough." Isaac raised a hand and flexed his fingers, revealing the glint of a bluish metal ring.

The Onyx Ghost paused, then let the energy ball fizzle.

"Is that...?"

"A Ring of Greater Invulnerability," Isaac declared. "Which will negate the effect of any spell you can cast. You see, not only did I research you and your abilities extensively"—he smiled at the lich—"I also spent real-world Esteem to equip myself with the appropriate relics. *And* to remove their level requirements, where necessary. Cost quite a lot, too!"

"That ring won't protect you forever."

"True." Isaac inspected the ring, even as a hairline fracture began to form. "Not much time left, it seems."

"That's it," Nina griped. "I just lost consciousness. Isaac, hurry it up before I die!"

"I'm sorry, but I can't hear unconscious people."

"Move it, or I'll haunt you from the grave!"

"You should be grateful I'm not doing this...in character," Isaac replied, giving the end of the sentence a scratchy quality.

"He does have a point there," Grace admitted.

The ring cracked audibly.

"Your time is running out, little moth," the lich taunted.

"Yes, I suppose you have a point." Isaac reached into his cloak. "You know, this is kind of relaxing. The last ghost we had to deal with gave us *loads* more trouble." He pulled out a small, black crystal.

"Is that—" gasped the lich.

"A summoning shard. A very powerful one, too. Care to guess what's inside?"

Before the cyber-lich could answer, Isaac raised the shard over his head.

"Come forth, Greater Avatar of Singularity! Heed your servant's call!"

"G-g-greater?" the lich stammered.

Isaac crushed the shard, and black energy exploded from between his fingers. A huge, hovering orb of darkness manifested above and behind him, expanding until it dwarfed the top of the skyscraper. Black lightning crackled around the entity, and plasma wreathed it before expanding outward along eight points, coalescing into giant arms of fire.

"*I Answer And Obey,*" rumbled the greater avatar.

"Now!" Isaac pointed sharply at the lich, his cloak whipping outward. "Cast Graviton Grave!"

"*In Singularity's Name.*" The greater avatar brought all eight of its hands together and conjured a swirling vortex of darkness between its flaming palms.

"Oh dear," the lich breathed, moments before he vanished into a shrinking period of darkness, accompanied by a barely audible *squick* sound effect.

"That's all very impressive!" Nina griped. "But I'm still unconscious and dying!"

"Yes, about that." Isaac began searching the interior of his cloak once more. "I should have something in here to help."

Susan found the effect of the paralysis waning, so she propped herself up on a forearm.

"Isaac?"

"Yes?"

"Did you really just one-shot the last boss?"

He turned to her with a crafty smile. "I don't like to lose."